# Fury
# of the
# Fifth Angel

Written by Albert Hoffman
and Chris Hoffman

Copyright © 2013 Albert James Hoffman and Chris Hoffman.

All Rights Reserved.

No part of this publication may be reproduced, stored in a retrieval system, or transmitted, in any form or by any means, electronic, mechanical, photocopying, recording, or otherwise, without the written permission of the author.

First published by Dog Ear Publishing
4010 W. 86th Street, Ste H
Indianapolis, IN 46268
www.dogearpublishing.net

dog ear
PUBLISHING

ISBN: 978-1-4575-2429-5

This book is printed on acid-free paper.

This book is a work of fiction. Names, characters, businesses, organizations, places, events, and incidents either are the product of the authors' imagination or are used fictitiously. Any resemblance to actual events, or people, living or dead is entirely coincidental.

Printed in the United States of America

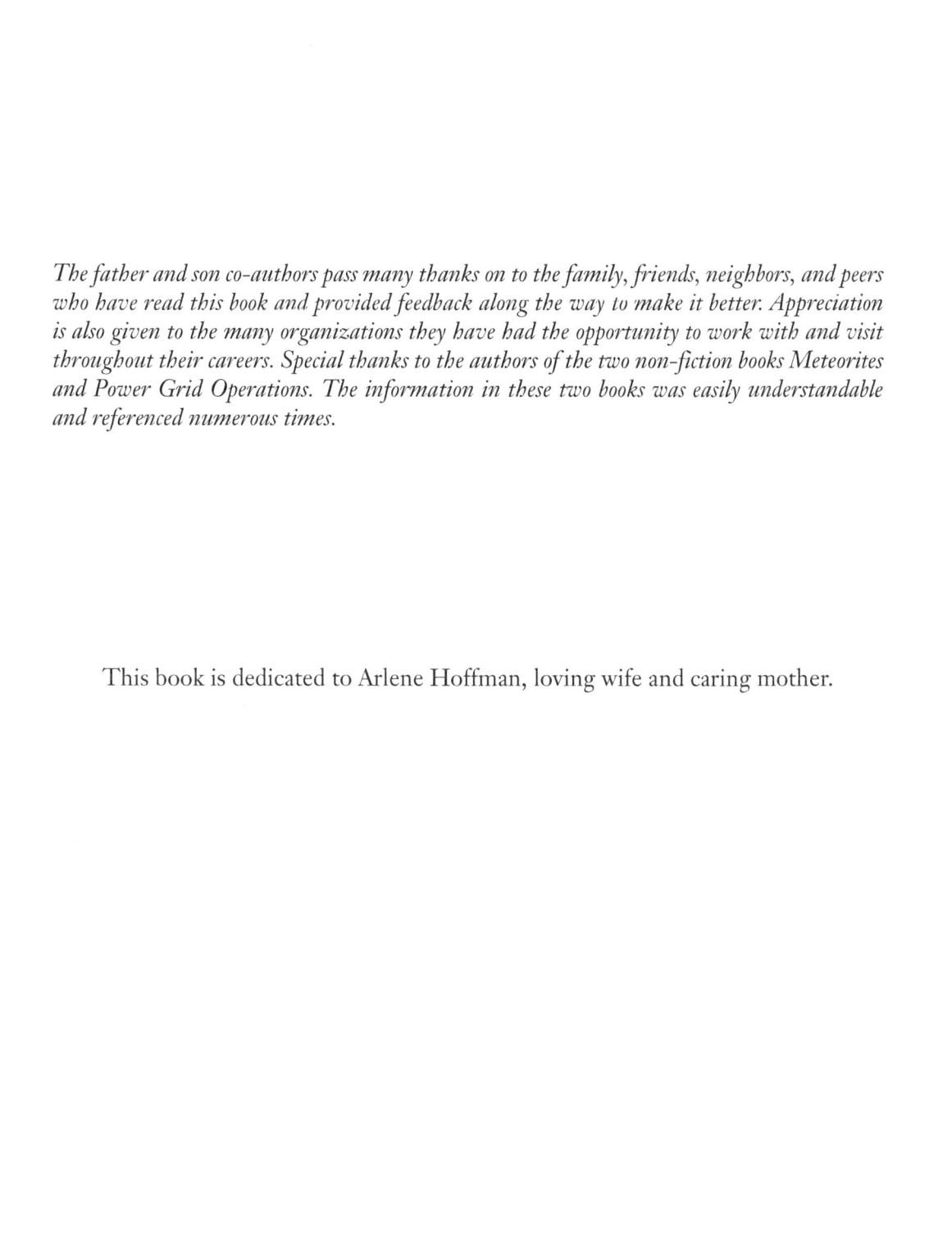

*The father and son co-authors pass many thanks on to the family, friends, neighbors, and peers who have read this book and provided feedback along the way to make it better. Appreciation is also given to the many organizations they have had the opportunity to work with and visit throughout their careers. Special thanks to the authors of the two non-fiction books Meteorites and Power Grid Operations. The information in these two books was easily understandable and referenced numerous times.*

This book is dedicated to Arlene Hoffman, loving wife and caring mother.

# Electrical Power Grid Foreword
## by Mike Terbrueggen

I travel often so reading in airports or planes is a common pastime. Most often I read technical material as I want to learn something from my reading. Fury of the Fifth Angel was a great surprise as not only did I learn a thing or two about interesting topics (like astronomy) but I also loved the story line.

I'm an electrical power systems engineer. After my education in Michigan and Colorado I took my first utility job in 1979. I have worked in power plants and power operations centers for various public and private utilities, and industry consultants. My current work involves the conduct of training seminars on power system operations. Over the past 25 years I have taught classes for thousands of power system engineers and operators. A character in this book is John Halloran who is a power grid operator and is representative of the many power system operators whose knowledge and dedication keeps our lights on.

The storyline weaves its way in and around the power grid industry as a whole in a very credible manner. The descriptions of how a power system operates are spot on and the people who operate these power systems are also very accurate. The authors will open many eyes to both how a power system operates and the vulnerabilities of these systems.

Since I travel a lot I've visited many of the locations described in the book and was pleased with how accurately the authors describe the various locals. I also live in Colorado and have visited all of the Colorado locations mentioned in the story. This is the first book I have every read that combines a complex technical field (power systems), deep personal relationships, political intrigue, and old-time religion into one fast paced story. I highly recommend Fury of the Fifth Angel. Take your time with it, absorb the different components and you'll love it as much as I did.

*Mike Terbrueggen is owner of O - T - S which is one of the most respected training organizations in North America for Power Grid Operations.*

# Astronomy Foreword by Dr. Edward Rhoads

Chelyabinsk, Russia recently dodged a cosmic bullet which gained national media attention and helped educate society. There are hundreds of thousands of asteroids which cross the Earth's orbit and most of them are the size of a football stadium. Astronomers have located at least half the asteroids that are larger than a kilometer in size. However, we have only found about one percent of the football stadium sized rocks and most of these rocks we only find AFTER they have a close encounter with the Earth. If one of these were on a collision course, we would not see it coming. A city could easily be destroyed in the blink of an eye with no warning and no chance to evacuate.

Every hundred to three hundred years an object the size of a football stadium hits the earth with enough energy to wipe out everything within twenty miles. When this happens, whether it occurs now or a hundred years from now, it will destroy a city without any warning. The loss of life and economic cost will truly be enormous. It is not a matter of if but when, where, and how much damage. The events portrayed in this book will occur someday. Again, it is not a matter of if, but when.

So, the question becomes can we prevent it? Sadly, the answer is currently no. The reason: presently less people work on finding these objects around the clock than work at your local diner. The funding for finding these objects is at best a meager few million dollars per year. There is no significant funding to research prevention. The likely destruction has the potential to be in the trillions, so I ask you the reader, what would you pay for insurance? To prevent this impact we would need to find these objects a decade or more in advance. To discover them we need better telescopes which cost hundreds of millions or better yet space based telescopes which cost more than a billion. Is that investment worthy if it has the potential to save trillions of dollars and millions of lives? So, what we do as a nation regarding this problem is up to each and every one of us. Our future is in the hands of you the reader because you choose the leaders who make the decisions regarding this issue. This book will help you to choose wisely.

*Dr. Edward Rhoads is an Astrophysicist lecturer at Indianapolis University Purdue University in Indianapolis and author of the ebook A Space Odd-yssy.*

Thursday February 11, 10:30 AM

NASA Complex, Houston, Texas

Ben Cohen sat quietly, staring intently at the video readout of observations made by the Spacewatch CCD mosaic detector array the night before. He was waiting, somewhat less than patiently, for a tiny smudge to appear. In his mind and in his heart, he prayed the smudge would not be there, and he worried over it. He had done all the calculations over and over again, and he knew exactly where they should appear. He had told his associates at Kitt Peak National Observatory exactly the area to scan; now all he could do was wait.

He watched the flashing light on his monitor as it updated the screen, unaware of the pain in his arthritic joints or that he was idly rubbing the long fingers of his sensitive hands together like a miser preparing to recount his neatly arranged piles of coin.

The Spacewatch CCD detector had methodically scanned an array of 4608 x 2048 13.5 micron-sized light-sensitive pixels in exact sequence, precisely recording their light intensity, and then repeated the entire process over and over again on a meticulously programmed schedule, as long as the window of "dark time" allowed. The observation had been made the previous evening on the 1.8 meter telescope located at the summit of the Kitt Peak observatory in Arizona, and the results had been transmitted via satellite to be stored on optical disk for one of the world's best known astronomers, Ben Cohen at NASA, Houston. His computer was organizing and reviewing all the data, comparing each scan with the previous scans, and displaying the results on the forty-inch monitor.

Ben's heart leapt as a slight smudge began to appear in the lower right-hand quadrant of the screen. From memory, he quickly located his benchmark stars, frowned, and tensed slightly. "Wait, Benjamin," he said to himself. "Wait until all the data is in before you scare yourself."

Four hours later, all the data was in. All the CCD scans had been analyzed, and the fright had turned to near panic. Ben Cohen's angels had indeed appeared, and they were right where they were supposed to be. That was the problem.

Ben reached for the phone and tapped in a four-digit speed-dial number, then listened to the beeping tones as the long-distance call went out.

"Professor Schmidt's office," came a pleasant feminine voice from the University of Colorado at Boulder.

"Yes, this is Dr. Benjamin Cohen calling. May I speak to Professor Schmidt?"

"I'm sorry, Dr. Cohen, the professor is instructing right now. Could he call you back?"

"No, that won't do at all. Could you please call him to the phone?" came Ben's brusque answer.

After what seemed to Ben to be an eternity of hold music, the voice of his old friend and colleague came on the line. "Karl Schmidt here."

"Karl, this is Ben. Can you come down to Houston right away? I think we have a problem."

"Ben, the semester is just starting, and I'm over my head in work. Can't this wait?"

"No."

After an association of nearly thirty-five years, Karl Schmidt knew that his friend would not ask him if it were not important, and an underlying tension, almost akin to fear, in Ben's voice made the decision for him. "I have a presentation to give this evening, then I'll catch the red-eye to Houston. I'll see you in the morning."

"Please don't delay, Karl. Good-bye."

Dr. Karl Schmidt stood, briefly staring at the dead phone. He did not like the feel of this conversation. He remained standing with a strange feeling of distress and anxiety beginning to move through his body.

Ben Cohen, in Houston, set the phone down very gently and walked around his desk and sat down slowly and carefully with an audible groan. He moved around in the chair until he had settled his aching bones into a semblance of comfort. The ancient wood-framed Morris chair was in many ways a mirror image of him. The chair's joints crackled and groaned just as his did. Its cushions had long since lost any likeness of color or pattern and were as shiny smooth as the top of his head. The chair's wooden arms were curved at the ends and conformed perfectly to Ben's arthritic hands.

Ben accepted these assorted pains as a necessary evil and simply the result of too many years spent in freezing-cold observatories studying his beloved and eternal stars. They were merely physical discomforts when compared to the tumult in his mind.

Ben shook his head in an attempt to clear his mind and was rewarded by a streak of intense pain running down his neck. Seeking some comfort, he reached over to the smoking stand next to his chair. He pondered for a moment, then selected his favorite pipe. It was a well-worn churchwarden style, and its bowl had been burned to a deep black and the stem well chewed. Ben used a small penknife to clean the burned out ash from the bowl and tapped the burnt ashes into the small handmade pottery ashtray that was the last gift he had ever received from his granddaughter. He compressed an aromatic cherry blend of tobacco into the bowl, struck a wooden matchstick into flame and puffed rapidly until he had a good light. He then drew in a deep puff, inhaled the smoke and exhaled through his nose, and then took several more.

Enjoying the rush and relaxation from the tobacco, Ben found the sweet spot in his chair, and a half smile formed on his lips as his mind's eye began to remember his beloved granddaughter sitting on his lap, passing her tiny fingers through the streams of his pipe smoke. Ben chuckled to himself for the first time in days as he pictured his granddaughter sitting with him. Then, the emotions suddenly changed and tears sprung from his eyes as he recalled those terrible days. Pictures flashed in his mind, streaming, one by one, like thumbing through a stack of old photographs.

All joy in Ben's life had ended that fateful day. Responding to the police call, Ben had rushed to the accident scene to see his daughter, Cindy, covered by a blanket in the driver's seat. EMTs had been working on a small bloody bundle by the crushed car. With a roar, Ben had fallen to his knees, pushed the EMTs away, and lifted Ellie's body into his arms. Her eyes had opened briefly and her mouth had curled into a small smile. Her tiny hand had reached up to touch his nose, and she had said, "Pop Pop," then closed her eyes for the last time. In that instant, a black cloud had fallen over Ben's mind, obliterating anything good or happy.

For the next several months, Ben had stumbled through life in a daze. He had buried his beloved girls, then attended the killer's arraignment and the subsequent trial with his deep, dark rage growing daily. The scruffy, unshaven slob who had stumbled in a substance-induced trance at the accident scene had been, amazingly, replaced by a clean-shaven, short-haired, bright and alert young man in a perfect black suit and tie in the courtroom. His attorney had claimed that his condition at the accident had been caused by a severe prescription drug reaction, which Ben had discovered later was a complete lie. Ben had learned, far too late to make a difference, that the district attorney, judge in the case, and father of the lazy shit-for-brains boy who had killed his family were all lifelong friends.

Ben had been crushed by the miscarriage of justice and depressed by what he perceived as a complete collapse of morality, justice, honor, and respect of mankind. He had wandered around his small home, neglected himself and his work, and sunk deeper into depression until the previous week, when a small report from the University of Arizona observatory at Kitt Peak had caught his eye. The report supported a research study that he had done several years ago on short-period comets. The study supported his original calculations that there existed several of these ancient comets that could become near–earth-crossing objects in the foreseeable future.

Coming out of his funk and the horrible memories, Ben got up and started to review his old calculations and analyze the new data from the CCD mosaic detector. He stupidly began to daydream, wishing one of these comets could punish those bastards who had caused him the grief he had lived with for so long.

\* \* \*

Professor Karl Schmidt stood at the podium, casually looking over the group of freshman astronomy students slowly filling the seats of the University of Colorado's Fiske Planetarium. He was vaguely pleased to observe that their mode of dress had shifted from the baggy, oversized and mismatched grunge style of a few years before to a considerably more traditional western style. As he waited, he was acutely aware of the airline tickets nestled in his breast pocket for the 11:28 p.m. Delta flight from Denver to Houston and of the mysterious reason for his hurried trip. When the last few students were seated, he tapped several times on the microphone and began.

"Good evening, children."

In the back row of seats, Selena Escobedo nudged her new friend, Beth DeSalvo, in the ribs and they both giggled at being called children. Professor Schmidt was probably the only instructor on the entire campus who could get away with calling these young men and women by that word, and only because of his grandfatherly appearance and reputation for kindly and gently leading his freshman students through the galaxy.

"Tonight you are going to enjoy a firsthand view of the most spectacular meteor shower in history, the Leonid shower of November 16, 1996. It may please you to know that on that very evening, I was camped out on the Mojave Desert, curled up snugly in a sleeping bag and rewarded for my efforts with a completely overcast sky." His little joke was received with a few polite snickers.

Seated at the U-shaped operating console for the Fiske planetarium projector, Rod Foster picked up his cue, dimming the lights in the dome-shaped room and starting the show. Professor Schmidt noted that a few couples took the opportunity to move a little closer and hold hands.

"What we are observing now is the beginning of the Leonid shower between 1:30 and 2:30 a.m. You will notice that the meteors all originate from that strange little cluster of stars to the left of the entrance, where you may see the laser designator, which you will soon learn is the constellation Leo, the lion." As if on cue, a bright streak of light streaked from the indicated constellation and crossed the night sky, followed by a second and third.

"Where do these meteors come from, you ask. Well, I'll tell you." Professor Schmidt regularly moved things along by asking and answering his own questions. "They come from comets."

"I thought comets were frozen balls of ice?" came a voice from the back of the room.

"Excellent, excellent." Professor Schmidt was pleased that he was getting student participation this early. "Big frozen snowballs are what they are, but these are snowballs that are full of stones, as if they were made from snow scraped off the roadside."

Suddenly, the dark night sky disappeared and was replaced by a bright object, glowing and streaming off long tendrils of colored light. "What you are observing now is a comet nucleus, which is passing through the inner planets and receiving tremendous solar heating, which vaporizes the primordial ices on the dayside. This off-gassing releases the silicate particles trapped in the ice, which fall behind to form a stream in almost exactly the same orbit as the comet itself. After many passes through the inner planets, the comet will have formed a dust trail throughout its entire orbit."

The sky filled with streaks of light flashing across the planetarium's ceiling. "We are now viewing the Leonids from 2:30 to 3:30 a.m., in which time we should observe over 300 meteors. Remember that the Leonids have been in progress for two weeks already and will continue for another few weeks."

"Why so many tonight, Professor?"

"We believe that the Leonids are a relatively young stream and not yet widely dispersed throughout the entire orbit. This may also account for a great variety in size of individual meteors. Leonids also follow an extremely elongated orbit, which is greatly inclined relative to the plane of the planets. This inclination causes the Leonid meteors to approach Earth almost head on. This elongated orbit indicates that the Leonid stream was laid down by a very ancient long-period comet, which may not have passed through the inner solar system since the beginning of recorded history."

A barely noticeable click on the video equipment preceded an increase in the meteor shower's intensity. "You are now observing the Leonids in the period from 4:00 to 4:30 a.m., with an increase in activity up to thirty per minute. Leonids usually contain typical naked-eye meteors, about the size of a grain of sand, but since they are young and lumpy still, they are capable of producing some truly spectacular displays. They arrive annually in mid-November, and the large displays have a period of approximately thirty-four years."

Suddenly, the sky was lit by the flash of a brilliant fireball, bringing oohs and aahs from the students. The intensity of the shower increased rapidly to thirty to forty per second. The students sat in shocked surprise as meteors flashed by in an uninterrupted stream. Professor Schmidt smiled, pleased at his choreography. "What you have just witnessed was an air burst, or fireball, as bright as a first-quarter Moon."

"Was anyone hurt by these meteors, Professor?" asked Selena Escobedo.

"An excellent question, but no. No one has reported being injured by a meteor shower. In fact, no meteorite strike has ever been associated with a shower. On the rare occasions where there was a coincident strike, it was found to have come from another direction and was not associated with the shower at all. Their composition is another factor. Spectrographic analysis of the luminous trails of meteors indicates that this cometary debris is composed of ordinary silicate and carbon-bearing rocky material. When this relatively soft material enters Earth's atmosphere at speeds as high as thirty to fifty-five kilometers per second, its fate is to burn up, or as in the example that we just observed, explode."

"Then what are the meteors that don't burn up made of?"

"A solid body that survives its trip through the atmosphere to the surface of the earth is called a meteorite, and its composition is startlingly different. There are more than 15,000 authenticated meteorites in collections, and scientists have had ample time to study them. They fall into three classifications. The strongest of these are the irons, which are made up of a naturally occurring alloy of stainless steel, containing iron, nickel, and a number of precious metals, particularly those of the platinum family. The second class includes stony-irons, which are made up of familiar silicate material with up to fifty percent irons. The last class is stony meteorites, which frequently contain from traces to up to thirty percent iron. These can be subdivided into over fifty groups by chemical composition."

"What are the percentages, Professor?"

"That is another subject altogether, and time is short, but as long as you're interested, I'll touch on it briefly." As the professor spoke, the meteor shower overhead increased in intensity. "Five out of six meteorites recovered are strong stones called ordinary chondrites. These contain anywhere up to thirty percent of iron. The remainder are divided between the irons, which are extremely durable, and soft stones called carbonaceous chondrites, which are not. One interesting fact is that in many primitive societies, iron meteorites were prized for use in making tools and weapons.

In colonial America, they were called bog iron because they could be easily recovered from swamps and shallow ponds and because they could be heated and hammered into useful items. One last thing is that meteorites contain an inordinately larger amount of sulfur than terrestrial rock does, meaning they give off an unpleasant odor when heated."

"Thank you, Professor."

"My pleasure." Professor Schmidt made note that even as he had explained about meteorites, his students' eyes had remained on the meteor shower overhead and swiveled about a lot so as not to miss anything.

"In closing, I'd like to state that under a bombardment like this, it is not hard to understand how the earth can gain ten tons of weight a day of extraterrestrial material. It is also not too late to reserve the evenings of November 16 and 17 this year to go up into the mountains and see a repeat of this show firsthand."

After the last of the students had left and Rod Foster had finally locked the planetarium doors, Professor Karl Schmidt hurried to his car for the hour-long ride to the Denver airport and his flight to Houston. He couldn't shake a feeling of foreboding over the reason for Ben Cohen's sudden summons and the necessity for his flying out at this late hour. He packed a comfortable old pipe with tobacco and lit it carefully. He enjoyed the sweet smelling smoke as he started the car and, out of habit, scanned the sky. There, in a quadrant that contained no notable constellations, came a bright white streak, which blinked out almost as quickly as it had appeared.

## Sunday, February 14

### The White House, Washington, DC

President Jameson Coleridge took the renowned astronomer's thin and arthritic right hand in his own much larger hands and held it gently. "Thank you, Professor Cohen, for your briefing. I would take it as a personal favor if you would make yourself available to me and the people at NASA while we work to prepare for the situation you have just described."

"Thank you, Mr. President, and yes, I will be more than happy to help in any way I can."

The president released Cohen's hand, and the aging astronomer turned and walked stiffly out of the Oval Office. An impeccably uniformed Marine guard fell into step with him. "Sir, the president has asked me to escort you to your limousine."

"Thank you, young man, that would be nice."

Jameson Coleridge heard none of this as he turned and closed the door. His mind was awash with the information that Ben Cohen had just delivered and with reeling thoughts of what could and should be done. As he reached his desk and was turning to sit down, his chief of staff asked, "What would you like me to do to get the ball rolling, sir?"

The president paused and considered his response, then said, "Nothing."

"Nothing, sir?"

"That's right, Amos. Nothing at all, for now. We need time to study this situation, consult with our allies, and consider our enemies. We need time to know the appropriate way to act. Until all that is done, we do nothing. Understood?"

"Yes, sir."

"Just one more thing before you go, Amos" the president said in a puzzled tone.

"Yes, sir?"

"I find all of this information fascinating and alarming at the same time. What I fail to understand is how some pissant kid in East Bumfuck, Texas, discovers this anomaly and reports it to the Texas stargazers, National Security Administration gets a hit on their telephone scans, they then tell the FBI, who investigates it, and I don't know a dammed thing about it!" Jameson Coleridge's concern and frustration showed as he hit his hand on the desk softly and then said, "Go home, Amos. Enjoy what's left of Valentine's Day," the president ordered. "We'll talk more tomorrow. We have a lot to think about."

## Tuesday, February 16

The big black Chevrolet SUV was flying down the dusty rutted West Texas road. The driver was a burly, fair-haired man hunched over the steering wheel, concentrating on his driving, while his partner, a slender Hispanic man, held on for dear life and said through clenched teeth, "Slow down for Christ's sake, Dick!"

FBI Agent Dick Morgan just smiled at the discomfort of his partner, Manny Riviera, and mashed down a bit harder on the accelerator. "How much further, Manny?" he asked, knowing he was driving recklessly for no real good reason.

"Less than a mile if we live that long."

"What's your preliminary report on the kid?" Dick asked, in complete control of himself and the speeding vehicle.

"Enough to know this is a wild goose chase," Manny replied, still through clenched teeth. "He's a good kid, from all information. As far as I can find out, he's a good student, especially in math and science, well liked, never been in trouble. Kind of quiet, though, and stays to himself, but not in a weird way that would raise any flags. His mother, on the other hand, is a typical local yocal and dates anybody who comes along and shows her the least bit of interest. The boy has had a tough time at home."

"Then where did he get the money to buy a scope big enough to see what he shouldn't see?"

"Found it broken up in the county landfill and repaired it. Proud as hell of it, too. He brags it up at school, and he is the darling of the science teacher."

"How is the teacher, a good guy?" Dick asked.

"A great gal you should say. She's good-looking with a great body that could knock your eyes out. He's her pet."

"Sounds like something to look into." Dick chuckled.

"Just up ahead on the right! I know you're driving like an ass to make me squirm, but you need to slow down quick!"

Dick slammed on the brakes, cut the wheel to the right, and skidded to a stop in front of a ramshackle old Texas farmhouse after scattering gravel and dust across what passed for a front lawn.

Approaching the house, Dick Morgan let his eyes take in the details. Old, dilapidated, unpainted windows were broken and patched with cardboard. The screen door hung half off, and the wreck that passed for a front porch sagged in all directions. Dick nearly fell on his face when the first step he took collapsed and he scraped his shin on the second. "What the fuck is this?" he cursed angrily in mild pain. He regained his balance and pulled up his pant leg to see the damage.

"Been meanin' to get that there step fixed for a while now. Guess I'm a little late. Sorry about that. I'll get my boy right on it, though. Hope you didn't ruin them nice trousers."

The words tumbled out of the gap-toothed mouth of an unkempt woman of indeterminate age. Her bleached blond hair hung in strings, and she looked as if she had not been introduced to a bar of soap for a while.

"Martha Simms's my name. Who might you gentlemen be lookin' for?"

"I'm Dick Morgan from Dallas. I'd like to see Billy Joe Simms."

"What's he got into now?" Martha asked with an evil scowl on her face. "Has that slut science teacher got him in some kind of trouble?"

"Nothing like that," Dick replied in a soothing voice. "Just a science project he has been working on."

Despite the quiet voice, Martha knew from experience that Dick was not a man to be trifled with, so she said, "Just need to talk, is all?"

"Just get him out here and you'll find out."

"Y'all might's well come on in, and I'll get 'im." Martha stepped inside and shouted, "Billy Joe Simms, get your bony ass in here. You got some important-lookin' company."

Out in the dog trot at the back of the house, Billy looked up from the work he was doing on a battered old workbench and answered, "Be there in a minute, Ma!"

"You come this very minute, or I'll come out there and whup up on you, boy."

Billy Joe had ample knowledge of what that meant, and he quickly swept several electronic circuit boards into a drawer, got up, and headed toward the house. Coming in through the battered back door, Billy saw the two men dressed in business suits who were waiting for him. One was big with sandy hair and the hard eyes of someone who was used to getting his way. The other was Hispanic, much smaller, but equally scary. "I'm Billy Joe Simms, sir. What can I do for you?" he asked, looking Dick straight in the eyes.

Dick began, "I'm Richard Morgan, and my friend is Manuel Riviera. We're from the Texas Astronomical Society of Dallas," he lied. "We are here in response to a letter that you sent us not to long ago."

"I never knew that you sent out no letter, Billy Joe. How come you did that?"

"Ms. Simms, I'll ask the questions," Dick Morgan said with unquestioning authority. Martha's jaw clapped shut in surprise.

Manny thought he should step in to smooth out Dick's abrasiveness. "Billy, we are here, very simply, to congratulate you on the sighting that you reported of asteroid BQ. Finding the anomaly that is traveling behind it in its debris steam was some excellent work."

"I knowed that Billy Joe was doin' important work out back," Martha exclaimed.

Without even noticing her, Manny continued, "We would like very much to discuss your sighting and to see the equipment that you used. It is quite a wonderful finding and was well worth reporting."

Billy Joe's heart was pounding as fast as his head was spinning. He was in no way accustomed to any words of praise except maybe from Miss Beardsly at school.

Manny Rivera was interested in astronomy and considered himself an amateur astronomer at best but was curious as to how a young boy with a junkyard scope had discovered a cluster of debris at such a distance. In his quiet, gentle way, he probed Billy until the boy explained.

"I was doing good with the scope until one night, suddenly nothing would work. I fiddled around for a while, then got mad and gave the scope a kick. My science teacher calls it a left-foot adjustment. Then I felt bad and set it up again, and when I looked through it, everything was good and clear and I saw them. I watched until they went out of sight, got all my measurements and star coordinates and all. Next night, it went back down and hasn't worked since. So I wrote to you to see if anyone else had seen that little cluster."

Manny was surprised at the boy's outburst but happy with the answer. "I think that we can help with your problem," he said, smiling, liking the boy and patting him on the back.

Dick maintained his composure, glad that Manny had stepped in, and delighted at the openmouthed shock on Martha's face as she calculated what all this might be worth in dollars and looked as if she would drool down the front of the dirty tee shirt she wore that read, "Stinnett, Texas….I'd rather be in Hell."

Manny and Dick spent a full two hours with Billy Joe, gently gleaning all they needed to know. They assured him that they would forward details of his discovery to NASA and the International Astronomical Society, stressing to him that he should remain quiet about it until findings could be published.

They wrapped up with a cash "reward" of $5,000 in a check, which Martha promptly snatched from Billy Joe's hand, and a pamphlet extolling the virtues of the Celestron NexStar Telescope that he would be receiving by mail soon.

Driving back at a more moderate pace, the two FBI agents congratulated themselves on a job well done and were happy that they could transmit an all-is-well-in-Texas back to Washington—even if they were not so sure what "well" was.

## Monday, March 1

"Good evening, my friends. This is Reverend Randall Davis, speaking to you on WVM-TV from beautiful downtown Wheeling, West Virginia. Tonight's program is very special. I am going to depart from my usual format because I have a message of extreme importance for you, which has come to me in a most unusual and divine way. So please, gather your family around you, and listen most carefully to my words. And by all means, if you have the ability to record this show, then please take a moment now to do so. I am hopeful you will share these words with as many friends and family members as possible."

Reverend Davis paused, waiting for a short time so his faithful followers could prepare to record his words. Those viewers who followed his show regularly, and many people did, noticed immediately that he was not speaking from his study at home as usual but was standing straight and tall on the studio set, holding his Bible in his hands. Randall P. Davis was not the run-of-the-mill televangelist. He was not bombastic or aggressive in his manner, and he did not continually preach hellfire-and-brimstone sermons with the threat of damnation held high to frighten his viewers and garner extra contributions. His television ministry was much the same as his ministry to his own flock: down-to-earth and honest. That was why his viewers believed his words and did his bidding.

Reverend Davis looked directly into the camera, drew himself up to his full six-foot, two-inch height, and, in his most calm and soothing voice, began, "Listen closely to these words, my friends, for I believe in my heart they are the words of God, given to you through me."

Allan Marshall sat up in his seat in the control room at WVM-TV and turned up his audio just a little. Al worked a steady night shift as engineer at WVM-TV and usually tuned out the commercial-free fill-in shows the station broadcast as a public service in the early morning hours. He had heard them all a hundred times before, but he always listened to Reverend Randy's Sunday sermons.

Reverend Randy's shows were not commercial-free and were actually broadcast from midnight on Sunday to 1:00 a.m. on Monday, and Al liked them a lot. Apparently, he was not alone, because the show had been picked up by a number of other small stations and had been reasonably popular. Al also liked and respected Randall P. Davis as a man of great personal honor and dignity, as well as a man of God. In the three years that Reverend Randy had been broadcasting, Al had never heard him claim or even imitate that he was speaking for God directly. This morning's show was going to be different, very different, but then, it had been from the beginning.

Al Marshall had been instrumental in convincing the station manager to allow Reverend Randall to record his programs at home in his own study for broadcast later. Al had taken his own time to instruct Randy in the setup and use of the remote equipment, which Randy typically picked up from the station on Saturday and returned Sunday afternoon, along with the flash drive containing the recording. Al had even designed and constructed a special foot-control device for the video camera so Randy could operate it while seated at his desk.

Randy's old-fashioned, wood-paneled study made an excellent backdrop for the show, and making the video at home allowed the reverend to do the show and still get a good night's sleep. It made the night shift easier for Al, who normally only had to insert the flash drive and click the mouse on the play icon. It saved the station the expense of a cameraman. Everyone was happy with the arrangement. This arrangement had worked well and been quite successful for many months, but tonight, this routine would change forever.

This entire week had been different. Early on Sunday afternoon, Reverend Randy had called the station manager at his home, requesting permission to do the show live from the studio this morning. Al had been surprised to find a cameraman setting up for the broadcast when he had arrived for work just before eleven p.m. He had thought that Randy must be gathering up a pretty respectable audience to have the station manager authorize overtime pay for a cameraman.

Tonight, Reverend Davis spoke with a new note of seriousness in his voice and a glow of complete conviction in his eyes. "My friends, you are all well aware it is my normal practice each Sunday to relay to you the same sermon that I delivered to my congregation in the morning, and then to discuss their reactions to it. This will not be the case tonight, and I would like to briefly explain why.

"While preparing for my sermon this week, I had great difficulty in choosing a subject and writing the text. While this is highly unusual for me, I was not greatly troubled by it at the time and simply applied myself more diligently to the work at hand. While doing so, however, I could not escape the feeling that something was gently drawing my mind away from the subject that I had chosen and guiding me along another, very different, path. I did not accept this guidance, however, and continued on my own way."

"I completed my sermon on time, but only with the greatest of difficulty and without my usual feeling of a job well done. When I delivered it to my congregation this morning, it did not ring true to me or to them. They could sense that my words were forced and that my heart was not in the message. I accepted then for certain that there was another message I should have been giving."

"After church was over, several of my parishioners actually inquired as to the state of my health or if I had a problem they could help with. I did, but I could not tell them about it, and they could not help. The task is mine alone."

"Again this afternoon, when it came time for me to record today's sermon and prepare it for broadcast, I attempted to do so but found that I could not do it at all.

No matter how hard, or how many times, I tried, my voice was stilled; my mind became a blank slate."

Anyone who was watching Reverend Randy this morning could see in his deep brown eyes and craggy, almost Lincolnesque, features the torment he felt as he tried to find the proper words to say. He looked down for a moment and paused, gathering his resolve.

When Reverend Randall looked up again, his eyes were aglow with honest emotion, and it was clear that his mind was finally unfettered. He allowed his thoughts and words to flow freely. "I knew in my heart that I needed to clear my mind and my spirit, and that I needed some space to do this. I dressed quickly and went outside to take a long walk. I wandered for a time through the fields and woods behind my church. Eventually, I lost all track of time, until I found myself on top of Blueberry Hill, at a place where I have often gone in the past to meditate and find my peace. There, I fell to my knees and stared up at the heavens, praying to God for a sign. I know that it was arrogant of me to ask God to give me a sign, when in my heart I already knew the correctness of my calling, but I asked anyway, and He replied. I continued staring up at the sky for a long while, until I was surprised to see a pinprick of light streaking across the afternoon sky. It lasted only a moment, but I knew then it was God's messenger and that the message that had been growing in my mind and heart must be told."

"I don't know how long I remained there, but when I became aware of myself, it was early evening and well past time for me to be heading home. As I arrived home and was about to enter, I again looked up at the sky and saw another of God's messengers telling me to do what I already knew was right."

"I am not an astronomer, and I don't know if this is a time when periodic meteorites normally occur, but I knew quite clearly what I felt at that moment. It was as if a great weight had been lifted from my shoulders and a veil was raised from my mind." Reverend Randall P. Davis stopped speaking but continued to look intently into the camera. It was as if his eyes could bore through space and time and into the souls and minds of everyone watching.

Al Marshall sat at his console, staring at the monitor, unmindful of anything going on around him. He, too, was mesmerized by the power and sincerity of the words that were being spoken.

The reverend continued. "At that moment, I was reminded of my own late father and how he had often sought guidance from the Lord. And I knew then what I must do, just as clearly as I saw the shooting stars in the sky. I decided I must let the Lord direct the message for me tonight, and I must do it as I had seen my father do so many times."

"I retrieved my father's old Bible from the shelf in my study and sat down at my desk. Holding it between my hands, I stood it on its spine, as I had seen him do, and raised my eyes to the sky, asking the Lord for his guidance. I could feel the old leather cover warming in my hands, and when I released the Bible from my grasp, it stood upright on edge for several seconds before settling to the desk. When I opened the Bible and selected a page at random, it was page 497, The Revelation of Saint John the Divine, chapter 9. My eyes fell on verse 1, and I read from it as follows: "'And the fifth angel sounded, and I saw a star fall from the heavens unto the earth, and to him was given the key to the bottomless pit.'"

"I knew at that moment, as clearly as I know my children's faces, that the Lord has placed a heavy load upon my shoulders. He has guided my hand this day so I might understand the end time is soon to be upon us. I knew also that it was upon me to give this message out to His faithful so you may prepare for that day and be saved."

Al Marshall stared at his monitor and could see the complete belief and sincerity there. He glanced over at the cameraman and saw that he, too, was totally engrossed in the reverend's words. Randy had always delivered his sermons in plain language before, simple and straightforward. Tonight, however, he was speaking in an old-fashioned and almost biblical manner, which was at once very convincing but, at the same time, a little frightening. No one who was watching him that night could help but believe him.

Al was so mesmerized by Reverend Randy's performance tonight that he didn't notice when the show ran seven minutes over time, and no one in the audience or any of the show's sponsors called in to complain about it, but many people across America got up from their chairs and went to their windows to study the early morning skies.

\* \* \*

Raschad Jamputra jumped slightly as the gold phone rang at 01:50. She snatched up the receiver and answered briskly, "Electronic Surveillance. Raschad speaking."

The Federal Bureau of Investigation gold phone was reserved for internal priority messages and almost never rang at this hour of the morning. Raschad knew that when it did, whoever was on duty had better be sharp, or be prepared to pay the consequences.

"This is Morgan, Houston office. Do you people monitor WVM-TV out of Wheeling at all?" Raschad recognized the name immediately, as she was familiar with Dick Morgan's reputation as an old-school hard-ass, and her heartbeat began to accelerate.

"Yes, sir, we do. There are some hillbilly militia down there who sometimes purchase air time in the early morning hours to spread their word," she answered briskly.

"Good. Run a recording of WVM from midnight to 01:30 and get it over to Amos Bellinger at the Watergate Apartments immediately. Do you understand?"

"Yes, sir," Raschad answered. Before she could repeat the order back to him, she realized that Morgan had already hung up.

Raschad's heart had sunk into the pit of her stomach at the mention of Amos Bellinger's name. If Dick Morgan was a hard-ass, and he definitely was, then Amos Bellinger was the crown prince of them all. A slight sheen of perspiration began to form on her forehead as she quickly found the requested show and set up to copy it. *Don't screw this one up, girl,*" she thought as she called for a special messenger to deliver the encrypted video flash drive, *"or you'll be selling jewelry in the mall tomorrow."*

The encrypted 16GB Aegis Secure Key flash drive was hand-delivered to the president's chief of staff in less than an hour.

\* \* \*

Amos Bellinger closed his door behind the departing messenger and padded softly on bare feet over to his media entertainment system. He inserted the encrypted flash drive into the appropriate slot, typed the password he knew from memory, and clicked play, watching idly as *The Hour of Devotion with Reverend Randall P. Davis* was introduced. He fished the few remaining ice cubes from the insulated bucket and poured a solid three fingers of bourbon over them before taking a seat in front of the TV and turning the sound up to a level he could hear.

For the next hour plus a few minutes, Amos was completely engrossed, his drink barely touched, as the ice melted into the bourbon. When the show was over, he punched the rewind button on the remote and sat back in his chair, considerably more concerned than he had been when Dick Morgan had first called him about Reverend Randy. Davis was a natural preacher who had delivered a very believable show. He was either a consummate actor or a entirely honest man—which was infinitely more problematic. An actor could be exposed as such and his character discredited publicly, or, even better, he could be threatened with exposure and manipulated to do Amos's bidding.

In contrast, it would take considerable time to create sufficient disinformation on the good pastor to prove to a loyal audience of long standing that their spiritual leader had feet of clay. Amos did not have that kind of time. Gritting his teeth in frustration, he mashed down on the play button again. This time he cut off the sound and just watched the picture, concentrating on Reverend Davis's face.

"There's no need to watch it again," came the soft feminine voice from behind him, followed by a soft kiss on his bald head and hands that slid tenderly over his shoulders and down his chest. Her sweet scent almost completely erased his train of thought. "Going over it won't alter the fact that he's an honest man with a calling, and even you can't change that."

Amos Bellinger had been so engrossed by Reverend Davis's sermon that he had forgotten about Lisa Howard sleeping in his bedroom. She had brought him back to reality both by her presence and her completely correct appraisal of the situation.

"But that's just the problem, Lisa; he is just as you say, an honest man. That's why I turned off the sound. Just watch his face, and you can see the belief in his eyes, and his concern for people is written clearly in the muscles of his jaw. If I can see this, then others will see it, too—and that's precisely why I am concerned."

"But there must be a hundred other preachers out there who are prophesying doom from the Extinctor and warning everyone to go underground or to the mountains or anywhere safe, right after they send in their check or transfer funds from their accounts. If there is such a place."

"Yes, there are hundreds, but they are phony, and that is obvious to anyone with half a mind. They're charlatans simply seeking to line their pockets by invoking doom and gloom, and any discerning viewer can easily see that. I can have the FBI pay them a visit and put on a little pressure. After that, they'll stay in line. Reverend Randall P. Davis is another matter altogether. He is obviously honest and sincere in his concern, and people will be able to see that and believe what he's saying. That's what makes him so dangerous, and also why he'll require some special attention."

"Come back to bed, and deal with Reverend Randy in the morning," Lisa told him.

"How much of it did you watch?"

"Enough to know that we've got a busy day ahead of us tomorrow, but more importantly, darling, we've got some unfinished business in the next room."

"I guess you're right." Amos managed with a distant chuckle.

Later, as Amos was drifting off toward sleep with Lisa's short, dark curls nestled against his shoulder, he allowed his mind to drift back to the prophetic words of Reverend Randall P. Davis.

\* \* \*

President Jameson Coleridge and Chief of Staff Amos Bellinger were lifelong friends who had joined forces to forge an unbeatable machine when Coleridge had decided to make a run for the White House. They had been a political upstart at the time, but Amos had managed a brilliant campaign, and as a result, Coleridge, a one-term governor from Alaska, had come from out of nowhere to win his party's nomination in a riotous convention and then win a hotly contested election, mainly on his rugged good looks and rural sincerity, along with his promise of complete honesty, fiscal responsibility, full communication with Americans, and less government—promises he had scrupulously maintained...until now.

Amos could still remember the hot flush of anger that had seized him when his good friend had selected a twerp of a Harvard MBA to be his chief of staff, and the seething need for revenge that had followed this affront. There had been little satisfaction in it for Amos when the twerp had proven to be grossly incompetent, unable to keep his mouth shut in public, and unable to stay out of bed with a college buddy, all of which had cost him his job and had promoted Amos to the position he honestly believed he had earned and richly deserved from the very beginning.

To his credit, Coleridge had done a good job as president with Amos's help, but he had still suffered all the indignities that could be heaped upon him by a hostile press. He had heard all the rude jokes about his being a Jimmy Carter with an iceberg up his ass, or having a big pair of snowballs in his shorts, but those didn't bother him. What did bother him greatly was having his attractive wife, Mallory, referred to as the "Ice Queen" out of jealousy for her excellent mind and austere ash-blonde beauty, or as "Snow Cones" for her ample bosom. There was simply no respect in the press corps anymore.

Coleridge had won the election fairly, and he had thoroughly intended to do a good job as president, despite all the obstacles thrown at him by an unfavorable Congress controlled by the opposition party. He had also been realistic enough to know that the road to Hell was paved with intentions every bit as good as his own, and that what he wanted for his presidency and what he would be allowed to do with it were going to be vastly different. He was right.

\* \* \*

New York Independent System Operations (NYISO) Control Center is a central coordination point for all of New York State's electric utilities. The organizations control center is located in a cavernous room inside a sedate brick building in Albany, New York. Within this room, five power grid operators labor through a twelve-hour shift, controlling the flow of energy through the bulk electric power system serving the entire state of New York, ensuring continuity of vital electric service. Twenty-four hours a day, seven days a week, these power grid operators monitor the megawatt flows on all critical transmission lines in the state and on all lines that connect New York State to adjacent companies. They constantly modify schedules of power purchased by the electric market participants in order to maintain safe transmission line loadings and to regulate system voltages and reserve power.

Seated at five consoles facing an eighty-foot semicircular dynamic system map board that reaches twenty feet high, and utilizing two huge computer systems, fifty full-color computer monitors, and hundreds of telephone and telemetering circuits, the operators provide for both system security and economic operation of the state's electric utilities. The lights never go out in this room, as there are backup supplies to the backup supplies and the phones rarely stop ringing as generation is shifted from place to place to most economically serve the needs of consumers in New York State and to control power line flows and critical voltages. Millions of dollars of electricity are traded within and outside of New York State, and system conditions are constantly balanced to a fine degree.

John Halloran glanced up over the tops of his computer monitors at his operator, Joe Krug. Krug's neck was rapidly turning bright red above his tight collar as he sorted through page after page of power contracts. He appeared to be ready to blow his stack, even though the shift had just begun. John knew that he had to do something to defuse the situation.

"What's the problem, Joe? Why can't we get the Central-East interface power flows down?"

"Because we've got an unbelievable mess of overlapping contracts here, and I can't identify the originators of the two contracts to Con Edison that will work to reduce Central-East the best. I've just spent the past ten minutes talking to the brokers who set up the contracts, and all I get from them is a damned runaround. They either can't or won't identify who the originators are, so they dummy up and hope I'll cut somebody else. Just give me a minute to wade through this damned labyrinth of intervening parties, and I'll get the cuts made," Joe Krug answered with a frustrated shrug.

John suppressed his own frustration with a supreme effort of will. He knew Joe was a good operator and that he was simply overloaded with multiparty contracts for power, transmission service, ancillary service, reserve, and capacity. In the best of times, these could be difficult, but tonight, they were overwhelming.

All this considered, John knew he had to take action. He couldn't allow his system to run over a stability limit without the very real danger of suffering a contingency loss of a major generator or element of his transmission system that could cause instability or voltage collapse. Voltages were already beginning to decline in steady state at several major substations. He made his decision and acted on it. "No time for that now, Joe. I've got to go into alert state for Central-East stability, so just put Ontario and Hydro Quebec under Emergency Operating Procedure 3-2 and we'll let the billing department straighten the dollars out after the fact. Log the cuts on my authority."

"Thanks, John. I'll get right on it." The look of relief on Joe's face was almost embarrassing.

John reached over to his telephone console and depressed the red button marked "Hot Line." An alarm bell rang, and John glanced up at his annunciator panel to watch a series of eight indicator lights begin to go from white to green as utility company system operators picked up their hotline phones and listened for his message.

The New York ISO hotline phone was a one-of-a-kind system, engineered to enable the shift supervisor to communicate with all member companies quickly by depressing only one phone button. Because the system was designed for strictly one-way communication from the NYISO to the member companies, indicator lights were needed to allow the shift supervisor to know when all eight companies were online and listening. If a company had a question about the hotline message, the company with the question would call the NYISO back on another line.

When all eight lights were green, John said, "Okay, folks, the system is operating in an alert state at this time, call it 19:15, due to exceeding the Central-East interface transient stability limits. We're currently in the process of making transaction cuts to reduce the cross-state flows, so please pick up your generation to the security base points at emergency response rate so dispatch can solve the overload. I repeat: alert state for Central-East transfers. End of message." John released the red button, and, one by one, the green lights on the annunciator panel blinked out.

John watched his security monitor screen as slowly, over a period of several minutes, generators in the southeastern portion of New York State responded to the reduction in contract power and increased their generator unit loading. Slowly, the amount of power flowing across the group of transmission lines that formed the Central-to-East transmission interface decreased and the violation cleared. John breathed a sigh of relief. A quick scan of his voltage profile showed significant improvement.

After waiting for a few more minutes just to be sure that the system had stabilized, John again depressed the red button. Seven men and one woman scattered throughout the state, picked up their red phones to listen. "At 19:32, the alert state is terminated. All flows are now within acceptable limits. The system remains in a warning state, however, due to loss of our backup satellite communications system. I'll keep you informed of any change in this situation. End of message."

John released his hotline button and, through the habit of many years in operations, allowed his eyes to scan the system voltage profile before returning to the more routine work of running the shift. *"Alright, bad boy, let's get you put to bed for the night,"* John thought. He enjoyed thinking of the power system as a huge animal that had all the needs and wants of a human being. This creature had to be controlled and made to conform to certain rules of operation, and it was his job to control it.

In fact, the load curve of an electric power system does conform exactly to the life cycle, needs, and wants of its very human customers. If you understood people and could read *TV Guide*, you could anticipate load trends very well.

At this time of night, the system load was climbing toward the evening peak, as people were busily cleaning up after dinner, showering, loading dishwashers, and settling down for an evening of homework, television, and internet surfing. Soon, stores would be closing, office cleaning crews would be going home, restaurants and shopping malls would be closing, and people would be preparing for bed. After the brief peak at suppertime, the load would trend steadily down until after the eleven o'clock news, when it would drop sharply. After the late-night comedian shows, the load would bottom out.

Around 05:00, the creature would begin to stir as early risers began their day. As people were preparing for work, the load would climb steadily. Between seven and nine o'clock, as factories, offices, stores, and schools opened and plugged into the system, the load would scream up at an alarming rate. The creature would demand more and more electricity until noon, after which it would stay quite constant until the evening peak load for the day. Just a nice reasonable predictable daily cycle. A good operator knew the beast and his moods and was prepared to respond to them, and John Halloran was a very good power grid operator.

He had finally gotten a free moment to start on his paperwork when the outside phone line rang. He depressed the corresponding button on his phone console. "New York ISO. Halloran speaking."

"Hi, John, this is Devon at the Space Weather Prediction Center, I have an SMD alert for you." The voice on the phone from the SWPC in Boulder, Colorado, was soft and friendly and very feminine, and just exactly what John needed to pique his attention level.

"Devon, go ahead."

"A solar magnetic disturbance of K-6 intensity was observed from 22:30 to 00:30 Universal time on March 1. Additional events of K-6 or greater are possible through 20:00 UT on March 5. That's all, John, and I already know your initials."

"Just a second, Dev. Do you have a minute for a quick question?"

"Sure, John," she groaned, a fine edge of sarcasm creeping into her voice. "The weather in Colorado has been fine. It snows every day. The spring skiing is great! You've been promising to come out here to enjoy it with me all winter, and I haven't even met you yet."

John Halloran and Devon Grant had developed a cordial phone friendship over the past six months and were comfortable bantering with one another. Devon was new at her job as a solar technician for SWPC and had been very curious about the effect of solar magnetic disturbances on electric power systems. Many of her priority-one customers were electric utilities and larger regional transmission organizations like PJM and MISO and ISO's like New York, and she wanted to know why.

John had always remembered that his company had provided training regarding when the Hydro Quebec system was blacked out by the effects of a solar magnetic disturbance on some very critical voltage-control equipment, and he had been interested in SMDs ever since. For that reason, he had very good-naturedly tutored Devon on elementary electric system operations and, at this point, had taught her as much as she could understand about the problems that SMDs can cause on the interconnected power systems of the northeastern US and Canada, while at the same time learning from her about the sun. Through this exchange of information, a trusting relationship had grown. Because many of their conversations had to be on the unrecorded phones installed for operators' private use, the sharing of unpublished phone numbers added a touch of intimacy and trust.

"No, Dev, this is business, sort of."

"Oh well, that does make a whole big difference, John, sort of. Go ahead, ask away."

"Well, I already know that SWPC primarily monitors activity on the sun and the effects it will have here on Earth, but I was wondering if SWPC might also have information about anything else unusual going on up there that might be even vaguely classified as unusual."

"It's our job to monitor and report on everything in the Solar-Earth environment, John. What is it you need to know?"

"Well, earlier this evening, Hughes Aerospace had to terminate our backup telephone communication system while they switched us over to another satellite. We've had the system for ten years now, and this is the first time they've had to shut it down on us. I know that a K-6 disturbance is not a major storm, so there must be something else that's causing the shutdown. I was wondering if you might know what that something else might be or if Hughes is just pulling my chain and dropping my communications system for their own reasons."

At the Space Weather Prediction Center, a strong hand suddenly gripped Devon's shoulder from behind, causing her to jump in her seat at the solar technician's console and to emit a tiny yelp of surprise.

"Devon, what was that noise? Are you all right?" John asked.

"Yes, I'm okay," she answered while a bony hand jabbed a long, thin finger at a bright yellow memo sheet taped to her console top, just below a television monitor displaying a graph of recent solar activity.

After a short hesitation, she came back. "No, John. We do not think there is any relationship between the current SMDs and your communications shutdown." A degree of stress had suddenly become apparent in her voice, and John had a strong feeling that she was purposely avoiding a direct answer to his question. Even though this behavior was quite out of character for Devon, he felt the need for an answer and decided to press the issue.

"I have one more question, if you don't mind," John continued, ignoring her stress. "Driving to work for the past couple of nights, I've noticed what appears to me to be an unusually large number of shooting stars. Is there a periodic meteor shower going on presently? And if so, could this have had any effect on the Hughes satellite?"

This time, her hesitation was substantially longer, and John was sure he heard muffled voices in the background. He waited for a few moments, and when he got no response, he said, "Hello, Dev....Are you still there?"

"Oh yes, John, hold on one minute please." Her usually soft and rather quiet voice had taken on a definite edge.

When Devon came back on the line, her manner and tone of voice were completely changed. She was no longer the friendly, open Devon Grant he had come to know but instead was very closed and businesslike.

"You already know that the SWPC is part of the National Oceanographic and Atmospheric Administration and that we monitor all activity in the solar-terrestrial region, but we are also the world and national warning center for disturbances in the space environment. If anything unusual was occurring, we would know about it, and we would report this to our customers. We also work closely with the US Air Force Space Forecast Center and the 50th Space Weather Squadron in Colorado Springs. We would know from them of any satellite problems, either military or civilian. There are none to report at this time."

Her response had suddenly taken on all the charm and grace of a public-relations message, and she was delivering it with the boundless enthusiasm of a rusty robot. This again was not like the Devon he had come to know, but John decided to press on. "And that's all you have to say?"

At the Space Weather Prediction Center, Devon Grant had shaken off the hand that had gripped her shoulder, and she swiveled her chair around to look up at Jason Shellcroft. The SWPC operations manager again pointed firmly to the printed sheet in front of her and shook his head. The set look on his face and his determined manner left no room for negotiation. She glanced over at Art Capiletti, her shift forecaster, but Art was deep in conversation with Air Force Lt. Colonel Mark Persons and did not notice her concerned look. Both men were studying a stack of plots and graphs on Art's desk, and both wore expressions of concern that Devon was curious about, but then, she was curious about a lot of things.

Military personnel were a common sight at SWPC, and several Air Force men were on the staff, but Colonel Persons was new. He had been pulled off temporary duty at Colorado Springs and reassigned to SWPC only a few days ago. By the way they were talking, Devon had to believe there was a significant event taking place that was not being shared with her.

John Halloran was correct in that a simple K-6 SMD was not a significant event, but Art had called the colonel in to work earlier tonight, and the two men had been in deep conversation ever since. There had to be a reason. The SWPC operations room was not large, but even in this small room, they had not shared any information with her, and try as she might, she could not eavesdrop well enough to get a clue.

Jason Shellcroft once again nudged Devon on the shoulder and pointed his finger firmly at the printed page on her desk. He nodded his head so emphatically this time that his half glasses slid down his nose comically. Devon would have laughed out loud if she hadn't been so angry with him. His look clearly said, "Read the message exactly as printed, or else," so Devon began to read.

"John?"

"Yes."

"I'm sorry for the delay. We have no information at the present time on any meteor showers in progress. I've put you on our first priority list for notification should anything of an unusual nature occur that could in any way affect your operations."

Her message still had a prerecorded sound, but the stress level in her voice had definitely gone up another order of magnitude. John decided there was no use in pressing the issue any further. He might be probing into things that were none of his business, and he did not want to compromise their new friendship.

"No problem," he said. "I was just curious because I have to declare an alert state on my system whenever I lose a major communication path, so I like to keep tabs on any potential problems. Thanks anyway. Have a good night."

"Bye," Devon said wistfully.

"One more thing, if it's not too much trouble. I've got some time coming to me, and I was thinking about coming out there to do some spring skiing. How's the weather and the snow conditions?"

Devon had to chuckle at his quick joke and how it removed the tension from their present situation, liking him greatly for this thoughtfulness. There was no hesitation in her response at all. "Snow is great, so is the weather, so quit making promises and come on out."

"Sounds good to me."

"Bye again, John."

Devon turned quickly to face Mr. Shellcroft and give him a piece of her mind. She did not like the new rules he was imposing, and she liked it even less having him grab her shoulder, and she meant to tell him so. He may be the boss, but he could not put hands on her, but the look on his face and his angry words cut her off completely.

"Ms. Grant," he began, "you are well aware of the new informational guidelines, and if you value your job at all, you will follow them to the letter. Also, I have not previously commented on your obviously personal conversations with your friend at the New York ISO, but in the future, they will cease. *Do you understand?*"

In the face of such uncharacteristic anger from a normally mild-mannered man, Devon's angry retort froze in her throat. "Yes, sir," was all she could say.

"Good." With that, Jason Shellcroft turned on his heel and walked stiffly away.

Devon watched Mr. Shellcroft's ramrod-straight back as he walked stiffly from the operations center. "*Tight ass!*" she thought as he disappeared.

When Art finished his conversation with Colonel Persons, he glanced over at Devon and noticed the angry expression on her face. A look of almost fatherly concern came over his weatherworn features as he ran his hands across his face and up into his hair. He arched his bushy eyebrows as if to say, "What's up, girl?"

When she was sure she had his attention, she covered the mouthpiece on her phone and said softly, "New York ISO wanted to know about meteorites."

Art glanced briefly at Lt. Colonel Persons with a strange conspiratorial expression on his face, then shook his head emphatically with a no. His expression told her he did not like this any more than she did, but orders were orders. "Leave this one alone, Devon. I can't say any more right now, but just leave it alone!"

\* \* \*

Solar magnetic disturbances are changes in the earth's magnetic field caused by magnetic fluxes ejected from the surface of the sun during periods of sunspot activity. There is always a fairly constant flow of charged electronic and magnetic particles away from the sun, toward the earth, and beyond into space. This flow is referred to by astronomers as the solar wind, and it carries the solar magnetic fluxes to Earth, where these charged magnetic particles can cause numerous problems with orbiting satellites, radio frequency communications, railroad signaling devices, and navigational equipment. The magnetic fluxes are also responsible for the stunningly beautiful auroral displays at the north and south polar regions, and they can also cause a number of problems on highly integrated electric power systems.

During an intense magnetic storm of K-9 intensity on March 13, 1989, geomagnetic-induced ground currents, caused by the SMD, were responsible for a series of severe voltage swings and several relay mis-operations that caused a province-wide blackout in Quebec, Canada. This particularly intense magnetic storm was also responsible for considerable equipment damage on the interconnected power systems in parts of the northeast United States and Canada. Vivid auroral displays, normally only apparent in the polar regions, were seen as far south as Florida. Since that date, the New York Independent System Operations Center, which was then known as the New York Power Pool, had become an SWPC priority-one customer and the service center had begun reporting SMD alerts and forecasts directly to the New York ISO operators.

When notified of a disturbance of K-5 intensity or higher, New York ISO logs this information and notifies all of its member companies and the adjacent operating areas of the Northeast Power Coordinating Council. These areas will then take any actions they deem necessary to protect the integrity of their systems. These notifications are a well-established routine.

While making such notifications, John was able to use part of his mind to consider some of the stranger aspects of his recent telephone conversation with Devon Grant at SWPC.

John Halloran had been an operator at the NYISO for more than ten years, and in that time, he had sharpened his communications skills to a fine degree. The job of operating a tightly integrated electric power system is a highly technical and difficult one, made more difficult by the fact that the operators have no physical control of any of the elements on the system. The power grid must be operated by using voice communication with member-system operators as the only tool.

As another result of these physical limitations, the power system operator must develop a second ear, trained to pick up any slight nuances of speech or changes in voice patterns that can give an indication of the level of stress in an individual or a situation. These sure signs of an operator's emotional state can often dictate the need for prompt action far better than words alone can.

When the continuity of electric power supply to millions of people is at stake, and with all of his or her communications recorded, an operator learns quickly to be clear and concise in communication and to use the unspoken word as routinely as the spoken. Quite often, what is not said speaks more loudly than what is said. For many years, power system operators' communication skills and job stress levels have been frequently compared to those of air traffic controllers, and rightly so.

Devon Grant had sounded to John Halloran as if she had been reading someone else's words and, more significant to John, that she had been uncomfortable with them. He knew Devon well enough to have asked her about it, but he felt this was not the proper time. He knew she was uncomfortable with her actions, but as to why, John didn't have a clue.

Since the Federal Energy Regulatory Commission rulings of 1996, orders 888 and 889 had mandated deregulation of utility service areas, the climate in the American power industry has been one of rapid change and conflicting priorities. Federal deregulation has placed public utilities into a difficult situation. By granting newly constructed non-utility generators free access to the bulk power transmission system, which was built and is maintained by the utilities, and then mandating that their energy must be purchased whenever it is available. Deregulation has helped contribute to force utilities into the difficult situation of being obligated to shut down their own generating units while purchasing power generated far from the utility load centers. This mandate has not had the desired effect of drastically lowering electric rates to the consumer, and it has caused the power grid operators many serious problems.

Power marketers of wholesale electricity have entered the marketplace by creating intense competition for every megawatt of available transmission capacity. Bulk power system flows and voltages that were once easily manageable are now difficult to control, and for the power system operator, this has only served to complicate an already difficult situation. Where once system security was an operator's paramount concern and preventing widespread power outages was the overriding goal, now, economy and compliance are king. The power engineer has been replaced by the lawyer, the HR department, and the accountant.

Because of this situation, John Halloran quickly became much too busy attending to his own system's problems to concern himself with the strange conversation he had just concluded with a fine lady two time zones away. He was forced to put the conversation out of his mind to tend to the world of power flows, distribution factors, megawatts, dollars, and voltages. This trend continued unchanged for several more hours of his night shift.

## Tuesday March 2

Reverend Randall P. Davis could not sleep. Instead of resting in his comfortable bed, cuddled next to his wife, Ruth, he was pacing the floor in his study, agonizing over the surprising reactions to his show on the day before. Randy did not doubt for an instant the truth of his message or his need to give warning to his faithful followers; what surprised him was the powerful response he was receiving.

Since his show had been broadcast, the phone lines at the studio had been overloaded with calls from his followers praising him and seeking more information. His home phone had been deluged with calls, and today, his e-mail in-box was simply unmanageable. He was prepared to do the work of the Lord but woefully unprepared for this kind of notoriety. He was also not prepared for the men who had arrived earlier and were sitting in an unmarked car across the street from the parsonage, or for the men who had paid a visit to his station manager, prompting a halfhearted censure of his material. Randy knew the station manager was under some sort of pressure to censor his material but reluctant to do so because of the very positive audience response.

He glanced at the clock, which read four thirty a.m. Without thought, he turned the page on his desk calendar to Tuesday, March 2, and moved idly to the window, staring up at the night sky. Randy Davis was rewarded by the sight of a bright blue-white streak across the sky, followed by two more. "*I see your messengers, Lord,*" Randy thought. "*But I don't know if my course of action is what it should be.*"

Randy lowered his forehead against the cold pane of glass in the window and prayed, "Lord, please show me the way to go. I know what needs to be said, Lord. Please give me the wisdom to say it properly."

\* \* \*

Devon Grant glanced over at Don Steward, the solar forecaster on the midnight shift, and assured herself that he was sufficiently involved in updating his data and trying to stay awake to notice an unscheduled call. While Reverend Randall, 1,500 miles away, continued to pray with his head pressed hard against his study window pane, Devon pressed the speed dial for NYISO.

"ISO, Halloran," came the sleepy voice from across the continent.

"John, this is Devon. Can you talk?"

"Certainly…and thank you."

"Thank you for what?"

"Thank you for calling and preventing me from bruising my forehead on the desk after falling asleep."

"You're welcome, John. But get serious."

"I am serious. At least as serious as I can be at four thirty in the morning."

"I want to talk to you about the call earlier."

"Yeah, but aren't you supposed to be home in bed? Your shift ended at midnight."

"My relief called in sick and I have to split the mids with the day-shift guy. He'll be here in a couple of hours. Now, can I talk?"

"Go ahead."

"First, I want to apologize for the runaround I had to give you. It wasn't my idea."

"I know."

"How the hell could you know?"

"In this job, you don't survive unless you learn to hear what isn't said or know when whoever you are talking to is using someone else's words."

"I don't understand."

"Well, there are many situations where a system operator has a situation on his hands where he needs help but doesn't want to ask for it. If you have gotten to know him well enough, you can sense the stress in his voice and find a way to help without his asking. There are other times where an operator has to refuse an ISO request or do something that is contrary to compliance policy. Almost always when I get that call, I can hear them speaking words I know belong to someone else. Sometimes a system operator will purposely change his manner of speech or use a catch phrase to tell me his boss is making him do something he doesn't agree with. I could hear that in your voice tonight."

"So you knew Shellcroft was making me read those stupid informational memorandums of his."

"I have no idea who Shellcroft is, but I knew the words you were saying were not yours. I kept pressing until I thought I might get you in trouble."

"He did chew me out a little before he went home, but not too badly. He told me in no uncertain terms not to call you again."

"He didn't make much of an impression then, did he?"

"What?"

"He told you directly not to call me, didn't he?"

"Yes."

"And what are we doing right now?"

"Oh, that.…Well, he never checks the voice recordings for this hour of the morning, and I had to let you know it wasn't me talking."

"I knew there was someone else there. We've talked enough for me to recognize when your speech patterns change. Your voice got a little higher, with a brittle edge to it. I think you were rather pissed."

"That's amazing," she said.

"Not so amazing. The NYISO has a good training program. They always manage to provide several communication courses each year. We have to be every bit as clear and concise as an air traffic controller does because lives depend on what we do as much as what they do."

"I'm sorry, John, but I just don't see that correlation. Losing power can be damned inconvenient, but not deadly."

"Would you say that if you were ill, at home on a ventilator or on dialysis or on a computer-controlled medication or chemotherapy? You probably have no idea how many people are on life support of one kind or another right there in Boulder, but I'm sure that Public Service Company of Colorado does. The good old health care system won't let you stay in the hospital one day longer than absolutely necessary. I think they'd do open-heart surgery as an outpatient procedure if they could.

"Utilities have to keep track of these people so that if we have to shut down customer load in an emergency to save the system, we try not to cut off any area that has a life-support person in it or a hospital, police station, nursing home, ambulance, rescue squad, or a telecommunications company or even a computer manufacturer. The list goes on and on and on."

"I thought all those people had emergency generators or something like that."

"Some do, and some don't, but most of them are rarely tested and have a limited-time duration because of fuel. If a utility company knows there will be an outage for scheduled work or if a hurricane or ice storm threatens, we will hook up one of our own portable generators to supply anyone that we know is on life support until regular service is restored."

"Wow, I had no idea."

"Most people don't." Do you remember the heat storm we had a couple of summers ago, Dev?"

"Wow, do I. I thought it would never cool off."

"Did you know that over a hundred people died of heat prostration in New York City alone? These were just the people who didn't have any access to air-conditioning. Imagine what the death toll might have been if there was a major power outage causing no air-conditioning city-wide in hundred-degree weather."

"I can't imagine."

"Neither can I, but the thought is in every power grid operator's mind because he owns part of the responsibility for keeping the system up and running."

"That's why you take the SMDs so seriously, then?"

"Exactly, Dev. Anything that can jeopardize the security of the power system, we take very seriously."

"Oh John, that makes me feel even worse about not being truthful with you earlier."

"The choice wasn't yours, Dev. I know how you feel. Ever since the Federal Energy Regulatory Commission ordered deregulation for utilities, I haven't liked the changes forced on system operations. Too much emphasis on economy and not enough on security. Too damned many lawyers and accountants making the rules and not enough good engineering judgment along with some old-fashioned common sense."

There was a lull in the conversation. Then, after both of them had thought things over, Devon said, "I'm going to have to get off now, John. I've got my shift-check list to catch up on. Will I talk to you soon?"

"Absolutely. I'll talk to you tomorrow. And keep your eye on the weather reports."

"That one's getting a little stale, John." Devon's voice sounded a little frustrated.

After a moment's thought, John answered, "I hear you."

"You'd better. Goodnight, John."

"Night, Dev."

\* \* \*

John Halloran was tired from working Monday evening into Tuesday morning and was ready to go home, but he continued to busily feed "the beast" that the New York power system had become this early Tuesday morning. He was inserting transmission voltage capacitors and urging the generating companies to move their generation up with the rapidly increasing load. It seemed as if everyone in the entire state had gotten up and turned on their coffee makers at the same time. An alarm sounded, and John looked up to see that the vehicle gate had opened. A glance at the security TV monitor showed Bud Flynn, his relief, had finally gotten to work. His transmission and generation dispatchers had been relieved at the normal time and were already well on their way home. Late or not, John was happy to see Bud come through the gate.

Bud was a man to whom life was a game to be played to the fullest, and he did just that. Even though he had worked shifts for many years, he had never gotten the clue that he couldn't party all night, still work day shift, and be on time. This attitude, among others, did not endear him to the men who had to wait until he arrived at work so they could go home.

Bud came bounding through the control room door promptly at 7:15, with his shirttail out, as usual, and his neck tie still in his pocket. His hair looked as if it had been combed with an eggbeater, and there were several bloodstained pieces of tissue plastered on shaving cuts. In other words, he looked quite normal for Bud, and John greeted him with a frown that fit the circumstance.

"Sorry I'm late again, Johnny. I'll make it up to you next week." Bud always said this but never did it. "What's the state of our mighty system this morning?" Bud asked, not really caring.

He went directly to the coffeepot to pour himself a cup, spilling more than a little on the counter. He rooted around the coffee area until he finally found an obviously day-old doughnut, which he immediately began to eat, scattering powdered sugar on the dark blue carpet. John had a flashback of the time when he had kept a doughnut in his desk drawer until it was a week old and hard as a rock. He had left it next to the coffeepot just in time for Bud's typical tardy arrival. Much to John's chagrin, Bud had picked up the doughnut, tested it for freshness, and then simply dunked it in his coffee until it was soft enough to eat. This had certainly not been the outcome John had desired.

When Bud finally got around to coming over to the shift supervisor's console to relieve John, it was a day late and a dollar short. John was completely frustrated. Bud exhibited a complete lack of concern as he spilled more of his coffee on the daily transmission outage log and left a trail of powdered sugar across the desk. Then he finally flopped into a chair and began to pay a little attention to what John was saying.

It was extremely difficult for John to hide his anger at Bud's selfish attitude, so he simply gritted his teeth, shrugged it off as always, and gave Bud the information necessary to take over the shift. "It's been the usual pain in the ass of a night. All the companies are busily trying to outdo the others by making short-term power contracts with energy traders and each other, totally without any regard for system conditions. It's rapidly becoming damned near impossible for the generation dispatcher to set up workable hourly schedules and for us to maintain the transmission system within limits. I had two alert states last night for Central-East and one for Oakton voltage, both due to overscheduling.

"Our generation commitment plan looks adequate for the day, except for the Hudson Valley. All we have on there are the two Indian Point units; everything else is on economy shutdown. That leaves us enough on line to meet our load and reserve requirements, but we're stretched pretty thin for voltage control. Speaking of voltage, you had better watch it closely, because it's been up and down all night across the system.

"I'm forecasting a 28,500 megawatt load for the peak today. We also have an SMD of K-6 through March fifth at 16:00. That reminds me, Hughes Aerospace shut down our backup communications for several hours yesterday evening. They had to switch over satellites, and we were in warning state for that time. SWPC says it was not the SMD that caused it. Otherwise, the system's been pretty quiet."

"Go home and get some rest," Bud said, still only half-listening as he sucked the powdered sugar off his fingers, then wiped his hands on his pants.

"See you later," John answered. John thought to himself that tonight would be an excellent time to get some of his late time back. "Don't wait up," he said, but Bud was already back in the coffee room with his head in the refrigerator, looking for more food to scrounge. John figured Bud's next move would be to check the refrigerator in the staff kitchen and, if nothing showed up there, the candy machine was a last resort. Bud's idea of the three main food groups were sugar, salt, and preservatives.

John took several deep breaths of the chilly March air as soon as he got outside the staff door. It felt good to be out of the seat after twelve hours in the pressure cooker, and better still to breath the clean crisp air. He climbed into his old blue Chevy pickup and kicked over the starter. As ancient as she was, the engine caught immediately and purred idling as John let her warm up a little before leaving the staff parking lot. Then he dropped her into first gear and headed out the gate of the ISO and back into the world.

It's hard to explain the affinity a man can grow for an old pickup truck, but John felt it strongly this morning for his rolling bucket of rust. The truck felt to him like an old friend, familiar and trusted. Since he had bought her twelve years ago, she had gone through one set of transmission carrier bearings and several sets of mufflers, brakes, and tires but had never once failed to start for him on a cold winter morning or to get him home in the wee hours of the morning, no matter how bad the weather or his own condition. In all that time, he'd had a lot better luck with the pickup truck than he'd ever had in his relationships with the opposite sex. The old truck didn't spring a leak if he forgot her birthday, or break down altogether if he didn't buy a valentine. The pickup also didn't want to move in together and bring a damned cat along. John had been through one long and painful relationship and several shorter, less committed ones. None of them had worked out, and all had ended badly. Several considerably more than casual acquaintances had been all right, but none of the women had stuck with him. The old pickup did.

Rambling on in the mind is not an unusual thing for a shift worker to do after a nights' work, and neither is the lack of attention that allowed the plain blue Ford sedan to slip in behind John without any particular notice on his part. The car and its two occupants followed him at a discreet distance down New York Route 20 toward the town of Duanesburg and the diner of the same name for breakfast.

"You better find yourself a day job and get off that shift work, Johnny boy. You look like hell this morning," greeted Sally Prentiss, the red-haired waitress at the Duanesburg Diner.

"Thanks for the kind words, Sal," John answered. "It makes me feel better just to hear your voice." *It doesn't hurt my eyes any, either,* John thought as he slid onto a stool at the counter.

"It don't make you look any better, though," she retorted, smiling, after which she wrinkled her nose and asked, "You having the usual?"

"Turkey on white toast, light on the mayo, and a glass of milk," John confirmed.

"Unreal. What a ridiculous breakfast." She grimaced.

"Just the ticket for sleeping after night shifts." John smiled. "Mother Nature's sleeping pill."

"Maybe so, but it's still weird," Sal muttered, moving down the counter to draw a big glass of cold milk. "Tom on toast, light mayo. He's on nights again," she called into the kitchen.

Jim Bradley's smiling black face appeared in the kitchen pass-through. "Good morning, Johnny," he called.

"Morning, Jim."

Sally Prentiss was an old friend, and she enjoyed the morning banter as much as John did. She had a temper to match her hair color, but she also had a heart as big as her bust line; and that more than made up for taking the sharp edge of her tongue every now and again. As John was a bachelor who did not enjoy either cooking or eating alone, the diner had become akin to a second home to him, and he knew Sally's work schedule as well as he knew his own. He could always come in here and cry in his milk about how lousy his bosses were or how badly some girl had treated him and Sally would offer a kind, if sometimes a little salty, word of comfort for him.

Occasionally when he was deep in the pits, she would lean both elbows on the counter and treat him to some of her sage advice, along with a view of some truly outstanding cleavage. John looked; he couldn't help himself. Sally knew he looked, and didn't mind at all. It was their private little game, and they both rather enjoyed it. Sally's advice and the view down the top of her uniform had saved John's sanity on more than one occasion. John had made a few attempts to advance their relationship beyond the over-the-counter bantering stage, but he had always been kindly but firmly rebuffed, so they had remained just friends.

"Eat up, boy. Then home to bed for you," Sally said with a smile.

"You coming along?" John teased with a wink.

"In your dreams, buster," she said, smiling again, more slowly this time.

"Try me."

"One of these days, when your health is stronger and I'm sure your life insurance is paid up, I may give it some consideration. Hey, that reminds me! I am still your beneficiary, aren't I?" she came back.

"Who else? Hell, I keep the policy under my pillow just in case." That won a good hearty laugh from the redhead.

In a much more serious move, Sally leaned her hip on the counter and bent over close to John. "Do you know those two suits sitting in the booth by the door?" She nodded her head in the general direction of the exit. "I can't figure out if they're in love with me or you."

"With you here, Sal, they don't even see me," John said, smiling and meaning it, as he casually looked back over his shoulder.

There were two strange men dressed in business suits and similar striped neckties. They were indeed sitting in the booth she had indicated, both looking quite uncomfortable and out of place in a local diner loaded with workmen dressed in plaid flannel shirts, work boots, and baseball caps. They looked away when John glanced over at them.

"Never saw them before," John said.

"I thought they might be big shots from your job."

"No, I never laid eyes on them before, Sal, so you must be the object of their admiration. Not that I can blame them," John flirted as he rose to leave. "See you tomorrow, Sal," he said, finishing his milk with a gulp.

"You should be so lucky." She smiled warmly and winked as John paid his bill and left.

John's biorhythms were doing a crash dive in preparation for sleep as he started the pickup and drove around the back of the diner to avoid the traffic light. His home was just a few miles up New York Route 7 and then a half mile west on Lone Pine Road. His small house had been built in the 1930s by the owners of the original homestead there as a home for grandparents after the children had taken over operation of the family farm. It was the only dwelling remaining on the original property, as the main farmhouse had burned down in the early 1970s. When John had purchased the house, along with one acre of land, the remaining property and farm buildings had been pieced off to local farmers with adjacent parcels of land, and that was just fine with John. The little house was all he needed.

Sally Prentiss had suggested he buy the little house when he had been in the depths of a huge depression. It was shortly after his parents had been killed in a terrible car accident and his last effort into the realm of romance had been vastly unsuccessful. John had been deep in the pits. Sally had been very, very right. Without realizing it, he had outgrown the lifestyle of the singles' apartments where he had lived at the time, and the house had provided a center for his life that had been missing for too long a time. John had been happily renovating, redecorating, and landscaping ever since.

John's two crowning projects had been raising the roof on the back of the house to install a Dutch dormer with the help of several guys from the NYISO and a half keg of beer, and then later adding a small but comfortable front porch with the same crew. The dormer provided him with a large master bedroom and bath upstairs with windows looking out on the Helderberg Mountains, and the porch provided him with both serenity and community. John loved to sit outside on warm evenings. Quite often, his neighbors would see him there and stop in for a visit. Life was good again.

John checked the rearview mirror just before turning into the driveway, hit the button for the garage door opener, and pulled straight inside. He went right to bed and promptly forgot about everything but the hours of good sleep ahead. He was just in the process of nodding off when the phone rang.

"Hello," he answered unhappily.

"Johnny, forget about sleeping and take a look out your window," said Sally Prentiss with no preamble.

"What the hell for?" John grumbled, throwing off the covers and moving to the window as instructed.

"Them two suits that were sitting by the door took off after you like a pair of scalded cats, so I thought I'd give you a heads up. Seems like kind of strange behavior to me."

"Thanks, Sal, but I can't imagine what they could want with me. Must just be a coincidence."

"Have it your way, but I still don't like the looks of it," Sally answered, obviously unconvinced.

"See you tomorrow, Sally."

"Sleep tight, John."

John continued to look out his front bedroom window for a moment and was rewarded by the sight of a plain blue Ford sedan cruising slowly past his driveway. John knew most of the cars belonging to people on his road, and this one was not familiar. Neither were the two men in dark suits sitting in the front seat.

\* \* \*

Devon Grant could not sleep. No matter how many times she rolled over and plumped up her pillow or how many new positions she tried, her mind would not shut down, and sleep would not come. Her usual glass of warm milk and half a Unisom pill had done nothing to relax her thought processes, and no matter how hard she tried, sleep remained elusive. She rolled over again, disgusted, and tried yet another position.

A few minutes later, she tore off her flowered sleep mask in complete frustration and swung her feet to the floor. Devon noticed the digital alarm clock on her night table read 11:28 a.m., as her feet felt around the floor for her scuffs. She had been trying for sleep since 8:30 a.m. to no avail, and it was time for a different tack. The brilliant Colorado sun was shining through the window blinds and making golden stripes on her bedroom wall. The traffic on Arapaho Avenue at the front of her apartment complex was making a steady hum, but neither of these things was what denied her sleep.

The events of the past few days had been running through her mind like a CD on a loop, and each rerun brought more questions to her mind—the same questions over and over again, and no answers.

"Why had Mr. Shellcroft been working in the building until after midnight for the past few days, and why had such a normally mild-mannered man grabbed her by the shoulder last night and insisted she read the garbage on his memo? Why had Art Capiletti been so busy and distracted that he had ignored her hand-waving signals? What had he and Lt. Colonel Persons been discussing so seriously, and why had the colonel been called in the first place?" All were questions with no answers to satisfy her curious mind.

The situation just wasn't fair. John Halloran was a good person and a friend, and Devon felt guilty for misleading him. His question was certainly relevant, and well within the expertise of SWPC to answer. Why had Mr. Shellcroft made her read that foolish typewritten memo back to John, especially when it wasn't completely true? Devon knew for a fact that several satellite operators had reported declining solar cell output on their satellites and had experienced some unexplained failures. She knew, from her training, that the likely cause of the failures was abrasion of exposed surfaces caused by clouds of space dust that occur during cometary passings. Other priority clients had inquired as to a probable cause also and had been given the same answer. She was ashamed that she had been forced to lie to them.

A number of problems were also showing up on military satellites, and this was likely the reason Lt.Colonel Persons was spending so much time at the Space Environment Lab. Satellite operators were priority-one customers of SWPC just as the NYISO was. They had legitimate questions about these unusual occurrences, and they were not being given the usual, correct answers. Why was Mr. Shellcroft so upset and cross recently—and especially after he had carelessly left that memo from Washington on her desk the other night? He had gotten very angry when he had caught her reading it. He had become a nervous wreck when he had realized she had seen the part of the memo on the increase in micrometeorite activity. Devon wondered a little nervously if she might have done anything else to bring his evil mood on. The questions kept popping into her mind, and she knew they would continue, so she just shook her head, tossing her hair and did the only thing possible for her to do in this situation. She got up.

Devon stripped off her nightgown and threw it on the rumpled bed. She quickly donned a pair of black lycra tights, with gray jogging shorts over them, a tee shirt with a Rocky Mountain High logo on it, and a loose, bright yellow turtleneck sweatshirt. "I probably look like a bumblebee," she said to herself as she headed downstairs for her run. "*I sure hope this clears my head,*" she thought as she grabbed a light jacket and went out the back door of the apartment building and into the parking lot.

Devon Grant was twenty-seven years old and had grown up in Cape May, New Jersey. Her life had taken its first turn when her father's drinking habit and the salesman's job that kept him away from home so much had collided with her mother's overly lavish spending and philandering ways. The whole mess had ended in a divorce. That in itself would have been bad enough, but it had degenerated into a publicly humiliating and acrimonious scandal that had aired every piece of the family's dirty laundry for the entire town to see. Devon had been everlastingly grateful when her mother had been awarded custody and had immediately removed her from Cape May Central High School to enroll her in a private prep school in Rahway. She had never returned.

After graduating from Princeton University with a degree in liberal arts, she'd had no particular career goals in sight and needed something to do. During her four years of study, she had taken three astronomy and geology courses, partly to fulfill her science requirements and partly because her father had been an amateur stargazer, when he had been sober enough. Those classes had also been a reason to be in the science center because she was fascinated with the handsome young professor who taught geology. Her motivation for taking them aside, Devon found the subjects fascinating and had done well in both subjects.

Devon was a beautiful young woman, and she had skillfully avoided Professor Holden's advances as an undergraduate, so it had not been difficult for her to regain his attention as a graduate student. Soon after she had done so, she had also been awarded an earth science fellowship for two years, working with Professor Holden, naturally.

Steve Holden, professor of geology, had the most perfectly unkempt dirty-blonde hair and the deepest blue eyes Devon had ever seen. They went perfectly with his deep tan and studiously casual mode of dress. Steve and Devon were not long into their relationship when Devon discovered that Steve instructed in anatomy almost as much as in geology. Many of the hills and valleys he explored definitely did not have rocks or vegetation on them. If she had thought very much about it beforehand, she would have realized that a man who spends his time exploring caves cannot develop a killer tan.

She soon became aware that what Steve Holden did study in his spare time was undergraduate female students and he had not altered this practice as promised when they had become a couple. Devon had ended their relationship by telling him exactly where he could use his rock hammer in the future.

Unfortunately, therefore, neither the fellowship nor the professor had turned out to be very satisfying, nor did either one hold any great hope for a long-term future to Devon. Devon had begun to be a little concerned about what that future might be when one day, she had been idly thumbing through *Astronomy* magazine and noticed an ad for a job as solar technician at the Space Weather Prediction Center. She had immediately applied and been awarded the position in Boulder, Colorado, but not without some help from her former boyfriend. So here she was, a new girl in town, with a new job that was slightly over her head, and a perplexing situation running around in her brain.

This morning, her mind was so filled with thoughts about the night before that Devon never thought to look out of her window before leaving to run. If she had, she might have noticed the gray Chevrolet parked on the corner of Arapaho and 9th Street with two men sitting in it, just watching.

* * *

"I would like to know…just what the hell we are doing, sitting here all day waiting for someone upstairs to finish her nap, when there are plenty of useful things we could be doing back in Denver," said the slightly built Hispanic man in the passenger seat of the charcoal gray Impala with the US government plates.

"Getting paid, aren't we, Dommy?" replied Frank Muller from the driver's seat. Frank was a big bear of a man who dwarfed his diminutive partner of many years. He just smiled with almost fatherly indulgence at Dommy's impatience.

"No matter," replied Domingo Ortiz. "I hate cooling my heels for no good reason."

"The good reason is that Vito is the boss and he called us in the middle of the night and told us to do it," replied Muller. "If you're so damned antsy, take a walk down the street and get us some lunch."

"I'll do that, partner. Same old, same old?"

"That'll do it for me."

Dommy Ortiz got out of the car and started to walk down 9th Street toward Canyon Boulevard and the orange Burger King sign. *Those nasty Whoppers are gonna kill Frank before any of the bad guys get a chance,* he thought. As he stretched the surveillance kinks out of his wiry five-foot, seven-inch frame, Ortiz cut his eyes steadily from left to right and up and down the street, just as he had been taught at the FBI Academy in Quantico, Virginia. He appeared to be walking casually down the street, but he didn't miss a thing as he moved. Then a flash of yellow coming from the parking lot at the rear of the Elk Ridge Apartments caught his eye and he stopped dead in his tracks, watching a young woman jog out of the lot right in front of him and across Arapaho Avenue. The mark was on the move.

Without conscious thought, Dommy Ortiz spun on his heels to head back to the car at a dead run. Frank Muller had also spotted Devon leaving the parking lot and had been slightly dismayed at his partner's quick move. He already had the motor running. "She's out for a run," Dom panted through clenched teeth as he swung into the passenger seat. Frank was already rolling.

"Nice move back there, partner," Frank muttered sarcastically as he edged out into traffic. "No way she didn't see you beat your skinny ass back to the car."

"Just drive," Dom said with a grimace, knowing Frank was right, and not liking it one bit.

Frank Muller had been a federal agent for more than twenty years, and he knew his way around the streets. His short-cut sandy-colored hair was well shot with gray, and his blue eyes crinkled at the corners. He sat in the driver's seat with his butt over against the door and his big body curled around the steering wheel like a black bear wrapped around a honey tree. For all his bulk, he handled the car with precision, allowing just enough distance between the Impala and the young woman in the yellow top.

As Devon steadily increased her pace, Frank stayed well back and ran through his mind a catalogue of all the jogging paths in Boulder that would be snow free and useable at this time of year. If he could discover what her possible destination might be, he would be able to reestablish surveillance without arousing any more curiosity on her part. Traffic in Boulder moved at a brisk pace, and college students did not have a great deal of patience with slow drivers. Frank knew very well that he could not continue driving this slowly without arousing Devon's attention or the ire of other drivers. He had already been cut off twice and flipped the bird more times than that.

Boulder, Colorado, is a busy and bustling little jewel of a city filled with parks, and Frank knew Devon might be headed for any one of several parks nearby. He watched as Devon crossed the bridge over Boulder Creek and turned right. Then Frank was sure. "She's headed for Central Park," Frank muttered to himself. "They keep the paths clean there, and we can drive straight up there from here. If we park at the Boulder Art Center, we can overlook almost the entire jogging path." He accelerated to resume the normal traffic pace and then moved ahead.

\* \* \*

Frank had been correct is his original assessment of Dommy's sudden dash back to the car. Devon Grant had spotted the slightly built Hispanic man spin about and run, and thought it a little strange. She continued to ponder this as she watched that same car drive past her with the two men in it. Neither man paid her the slightest attention, however, and they continued to go straight up 9th Street. She began to relax and enjoy her run.

When she reached the park, she took the jogging path to the right and settled into a nice rhythmic pace, enjoying the pleasant green scenery along Boulder Creek. The warm sunshine was relaxing, and she let her mind drift clear, concentrating only on the pounding of her shoes on the running path.

Boulder was a wonderful city for a runner because of its many fine parks, which helped to eliminate crowding, and they all provided excellent scenery, including many magnificent views of the Flatirons rising in the distance. Devon took in one great lungful after another of the clean, dry air, savoring the view, until she caught the reflection of the noonday sun glinting off something shiny in the near distance. As her eye followed the flash, her heart sank into her stomach. She realized the reflection was caused by the same gray car that she had seen earlier. The men had apparently looped around two blocks on Walnut Street and come back down 13th. They were just backing into a parking spot beside the Boulder Art Center, which would provide them with a view of the entire park. Devon was now certain the same two men were sitting in the car and watching her run, and this gave her chills.

On a sudden impulse, she sprinted and made a quick left onto a rarely used path that would take her through a small patch of woods and eventually back to her apartment by another route. As she continued her run, Devon wore a smug smile of satisfaction that she had shaken off the men who were following her and that they would never be able to follow her home. She didn't even consider the fact that they already knew where she lived and that all she had accomplished was to tip them off that she knew they were following her.

\* \* \*

"We're blown," Frank Muller groaned through his teeth. His heavy fist slowly pounded the steering wheel.

"My fault!" Dom exclaimed. "The boss ain't gonna be happy about this."

"That little gal is sharper than we gave her credit for," Frank said, calming down slightly. "We'd better get the girls to keep an eye on the apartment until we find a place with some cover to watch her. I don't want her taking another run."

"I'll call it in," Dom said. "Then I'll hang out at the senior center across the street."

"You'll fit right in there," Frank joked.

"Smartass."

"And watch those old ladies there. If you get too frisky, I'll have to tell Maria on you."

"Yeah, yeah, do what you got to do," Dom said with a smile, still mad at himself for being the reason their cover was blown.

\* \* \*

"Mr. Shellcroft, it's about time you start giving me some straight answers on just what the hell is going on here," Vito Pianese said in his best scare-the-hell-out-of-you voice. "And you'd better do it in words of one syllable or less. Make it clear, concise, complete, and immediate." Vito jutted his chin out and fixed his dark Mediterranean eyes directly into Jason Shellcroft's watery blue ones. He put on his best "cut the bullshit" look.

Vito was second in command of the Federal Bureau of Investigation field office in Denver, Colorado, and was a veteran of more than twenty-five years of service. He had worked his way up through the ranks and could be a very formidable and intimidating presence. He said only two more words: "Now talk!"

"I don't know if I'm completely clear on the entire situation myself…and I'm not exactly sure how much of what I do know that I can tell you." Shellcroft hedged and stammered, clearly shrinking back from the hard brown eyes glaring down on him.

"Well then, I think that I'll just collect my agents and go back to Denver, where we can get some real work done," Vito threatened and began to get up. He was not sure he could legally carry out this threat, but the look on Shellcroft's face was enough to convince him that the pretense was going in the right direction.

Vito was still more than a little pissed at having been roused in the middle of the night, torn from a sound sleep, to put together a surveillance team and head immediately to Boulder for an assignment that had all the earmarks of a fool's errand. He had no clue why his men were watching a seemingly innocent young woman, but he was damned straight going to find out.

"No, no," Shellcroft stammered as he sat upright in his chair and pushed his granny glasses back up on his straight, sharp nose. He was fairly flushed with agitation. "That will never do. Your instructions came directly from Washington, just as mine did, from someone high up."

"Then you had better fill me in so I can do my job, as ordered by that someone from high up," Vito said in his most gentle and reasonable growl.

The rapid mood shift approach had worked as predictably well as Vito had known it would. He had perfected this technique over the years, and it was his stock-in-trade. Shellcroft deflated immediately and began to spill out words like a fountain.

"The Space Environment Lab is one of eleven labs operated by the National Oceanographic and Atmospheric Administration. We conduct research here on solar-terrestrial physics and develop techniques for forecasting solar and geophysical disturbances. We provide real-time monitoring and forecasting of solar and geophysical events." Shellcroft was quoting dogma straight out of the Space Weather Prediction Center public relations brochure.

"Cut the shit and get to the real story. I'm not some Boy Scout leader here for a tour," Vito cut in, aggressive and bristling again.

"Yes, but from here it gets rather complicated."

"Start at the beginning. Keep it clear, concise and in words of one syllable, like I told you before."

"I supervise the Space Environment Service branch, which includes the Space Weather Prediction Center and the Space Environment Lab. We are, in effect, the nation's space weather channel. We provide forecasts of geomagnetic activity to agencies and businesses affected by rapid changes in the earth's magnetic field. These include many satellite operators, including the military, electric power systems, pipeline operators, plus railroads and communication systems."

"Go on," Vito coaxed gently, not hearing what he needed to know, but not wanting to stop the flow of information, either.

"There has been a marked increase in meteorite and micrometeorite activity, beginning a week or so ago. Lots of shooting stars, if you will. This meteor shower is similar in all ways to other periodic meteor showers that occur when the earth crosses the trail of debris left behind by old comets, but none of the known showers occur at this time of year. This one appears to be new and has a couple of astronomers curious."

"Curious about what?"

"This new shower is similar in some ways to the Leonid showers, in that it appears to be crossing the earth's plane at a very low angle. This could mean that we may well be in the stream for a few weeks' time, and we don't know anything about the particles' sizes or density."

"Explain that, please," Vito pursued, now very interested.

"This may make it a little clearer for you. Each year, we pass through the meteorite stream of Halley's Comet twice. Halley's is a short-period comet. When we pass through the meteorite stream in October, we observe what is called the Orionid meteor shower. When we pass through the stream again in May, we experience the Eta Aquirids."

"Where does this meteorite stream come from?" Vito asked.

"Picture a comet to be similar to a dirty ice ball, made up of about twenty percent frozen gasses like carbon dioxide, methane, and ammonia, and eighty percent water ice. Within this ice ball are solid particles of widely varying sizes which may be either stony or metallic in nature, left over from the birth of our solar system."

"Metallic?"

"Yes, metallic meteorites are mostly composed of nickel-iron with many other metals mixed in, including platinum, iridium, and germanium, but that's another story."

"I can't seem to get this one straight yet. One time you're calling them comets; in the next breath, you're calling them meteors, then meteorites. Which one are they?" Vito grumbled.

"Asteroids and comets are differentiated by astronomers on the basis of their appearance. If the object has a tail or visible atmosphere, it is called a comet. If it doesn't, it's called an asteroid. Both of them could be properly referred to as meteoroids when they are in space. If they enter the atmosphere, they are called meteors, and if they contact the earth's surface, they are meteorites. Is that any clearer?"

"Continue," Vito groaned, not liking to be talked down to, but needing this education to do his job and get back to the action in Denver.

"Each time a comet passes through our solar system and, relatively speaking, close to the sun, it is heated and loses some of its frozen mass through off-gassing. Any debris that is released by this loss of mass falls away and becomes part of the meteor stream remaining in the comet's orbit. While the last stages of a comet's life are not well understood, one theory holds that as the volatile gasses are depleted, a crust forms over the nucleus and allows the interior to remain bonded together."

"Where does all this junk come from?" Vito questioned.

"Comets are believed to be made up of the remains of material that formed the solar system and orbit in the far reaches of our solar system, far out beyond Pluto in an area called the Oort cloud, or in an area closer in called the Kuiper belt. Out there, the deep cold of interstellar space can preserve the comets' primitive chemistry, and it is not until something disturbs their orbits that they come closer to the sun and begin to disintegrate."

"So what's your point?" Vito begrudged, not liking his obvious lack of knowledge. "What can we expect from this encounter?"

"Nothing of any significance, as far as I know. We experience meteor showers regularly and have never been struck by one; otherwise, they would be called meteorite showers." Shellcroft smiled at his poor little joke. Vito was not amused.

"Then why all the uproar?"

"I don't honestly know. It must be that something else is going on up there that I haven't been told about."

"Obviously, but what?"

"Possibly some other NEO."

"Okay, so what's an NEO, and will you please speak English for a change?"

"NEOs are near-Earth objects—asteroids and comets whose orbits bring them near Earth. There are thousands of them out there, and some of them come pretty close. Perhaps a new one has been discovered."

"Why wouldn't we already know about it? Haven't we got the technology or expertise to locate and catalogue them?"

"We have both in abundance. What we lack is the leadership in Washington to establish the priority or willingness to spend large amounts of money on something that doesn't guarantee an instant return. There was a great deal of interest back in 1990 when the huge impact crater at Chicxulub in the Yucatan peninsula was discovered and it was determined that it was large enough to cause the extinction of the dinosaurs. The Spacewatch Survey was started to locate and catalogue NEOs. When Comet Shoemaker-Levy crashed into Jupiter in 1994, it caused the most spectacular demonstration to date of just how fragile our environment is and how dramatically a small impactor can disrupt it.

"Congress responded with funds to enlarge the Spacewatch Survey and begin a comprehensive system of observatories and a data-collection and cataloguing program. Then came the budget wars during an election year, and the funds were slashed. They never came back, and the survey was never completed. Since then, a few dedicated astronomers have continued the work on their own by begging, borrowing, and stealing telescope and computer time from other paying projects."

"Ouch! No wonder Big Brother wants to keep this at a low profile."

"That speaks volumes, Mr. Pianese, volumes. For shortsighted political reasons, we did not heed the danger signs. Now since our leaders can't explain away the program cuts, they respond by placing a gag order on reporting the situation until it can be verified that the earth is safe. They compound a misdemeanor with a felony."

"Do you mean to say that we may not be safe?"

"Given our present situation, what other conclusion can we draw?"

Vito shook his head, trying to take in the scope of what he had just heard. "Now just where does Miss Grant fit into the scheme of things?"

"That gets us back to the original problem. Three days ago, I received a priority message direct from the secretary of interior, hand-delivered by special messenger. This kind of extravagance is unheard of. The message prohibited us from discussing anything about the new meteor shower or anything even faintly associated with it. The secretary was kind enough to provide us with some simple cover stories to give out should we be questioned on the subject—which, by the way, were complete bull. We are using them, however, and we have received a number of questions."

"That still doesn't explain about Miss Grant."

"Over the past six months, Miss Grant has developed a friendship with a power grid operator from New York, one of our priority-one customers. Miss Grant is a new employee, and her natural curiosity has been beneficial to learning her job, but recently, she has been asking some very pointed questions about recent events which she has no concern, and now the New York operator is also asking questions."

"Miss Grant has had an opportunity to read part of a memo from the secretary on the subject, which I inadvertently left on her desk. That was my error, but I admonished her at the time and instructed her that this was extremely sensitive information and in no way to be discussed with anyone. After last night, when I believed that she almost gave out some of this information to her friend at the NY operations center, I began to question her trustworthiness to maintain security. I have taken the opportunity to audit her recorded conversations, and you may listen to them, if you wish. They verify that she did not actually breach security, but she still makes me nervous."

"I don't know what she knows or suspects, but she has a sufficient background to make some quite accurate and apparently dangerous assumptions. Washington does not want this to happen. I've never been briefed on the reasoning behind the gag order, but when I notified my superior of her behavior, you suddenly showed up. That's all I know."

"That was excellent, Mr. Shellcroft. See how well you can do with just a little encouragement?" Vito oozed with a satisfied grin. "I'm still a bit confused about how one seemingly innocent phone conversation about shooting stars can be cause for FBI surveillance. Just how long do you anticipate this event will last?" Vito asked.

"I don't really know…and I don't really care," Shellcroft responded with unusual vigor. "I just want to be left alone to do my job, and possibly get some decent sleep after this mess clears up."

Vito Pianese pulled his most serious special-agent face and said, "Now that we have some facts, I think I can see a reasonable course of action to take. Here's the way I see it: We'll maintain surveillance on Miss Grant for a few more days. We have her phone monitored, so we'll know if she makes any unusual calls. If nothing develops in that time, I think it's safe to assume this was an innocent conversation, and we can then suspend operations and return to Denver. I'm sure you can monitor her actions here at the center to ensure security is maintained on your end, Mr. Shellcroft. In the meantime, I can talk to some friends in Washington to try and get a better idea of just what we are dealing with."

\* \* \*

David Van Patten looked grim as he stamped his cigarette out in the already overflowing ashtray. "Damnit, Ben…I never expected things to come to a head this early in the game. You only discovered them a few weeks ago."

"It's not the cluster causing the current turmoil in Washington, David. It's their own institutional paranoia. They're so concerned the general public will find out their little secret and panic that they panic themselves."

"I can understand some of their concerns, Ben, but what a furor over a small-time televangelist from Wheeling, of all places."

"Although I don't ascribe to the teachings of this backwoods preacher or even acknowledge his existence, I do wonder at the accuracy of his predictions and his source. I fully realize that Southern Baptists just love to preach Revelations, but his forecast was more than that. I watched a recording of his show, and the way he used the biblical references to support his theory was uncannily accurate," Dr. Benjamin Cohen answered. "It's enough to make a person wonder."

"But he preaches the earth will be struck repeatedly; while your calculations indicate a close encounter but a clean miss."

"My calculations place the asteroid cluster's perihelion distance from the sun at 0.9825 AU. As you know, David, the earth's mean distance from the sun is 1.000 AU. That, my friend, is a very close encounter and does not take into consideration the gravitational attraction of the earth and the moon, sideward drift of the cluster, or an unintentional error in calculation by an old man. The federal government has every right to be concerned, and Reverend Randall may yet be correct."

"If that news got out, then every person in the world would start building an asteroid shelter."

"That's true, David, so all we can do is keep your friends in Washington happy by leaving the rest of the world in the dark. But sooner or later, another astronomer in another part of the world will spot them in the stream and do the calculations that we did. If whatever authority he answers to can't keep him quiet, then the world will find out what's coming, and we had better have our bases covered when they do."

"So here we stand," David said, grinding his teeth in frustration and reaching for a fresh pack of cigarettes. "By all the best scientific calculations, we're safe, and yet we worry the fact that one backwoods country preacher is getting his listeners to look up at the sky in fear."

"David, there's no way we can prevent people from staring up at the sky. The heavens have fascinated mankind ever since time began, and if men look up, they will see shooting stars in an average of eight or ten an hour on a typical night. If they have studied the skies before then, they will surely notice they are seeing more than usual, and they will wonder about it. They may even go to the internet to see if a periodic shower is occurring. When they see that no meteor shower is predicted, they will start asking questions. This cannot be avoided. It's a matter of human nature. The universe is a large place, David, and who can know what awaits us out there?"

David Van Patten wrinkled his eyebrows and stared briefly at the aging astronomer bent over in concentration, filling the bowl of his pipe with a mixture of tobacco.

"Is it possible this incident in Boulder may just be coincidental?"

"They have done nothing illegal, nor have they made any move to go public with whatever it is they suspect," Dr. Cohen answered.

"It may very well be, and I sincerely hope it is, but the truth is bound to get out sooner or later, and we have to be prepared for that day," David challenged.

"What do your friends in Washington have to say?" Dr. Cohen questioned.

"Don't you mean *our* friends?"

"No, they're your friends, David. I merely work for them."

David wondered at Professor Cohen's strange statements. "Washington is not saying anything at all…just to keep a lid on things until the president has a chance to discuss the situation with all concerned and formulate a joint plan of action. The only positive move I was able to coerce out of them was to have the director of civil defense begin quietly building up stocks of supplies and have National Guard units begin preparing for disaster response. Beyond that, nothing. Just sit tight and wait for further instructions."

"Well, then, we'll wait a little while longer. But I tell you, and you can relay it to the powers that be if you wish, I do not believe this is information that should be shared with the general public."

"I don't understand your thinking, Ben," David posed respectfully. "If a chunk of asteroid was going to fall on your house or your neighbor's house or even in your community, wouldn't you want to know about it so that you could prepare?"

"For myself, no," the professor laughed. "I'm too old and far too decrepit to fight that particular battle. As for others, I suppose I would want to be selective and try to assure myself that only the best survive. As for large suburban communities and cities, definitely no. While the better elements of our society would work to prepare for survival, the less savory elements would arm themselves so they could take control and prey on the weak. They crave power and understand how to use it, and in the end, they could cause more damage and suffering than the meteorites themselves."

"I still can't subscribe to your theory, Ben, and I'm glad it's all academic, anyway. I hope to have some new data from Hubble for you soon," David answered as he reached for yet another cigarette.

"My good friend, you should quit those deadly things." Benjamin Cohen rose slowly and painfully from the chair, crossing the well-appointed office at the NASA complex in Houston to retrieve his coat.

"Your arthritis is bothering you pretty badly, isn't it?" asked David.

"Too many years in cold and drafty observatories can do this to one's bones. It is an occupational hazard for astronomers, and I must bear it," Ben justified. "I'll be waiting to hear from you."

"Ben, have you given any thought to what would happen if we were struck by a meteorite of significant size?" David posed.

"I have thought of little else lately, but I wonder at the futility of it. Perhaps I'm just too old and disillusioned." Ben Cohen thought for a moment, then put his coat down and looked directly into David Van Patten's eyes. "David, there's a book I've read several times, just for the pure pleasure of it. It's named "*Lucifer's Hammer*" and was written many many decades ago by Larry Niven and Jerry Pournelle. It is a wonderful disaster story about a big comet that strikes the earth and about what the survivors must do to adapt to the privations of a more primitive society without the benefit of modern conveniences. It is a classic struggle of good against evil, replete with heroism and cannibalism. In the end, mankind rises above all the death and destruction to survive against the odds. It seems that we have a similar situation here, my friend, but I don't think it's Lucifer who is wielding the hammer this time; I think it is God. So does Reverend Davis."

"Ben, I thought you weren't a religious person?" David suggested, becoming more curious by the moment at the direction the conversation was taking.

"Religion has nothing to do with this; it's retribution, pure and simple," Ben replied harshly. "Take a hard look at our civilization, and you'll see what I mean."

Ben Cohen rubbed the swollen knuckles of his hands together and warmed to his subject. "I read in the papers a few years ago about three men in Detroit who beat a woman senseless on a bridge and then threw her off it into the river. A crowd of people had gathered, and instead of coming to her aid, they actually cheered the attackers on. This is an unconscionable act. How many times have you heard or read of people, women in particular, being attacked in our cities while people living in the surrounding buildings simply look out their windows to see what is happening, then draw their blinds and turn up the TV? They don't want to get involved.

"Our judiciary regularly releases men from prison who have previously beaten their families and threatened to kill their wives. The families are mistakenly not notified of their release and often come to harm because of it. In one case I read about, the wife ran screaming from her home while her husband stabbed her repeatedly. Her neighbors stood by doing nothing and watched her be killed.

"Our youth don't respect their elders or any of our institutions, and they may have good reason not to. They see our national leaders lie, cheat, steal, and molest, and get away with it. They blame us for the failure of our culture. Young people run wild, using illegal drugs, joining gangs to obtain the identity their parents have failed to give them, and then go around shooting each other from cars.

"An ever-increasing portion of our population will not work and prefer to be supported by the working public. Our welfare system almost forces them to do this. Another section of our population does nothing but work in order to acquire things that have no real value, and their families are neglected in the process.

"Racial prejudice continues to rear its ugly head occasionally, and many of our cities are powder kegs simply waiting for a fuse. Ethnic warfare is commonplace around the world. Man's inhumanity to man is rampant, and no one knows how to stop it."

Dr. Benjamin Cohen had really warmed to his subject now. He was rapidly ticking off mankind's faults as if he had stored them up for just this occasion. "Sexually transmitted diseases are pandemic, and despite all the education available and supplies of condoms piling up like multicolor mountains in our schools, incidence of these diseases remains on the rise. We cannot, as a people, restrain our self-satisfaction and self-indulgence, even at the risk of our own lives.

"I think we are a failed species, David, just like the dinosaurs, and I think we're headed for extinction, just like them. There's a popular theory that the earth was struck in the late Jurassic period and that worldwide climatological changes caused by it brought about the demise of the dinosaurs. I believe that God is disgusted with his chosen people and is sending us down the same path, and these runaway asteroids are his weapon of choice.

"Read your Bible, David, and you will see that when God has gotten angry with his people in the past, he has used many different forces to clean up the slate. We are again bowing down to false idols, lusting for money, power, fame, and each other's wives. We no longer love our neighbors, and we're bad stewards in general. This may be the time for a new beginning."

Alarm bells were going off in David's head, and he decided to push Dr. Cohen a little more. "Ben, I know you're tired and depressed, but surely, from what I've heard, a meteor strike will not destroy all of mankind."

"Meteors don't have to do the deed, David. They merely create the proper circumstances. Mankind will do it to himself."

Ben Cohen regained his coat and prepared to leave. "Think a moment about what I've said, David, and I think you'll agree."

When Ben had left, David sat for a long time, mulling over their conversation in his head. Ben Cohen was a longtime friend, and David didn't like the direction his thoughts were going. Ben's own calculations proved that all of the newly discovered asteroids were going to pass the earth by a comfortable margin, yet he was acting as if they were actually going to hit. David decided to do some checking on his own before telling anyone else about his uncertainties.

\* \* \*

"What's new in the wonderful world of undependable system operations? Oh sorry, I mean independent system operations?" John Halloran teased, grinning at his own stupid little joke as he entered the control room promptly at 7:15 p.m. After a good sleep, a long lazy shower, and a nice steak grilled to order on the barbecue, he felt rejuvenated. The extra time he had allowed himself to sleep in order to regain some of the time Bud owed him didn't hurt his mood at all.

"Same old pain-in-the-ass system you left me this morning," Bud complained. "Twenty-six thousand three hundred megawatts is a good load for the peak this evening. Con Edison is buying megawatts from everybody in the western world with their usual lack of regard for how we will get it through the system. We've had to make contract cuts almost every hour…mostly from Quebec, and they're okay with that because they don't like too many megawatts loaded on the DC tie during an SMD any more than I do. I've had some minor voltage swings, but nothing much otherwise. Central Hudson is seeing some big swings on their ground-induced current recorders, but overall, things are just as you left them."

"Have a good night, and get to bed early for a change," John told him.

"Too much bed and no company makes Buddy a really dull boy," Bud quipped as he left. John had the feeling Bud was going to be late again tomorrow morning.

"Speaking of fun, you had a call from a woman. I didn't think that you did that anymore," Bud poked on the way out the door.

"Did what?" John asked.

"Piss off the ladies. She sounded more than a little torqued up to me. Her number is on the phone pad. See you." In a flash, Bud was gone.

John grabbed the phone pad to see the number beginning with a 303 area code. He took out the SMD report folder from the lazy susan behind the desk, and, sure enough, it was the same area code as SWPC listed under NOAA in Boulder, Colorado.

Although he wanted to call Devon immediately, John had to get his shift started with the system set up to his satisfaction before he would be free. It was an hour into the shift before he could make the call. After a minute's consideration, he punched in the number on the unrecorded phone at the shift supervisor's console. Things were pretty quiet system-wise, and John was really curious about this mysterious call.

She answered on the third ring, with a tentative "Hello?"

"This is John Halloran speaking. Who is this, please?" he came back quickly.

"Hi, John, this is Devon. When we talked last night, there were some things I didn't tell you," she answered, sounding a little more settled.

"That's alright. Sorry I didn't recognize your voice, but it's nice to hear from you again," John said, intrigued by her call. "What else did you want to talk to me about?" He was hoping it was more than just business.

"I don't really know where to begin, but I've had somewhat of a strange day," Devon answered. "And I started wondering if your day was the same."

"I've had more than a few of those days myself, especially after night shifts," John confirmed. "Why don't you just tell me about yours, and then we can compare notes."

"Well, it started this morning when I couldn't get to sleep. I was upset about a lot of little things that have been happening at work lately and just couldn't settle down. After tossing and turning for a while, I thought I would take a run in the park to get myself tired and relaxed enough to sleep. When I left my apartment, I saw two men just sitting in a car in my parking lot, and I thought that seemed strange. Then I started getting a little paranoid and thought they were following me. But I kept running and then I didn't see them, so I figured I was just losing it, but I looked up and there they were again, so I picked up my pace and took a shortcut through the woods to get home the back way."

"Where were they parked when you first saw them?" John asked.

"On 9th Street, right across from the front of my building," she answered.

"Devon, if they were parked in front of your building, that means they know where you live," John warned.

"Damn it," she exclaimed. "Why didn't I think of that? I guess I wasn't so smart after all, was I?" Devon paused to ponder the thought that she hadn't outsmarted her followers.

John wanted badly to cheer her up, but he had a nagging memory of the two strangers in the diner at breakfast. "Devon, what make of car was it that followed you?" he inquired.

"It was a new gray Chevrolet Impala…you know, those ugly ones that only the police and government agencies seem to buy. Oh, my God! Do you think the police were following me?"

"I don't know, but I had two men following me this morning," he added. "And now that you mention it, they were acting a little suspicious. They came into the diner where I have breakfast most mornings. It's a local place, and you get to know most of the faces you see in there. The two of them just looked out of place, waiting for something."

"Oh!"

"Devon, is this an unrecorded phone?" John asked, suddenly feeling a bit paranoid.

"Yes, it's an unrecorded line in the hall just outside the lab," she confirmed.

"Good deal. Was there anything else out of the ordinary you remember?" he pushed.

"Only that a slightly built Hispanic-looking man in a rumpled suit did a 360 to run back to his car when I started out for my run," she answered.

"Anything different when you came into work tonight?"

"No, nothing I can think of, but I was pretty relaxed at work, thinking that I'd outsmarted them, or so I thought, and I wasn't really looking for anything."

"Me neither." John compared, "I saw the car, and two men, but I didn't think a thing of it until now. There is nothing in my life to cause it."

"I probably wouldn't have either, but my boss, Mr. Shellcroft, has been acting really odd for the past week or so, and he was quite rude to me last night when we were talking. That just isn't like him. He's been working late for the past few nights, and last night, he stopped by the forecast center on his way home. He came to my console and chatted me up briefly, then went to talk to Art Capiletti, the shift forecaster. Mr. Shellcroft took him aside, and they had quite a little private conversation. He forgot he laid some papers down on my desk when he walked in, so I glanced at them to see if there were any memos for me or not. There weren't, but I did see one on the increased incidence of meteorite sightings that you were asking about, so I started to read it. Mr. Shellcroft got extremely agitated when he saw me reading it, and he grabbed all the papers back. He swore me to secrecy about whatever he thought I saw. Actually, what I was able to see only speculated about the possibility of that huge asteroid, the one the media are calling "the Mountain" having collided with a smaller one in the belt between Mars and Jupiter and sending a shower of debris off into space, which may cause a marked increase in meteorite activity. But that would happen sometime in the future, which doesn't explain the ones we are seeing now. That was as far as I got, but he was really ticked." Devon sounded both frustrated and perplexed.

"It didn't work, did it?"

"What didn't work, John?"

"Your bosses swearing you to secrecy."

"Don't kid around, John. I need to know who I can trust," Devon continued, on a roll now. "I'm not an astronomer. In fact, I barely had enough background to get this job in the first place. But if that memo was correct and not just some harebrained theory, and if those pieces of asteroid are going to come close to Earth, then there will be adequate time to track them. There is nothing that could account for the meteorites you are observing now, which probably caused your satellite problems. My question is, what else is going on up there? And why hasn't the government said anything about it? Why on earth would Washington cover anything like this up?" Devon finished with a rush.

"I don't know why they would. And if you think about it, we really don't know for certain that anything is going to happen. There might not be anything to cover up. Also, with all the doom-and-gloom stories appearing on TV and in movies lately, it may be that people are simply on overload. Some of this stuff is really pretty scary."

By this time, John had phones ringing and the other ISO operators already on the line. *Duty calls*, John thought, reluctant to end the conversation. "Listen, Devon," he said, "I'm going to have to get off now; I've got three calls waiting. Why don't we talk tomorrow night and see if anything out of the ordinary happens today. I'm not working, but you can call me, about six p.m. my time. Can you copy this?"

"Yes."

"Area code 518-515-1122. Got that?"

"Got it, John. Call you tomorrow. Wait, John, is this your cell phone?" Devon asked, starting to think now.

"No. It's a diner in town. I'll catch supper there and wait for you to call. It's my home away from home. I am embarrassed to tell you I don't have a cell. I am usually one of three places: work, home, or the diner. When I am somewhere else, the last thing I want to do is answer the phone. I know I am going to have to cave and get one sooner or later."

"That's okay. I knocked mine in the toilet last week, so I am without one, too, until my two-year Verizon contract allows me to get another for free, but I have to wait until April fourth. It's killing me. I love my phone; I wish I bought the insurance for it. Okay sorry, I will let you go;, I'll call you about 18:00 Eastern time, okay?"

"That's good for me."

"Bye," she said.

"Bye." John hung up and immediately got busy with waiting calls. Not until a long time later did he get some time to think about this strange conversation. John really didn't know what to make of it, but he decided he didn't mind Devon calling back at all.

Bud Flynn had been correct in his observation that John didn't have much to do with the fairer sex of late. Since his last and most disastrous affair with Cheryl, which had been well over two years ago, John had stayed pretty much to himself. One thing was for certain, he would be a lot more careful and observant this morning. Maybe there was something going on after all—and for some perverse reason, he almost hoped that there was.

\* \* \*

On an isolated desert road about three miles outside Verdi, Nevada, Sharon Bates and Stanley Patowski cuddled close together both for comfort and to ward off the cold Nevada night. In a fluffy down sleeping bag in the back of his van, they watched the stars. They were sleepy and relaxed after their second lovemaking of the evening, and neither was anxious to return home to their respective spouses. "*It was nice*," Sharon thought, *"to lay here all naked on the soft bed that Stanley had tricked out in the back of the van."* Stanley had told his wife he had done it for camping and fishing, but Sharon knew better…much, much better. She also knew she had best start Stanley heading for home, before he got in trouble with Emily again.

Sharon gently poked him in the ribs with her index finger and said, "Get with the program; it's time to go home."

"Oh, God…is it that late already?" he asked sleepily while lovingly running his hand down the deep groove in the middle of her back.

"Unfortunately, yes, it is," Sharon stated matter-of-factly.

"This sucks," he moaned, his voice muffled in her hair as he kissed her neck.

"I know, but it is what it is. Now let's get moving." She shrugged in resignation as she watched him stretch his long, lanky body out to full length.

Stanley was right in the middle of that big stretch when a strange hissing and rumbling noise from outside the van got his full attention. Then immediately something hit the front of the van with an explosive impact. The van slid down the ditch and rolled over onto its roof, tumbling the shocked lovers into a pile of clothes, sleeping bag, and assorted empty fast-food containers. Stanley Patowski's pride and joy had come to an abrupt stop with its engine smoking and the smell of gasoline permeating the air.

Fortunately for the cheating lovers, the passenger-side sliding door had popped open on the uphill slope of the ditch. "What happened, Stanley?" Sharon asked in a dazed, yet terrified voice. "Is it your wife?" she blurted out with a surprising sense of guilt.

"Just get out of here, and like now, Sharon!"

Sharon responded instantly to the urgency in his voice, and they were both able to scramble out of the van into the sagebrush just before the gas tank exploded, leaving them running for cover, buck naked, in the cold desert morning air, wondering how the hell they were going to explain this mess to their respective mates.

\* \* \*

Amos Bellinger stretched hugely before getting up from his battered old leather recliner to answer the doorbell. His apartment was located in the newly remodeled Watergate complex, near the White House. Amos's place was Spartan in decor but comfortable in an intensely masculine way, and it suited him just fine. He opened the door and greeted David Van Patten of NASA and Dick Morgan of the FBI. Both men had just flown up from Houston. Dick was here to coordinate surveillance activities, and David to address a meeting scheduled by the president on civil defense measures. Amos had invited them to stop in for an informal chat when they arrived in Washington, which amounted to a direct order from the president.

When they were all settled in with fresh drinks in their hands, cigars lit, and ties loosened, Dick began in his usual brisk businesslike manner. "Amos, I know that the chief is concerned, but we've got security clamped down tighter than a bull's ass in fly season. There's no need for him to worry."

"He still does, Dick, so fill me in."

"The kid in Texas with his junk yard telescope is taking an extensive tour of NASA facilities in Houston at government expense, all of which he finds fascinating. When he gets home, he'll find a bunch of new toys to keep him occupied from looking far out into deep space. No more snooping around for NEOs for this kid. But of course we'll continue to keep an eye on him, just in case."

"That would be a good idea," Amos muttered.

"John Halloran and Devon Grant, from New York and Colorado, respectively, are being closely monitored. At this point, they seem to me to be more curious than dangerous, but since surveillance is in place, we'll continue until we're absolutely sure of them. I think Shellcroft is an asshole for blowing the whistle on them and the surveillance is a supreme waste of time, money, and personnel. It is being maintained, however, and will continue to be. Vito Pianese is in charge out there, and he's a good man. He reports they are both sharp people with responsible jobs, and keeping a close watch on them without arousing their curiosity even further is going to be tricky."

"Reverend Randall P. Davis is another story. He is a good and godly man who believes completely that he has been given a mission by a higher power than even the president of the United States, and he means to obey. The FBI has contacted him and, without giving up too many details, appealed to his sense of loyalty to the government and the nation. We have made it quite clear to him that if he continues to preach on this subject, he may do irreparable harm to the country. He is guided by a higher power, however…what the psychobabblers like to call "other-directed"…and he politely, but stubbornly, refuses to change his course, so we have had to sit on him a little. We currently have two men in his house, two more outside, and several agents on roving surveillance. With shadowing all the other doomsayers, it's stretching our resources pretty thin, but I made sure we sent some good men to monitor Reverend Randy. We also have the TV station buttoned up tight. We are continuing to closely monitor all radio, internet, television, and print media for any other potential trouble spots. That about wraps it up for me."

"That's great, Dick. Please stay on it and keep us informed of any changes," Amos said, taking a sip of his whiskey. "What about you, David? Are you all set for tomorrow?"

"I'm as ready as I can be. Ben Cohen volunteered to come up with us, and he and I are going to share the duty on your civil defense committee. For my part, I'm all set, but I'm a little worried about Ben."

"What seems to be his trouble, David?" Amos asked, a small wrinkle of concern appearing between his eyes.

"I can't really put my finger on it, Amos, but he has been distracted and sometimes distant lately. He's an old man and he's working very hard, so I can't be sure if he's just worn out or if he has something deeper on his mind. You are well aware of all the tragedy he's had in his life, and I believe that it's taking a toll on him. He really hasn't been the same since his daughter and granddaughter were in that terrible accident a while back, and I wonder if he isn't driving himself hard just to forget."

"Do you think his present condition has affected the quality of his work?" Amos asked, concern becoming obvious on his features.

"I don't believe so."

"Don't just think so, David. Check and make absolutely sure, and please keep me informed about this. Ben's calculations are crucial," Amos almost growled. "The president puts great stock in him, and I wouldn't want anything to happen."

"Will do," David reassured, thinking but not saying, *and you think I'm not concerned, you arrogant asshole? It was me who brought it up, remember?*

The tone of the meeting then shifted down to a more amiable level of small talk, mostly between Amos and Dick Morgan. David Van Patten subsided into a sullen silence until the lateness of the hour drove them all to their beds. They needed to catch a few hours of sleep before their busy day tomorrow.

Amos was pleased with what he had heard in the meeting and in the small talk afterward. He was most pleased with David's sullen behavior. "*Good,*" he thought. "*I need him to be pissed off to keep him on his toes.*" He allowed himself another drop of his favorite 101-proof bourbon, Wild Turkey, before falling into bed wondering what to do about Ben Cohen. Ben was the key to everything.

## Wednesday, March 3

"She's getting up," Dommy Ortiz said, staring intently into the Barska 20-60x60 spotting scope. "Goddamn, she's a great looker, Frank."

"Keep your eyes in your head and your hands out of your pockets, you Puerto Rican pervert," directed a somewhat sour Frank Muller. Frank was having a hard time spying on a young woman who was just about his daughter's age and who in some ways even reminded him of Cathy.

"Just some fringe benefits, compadre," answered Ortiz. "And by the way, I'm not a Rico or a pervert. But I'm not blind, either."

"Then give the girl some privacy and simply maintain light surveillance, as ordered," Frank growled. He had relocated his surveillance team to the fourth floor of the Boulder Senior Center, which was directly across the road from her apartment. Their location was on the same floor as Devon Grant's apartment, but the viewpoint was offset by a slight angle, which allowed them to see most of her one-bedroom apartment through the front picture window. Through the partially drawn blinds, they could see across her living room toward the bedroom, which conveniently had mirrored sliding doors on the closet through which they could get a partial view of the bathroom through the bedroom door. Not an ideal setup, but better than nothing.

"She looks a lot better with her clothes off," Ortiz mumbled. "She's got one fine set of knockers. Never noticed them when she's got clothes on."

"Spare me the lurid details," Frank said, barely concealing his mounting anger.

"Chill out, partner. She's in the shower, and I can't see her anymore," Ortiz said, looking up from the spotting scope eyepiece. "Our orders were to keep her in sight, weren't they?"

"That may be true, Dommy, but you're crossing the line between surveillance and being a peeping tom. Besides that, she's just about my Cathy's age, and it just gives me the creeps to think of someone peeping into her place, for whatever good reason."

"Sorry, partner. I didn't think it bothered you in that way. I'll keep my running commentary down," said Ortiz, bending again to the eyepiece to check the progress of Devon's shower. Frank did not miss the fact that Dommy had not said he would stop looking, just stop talking about it. After a few moments passed, Dom exclaimed, "She's out of the shower and getting dressed. That must be a world speed record for showering. I wish my daughters would get done that fast."

Devon was selecting her outfit with as much care as if she were going out on a date, instead of simply calling a man who could not see or appreciate it and whom she had never met in person. She had to be careful also because Art Capiletti would notice if she came to work on the night shift all dressed up instead of wearing her usual blue jeans. That might raise some eyebrows and possibly even require an explanation. Devon thought briefly that she had enough problems at work as it was, without getting the rumor mill going.

A trim pair of blue slacks and a soft cream-colored blouse were her choice—loose enough so as not to accentuate her fine figure, but not so loose as to hide it completely, either. She added some jewelry and a comfortable pair of flats to minimize her five-foot, seven-inch height, and she was ready. *One must dress unobtrusively if one does not want to attract attention. Plenty of time for that later. Now a little makeup, grab a bagel from the fridge, and I'll be ready to go.* Devon was surprised at the little thrill of anticipation she felt at the thought of talking to John again. After that, she would treat herself to a little dinner out and walk the mall a bit. Then maybe go in to work a little early; she had a few things on her mind that she would like to do.

"What's going on over there, Dommy?" Frank asked.

"Nothing much, just packing up to leave for work, I would guess," Ortiz replied. "Better cue Kim in so she can pick her up. I didn't expect her to be going out this early."

Kim Yamaguci was one of the replacements called in when Devon had picked up their original surveillance. She was a slightly built Japanese American and a dedicated runner. This had served them well earlier when Devon had gone to the park to run. Kim had simply joined her on the jogging path and run behind her, far enough back not to attract unwanted attention, but close enough not to lose contact. Kim even had a two-way radio that was made up to look like an iPod so she could stay in communication. She had called to Devon once to stop when she had seen that one of Devon's running shoes was untied. Some pair of balls on that girl.

Kim picked up Devon's white Toyota Prius as she pulled out of the apartment parking lot, and expertly swung her beat-up Honda Civic into the traffic stream several car lengths behind. The subject did not seem to be suspicious, so Kim relaxed behind the wheel to the point that she almost missed it when Devon turned into the Downtown Boulder Mall public parking lot on 11th Street just a few blocks from her apartment.

Devon pulled up and parked next to a rare group of public phones. Kim was forced to drive right on by, even at the risk of exposing herself. After cruising around the lot for a few minutes, however, she was able to park a few rows away to observe.

Kim rolled down her window and lit up a cigarette, almost choking on the smoke. With the near-total ban on smoking in public places, smoking in the car had become a very good cover. Employees and visitors alike were now forced to go out to their own cars to grab a smoke in private. It seemed strange to her, but in Boulder, she had noticed that many people did not even smoke inside their own houses. It was a common sight to see people standing on their front porches or in their driveways, shivering with the cold, just to cop a smoke outside.

All the while she was carefully lighting up and blowing the smoke out the window, she was also watching Devon punch in a number. Kim knew that it was long distance by counting the number of digits. She noticed that Devon used her phone card, so it would be easy to trace the number.

"Hello, this is John Halloran."

"Hi. Devon here."

"Hello there. You're right on time," answered John, quite surprised at the slight surge of emotion he felt at hearing her voice. This was crazy, he thought, having feelings for a girl that he had never met, who lived nearly two thousand miles away. But they were there, nonetheless.

"You said to call at 18:00, so here I am."

"Did anything unusual happen today?" John inquired.

"No, nothing I can put my finger on. I just have a feeling of being watched," Devon said.

"Anything in particular to give you that feeling?"

"No, just a feeling. Anything happen with you?"

"Yes and no, if that makes any sense," John offered.

"Nothing makes much sense lately," she said. "Would you care to explain that a little better?"

"Well…" John hesitated for a moment, collecting his thoughts, then continued, "I live out in the country, on sort of a back road that normally has very little traffic. It's not a through road, so just about the only people who use it are folks who live there, and over the years, I have gotten to know their cars pretty well. This afternoon, I was sitting on my front porch and I saw a black van go by slowly. Not just once, but three times. None of my neighbors have a black van. On the first pass, he slowed down at my driveway, but not so on the next two. I can't decide if it is something significant or just some kids out for a joy ride. Maybe I'm just being paranoid."

"If it's paranoia, then we've both got it," Devon chimed in. "It's just like me feeling like I'm being watched."

"I'll keep an eye on the road and see if it happens again, and I'll tell you about it tomorrow night."

"Then there will be a tomorrow night?" Devon questioned. John thought he detected a small lilt of pleasure in her voice.

"It's okay by me, if you're willing."

"Yes, definitely," Devon agreed.

"I'll call you tomorrow, then."

"Great," Devon replied, grinning a little.

"Tell me about how things are at work," John inquired, not wanting to end the conversation just yet.

"It's still about the same. My boss, Mr. Shellcroft, is still acting very nervous and more than a little short-tempered, but he came over and apologized for the other night, you know, when we were talking. He blamed overwork and stress. But he still won't allow us to report anything more than routine information," Devon said.

"Just following orders," John reminded.

"I guess. You know we've always been honest and helpful here, John; that's our job. We've never operated this way before, and it's bugging me. Just out of curiosity, I dug out some of my old astronomy textbooks today. This is definitely not the time of year for any of the known periodic meteor showers. They are the ones that are predictable and named after the constellations in which they appear. We should only be seeing four or five meteorites in any given hour. I watched last night and saw fourteen."

"Did you make a wish on them?" John joked.

"None of your business. If you tell, they won't come true."

"Okay, then. Why don't you just keep your eyes open tonight, and we'll talk again tomorrow night. What number should I use?" John asked.

"Call me at 303-146-5505. What time is good for you?" she questioned further.

"I have tomorrow off, so any time is good for me."

"I'm still on night shifts, so how about 20:00 here, that would be 22:00 back east, is that too late?"

"I don't think I'll turn into a pumpkin if I stay up that late," John said, smiling into the phone.

"Good night then, John, and thanks for taking the time to talk to me. I realize this may all be just a silly misunderstanding, but I feel better knowing there is someone out there who understands me and I can call if I need to," Devon confided, not really wanting to end the conversation.

"If you need to get a hold of me any time before then, use this number and just leave a message. I'm in here almost every day."

"That's great, John. Thanks. Well, I guess I'll hear from you tomorrow. Good night," Devon said.

"Have a good night Devon and keep your eyes open."

"Will do, Good night."

Devon climbed into her car and drove through the Boulder Mall parking lot out onto Broadway toward work. A squeal of brakes behind her caught Devon's attention. Looking back in her rearview mirror, she saw an Asian girl in a Honda Civic had just cut a car off while pulling out of the mall parking and was now on the receiving end of some fist-shaking abuse from its driver. She thought there was something vaguely familiar about the girl in the Civic... Devon's mind flashed back over the past few days. *That's the girl who was jogging at the park yesterday who told me about my shoelace being untied. How weird is that?*

Devon drove slowly and carefully, making a U-turn east on Walnut, south on 14th Street, back south on Canyon, and west again on Broadway to the SWPC building, all while keeping a careful watch on the Civic. The beat-up car with the Asian driver at the wheel stayed carefully alternating between two or three car lengths behind her all the way. As Devon pulled into the staff parking lot, the Civic drove on by without the girl giving Devon a second glance. *Still*, she thought, this is something to tell John tomorrow night. Devon was not really surprised to realize that she was looking forward to John's call. She had not had the time or the inclination to analyze her feelings about him until now, and now that she did, she was still unsure as to just what they were. She did know, however, that she enjoyed talking to him and sharing the mystery, and she would leave it at that.

Devon had to admit, if only to herself, that she had sadly neglected her social life since moving to Boulder six months before. Devon had immersed herself into setting up her new apartment and learning a new job that challenged her abilities every day. She was a very attractive young woman and had not lacked for interest from many of the young men at SWPC, and she had occasionally socialized with them after work, but she was not ready to pair off just yet. Consequently, she had not taken up any of their offers for anything more than a casual date. Maybe it was time for a little serious attention from the masculine gender.

\* \* \*

"I think she spotted me coming out of the mall," Kim said. "I was watching her and didn't see that old guy coming. When I cut him off, he really leaned on the horn and gave me hell. I think she may have picked me up then, because she took a strange route to work and drove extra carefully. I think she was checking me out in her rearview mirror. Sorry about that, boss."

"No big problem, Kim," Frank Muller reassured her. "We'll just have to switch to Christine on close surveillance for a while and have you lay back. We still need you to cover her when she goes running, however."

This was good, because her partner, Christine DeMarco, was at least thirty pounds overweight from too much pasta and too little exercise. Chris was a great girl, but she'd look out of place on the jogging paths. "Have Chris pick her up after work in the morning, and you cover the back of the apartment," Frank directed.

\* \* \*

The fireplace in the Oval Office of the White House was crackling but went unnoticed as three men huddled around a coffee table, deep in conversation. All three had their collars open and sleeves rolled up, here to do business, not look smart. A handsome man of average height and build with a full head of dark hair and a nicely tanned complexion rose and stretched. Jameson Coleridge was the president of the United States, and he had an abundance of problems. Unfortunately, the meteorite stream behind the Mountain was hurtling through space at cometary speed on a course that would bring the third planet from the sun into a close encounter.

"David, you mentioned earlier that you had some concerns about Ben Cohen's condition. Would you care to elaborate on that?" Jameson Coleridge asked cordially enough, but with an edge of concerned authority in his voice.

"Sir, for the past few months, I have noticed a subtle change in Ben's physical health, as well as a shift in attitude. At our last meeting together, I developed a strong feeling—and at this point, that is all it is—that he is deteriorating more rapidly. When discussing scientific matters, he was completely calm and competent, as usual, but when I mentioned your plans to announce our passage through the meteorite stream, he became very agitated and quite adamant about believing the government should not inform the American public at all.

"He began to count off society's faults, as if he had been storing them up like a chipmunk for just such an opportunity. I've known Ben Cohen for a long time, and I know he has had more than his share of personal tragedy. I don't believe that he has ever fully recovered from the tragic death of his daughter and granddaughter."

"Yes," Coleridge agreed. "Drunk and stoned driver, right?"

"Yes, sir, but Ben never shared any of the details of the tragedy with me or with anyone else I know of. He just did what he had to do and kept it all inside."

"Go on, please."

"He seems convinced that God is angry with mankind for all of our faults and sins and that He is using asteroids as his instrument of retribution. The meteorite stream is God's weapon of choice to wipe the slate clean and start again."

"What in the world? Isn't one runaway preacher enough?" Amos Bellinger almost shouted. "Now you say Ben is joining him."

"Not exactly, but even though he quietly disclaims any belief in Christ, he seems almost convinced that God is using Reverend Davis as his agent to warn the faithful with the apparent accuracy of his predictions."

"What else?" the president asked, knowing there was more.

"Sir, he believes any damage done to society by meteors would only be incidental to the damage we would do to ourselves."

"For once tonight, I fully agree with him. That is exactly why I am trying to delay my public announcement until exactly the right moment. Panic and civil disturbance are not an attractive outcome, and I need time to complete civil defense preparations."

"I understand your position, Mr. President, but I cannot agree," David said, more than a little fearful of disagreeing with the president. He swallowed hard and continued stubbornly, "The Ben Cohen I used to know would never consider allowing the American people to be exposed to this kind of danger without allowing time for personal preparations. I think making your announcement too late will precipitate more panic due to the lack of time to adequately plan and prepare."

"I appreciate your candor, David, but there are too many considerations to be dealt with before the time is right."

"I understand fully, Mr. President."

"What will you tell the Disaster Preparedness Committee?"

"Only as much as they need to know to get their jobs done. Ben has asked to be the first to address the committee, and he will brief them on the astronomy and the historical aspects, and probably scare the living hell out of them. I'll follow the next day with whatever additional information they need and press them to hurry," David answered.

"That's important, David. Press them hard. They must understand the need for immediate action."

"Yes, sir. I will," David offered, flushed with relief at not being fired on the spot.

"And David…"

"Yes, Mr. President?" He was thinking, *Here it comes… the axe…*

"Feel free to take whatever actions you deem appropriate to see that your family is safe and secure."

"Thank you, sir, but I've already done that."

Jameson Coleridge smiled for the first time that night. "Again, David, thank you for your candor. A president needs that at a time like this."

"You're welcome, sir."

The president then turned to his chief of staff and said, "Amos, before I go public, I have to know where we are vulnerable. The media is going to make hamburger out of me in any case, but I have to know where the skeletons are buried before they do." Jameson Coleridge mixed metaphors as he noticed the obvious tightening of David Van Patten's jaw muscles.

"I think they'll go after the cuts we made in NASA's budget a few years back. David can probably give us a feel for the effect these cuts made."

"David?"

"At the time, the cuts were painful but not disastrous. In light of current events, that may not be the case now. I won't go into the sequence of discoveries that presaged America's thinking prior to the budget wars; let's just say we discovered that we live on a dangerous piece of real estate. At the time, we believed the probability of Earth being struck by a comet or asteroid of significant size was extremely small, but we discovered that the consequences would be devastating. A decision was made at that time that it would be prudent to assess the threat first and then to search for a way to deal with it.

"The congress agreed with us, and they commissioned and funded a preliminary study on developing a system to locate and catalogue any near-Earth objects, NEOs, and assess their threat potential. From this study, the Spaceguard Survey began and the Space Guard System was proposed.

"The initial phase of Spaceguard was to coordinate activities at a number of existing observatories in both the northern and southern hemispheres which had existing equipment capabilities to detect objects of one kilometer in diameter. Each observatory was assigned a portion of sky to monitor and report on. The initial results were impressive, to say the least.

"The survey was scheduled to follow up with observations of the newly discovered objects using planetary radar to refine data on orbits, and later observations to establish exact sizes and physical properties. With the construction of some new observatories to fill in the gaps, we would have been able to scan the entire sky." David paused briefly before continuing.

"The whole project would have cost approximately four hundred million dollars to set up and twenty to thirty million per year to maintain and could have been in operation fully less than a decade ago, but funding was cut along with other NASA projects and it never got done.

"If you're looking for potential problem areas to explain to the media, you can add the Hubble orbital telescope upgrade and the Voyager 9B and Intrepid 1 deep-space probe projects, which were also canceled. We don't need to add the cancellation of the space shuttle. The cancellation of the space-shuttle program was very publicized and more traumatic to the public that any of us imagined. None of the last three projects was specifically targeted on NEOs—sorry, near-Earth objects, or comet studies, but any good science editor could find many ways they would be helpful in our current situation." A trace of bitterness was apparent in David's voice.

"Thank you again for being candid with me, David." The president lapsed into deep thought and sat quietly for several minutes, after which he sat up straight and said, "Amos, get our science people working on this first thing in the morning. We need some damage control; Ben and David are going to be much too busy to deal with it.

"David, thank you for your help tonight. You might as well try and get some rest. Amos and I have some civil defense items to discuss, then we'll turn in also. Please tell Ben that I need an ETA as soon as it's feasible. I have too many things to do which I can't start until I have a time frame to work with."

"Yes, sir."

"Also, I need you to be at your best in the meeting tomorrow. Lay it all out for our experts, then drive them hard to help us find more effective ways to provide for the survival of our nation and the American people. I can't stress too strongly how important this is."

"Yes, sir. You can count on it."

As David rose to leave, the president gave him a friendly smile, then turned to Amos and began working as if David were already gone. Perhaps in his mind, David was gone.

"Amos, tell me about the preparations we've made so far."

"We are taking a number of actions that will put the nation as a whole on a much better footing for survival should events come to that. First, we have terminated all grain and foodstuff exports, and have arranged to have as much as feasible shipped back inland away from the seacoasts, to protect them from tidal wave damage in the likely event of an ocean strike. We are funding an American Red Cross effort to fill out their disaster relief supplies, and blood banks. We have been quietly in contact with the mayors of all large cities, and are funding their disaster relief re-supply. They are also coordinating with their State National Guard to have as many units on active duty for crowd and traffic-control assistance as they deem necessary. Many of them are blending National Guardsmen with police units for training already."

"The Military have responded magnificently, so far. The Navy is loading all available ships with survival equipment and supplies, the nuclear units in particular. They plan to have these ships disbursed over the oceans to allow for a greater chance of survival from random strikes," Amos Bellinger answered.

"Won't they have to be concerned with tidal waves from an ocean strike?" The President asked.

"No sir, the Navy tells me that in the mid-ocean, a tsunami, or Seismic Sea Wave if you will, appears as simply a long, rounded swell of one to five feet. Naval ships can easily sail over it. The tsunami does not rise up and break until it reaches the shallower waters of the Continental Shelf."

"That's one good thing. Please go on."

"All military branches are setting up to use their bases, armories and reserve training centers for public assistance. We have been quietly reopening several closed military bases and are currently re-staffing them with security forces. The thinking is to use them for refugees and as detention centers as needed. They have security and warehousing and are situated all across the country. Most bases have hospital facilities, and most also have a source of emergency electrical supply.

"All military personnel involved have done a wonderful job of searching their inventories for anything that might be useful. The Army found two warehouses full of infantry rations dating from the Gulf War. This surplus has been tested and found to be safe and is currently being distributed. Good old K rations may not be haute cuisine, but they will keep people alive.

"The Air Force found ten thousand metal cots and pads in storage and are distributing them also. The story goes on and on. We are setting up to utilize the facilities and staffs of the American Red Cross and Salvation Army to establish evacuation centers, food kitchens, and emergency shelters for housing and medical care. These two organizations are trained and much more experienced, after Hurricane Katrina and Hurricane Sandy, in warehousing and distributing disaster aid where and when necessary."

"You've been busy, Amos."

"That's a fact. We are also working on emergency evacuation plans for trained medical personnel from coastal cities vulnerable to sea waves. If all goes according to plan, they will be relocated to military bases and, in some cases, used for replacements in Army MASH units."

"What about security?"

"We are telling people only what we must in order to bring them on board, and swearing them to secrecy under the National Security Act."

"That is all very reassuring, but people will talk; it always happens." The president continued to pace the pale blue carpet. "We still have to decide upon the optimum time to release this information to the general public." Jameson Coleridge raised his hand to stifle any interruption. "I'm well aware of all the arguments against doing so at an early date, and I'm sure that your assessments are impeccable, but I still have a responsibility to the American people who trusted me enough to put me here not to leave them personally unprepared for a disaster of epic proportions. This is a huge responsibility, Amos. I must keep my promise to the people."

"I fully agree, Mr. President," Amos Bellinger said quickly, "but now is not the time to do so."

"Should I wait until someone else does it for me?" the president asked, arching his remarkable eyebrows and looking directly into Amos Bellinger's eyes. "What about the naked couple in Nevada or that young boy in Texas with the junkyard telescope, or the Hubble telescope photographs we had touched up, or what Mrs. Coulter will do when she gets wind of this? We absolutely must contain that damned preacher from Wheeling. He stirred up too much of a fuss the other night. I'm told that despite the late hour, calls to local, state, and federal offices quadrupled after the show, and internet traffic has continued at a high level ever since.

"I understand that this isn't the time to go public, Amos, but I know this town. There are too many people here who would race to the media if they got even a sniff of something of this magnitude happening. I know the bureau is good at keeping a lid on things, but that absolutely must continue until we are ready, and then I will make the announcement myself. If one congressional aide talks to the wrong person or goes to the media, then where would we be?"

"All of them are being contained at present, sir, and will remain so as long as necessary for you to complete your preparations. When the time comes, we'll know it, and there are plenty of scientific justifications for waiting until we're absolutely sure."

"Shove your justifications up your ass, Amos. I will not be remembered in history as the President who held out critical information from his people, and let them be crushed under an unprecedented disaster."

"That will not be allowed to happen, sir."

"All right, Amos, we'll wait. But remember, I want to announce at the earliest possible time. Also remember whose ass is on the line if something goes wrong."

"Yes, sir; rest assured we will do just that." Amos spoke obediently, wondering if the president meant his own ass or Amos's ass was on the line.

## Thursday, March 4

Amos Bellinger stood at the head of the long oval table and looked down at the twelve assembled experts. They were all cabinet-level people or top assistants, and they were unusually subdued today. It was almost as if they already knew the degree of danger the nation was facing and were awed by it. Many of them had never been in the secure meeting room, four floors below ground level under the White House. They spoke quietly and cast glances at the photographs of presidents, generals, and admirals who had presided here. *Oh, well*, Amos thought, *time to get started*. He cleared his throat for attention.

"Good morning. Let's get down to business. We've got a busy schedule today. I believe you all have been introduced. We're here today to discuss the consequences of a discovery made by Dr. Benjamin Cohen and to assist the president in making some very difficult decisions on how to deal with it.

"Dr. Cohen's discovery has grave implications for the future of our society, and the president needs to have a clear understanding of what we and the rest of the world are facing. He would also like from you any specific actions we can take to be prepared for an event, should it occur. Perhaps it would be best if we start with Dr. Cohen's findings. Ben, you have the floor."

Dr. Benjamin Cohen rose from his seat near the head of the table and faced the group. Ben was a tall, lean man who moved slowly, as if his joints were all filled with ground glass, and whose swollen knuckles had long since stolen the agility from his hands. His overlong and nearly pure white hair was fine and unruly, giving him the look of a modern-day Merlin the magician, but his eyes still glowed with great intelligence and more than a little mischief. "Ladies and gentlemen," he began in a professorially resonant baritone, "I think it might be best if I go back to the very beginning. This will probably be a fairly long presentation, but I can assure you, not a dull one.

"Our story truly begins back in 1978, when two scientists named Luis and Walter Alvarez made a startling discovery while studying seabed cores for a largely extraterrestrial element called iridium. What they discovered was a band of clays that could be found at the same level all around the world which marked the boundary between the Cretaceous and Tertiary geologic eras. This time is coincidental with the extinction of the dinosaurs, which had ruled the earth for millions of years. This clay was not only distributed more or less evenly all around the world, but it also contained an unusually large proportion of iridium. In fact, it was roughly the same proportion of iridium that is found in nickel-iron meteorites. The Alvarez brothers calculated there was enough iridium in the boundary clays to equal the content of a meteorite of a ten-kilometer diameter.

"At first, the discovery was met with much skepticism, but as years passed and supporting data accumulated, the number of their supporters of an extraterrestrial cause for the great extinction grew. Then in 1991, the Chicxulub crater in the Yucatan Peninsula was discovered, and now we have an impact site of sufficient size to have done the deed.

"The impact of comet Shoemaker-Levy 9 on Jupiter in 1994 was probably the most watched astronomical event in history. All those observing were amazed at the tremendous heat and energy released as the meteors exploded in the Jovian atmosphere and at the amount of material ejected. The clouds created by the impacts still darken the skies over Jupiter. The event gave us a frightening look at what must have happened at Chicxulub, both in the immediate effect of the explosive impact and in the long-range ecological damage done to the planet.

"Could this happen to us here on Earth? The answer is a definite yes, and in fact, it has happened here on Earth many times before, and we have the craters to prove it. The heavily cratered surfaces of all the planets and moons in our solar system give mute testimony to the fact that we exist in an ocean of extraterrestrial objects. Sadly, however, we have discovered and plotted the orbits of very few of them. Unfortunately, on a typical night, there are probably more people working the night shift in your local diners than there are searching for near-Earth objects, NEOs, which have the potential to wipe out civilization as we know it." This last statement caused considerable shuffling and a rumble of subdued but angry comment around the table.

"Good," Dr. Cohen said, smiling. "I can see that I have caught your attention. I understand your anger, but it does nothing to alter the facts of the situation that we now face. Since 1972, the California Institute of Technology at its Mt. Palomar Observatory has been conducting a study of asteroids whose orbits bring them close to Earth. To date, they have located well over one hundred such asteroids and fifty-five comets and, in the process, mapped several thousand main-belt asteroids. A similar project at the Lowell Observatory in Arizona discovered comet SL-9 and well over two hundred NEOs. There are a number of other studies worldwide run by dedicated astronomers with very little funding, and they are meeting with success, but the Spaceguard project, which would have tied them together and coordinated results, was canceled due to lack of funds." The grumbling around the long oval table subsided into an awkward silence.

"Dr. Cohen," Liz Coulter, deputy administrator for the Nuclear Regulatory Commission, spoke out.

"Yes, Mrs. Coulter?" Ben answered.

"I thought that asteroids were all clustered in a belt out beyond Mars somewhere?" she posed. "And please call me Liz."

"Yes, you are correct, Liz. The asteroid belt is nearly a million miles wide and lies between the orbits of Mars and Jupiter. There are many other asteroids, however, that travel in greatly elongated and eccentric orbits that bring them near the sun and occasionally near the earth. The larger of these asteroids travel in predictable orbits, and we have located and named many of them after characters in Roman and Greek mythology. Ceres, for instance, is nearly one-third as large as the moon, and Eros is football-shaped and tumbles its way through space end over end. In 1972, a small asteroid actually bounced off the earth's atmosphere and caused a great streak of light across the sky, and we never saw the damned thing coming. But I'm digressing now. I think that when I finish, most of your questions will have been answered."

Warming to his subject, Ben Cohen continued. "Amy Chen, from Jet Propulsion Lab, has been leading a group of three astronomers, including Donald Grayson from the US Geological Survey and Dr. Karl Schmidt from the University of Colorado. They have been finding as many as eighty asteroids a year of a size that could eliminate the human race, or at least send us back to the dark ages. NASA estimates there are between one thousand and four thousand asteroids that cross the earth's orbit that are large enough to send mankind all the way back to the Stone Age. The record of comet or meteorite strikes is clearly written on the surfaces of all the inner planets, but most scientists and astronomers have believed the chance of a collision with one of these was very remote and not probable for twenty thousand years or more.

"It was Amy's group who first discovered the Mountain when it impacted a small asteroid in the belt and caused a perturbation in the area. Since its discovery, the Mountain has attracted the attention of most astronomers around the world."

"Dr. Cohen, I thought the asteroid you call the Mountain has passed the earth by a few millions of miles?" interjected Kurt Houser, Secretary of the Interior.

"That is correct, Mr. Secretary, and it is not the asteroid we are concerned about today. Also, contrary to our original belief, the Mountain in question is not one monolithic mass as we consider an asteroid to be but actually the head of an extremely old and burned-out comet. As such, it consists of many pieces of solid material accreted together by frozen gasses."

"What does that mean to us?" Secretary Hauser asked, obviously anxious to get to the heart of the matter.

"That takes us into the life history of comets," Ben Cohen continued, unperturbed. "Each time a comet makes its passage around the sun, some of its volatile gasses are burned off and stream away into space, creating the visible tail. In the process, particles that were frozen inside the comet's head are released and fall away to form what astronomers refer to as the meteorite stream, following behind. Since the Mountain has been renamed the Chen-Schmidt 1 comet and it is huge, the meteorite stream following it will be proportionately huge and may possibly contain pieces of some considerable size. Within the next several days, the earth will begin to pass through this stream, and it is here we may encounter a meteor shower the likes of which mankind has never seen. The possibility exists that this shower may contain meteors of sufficient size to become meteorites on contact with Earth."

"What about the meteors we are seeing right now?" Liz Coulter asked.

"The comet is large enough to have its own slight gravity, and I believe what we are observing is merely debris that is following along in the Mountain's gravitational field. What we may encounter in the stream could be much more significant."

"Thank you."

"Astronomers worldwide are searching nightly for any significant-sized asteroids in the stream, but the area of search is vast and our resources limited, leaving the possibility for one or more pieces of significant size to go by undetected."

"Why didn't we know about this stream sooner?" pressed Liz Coulter, her concerned expression not diminishing.

"Firstly, because we didn't realize that CS1 was actually a comet until very recently, and secondly, most of the debris in the stream is very tiny and hard to detect."

"Thank you again, I think," Liz replied.

"In any event," Dr. Cohen continued, "this is the situation we are faced with, and we have only a very short time to prepare. This, my friends, is up to you."

The end of Ben Cohen's speech was greeted with a stunned silence from around the table as everyone took a moment to digest what they had just heard and then with chaos as everyone tried to talk and ask questions at once.

"Amos, what the hell is the reason for the delay in informing the American public?" asked Kurt Houser over the rising protests of others around the table.

"Everyone, please calm down. I know you all want answers, and you'll have them, but what we need to do is stay focused and take the questions one at a time," Amos Bellinger answered with a calm that he did not really feel.

"Why don't you start out by answering Kurt's question and then tell us what has been done so far," suggested Katherine Meecham, Secretary of Health and Human Services.

Amos waited patiently until the noise level dropped and he had the attention of everyone around the table. "The delay was a joint decision made by the president and a number of heads of state of our allies in Europe and the Pacific. Defense and the CIA were included in the decision as well. All agreed that a delay was warranted to allow time to study various scenarios of both military and political natures and also to consult with our allies on the international implications. At present, we are realigning our military posture worldwide and making discreet improvements in civil defense preparedness. You have in your informational packets a list of civil defense preparations that are under way; beyond this, I am not at liberty to say any more. Please rest assured that we are doing everything possible at this time."

"Just what exactly do you want us to do, Amos?" questioned Liz Coulter. "If you don't intend to inform the general public to be prepared, then what is the sense of making preparations?"

"All in good time, Liz. First, we need to have a plan." Amos smiled charmingly. "The president has asked me to put three questions to you today and to request that we reconvene here tomorrow, with some suggested courses of action.

"First, the president would like your assessment of the optimum time for him to make a public announcement of the situation and its probable results.

"Second, please prepare your assessment for the possibility of physical damage to and disruption of civil and private services by the announcement of the possible impact of meteorites, and the same caused by the actual strikes themselves. You will need to include an assessment of civil damages caused by problems such as mass absenteeism from work, possible mass migration from urban areas, riots, looting, and the breakdown of civil restraints in general.

"Finally, be sure to prepare a comprehensive list of ways to prepare the civilian population of the United States to cope with an impending disaster. Please consider loss of civil restraint and/or control and damage to infrastructure. Consider the use of the military forces for civil control under martial law, problems with supply and demand of essential goods and services, and the many other challenges I am sure we haven't thought of as yet. Please discuss these questions with each other before you leave here today, and be prepared to reconvene here tomorrow morning. Thank you."

Amos Bellinger then gathered up his papers and exited with a huge display of dignity while pandemonium reigned supreme in the meeting room behind him. Turning to his executive assistant, he said, "Give them a few minutes to calm down, Lisa, then go back in there and take control. Make them think hard, because we're going to need all of their expertise before this is over."

Lisa Howard favored Amos with a weary smile and answered simply, "Yes, boss."

\* \* \*

"Morning, Johnny. How they hanging?" came the voice of Benny Butell, a shift supervisor at the NYISO, over the phone.

"One behind the other—same way you left them," John Halloran answered. "What's up?"

"Roger asked me to give you a call to see if you could come in today for a special assignment."

"What special assignment?" John asked, somewhat puzzled. Callouts like this were not common at the NYISO.

"I don't know," Benny replied, "but he's certainly had a wild hair in his ass since first thing this morning."

"I just finished changing the oil on my pickup and I'm filthy, so let me catch a quick shower, and I'll be right in," John said, really curious about what the problem could be.

"Don't rush on my account, John. I'm going to be here all day."

"See you in a few minutes."

John Halloran made the shower, shave, and drive in to the NYISO in near record time. Roger Adamski, the dispatching supervisor, was standing near the shift supervisor's console as John came in. Roger looked worried. "What's up, boss?" John asked.

"Come into the office," was all Roger said. He started walking across the control room floor toward his office.

"Sit down," Roger said when they got into the office. He started in immediately. "We got a call from the Nuclear Regulatory Commission just before noon today ordering us to prepare contingency plans for shutting down all of our nuclear generators.

"All of them?" John asked in disbelief.

"Yes, all of them. In two stages, boiling-water reactors going first, then the pressurized water units."

"But that's almost 6,000 megawatts of generation."

"That's not all. They also called ISO New England, and the two big dogs, MISO and PJM, with the same order."

"That's got to be well over 30,000 megawatts. What the hell would possess them to shut down all the nukes?"

"Damned if I know, but I need contingency plans on how we can best cover the shutdown, and I also need you to make arrangements for a meeting to include two people from each of the Northeast Power Coordinating Council areas and the Pennsylvania, Jersey, and Maryland Interconnection for tomorrow night. The meeting will address how we are all going to deal with the possible loss of all this generation. MISO will coordinate with the entities in the Midwest, so you don't need to include them yet," Roger replied.

"Should we include the larger independent power producers?" John asked.

"Not just yet. Let's get our game plan started and then invite them in when appropriate. I've been in touch with my Canadian counterparts at Hydro Quebec, Ontario, and New Brunswick. They are fully aware of our situation and are willing to help out. They said to give them a couple of hours and they will let us know how much help they can provide. Canadian Nuclear Safety Commission has not called for any shutdowns up there, but they are discussing it as well, so I am not taking any chances. Their help will be limited if they do get the ax. Jim Wilson is on the spare shift today, and I've got him calling all gas transmission companies to try and nail down all available natural gas supplies above what is already under contract. Take it from there and get on it."

"Okay, boss."

"Talk to George too," Roger said, absently returning to the pile of paperwork on his desk. "I asked him to start getting together some preliminary figures on how much fossil-fueled generation we can call back from maintenance and reserve shutdown, and how many megawatts we can delay taking off line for scheduled maintenance. We'll have to base load our gas turbine units and then use the top of the thermal units for control. It'll be expensive, but I don't see anything else to do."

"I'll get right on it," John reassured him, getting up and heading for George Brown's office. George was the ISO generation scheduler, and he was a great load forecaster, to add to his credentials. He had already begun to assemble the numbers John needed.

"One more thing, John," Roger called. "You are not to discuss this with anyone or share the information with anyone not cleared by me. Understood?"

"Yes." John understood the order, but not the reason behind it.

John spent the rest of the afternoon studying installed capability, maintenance histories, and fuel stocks and making arrangements for tomorrow's meeting. All in all, it was a damned busy day, and he left work at nine p.m. with his head so filled with numbers and crazy thoughts that he wouldn't have noticed a herd of elephants unless they trampled him.

\* \* \*

"She's leaving the parking lot now," Kim Yamaguci said into the radio. "Going across Arapaho on 9th Street."

"I've got her," Chris DeMarco replied. "Looks like she may be heading back to the Boulder Mall."

"I hope so," Frank Muller replied. "I left a little something at the public phone earlier. If she uses the same group, we should be able to catch the conversation."

"She's turning in to the mall now," Christine reported. "I'm going to stay on 11th Street and loop around to come in at the Broadway entrance. I'll pick her up from the other direction."

"Chris, give her plenty of room."

"I've got her in sight," Frank reported. "I'm in the mall parking lot about two rows east of her location, parked where the light is out, Chris. Stay loose, gang; this little lady is watching for us."

\* \* \*

Devon pulled the little white hybrid into a space a short way from the same group of phones she had used the previous night. She was a few minutes early, so she studied the parking lot carefully while she sat and waited. Devon was thinking about what she had done at work last night, and her stomach responded with a nervous flutter. She was surprised at her own audacity.

It had been a quiet night with only routine work to do, and Mr. Shellcroft had even gone home early for a change. She'd waited anxiously until around 03:00, when things tended to get a bit sleepy around the office and then slipped out, telling Art Capiletti she had to go to the ladies' room. She had actually moved quietly down the hall to try Mr. Shellcroft's office door. It had been unlocked. After checking over her shoulder that the coast was clear, Devon had slipped inside.

Leaving the lights off, she had waited for a few moments until her eyes adjusted, then slipped quietly over to the desk and studied the office. With a woman's keen eye for housekeeping, Devon had noticed immediately that things were not right. She had thought back to the day she had started work at SWPC. When she had reported to Mr. Shellcroft, she had been quite impressed by the neatness of his office: nothing out of place, papers and pencils neatly lined up on the desk, almost prissy in its perfection.

Tonight had been another story altogether. The desktop had been a jumble of Xerox copies. Pencils and colored pens had been scattered about, and, most curious of all, his middle desk drawer had been slightly ajar. Another flashback of her first day at SWPC had returned, and in her memory, Devon had clearly seen Jason Shellcroft rising to take her around to meet the staff at Space Environment Labs. He had stopped after closing his middle desk drawer to lock it and put the keys in his pants' pocket. He had even patted his trouser leg as if to assure himself that the keys were actually there.

Devon had quickly sifted through the copies on the desk and found nothing of any particular interest, mostly routine office communications and an article by Neil de Grasse Tyson copied from an astronomy magazine, a book titled *How I killed Pluto*, and some other technical publications. When she had slid open the desk drawer, she'd quickly sifted through the contents; in the back of the drawer, under some file folders and the usual office paraphernalia, had been a brown manila folder edged in red stripes. Devon had never seen one like it in this office, but it had appeared to be important, so she'd pulled it out and opened it carefully. Inside had been a letter from the office of the secretary of the Commerce Department ordering Mr. Shellcroft, in no uncertain terms, to continue applying the informational guidelines as per their recent phone conversation. Furthermore, he was to continue suppressing any inquiries on the subject by utilizing the attached list of acceptable explanations.

Attached to this had been a small pile of typewritten pages that contained vague and misleading answers to be used in response to many of the questions SWPC had been receiving from its customers. The acceptable answers had no basis in truth, however, and merely avoided the truth by applying a thin layer of half-truths and some out-and-out lies.

The letter closed by admonishing Mr. Shellcroft to continue maintaining maximum internal security. On one corner of the letter was a tiny trace of pale blue ink resembling a partial fingerprint. The color had looked vaguely familiar to Devon, and she had studied it for a second before realizing what it was. She had realized it was a smudge from the pale blue highlighters Mr. Shellcroft preferred to use. Without further thought, Devon had quickly returned to the papers on the desktop and gone through them, finding only three that were highlighted in blue.

She had gone quickly across the office to the copy machine and pressed the button to start. The copier had not started, however, and the green LED display had read, "Beginning warm-up cycle, ready to copy in two minutes." Devon had stamped her foot in frustration and waited. After what had seemed to be an eternity, the ready light had come on and she had quickly made copies of all three documents. She quickly replaced everything just as she had found it, closed the desk drawer, and left the office. She had stood outside for a moment, leaning against the doorjamb, waiting for her heart rate to return to normal.

Devon had been back to her desk in a minute. She had sat down with her heart still pounding in her chest. Later she had thought, she would take the time to look over the articles, and then she would have something concrete to talk to John about tonight.

When the mall phone rang, it startled Devon out of her reverie. She jumped a little, then snapped to attention and hurried to the phone. "John?" she answered quickly.

"Yes. Hi! How are you?" he asked.

"I'm good. What kind of a day did you have?"

"A really busy and really strange one," he answered. "How about yours?"

"You go first," Devon said. "Mine might be quite a long story." She was anxious to tell him but wanted his undivided attention when she did.

"Today was supposed to be my day off, but I got called in to work this morning to help the operations manager with a study the Nuclear Regulatory Commission demanded in a hurry. They want to know how New York would meet its load if all nuclear plants were shut down. Why the plants would be shut down, they didn't say;

nor did they order us to do so. Just a simple study, they said, but it has everyone concerned. It's very strange.

"This type of study does not fall under the authority of the NRC, but the Federal Energy Regulatory Commission undersigned it, so we have to comply. Under the old electric utility agreements, this study would have been a snap, but presently, all of our members have divided into two discrete companies—one generation company and one transmission/distribution company, so I had to call both business units to get the information I needed and verify that ancillary services such a voltage support and reserve generation would be adequate. We can make it okay in New York, but some other areas of the northeast may not be so well off.

"The study took me a long time to finish, and it was quite dark when I finally left work. I was really observant, but I couldn't spot any surveillance. How about you? Now it's time for your story."

"Well, this is totally unlike me," Devon began, "but I snooped around a little last night. I went into Mr. Shellcroft's office and looked in his desk. His office was a mess, which is a little unusual in itself because he is such a neat-freak. I looked around and found some sort of secret letter. It was from the secretary of commerce, and it ordered him, quite clearly, to continue using the approved government cover stories and to follow the guidelines on security. He was not to discuss something they both knew about, and had previously discussed on the phone, but the letter didn't state specifically what that was. He had highlighted some articles from a magazine, so I made copies of them. One was about what they called a ripple in the belt of asteroids where that huge asteroid called the Mountain plowed its way through, and the other was about some problems with the Hubble telescope causing a blurring on some photographs. I really don't think the articles are completely credible. First of all, the asteroids in the belt are always bumping into one another and we know the cause of this disturbance. My professor often referred to the asteroid belt as a cosmic grinding mill. In fact, many of the shooting stars we see on Earth are the result of collisions in the belt."

"Could it be possible that something other than the Mountain passed through there and was not seen or reported?" John asked.

"Yes, that is definitely possible; there are thousands, maybe millions, of undiscovered and unnamed objects out there comets, asteroids, and meteors. Some of them have been seen and recorded, but most of them we don't even know about. I remember a few years ago, a previously undiscovered asteroid passed within seven hundred thousand miles of the earth, a little closer than the Mountain, and I know that it seems like a large number, but in astronomical measurements, it is a very near miss.

"Then there is that article on the blurry shot from the Hubble Space Telescope. Sure Hubble had problems when it was first launched, but after the Atlantis shuttle astronauts did that wonderful repair job on it, it has been working flawlessly. Neither of the articles rings true to me."

"You're the expert, Devon. I don't have a clue, but someone appears to be unhappy that we are interested at all."

"Are you still being followed?" Devon asked.

"Not really followed. They know where I live and where I work, but I feel I'm being shadowed."

"I know what you mean. I feel like I'm being watched, but I cannot spot who it is," Devon compared.

"When I went for my walk this morning," John continued, "there was a car parked off the road about a half mile from my place. The hood was up and there was a handkerchief tied to the antenna, so it appeared to be a stalled vehicle, but when I stopped and looked a little closer, I noticed an empty binocular case on the floor in the back seat, and a bunch of food wrappers with it. The engine was stone cold. The car had apparently been there overnight. I'll admit some services are not too rapid in Schoharie County, but it doesn't take that long to get a tow for your car.

"I walked around in the hedgerow near where the car was parked and found a spot where the grass and leaves were all matted down. There were candy wrappers there also, along with chewed sunflower seeds. Someone spent a considerable time there. Looking across the fields from this spot, there was a clear view straight to the back of my house. I'm sure someone was watching me."

"Could this still be just a coincidence, John?" Devon asked. "Could we be jumping at shadows?"

"I don't know for sure, Devon. I hope that's all it is, but hunting season is closed, and bird watchers don't watch at night."

"This is really starting to add up to something, but I don't know what. What should I do with the papers I copied?"

"Get rid of them, Devon. You've read them and don't believe them, and you know a lot more about it than I do. Just destroy them."

"Should we use a different phone tomorrow?" Devon asked. "I remember seeing in a movie once that you shouldn't use the same phone or talk too long. Oh my God, the phones…"

"What about the phones?"

"Two of them are broken. The wires are ripped right out of the box, so I can only use this one," Devon shrieked. "They were all fine last night."

"Hang up," John said. "Call me tomorrow at the first place you called, at the same time. Do you remember?"

"Yes! Bye," she said, slamming down the receiver.

After breaking the connection, Devon hesitated for a moment, then unscrewed the mouthpiece as she had seen people do several times in the movies. Sure enough, right there inside the mouthpiece was a tiny round microphone. In a fit of anger, she pulled the microphone out, threw it onto the pavement, and smashed it with her foot.

In his car just a short distance away, Frank Muller cringed at the loss of that beautiful little piece of government equipment and then slowly removed the earpiece from his ear.

## Friday, March 5

Vito Pianese was not in a good mood this morning, not good at all. Shellcroft was sitting at his desk, looking like the cat that had eaten the canary. This did not please Vito, either. Something about Shellcroft's smug superiority got under Vito's skin and made him want to make Shellcroft sweat. Most of all, he just wanted to be home, working out of his own office in Denver, sleeping in his own bed with his own wife, and not dealing at all with this priss wearing the granny glasses. But his orders from the bureau were to maintain surveillance of Devon Grant and take no overt action, so that was what he would do. Watch but don't touch were the orders, and that's exactly what he would have his men do.

"Just tell me why the hell you left the papers in your desk and the drawer unlocked, Mr. Shellcroft?" Vito Pianese inquired with more venom than usual.

"Because I wanted to prove to you that I was right…there's more to Devon Grant, more than the 'sweet little miss innocent' she appears to be," Shellcroft came right back.

Shellcroft was a little feistier this morning, Vito thought. "That was not in the program," Vito growled, "and you should have checked with me before pulling this kind of stunt. I don't like people playing cowboy on me."

"There was nothing in any of the papers that she didn't already know if she really thought about it and did a little homework," Shellcroft justified, "but now I know for sure she's looking. I left the middle desk drawer open last night, and it was closed this morning. The counter on my Xerox machine showed three copies were made after I left the office. She worked the midnight shift, so she had access to my office. It could only have been her."

"And how many others were on the night shift last night?"

"I don't know the precise number, a few, maybe four I guess."

"And you think Devon Grant was the only one of them who could have snuck into your office and rifled your desk? Mr. Shellcroft, think again." Vito was delighted at the disappointment flooding over Shellcroft's face. It just about made his day. "I'll have my people tighten up surveillance a little," Vito snarled. "And I'll call New York to have them do the same." He was still not convinced that Devon was a threat, and he would have much preferred to close up shop here and return home, but decided to have forensics check Shellcrofts' office for fingerprints anyway

Vito longed for business as usual but had no idea that business as usual would never exist again.

\* \* \*

Kenny Smith stopped every single day for his morning coffee at the Speedway shop on US Route 36 in the village of Danville, Indiana. Kenny just loved Speedway coffee. It was so rich and creamy and nice. He felt very much the same way about Becky Crawford, who worked the morning shift behind the counter there. With her straight, dark blonde hair and flawless skin, she was just as creamy and nice as the coffee. That old lady, Tracey Bishop, who was supposed to work there never did much more than gossip with the customers and let Kenny do her job for her.

Becky was a pretty young girl who had come to Danville just a year or so ago from back east somewhere, no one knew for sure, because Becky didn't talk much about it. She enjoyed having a little fun once in a while and could hold a drink and tell a joke right along with the best of the boys in town, and she could dance them all into the ground. Her fun-loving nature generated a considerable amount of locker-room talk about her, and not all of it complimentary. Kenny just hated when the boys down at the Subway on East Main Street would make rude jokes about her, and he wouldn't stay around when they talked like that. That only served to make them stop talking about Becky and start ragging on Kenny about his being sweet on her. His face would burn with embarrassment as he walked away.

The men at the Happy Tyme Frozen Food Company, where Kenny worked, liked to joke about Becky too. They all claimed that she was easy and ran around a lot, but Kenny didn't believe a word of it. They were all just full of it, as far as Kenny was concerned.

Kenny may not have been the smartest guy in town, but he was wonderful with his hands and good at whatever he tried to do. He held down a steady job delivering frozen food for Happy Tyme for the past three years, even though he had the oldest truck and the least profitable route in the area. If any of his coworkers had thought about it for a minute, they would have realized that after those three years, they really knew very little about Kenny Smith. He did well in his work because he was quiet and agreeable and so polite that things just seemed to work out for him. He had a nice attic apartment in a big old house downtown, and his landlady was eighty years old. She liked Kenny, too, and let him do just about as he pleased around the place. He did the yard work and maintained the outside while she cooked his meals and did his washing. It was a perfect arrangement. It didn't matter to Kenny what the guys did or what they said about Becky, she was still his angel.

Kenny would always load up his truck for the next day's deliveries at night, right after work, even though that meant he would have to plug the freezer in at home to keep it frozen overnight. The gas engine on the reefer was too loud for the neighbors to put up with. Kenny cared about the electricity that his landlady paid for, but she said to never mind about it. She knew he did it just so he could have some extra time in the morning to spend at Speedway to help Becky out. The sight of those gorgeous eyes and pony tail wagging really jump-started his day.

The Speedway in Danville was a busy place in the mornings. Kenny always got there early to hang out and make up a fresh pot of coffee or two for Becky so she could stay behind the counter. This would usually win him a smile and a wink when he glanced over to see how busy she was. With any of the other boys in town, this would just be the prelude to their hitting on her for a date, but Kenny was different. He wouldn't know what to do on a real date, so he did it just to be nice.

"I made a couple of pots for you," he would say proudly when he finally came up to the counter.

"I know, Kenny," she would say and smile at him. "Thanks a lot. You are always so nice." She was so beautiful, she made Kenny feel warm all over.

Becky thought Kenny Smith was a nice-looking young man, although he didn't know it. He had nice regular features and a great tan from working so much outside. He was well liked by the men at Happy Tyme and respected by his employers for his honesty and thoroughness. He was a good worker, even though he often seemed to be going through life with a permanently puzzled expression on his face. Becky liked him and believed there was a lot more to him than he ever let her know.

At first, Kenny had been too shy to even tell Becky his name, but she had read it off the pocket of his Happy Tyme Food Company shirt. "What'll it be today, Kenny?" Becky would always ask with a nice smile for him.

"Lemme have a couple of packs of them Marlboro Reds," he would always answer.

"They have got a kick to them, don't they?" she would say back as she reached up to get them off the top row of the cigarette rack above the register. Kenny really didn't care what smokes he got, but he loved the way her Speedway shirt pulled tightly across her breasts when she got the smokes down off the very top rack for him.

"That will be eleven dollars and ninety cents," she would say next, and Kenny always had a twenty-dollar bill ready. It was a routine that was cast in stone between them.

"Have a nice day, Kenny," she would say as she gave him his change. And no matter how bad the weather or how crabby his customers were, Kenny Smith would have a nice day.

"And you do the same," he would always answer.

Then Kenny would climb up into the cab of his big old Dodge Power Wagon, stow his smokes in the glove box on top of the other packs he had accumulated, set down his coffee in the drink holder, which he would nurse all day long just so he could be reminded of sweet Becky, and then pick up his clipboard. It embarrassed him some to get into the bright pink truck with the big clown face on the side under the Happy Tyme logo, but mostly he ignored it. To anyone passing by, he appeared to be checking out his route, but in truth, he knew his route by heart, just like he knew all the country roads in the entire county. He could even remember from last week that Mrs. McCrudden wanted an extra two gallons of black raspberry ice cream because her "tennis daughter" was coming up for a visit from Florida and her son Mike and his family were coming in from Tivoli New York. Kenny didn't even look at the clipboard but took the time to steal an extra glance at Becky Crawford working behind the counter. This is why he parked in exactly the same place every day.

He kicked the big old Dodge over and started his route.

\* \* \*

Amos Bellinger once again looked down the long oval table at the somber group arrayed there in the White House situation room, several floors below the ground. They were a serious and unusually quiet group today, shuffling in their seats and rustling papers to kill time until the meeting began. *The hope of America and maybe of mankind,* he thought as he opened the meeting. "Good morning, everyone. Let's please cut the chatter and bring this meeting to order.

"You may be pleased to know that we have been designated by the president as the Select Committee on National Disaster Preparedness. A mighty-sounding name, but not nearly as mighty as the task that lays before us. As you all know, we are charged with preparing this nation for survival in a situation I'm sure we all find hard to comprehend, and to do it in a very short time span. We are charged by the president with reorganizing this nation's civil-defense establishment so that we can be better prepared in the event of a natural disaster, and designing a coping mechanism for our people. We are all aware of the impending dangers our nation faces, but what we do here will be applicable for any disaster of a national scale, at any time. At the last session, I left you with three questions to answer, and I trust you've done your homework.

"I'd like to introduce you to David Van Patten from NASA. David has been working closely with Dr. Cohen and is here today to start us off with the latest from Houston," Amos said.

David Van Patten unwound his long, lean frame from his usual slouch to a perfect posture seated position. "Thanks, Amos, for the dubious distinction of leading off." He started out with a little joke to break the ice and was rewarded with only a few polite chuckles. All around the table, however, everyone straightened up a little to hear the latest from the Houston Space Center.

"Fortunately or unfortunately, whichever way you look at the situation, nothing new has been discovered in the stream overnight, so there is nothing substantial to report from Houston." David's heart felt like a lump of lead from the necessity of lying to these good and honest people, orders or not.

"What about that van that was struck out in Nevada?" Liz Coulter asked.

"Houston believes the report of a meteorite hit is greatly exaggerated. Nevada State Police believe a mechanical defect caused the van's engine to explode and burn, not an extraterrestrial object," David replied, hating it.

"They believe, but you don't actually know, do you?" Liz Coulter came back.

"No, Mrs. Coulter, we don't actually know," he said, hating it more this time.

"Thank you."

"May I add, Mrs. Coulter, that every optical telescope, every radar telescope, and every tracking device available are all trained on and scanning areas of the CS1 meteor stream and no object of any substantive size has been located. I find it hard to conceive that anything could evade that kind of scrutiny."

"Hard to conceive, Mr. Van Patten, but not impossible. Is that correct?" Liz Coulter was a bulldog.

"No, not impossible."

"Thank you, David. We must deal in facts, not probabilities. In this case, I have to start considering shutting down all operating nuclear generating plants immediately and getting their fuel supply stored safely." Liz wore a worried look on her square, plain face.

Amos Bellinger sat bolt upright in his seat, "You did say 'consider,' not 'order,' didn't you, Liz? I don't want any orders to go out as yet. Any problems with that?" Amos inquired.

"More than you can imagine," she answered with a deeply concerned look.

"I would like to have an idea of just when the president is planning to release this information to the public," said James Calvin, a very dignified black man with a streak of pure white hair sweeping back from his pronounced widow's peak.

"The president is maintaining close contact with government and scientific people worldwide and is keeping his options open for now," Amos said, evasively.

"I understand his concerns, and some of his problems. I also can appreciate the stress that he is working under," James Calvin interjected. "But I must ask, because in the politically sensitive areas of our inner cities, the timing of the announcement is critical to the people's perception of being left out in the cold again."

"You're quite correct, James," Amos answered, "and as soon as I know, you will know also."

James Calvin's mind reeled with pictures of cities burning and Americans killing each other in Watts, Detroit, and East L.A. These were memories much too real for him to ignore.

"General Gates, I wonder if you would take some time to brief us on the military role to date," Amos said. "Tailspin" Tommy Gates was a big, raw-boned, four-star general from the United States Army. He had a round face with a ruddy complexion that usually wore a slightly amused and jovial expression. This benevolent exterior belied the excellent brain and iron will that lay behind it. Many a junior lieutenant and more than a few full colonels had been fooled by it and had lived to regret that bit of professional oversight.

Thomas Gates earned the nickname Tailspin the hard way, through multiple tours in Afghanistan and Iraq. Major Thomas Gates had taken his flight of three AH-64 Apache helicopters into an extremely hot landing zone to extract the remains of an infantry company under heavy fire and in danger of being overrun. He had just taken off after loading his airship to the combat maximum with wounded infantry when a lucky rebel gunner had shot away part of his tail rotor controls, putting him into a violent three-hundred-and-sixty–degree spin. He had only avoided becoming a ball of fire in the foreign country by the narrowest of margins as he had slowly fought the damaged controls until his craft was reasonably stable. The battle from which he was extracting wounded troops was going badly, and no one knew how long the landing zone would remain in friendly hands or when a relief flight could be brought in. This fact plus the need of his passengers for emergency medical attention made landing the damaged aircraft and waiting for help a less-than-optimal decision. His only other choice had been to battle the damaged aircraft through a grueling forty-minute flight back to his base at Bagram.

It required more than forty minutes of the toughest flying Major Thomas Gates had ever done. He was constantly balancing collective against cyclic controls while nursing his rudder and throttle. It had been impossible to coax the chopper to fly straight ahead, so the entire flight had consisted of an ongoing side slip from left to right and back again, always inching forward. His flight suit had been drenched in perspiration as he'd neared Bagram and called for a clear landing pad. He then made a dead straight approach and landed his fully loaded chopper as softly as if it were factory fresh.

The decorations and aviator wings he displayed above his left breast pocket along with the three stars on his blue combat infantry badge, which represented the number of conflicts he had served in and been an integral part of, had all been well and truly earned in his decades of service.

Thomas Gates cleared his throat for attention and began. "Ladies and gentlemen, I'll try to make this briefing as brief as the name implies. The president, as commander in chief, has tasked the United States military with three specific goals. First and foremost is the defense of the North American continent. The area has been designated by the president to begin at an exclusion zone located 150 miles south of the Panama Canal and to include all of the American continent northward to the Aleutian Islands of Alaska. This operation is under the command of United States forces in coordination with the armed forces of Canada and Mexico.

"Our second goal is to redeploy all overseas forces in a manner that will allow for protection of US possessions overseas and protection of our citizens abroad. This includes maintaining the security of supplies of all critical material at their source, and on all lanes of commerce back to the United States. We are tasked to accomplish this while returning as many forces as possible to the United States.

"Thirdly, we have been directed to prepare contingency plans for assistance in national civil defense. This is to include disaster relief of all categories, assistance to local constabulary in maintaining civil order, and maintaining the security of the national infrastructure. Admittedly, this last task seems somewhat nebulous, but planning has been in progress for several days and is progressing very well."

"General Gates, could you be a little more specific on just how the military plans to assist in maintaining civil order?" James Calvin asked.

"Certainly, Mr. Calvin. We are planning to divide the United States into ten civil defense zones. These would roughly coincide with the four time zones from east to west, each divided into northern and southern areas. The Canadian border north and Mexican border south would constitute the remaining two zones. Each will have an individual command responsible to the national command. Each zone will have its own supplies, communications, and sufficient troops to carry out the mission. Their orders are to provide disaster relief, when and where necessary, at the discretion of the zone commander. Each command will also provide assistance at the request of state or local authorities, in order to maintain civil control. We are not anticipating martial law or overriding any local authority, sir. We will, however, defend federal buildings, and also highways, and other facilities at our discretion."

"Will this include armed crowd or riot control in cities?" Calvin asked.

"Only upon request of the local authorities, and subject to rules of engagement authorized by the president," the general answered. "Our purpose is to protect lives and property, Mr. Calvin, not to start a shooting war in the inner cities."

"Thank you, General Gates. I just wanted to get that point clear in my own mind."

"The United States Navy has not been idle for the past week. They have been recommissioning all fleet ballistic missile submarines and calling those on patrol back into port."

"Wait a minute, general," said Barry Blumenthal, Undersecretary of the Interior. "I thought we were preparing for survival as a people, not for nuclear war."

"We are preparing for survival, Mr. Blumenthal," General Gates replied quickly. "The Navy is planning to remove as many offensive weapons from their fleet boats as possible and to reload them with food, medical supplies, and all classes of survival gear. You must remember that each submarine has onboard one of the finest nuclear electric generating plants in the world. It is our plan to have these boats out to sea as soon as they are loaded, under orders to return to shore when they are ordered to do so or when their commander deems it safe to do so. They are to locate to a safe harbor and settle indefinitely there to provide electrical power, supplies, and protection for the people in the area. Each boat will carry a normal crew plus a detachment of fully equipped Marines for local security."

"My apologies, General," said Barry Blumenthal. "I should have let you finish."

"Not necessary, sir," replied Tailspin Tommy. "That concludes my brief, unless there are any questions."

"My thanks also, General Gates. That was excellent," Amos cut in before any fireworks could start. "Now I wonder if we could hear from the Department of Energy."

"At DOE, we have been studying the situation with an eye toward stockpiling as much fuel as possible and developing an acceptable rationing system. Our intention is to limit fuel use to a level that will allow the country to make the stockpiled fuels last until supplies can be returned to pre-event levels. We hope to make the most efficient use of indigenous fuels and minimize the need for imports." Larry Valleau was on a roll, and he thoroughly enjoyed the spotlight. He had prepared well for today's meeting in both the quality and completeness of his report and in his personal appearance. He was a handsome man with a wonderful head of hair of which he was justifiably proud and which he had meticulously combed and coifed. "Our supply of electrical energy," he continued, "is of utmost importance, since so much of our lives are dependent upon it. Fortunately, our utilities are solidly interconnected nationwide and accustomed to cooperation both in routine operations and in restoration from damages. On the down side, however, an electric power system is a far more fragile thing than most of us realize, as the 2003 blackout has proven, as well as the huge blackouts in India a year ago. Additionally, power grids are susceptible to damage from any number of natural events. All utilities have emergency action plans for dealing with damages from hurricanes, tornadoes, earthquakes, ice storms, heat waves, and other natural disasters. These plans can easily be applied to meteor damage, and with their usual cooperative efforts, damages should be repaired and service restored within a reasonable time. We are, however, through secure channels, requesting that all utilities stock up on restoration equipment and be as prepared for problems as is humanly possible." He stopped to take a sip of his water.

"Integrity of the interconnected electric systems is not deemed by this office to be of major concern. Fuel stocks, on the other hand, are. At this time of year, stockpiles of fuel at electric generating plants are normally at their yearly low level. We have requested that utilities make every effort to bring their stockpiles of fuel up to full as soon as possible, claiming the potential threat of a Wildcat CSX and Norfolk Southern Railroad strike as the reason for purchasing fuels at uneconomic prices. The president has authorized the DOE to issue a tax credit to utilities to recover the extra cost of purchasing these fuels at unseasonal prices. Most seem to be responding to this request. Unfortunately, deregulation of utilities and division into separate and competitive business units is complicating and slowing the process somewhat.

"Our nuclear generating plants are another matter altogether. I'll turn you over to Dr. Elizabeth Coulter from the Nuclear Regulatory Commission, and she will bring you up to date on this situation. I will only add that DOE is undersigning all requests by the Nuclear Regulatory Commission for action in the nuclear industry." Larry Valleau smoothed his trouser creases as he resumed his seat and favored Liz Coulter with a conspirator's *I know what's coming* glance.

Elizabeth Coulter was a short, fair-skinned woman with a few streaks of gray in her lustrous dark brown hair. She was married to a colonel in the 82nd Airborne Division and, like him, would not put up with any nonsense. Liz had learned early in life that she could not get by on charm and good looks, so she had learned to capitalize on brains, grit, and hard work. Despite her diminutive size, she was a formidable presence, a ball of physical energy, and a PhD nuclear physicist from Cal Tech. She fixed each member of the select committee with a stern look as she began. She knew this presentation was going to be controversial. "Our nuclear generating plants present us with a monumental conflict of interest. On the one hand, we would like to keep all nuclear generating plants running at full output in order to conserve fossil fuels at other stations. As Larry indicated, fossil-fuel plants are at their seasonal low point for fuel stockpiles. We cannot, however, allow these nuclear generating plants to run any longer than it is safe to do so. We cannot risk the possibility of a breach in containment caused by a meteor strike to jeopardize public health with radioactive contamination. Therefore, I have been in contact with the Atomic Energy Control Board of Canada, and my colleagues there are in complete agreement that steps must be taken at the earliest possible time to eliminate this danger. The Canadians are considering shutting down their older heavy-water reactors in an orderly fashion. The provinces are not heavily dependent on nuclear energy to meet their electric demand, but their national government is preparing a megawatt-sharing arrangement anyway. However, these shutdowns may force curtailment of energy sales to the United States, on which several northern states are dependent." She paused and got ready to drop the bomb.

"Accordingly, I have had my office contact all independent system operators and regional transmission organizations, ISOs and RTOs if you will, along with regional regulatory agencies and requested that they study the impact of shutting down all nuclear generation on their systems. I have also requested them to prepare contingency plans toward that end."

"You did what?" Amos Bellinger roared. "Who authorized you to do such a thing?"

Liz had been prepared for this reaction. "No one had to authorize it, Mr. Bellinger," she responded with an aggressive jut of her chin. "It is within my authority to do so, and with all due respect, sir, I don't want to be responsible for a tragedy similar to Fukushima in Japan just a few short years ago."

"It's not within your authority to start a national panic," Amos responded with mounting anger.

"I indicated that this study was to be conducted with complete secrecy and nothing was to be shared with the media," Liz said.

"Reporters are always poking around nuclear plants looking for a fill-in story, and these industry professionals aren't cleared for security. There is bound to be a leak, and some hard questions will be raised. Is your office prepared to answer them?" Amos asked with a sour and positively furious look.

"We're ready," she said with a confidence that was faked beautifully.

The remainder of the meeting went very smoothly, with no one wanting to ruffle Amos Bellinger's feathers any more than Liz Coulter had already done. All responders were well prepared, and Amos was quite pleased with their progress. The subjects ranged from food and fuel stocks, transportation, and emergency medical supplies to tools and equipment and the means of guarding and distributing available supplies. As the meeting closed, Amos became concerned that the focus had been almost exclusively on the short term.

"I'd like to thank all of you for an excellent job done on short notice and under difficult conditions. I'm sure the president will also be pleased. If it is not a problem for anyone, I would like to meet again tomorrow for a progress report and to field any new ideas. Again, many thanks."

\* \* \*

"Well, Lizzie," Dan Coulter said into his office phone at Fort Bragg, North Carolina, "you really stirred up a hornet's nest with that one."

"I know," she replied. "I hope I was correct in claiming we are prepared to field all the questions that may arise."

"You'll handle them alright," Dan said. "You have never had a problem handling me."

"It's not me that I'm worried about, Dan. It's my staff who will have to handle the calls."

"Just brief them on the possible questions and give them the acceptable answers," Dan replied. "Then threaten to transfer them to duty in some remote area of Alaska if they screw up. It always works in the military."

"I wish you could get some leave," Liz said. "I would really like to see you tonight."

"I know, babe; that goes double for me," Dan cooed sincerely, his gruff voice going soft. "But things are more than crazy around here lately. We have had to deploy a brigade to Panama for special duty, and another is on alert for redeployment to another as yet undisclosed place. My regiment is now taking special crowd-control and anti-riot training. For Christ's sake, what's going on, Lizzie? We are airborne, not military police," Dan commented grumpily.

"Well, do good, Danny boy, and remember I love you," Liz said, hating not being able to tell him the reason for and importance of what he was doing.

"I will, Lizzy, and you do the same."

"Okay, I've got to go. Sleep well and get some damned leave soon."

"Second order of business, darling. You keep well also. Good night."

"Good night."

\* \* \*

Lisa Howard nuzzled her nose in the crinkled salt-and-pepper gray hairs on Amos Bellinger's chest. "That was quite a meeting today," she said, speaking into his chest.

"Uh-huh," Amos answered.

Lisa was disappointed with his less-than-enthusiastic answer, so she pinched his nipple hard, then twisted it, pulling out several chest hairs in the process. Then she kissed it gently to soothe it.

"What the hell did you do that for, Lisa? That freakin' hurt," Amos replied sulkily.

"No pain, no gain, sweetheart. You'll feel better shortly," she said, kissing a warm trail down his furry belly. "I knew we would have a good time tonight, you are always very amorous after a tough meeting," she replied.

"That's why you took a man with a high-stress job as your lover, I suppose," he mused.

"That and the fact that I always wanted to make love to a bald-headed man," Lisa said, taking a patch of his chest hairs in her teeth and tugging gently.

"Ouch, that hurts," Amos grumbled again.

"You didn't mind it a few minutes ago."

"That was then, and this is now," Amos said, moving on his side slightly to rub the bristly black hair on the back of his fingers across the erect nipple of her left breast, eliciting a small groan from deep in her throat. After enjoying the sensation for a moment longer, Lisa raised herself up to plant a deep, sensuous kiss on his mouth.

"Do you know there's something very sexy about a man with more hair on his face and body than on his head?" Lisa teased.

"I certainly hope so," he said as his hands began doing delicious things up and down her lush body, pausing here and there to pay attention to a few particularly sensitive areas that he had come to know quite well.

Now that she had his undivided attention and she could feel he was definitely rising to the occasion, she eased herself slowly on top of him.

"Amos, old boy," Lisa said between nibbling little kisses, "I think it's time to stop talking."

## Saturday, March 6

Devon Grant was jolted out of a deep sleep, startled by the feeling that she was not alone. A scream rose in her throat but was quickly stifled by the strong fingers closed over her mouth. Even in the darkness, she could sense a face was coming close to hers.

"Please don't make a sound, and look only at the ceiling." The deep, masculine voice, which was commanding without being frightening, continued, "I mean you no harm, Miss Grant, and if you will promise not to scream, I will take my hand off your mouth."

Devon nodded in the affirmative, and as promised, the fingers moved a fraction of an inch away from her lips. Devon could sense the residual scent of aftershave on them. "Miss Grant," came the soothing voice again, "I'll be brief, and then I'll be gone. I have only come here tonight to warn you that the little game you're playing with Mr. Shellcroft had best end now. Forces are at work that you can't even imagine, and if you continue, you may be placing yourself and your Mr. Halloran in danger. Let it go, and go back to being a nice, quiet employee."

"Who are you?" Devon asked softly into the palm of his hand. "Why are you doing this? Are you the one that we should be afraid of?" As usual, Devon's questions rolled out without giving time for an answer.

"I'm just a man who has a job to do. But I also have a daughter about your age, and I can picture her doing some of the same things that you are doing. I simply want to give you the same advice I would give her. Stop this foolishness so we can all go back to living our normal lives. I'm going to leave now. Please remain as you are for another five minutes."

Devon felt the shadowy presence leave the side of her bed and move swiftly and surely through the half-light and out of her bedroom. She could not resist a quick look but saw only the back of a tall, man going out her bedroom door. Only seconds later, she heard the soft thump of her apartment door closing.

Devon leaped from her bed and moved quickly across her bedroom to the back window overlooking the parking lot. A moment later, a man came from the building and walked away into the darkness, pausing momentarily to glance back over his left shoulder at her bedroom window. At that moment, Devon Grant came eye to eye with Frank Muller, Special Agent for the FBI. From this distance, he looked more like a big and bulky father figure than the sinister man who just had his hand over her mouth right there in her own bedroom. He held her eyes for a moment, then with a brief, slightly crooked smile, turned and proceeded with a rolling gait to the plain gray Impala parked in the back of the lot, conveniently away from the light.

Without a second's thought for the time of night or the time difference on the East Coast, Devon picked up the bedroom phone and dialed the New York number John had given her.

"Duanesburg Diner," answered a feminine voice.

"Hello, I'm looking for John Halloran. Is he there, by any chance?" Devon asked.

Sally Prentiss was slightly taken aback by the fear and tension that were obvious in the voice on the phone. She responded automatically with some banter, trying to defuse the situation. "He's here by virtue of the fact that it's six in the morning and he's looking for some breakfast," she answered. "That and the fact that he's been mooning about you, if you are who I think you are, and he can't seem to sleep too well anymore."

"Will you never learn to keep your mouth out of other people's business, Sal?" said John Halloran, reaching for the phone.

"My, my…aren't we testy this morning?" Sally answered as she handed over the phone, grinning widely, pleased at having struck a nerve.

"Devon, is that you?"

"Yes, it's me," she answered. "I'm so glad I found you. There was a man in my apartment just now, and I'm really freaked."

"What man? Who? How did he get in? Tell me what happened." John was almost shouting into the phone. Fear for Devon was rising in him like it had a life of its own.

"It was one of the men who have been following me. I don't know how he got in or out, but he woke me out of a sound sleep," Devon explained. "He put his hand over my mouth so I couldn't scream, and then he told me not to be afraid. He didn't hurt me at all, and his voice was so gentle that I didn't really feel afraid at the time. It was weird.

"He warned me to stop playing games with Shellcroft, if I knew what was good for me, and you too, and then he left. I don't think he meant me any harm, John. And I'm sure he's one of the men who have been following me, because I saw him get into the same gray Chevy Impala I saw that first day. I got a look at him in the parking lot as he left, and now that I think about it, I think he wanted me to see him. He said I reminded him of his daughter." Devon was firing off words like a machine gun, and John needed to slow her down to make some sense of her situation.

"Whoa there," John said, "slow down."

"OK. I am still just a little worked up," Devon said.

"Just calm down. Are you all right? He didn't hurt you at all?" John asked with obvious concern in his voice, which made Devon feel a little more secure and somehow quite pleased.

"No, I'm fine. Just a little upset, but I'm feeling better now just talking to you."

John felt horrible and wanted to be with her. "This is getting much too complicated to handle over the phone, Devon. I've got a couple of days off. If I were to fly out to Boulder today, could you meet me at the airport?" John asked. "You did say the skiing was good, didn't you?"

"Don't kid around about this, John." Devon's voice was firm.

"I'm not kidding."

"Today? Could you really come out, John?" Devon said excitedly, the pleasure unhidden in her voice. "Even if only for a day or two, it would be wonderful! But how can you even think about skiing at a time like this?"

"I was just kidding about the skiing, but I think that we conspirators should finally meet, don't you?"

"I'd love that, John! Fly into Denver, and I'll pick you up there. The connecting flight from Denver to Boulder can be pretty bumpy, and the drive will give us time to talk."

"I'll make the arrangements and call you back with flight numbers and times," John said, feeling better already.

"Wait, John," she said. "How will I know you?"

John pondered the question for a moment, then said, "I'll be wearing blue jeans, a gray fleece jacket, and a tan baseball cap with 'Eli T Iceman' on it," he answered. "And I won't be carrying skis."

"Okay," she said. "And thanks, John, for being patient with me." She had missed his meager attempt at a joke altogether.

"No problem. I'll call you in a while. No, wait a minute…are you calling from home?" he asked with intensity in his voice.

"Yes! Oh, damn it, John! I didn't even think!"

"Too late now," he said reassuringly. "I'll just call you at work in a few hours. I should have the arrangements made by then," John said, more to settle her down than anything else. They both knew if her phone was tapped, then whoever was following them already had all the information they needed. "Don't worry, Devon. Everything will be fine. Talk to you later."

"Thanks, John. Bye," she said and hung up.

"That must be one fine woman," said Sally Prentiss, leaning over on the counter and treating John to an unusually fine view of her magnificent cleavage.

"I think so," John answered, not noticing the view. "And I haven't even met her yet."

\* \* \*

William J. Appleby was a handsome young man just above six feet tall with chiseled features. He set out for a stroll, enjoying the unseasonably warm March air and a little game of cat and mouse with an attractive young woman walking just ahead of him. He admired the lively bounce of her trendy-cut auburn hair and the sensuous sway of her rounded bottom. They were both just about to brave the traffic on Charing Cross Road when it hit. Eight pounds of hot nickel-iron traveling at terminal velocity slammed into the old brick-and-stone building across the way, where Foyles Charing Cross Road Bookstore was located. There was a brief moment of noises resembling distant thunder and angry snakes just before the meteor blasted its way through the old run down roof and through three floors of the old brick building. The meteorite severed a gas line between the first and second floors, before exploding into the first floor storage room filled with old rare books and manuscripts. Within just a few moments, smoke and fire were billowing up all three stories and through the gaping hole in the roof. The crowd on the sidewalk recoiled from the shock of the impact.

William J. Appleby was never one to miss a perfect opportunity, so he quickly stepped around a few people who were riveted in place by what had happened and placed himself directly behind the young woman he had been admiring. She recovered from her initial shock and turned around in fright, bumping directly into him just as he had planned. He wrapped his arm around her to prevent her from falling, and held her a bit closer than may have been necessary. "Sorry," she said. "It's just so terrible."

"That's all right," he said, keeping his arm protectively around her shoulder. She allowed him to hold her soft warmth against him.

"I'm Billy Appleton, by the way" he said.

"Meave McCormak," she answered, still not moving away from him.

"I guess I'll buy no books at Foyles today," he said.

"Not likely."

With that obvious fact decided, they remained standing close and simply watched the growing crowd of onlookers. People were clearly frightened by the thought of something falling from the sky and creating such havoc. The onlookers also stood close together for comfort and chatted noisily to hide their fears.

Billy and Meave remained close to each other as the Soho Fire Station trucks arrived from nearby Shaftsbury Avenue, filling the air with bells and whistles blaring and ringing and drowning out any chance at normal conversation.

"Such a shame," Meave said a bit more loudly than normal, "all those rare books and such just going up in flames. I hope they've got them insured."

"Let's go somewhere quieter, don't you think?" Billy said into her ear, taking the opportunity to sample her cheap perfume and talk softly into her ear. "The Royal George Bar is just up the way a bit."

"Sure," Meave said as she allowed him to lead her by the hand through the gaggling crowd that was growing by the second.

William Appleby said nothing; he simply watched and learned. Soon, the gem of an idea formed in his fertile mind. Keeping his arm firmly around Meave, he moved off slowly, still observing the anxiety in the crowd. "Do you know about insurance, then?" he posed.

"Oh, just a little. I've been working as a temp at Heathrow Casualty for several months now. It's kind of boring, though."

"I should like to hear more about it. Do you have time for a bit of a drink before going back?"

"I don't mind if I ever go back," she said, falling into stride with him.

"We'll have to see about that," Appleby said, his mind a riot of profitable thoughts.

It took the London firefighters over an hour to get the fire under control. The fire also made the evening papers.

\* \* \*

John Halloran was dressed exactly as he had said he would be, and Devon Grant recognized him instantly. She knew she should signal him with a wave and a smile and go right up to him, but perversely, she wanted to wait a few minutes. She needed a little time just to study him without his knowing it. Her life had gotten so complicated so quickly that she needed this little time to adjust. Strangely enough, she was feeling shy and concerned he wouldn't like what he saw when she revealed herself. In her heart, she knew this wouldn't be so, because she had taken great care in dressing to pick him up, and she knew she looked her best. Hadn't she gotten several frankly admiring glances on the way to the arrival gate?

If only she could have read his mind, she would have seen that he was feeling just as vulnerable as she was and in fact, shared many of her exact same thoughts and anxieties. He was talking to another man as if they were old friends, and she wondered how that could be.

John's face was not pretty-boy handsome, but also not hard to look at. His features may not have been Hollywood perfect, but the whole picture was nice. He had light brown hair that was cut short and tended to lay close to his head. His eyes were possibly a little too close together, but his nose was nice and straight, and his mouth was proportionate to his face. He was at least six feet tall and looked fit enough. Devon noticed he had big hands and huge shoulders and that he handled his overnight bag as if it weighed nothing.

John's friend left with a handshake and a big smile, and John was left standing quietly by a large potted fern, looking over the crowd, obviously trying to figure out who among them might be Devon, when a very pretty young woman stepped out of the crowd and extended both her hands to him in a gesture of greeting. "Hi, John. I'm Devon," she said simply.

He took her hands instinctively and felt their warmth radiate up his arms and throughout his body, robbing him of his power of speech. John estimated that Devon Grant was in her mid-twenties, which made her about ten years younger than him, and so damned pretty it frankly scared the hell out of him. Just looking at her took his breath away. He grinned stupidly until she broke the silence for him.

"Not what you expected to see?" she asked with an impish grin, cocking her head slightly to the side and causing her blonde curls to toss.

"People never seem to be the way you picture them when you talk on the phone. You surprised me so much because you are exactly what I had envisioned." He lied gallantly and hoped she didn't see right through him. She was more than he had expected—much, much more.

"Not disappointed, then?" she asked.

"Not at all," John answered, still grinning stupidly and wishing he could somehow regain control of his facial muscles. "We can go," he said, making every attempt to get his thought processes operational again. "This is all of my luggage."

"Let's go, then."

As they turned to leave, John switched his overnight bag to his left hand and held on to Devon's small hand in the other. She glanced up at him briefly, then smiled and gave his hand a confirming squeeze before asking, "Who was that man you were talking to before I came over?"

"Oh, that was an electrical engineer from British Columbia Hydro in Canada who recognized my hat," John explained.

"When you told me you would be wearing a tan Eli T Iceman hat, I wondered what it was about."

John picked up where he had left off. "Eli T Iceman is short for ELI THE ICE MAN, which is an electrical memory aid that would bore you to death if I was to continue. But anyway, someone shortened the name up and put it on a hat. Since I got my hat, I've been meeting people from all across the world who recognize it and start conversations. I always wear it when I fly."

The Denver airport is a huge place, so the walk to the parking lot was a long one. Devon looked up at John and said, "So, I'm just exactly what you expected; is that it?"

"No, not really," John said, grudgingly admitting the truth. "I expected you to be tall and scholarly, and painfully thin, with dark hair and a long straight nose and dark-rimmed thick glasses."

"You're somewhat disappointed, then, I guess?" she came right back with a mischievous grin. "I really faked you out on that one. I suppose you're not exactly what I had expected, either."

"I know," John said. "You expected a big rednecked country hick with a plaid flannel shirt and lineman's boots to go with the baseball hat."

"No, not really." She smiled again. "I expected a more scholarly type. You were the one who was supposed to have the thick, dark-rimmed glasses. And, no I'm not disappointed at all."

That last comment and the way she said it were worth his best smile, and he was pleased when the smile was returned.

*  *  *

Keeping back a discreet fifty feet, Special Agent Angela Freece blended in well with the rest of the airport crowd. Earlier that day, Angie had been suddenly pulled off her regular assignment and ordered to keep John under surveillance. She had been forced to bully her way onto John's flight, using a combination of charm, defiance, and stubbornness along with her FBI identification card. All of these had barely allowed her to bump one passenger with a standby ticket and see her booked through Chicago to Denver, first class.

Angie was a petite five-feet four inches, with short dark hair and a very nice trim figure. Dressed in a smart business suit and sporting studious glasses she didn't really need, she was the picture of a successful young businesswoman. She was just idling along, keeping pace with the crowd and maintaining the subject in the periphery of her vision while she cut her eyes continually right to left, seeking a familiar face from the Denver office. She really hoped that it would be a certain familiar face.

*  *  *

The air at Denver's five-thousand-foot elevation was thin and had a definite nip to it as John and Devon walked across the short-term parking lot to Devon's car. There were piles of snow everywhere, attesting to the severity of the previous winter. John threw his flight bag into the back seat and got in. "Are you hungry?" Devon asked.

"I didn't eat much on the plane, but I can wait, if you know of a good place."

"There's a really nice local place just past the city on our way to Boulder. It's nothing fancy, but the food's good and the old high-backed booths are nice and private."

"Sounds good to me," John said, still smiling.

Devon returned his big grin and just shook her head a little as she started the car. She understood the grin, because she was surprised herself at how right it had felt just holding his hand as they had walked through the airport. She recognized the sudden warm comfortable feeling she was getting just being with him.

She hadn't realized she was still smiling until he asked, "What?" while looking into her soul through her eyes.

"Nothing," she said. "I guess I'm just surprised at how comfortable I feel after just meeting you a few minutes ago."

"Me too."

\* \* \*

Angela Freece looked up and down the service road for a familiar face. She had been told before leaving Albany she would be met by an agent from the Denver office with transportation. This was an absolute necessity to avoid the delays in renting a car. The subjects had gotten into a white Toyota Prius and were already heading for the ticket booth. She was feeling the tension and beginning to contemplate hailing a cab when a gray Chevrolet Impala pulled up in front of her and a familiar voice said, "Hey, lady, you wanna go for a ride in my rickshaw?" It was an old Buddy Hackett line, and she knew immediately who the comedian was.

"Frank Muller, you old snake, how *are* you doing?" Angela smiled as she slid into the seat next to him. She had first met Frank when she had been a student and he an instructor at the FBI Academy in Quantico, Virginia. They worked together for a few years on a drug case out of the Albany office, and he was therefore a known entity. He was also exactly who she had hoped would pick her up. Frank Muller was not a brilliant agent or a high-rising hotshot, but he was a good, steady man to have with you, and a comfortable man for her to be around.

"They're in that white Prius that's just pulling out," she said.

"I know the car, Angie. I've been following her for a few days," Frank answered. "I've also got a good idea of where she's going."

Frank fell in with traffic and followed Devon out of the airport and onto Pena Boulevard. He slid in comfortably and maintained his position well behind them.

"Did he pick you up on the flight?" Frank asked Angela as they drove.

"I don't think so," she said. "I sat in first class, so I got on after and off before he did," she explained.

"Good. Are you hungry?"

"No thanks; I ate."

"If they stop for something to eat, we'll just wait outside."

\* \* \*

On the ride from Denver, Devon wheeled her Prius onto Interstate 70 past the old Stapleton Airport, then onto I-270 bypassing the city, and then, after a short run on I-25 across the river, she took US Highway 36 toward Broomfield and Boulder. She kept up a steady flow of small talk, filling John in on local history and points of interest, and John found himself relaxing. Normally a quiet person, he enjoyed both her company and the scenery.

The Mountain View Rest lived up to its name in that it had an excellent view of the mountains and it was restful; otherwise, it was no more impressive than the Duanesburg Diner. It was just a truck stop on US Highway 36 northwest of Denver, and like in most truck stops, the food was hot, hearty, and generous in portion. So was the service. Now that they were comfortably seated in the high-backed old booths Devon had recommended for privacy, it was time to talk seriously.

"Did you notice the gray car behind us on the way from the airport?" John asked.

"Yes," Devon answered. "Pretty sure it's my 'friend' from last night, and it looks as if he brought someone new along for the ride."

"It seems like they're still watching, but that's it."

"Yes, same as usual for the past few days."

"Not quite the same," John continued. "I think his friend was on the plane with me from Albany. When I boarded, the Jetway for my flight was down for repairs and we had to walk across the tarmac and up portable stairs to get on the plane. This gave me a clear view of the departure gate through my window. I noticed her boarding late, as she had to run to even make the flight. She must've been seated in first class, because she never passed by me in coach. I didn't even give her a thought at the time."

"What do you think that means?" Devon asked.

"I think it confirms your phone is definitely bugged, and they knew I was coming here, so they found out what flight I was on and that they know how to travel well. That also means, whoever they are, they carry a lot of clout."

"So you think they have to be very well connected because they could get a tap on my phone and get on your flight so quickly too, right?" she asked.

"Yes, I do. They're probably FBI or something, and they must believe we know something they don't want us to know. They probably don't want us to go to the media, so as long as we stay away from the press, maybe they'll leave us alone. You agree so far?" John asked.

"Yes."

"I did a lot of thinking on the flight out here, and I believe you must be correct in your meteor theory. Why else would they go to all the trouble and expense of tailing us? They also apparently believe we know a lot more than we really do, but as long as we're not going to the media with it, they will leave us alone. I hope. What I can't figure out is why they're still shadowing us when the Mountain, or whatever you want to call it is past the earth now. We should be out of danger, shouldn't we? I'll be damned if I know. They probably also know or strongly suspect that you were in Shellcroft's office and that we have been discussing it on the phone," John said, taking a deep breath. That was quite a long speech for him in the presence of such attractive company. "Unless there is something else following it..."

"If the earth is going to get hit by a bunch of meteors or even have a close encounter, wouldn't the government want to tell the people about it so that they could get ready?" Devon asked. "People have a right to know."

"I thought so at first, too, but after thinking about it, it's not necessarily so," John answered. "First of all, how would people even prepare for a meteor shower? No one knows for certain if there's even going to be a strike…or where…or when…. Then what happens if knowing there's the possibility of a strike makes people crazy with fear and causes panic? Under those circumstances, the government would want to keep it quiet until the last possible minute to minimize the social upset. I'm sure they don't want a mass exodus of people fleeing from big cities out into the countryside. The government may fear riots and looting breaking out in the inner cities, just like there was in New York City after the electric blackout in 1977 or in Los Angeles after the Rodney King verdict. People have changed over the years, Devon. In the Northeast blackout of 1965, people were orderly; they helped each other, and some even enjoyed it. Nobody even thought of taking advantage of a bad situation.

"By 1977, when Con Edison went black for two days, attitudes had changed drastically. People rioted and looted in Harlem. What they couldn't carry off, they set on fire. There was a huge increase in crimes of passion. People can do some strange and dangerous things if they have an idea the world is coming to an end, or that they won't get caught or punished. The huge 2003 blackout was nearly all back together in less than fourteen hours, so it wasn't long enough to see the rotten elements of our society. If it was out another day, I hate to imagine the effects," John was on a roll.

"That may be a good thought, John. Have you read anything about all the crazy things people did when the comet Kohoutek was supposed to pass close to Earth? We looked at it when I was in school. Some people did terrible things just because they thought that they could get away with it—their chance to get even with society, I guess. I read half the hippies in California decided to go on a camping spree and ran away to the mountains."

"No," John said, "I wasn't aware of that one, but it sure is easy to believe."

"After we eat, let's pick up some newspapers and see if there's anything in them to confirm our thinking."

"Good idea," John answered, taking a big bite of his bison burger.

\* \* \*

Alice Coons sat on the front porch of her home at the Muddy Springs sheep station about thirty miles west of Alice Springs, deep in the Australian Outback. She loved to sit out here on late warm evenings to watch the stars come out and enjoy a bit of coolness before another blazing-hot day came upon her. The breeze through the crispy brown grasses whispered gently to her, and the distant white stars she adored were blocked from her view by a partly cloudy night. Alice was enjoying a sort of vacation, as her husband, Bob, and the rest of the hands had the sheep at summer camp in a bend of the small river that bordered the station where there was plenty of water and the grass was actually green. Alice was on her own, enjoying every minute of it.

"Blimey sakes, Ol' Winnie, we can't see any of them shooters we've been seeing the last few nights." she said aloud to her beloved bloodhound, who was contentedly curled up beside the rocker. Sir Winston Churchill just raised his big brown head for a moment, then, simply lay back down to resume sleeping. The cold-blue streaks had been zipping across the sky for the past few nights and she regretted she would not see them tonight. She loved sitting out there in the quiet and tranquil setting. She began to think of her husband as she shrugged her shawl close over her bony shoulders and snuggled down in the big old rocker. She dropped her hand and scratched Sir Winston behind one floppy brown ear, and he groaned a little in contentment.

A half hour later, Alice and Ol' Winnie were dead. She was taking the last swig of her customary evening cup of tea when Ol' Winnie's head rose in curiosity to something. Then it came. Just eighteen meters from the gas fueling pumps of the sheep station and only thirty five meters from her rocking chair it struck with such an overwhelming impact it caused a heat blast and shock wave that killed the two of them instantly. The gas pumps were also destroyed and the unannounced impact left a round crater in the sandy tenosol soil, and a wall of flames and smoke melting the Australian night into a living hell. Alice, Ol' Winnie, the beautiful Ghost Gum trees and everything else in the vicinity was gone forever.

\* \* \*

Conversation at the Fairview Senior Apartments' Saturday-night card game was considerably more animated than usual. The four widowed women who played every week were friends of long standing. All of them had lost their mate in turn, each had sold the house they could no longer maintain and each had taken a one-bedroom apartment in the complex that presently housed fifty-four women and two very lucky men. Located in a quiet suburb of Boston, the apartment complex was clean and well maintained, and rents were regulated to each person's ability to pay. The maintenance staff was always helpful, and no one got lonely there unless by choice.

Each lady took her turn at hosting the game and making the dessert and coffee that followed. It didn't matter who won or lost, because the proceeds of their weekly card games were pooled and saved up until there was enough in the kitty for the four girls to take a little trip together. The table would be covered in travel brochures as the girls decided where they wanted most to go. When they did travel, they always went on a package tour, and they frequently became known as the Boston Tea Party to the other travelers because of both their means of saving for the trip and their energetic nature. They did their homework and usually knew the best places to see, the least expensive places to eat, and where to go for a little fun. For this reason, they usually did have more fun than anyone else.

"Did you listen to Reverend Randy last week?" Paula Patowski asked no one in particular. "I thought the show was just wonderful, but a little frightening. I only wish my John had listened to him when he was alive; maybe he'd have stayed home a little more." She allowed herself a small grin and a snide chuckle over the shot she had given to her dead husband. Paula was the nominal leader of the Boston Tea Party because she was the biggest, the loudest, the hardest working, and a natural-born planner and leader.

"I saw it, Paula," answered Burtha Kurtz. "I took out my Bible and read Revelations again after he went off, and I watched the sky just like he said to do. I saw several shooting stars. Revelations has always frightened me."

"You girls are too much for me," said Wilma Krauss, shaking her head and tossing her tight blue curls, "always seeing the end of the earth in everything that's just plain natural. When I was a bit younger, I stayed out late many a night and saw many a shooting star. And I'm still here alive and kicking."

"We know all about that," Paula said, "And you were probably in the best position to see them, too."

"Well I guess that's why I don't get to see many of them anymore," Wilma replied, getting a good dirty laugh from the girls.

"Shut up and play your cards, will you," Annie Phillips said. "This hand is going to take all night. And I gotta pee."

"So what if the world does end?" posed Wilma. "We don't have much else to do at night anyway, do we? And you always have to pee."

They all got a good laugh out of that one, even little Annie.

The game continued good naturedly as it always did, and they broke up after coffee and some excellent apple-cranberry strudel at a little after ten o'clock, as usual. After her three good friends had gone home, yawning and ready for bed, Paula remained wide awake and concerned. While washing up and getting ready for bed, Paula mulled over in her mind all of the things that were happening lately, and she wondered what the world was coming to.

She had seen a news clip about her grandson Stanley out in Reno getting caught out in the desert buck naked with some woman who wasn't his wife. Paula just shook her head and thought Stanley would have been much better served if he had been at home listening to Reverend Randy last Sunday than out chasing some sleazy little tart out in the desert. *You young fool*, she thought. *You're just like your grandfather. Always looking around the corner for what you already have at home.*

Paula grinned a little sheepishly as she poured herself a generous shot of the Southern Comfort her doctor prescribed for her as a sleep aid. She shook her head and chuckled. Old age does have some benefits, after all. Doctor's orders.... Bottoms up!

\* \* \*

The floor of Devon Grant's apartment was strewn with newspapers as she and John spent the evening carefully examining every page to look for evidence to support their theory. "Here's a funny one," Devon said. "Two people were parked out in the desert near Reno, Nevada, when they claim something came out of the sky, hit their van, and knocked it off into a roadside ditch. The van burst into flames and they got out with their lives, but not their clothes. Ha! I bet there'll be some explaining to do on that one. The paper says local authorities believe a mechanical failure caused the engine to catch fire, which spread to the sagebrush, and that's what caused the gas tank to blow. They don't even begin to explain what smashed in the front of the van, but they're trying to collect damages from the couple for the cost of putting the fire out. That seems very strange to me. Nothing additional about it on the internet, either."

"Yeah, sure does," John answered casually. "Add that to the meteor that hit the bookstore in London, which we saw on the MSN homepage, and that makes a whopping two," he continued, somewhat disappointed.

"But, John," Devon said, "that's two within a few days. It's not unusual to go for ten or twenty years without hearing about even one meteorite strike."

"Really?" he said, brightening, "I guess we'll just have to keep looking."

"It's getting late, John," Devon said. "Maybe we should turn in. I'll get you a pillow and a blanket. It's certainly nice to have someone here tonight. Maybe I'll be able to get a little sleep."

"Mind if I grab a quick shower before turning in?" John asked.

"No, not at all," Devon replied, "but you have to go through my bedroom to get there. I put some extra towels out for you." Then Devon smiled sweetly and continued, "I'll make up the sofa while you're showering."

That was when it became clear to John exactly where he would be sleeping.

*   *   *

"Real cozy little domestic scene over there," Dommy Ortiz said as much to himself as anyone. "She's making up a bed for him on the sofa." He moaned a little as he straightened up from the spotting scope.

"What's the matter, Dommy?" Frank Muller asked. "Disappointed there's no smut to watch tonight, or is your back giving out on ya?"

"No fun tonight, boss. They're just settling in, and she's keeping the bedroom door closed."

"I still say we should go over and shake them down a little," said Roger Markson from across the room, where he had field stripped his 9mm Browning and was fastidiously cleaning it before reassembly. He and his partner, Sal Grizetti, were new men who had been assigned to the surveillance team just today. Roger obviously favored a more vigorous approach to criminal investigation, and Sal agreed with anything he said.

"Look but don't touch is still the word," Frank Muller said with finality. Frank had been somewhat puzzled about these two ever since they checked in. He had never met or heard of either one of them in all his years in the bureau, and they also didn't sound or act like bureau people. He made up his mind to keep an eye on both of them.

"That's all for me, guys," Dommy said. "I'm going to pack it in for the night. Wake me up when she gets up, so I can watch her shower." He actually enjoyed the stormy look he got from Frank. The other two special agents just chuckled grossly. "Wake up yourself, Ortiz. If you're asleep, you can't hog the scope," Markson chimed in. Grizetti just laughed on cue.

"I think I'll pack it in, too," Frank said. "You guys have got the midnight shift. Make sure you stay awake."

\* \* \*

Reverend Randall had never got gotten completely comfortable speaking out loud to a camera by himself. "Good evening, ladies and gentlemen. This is the Reverend Randall P. Davis, speaking to you tonight on station WVM-TV from beautiful downtown Wheeling, West Virginia." With a sigh of mounting frustration, Randy Davis clicked off his Sony IID flash memory digital camcorder and rested his forehead in his hands. He was extremely frustrated and confused on this chilly March evening. Three times before, he had started to record his Sunday-night TV sermon along the guidelines laid down for him by the FBI agents who had come to the parsonage last Monday, but somehow, he just couldn't do it. Randy Davis was a devout and a patriotic man, honoring both God and country. Now these two cornerstones of his life were in conflict, and Randy didn't know how to deal with it. His mind went blank.

Last Sunday on the show, he had spoken from his heart and from the depths of his belief and had thereby gotten himself and his family in deep trouble. Monday, two men had appeared at the parsonage door, flashing him identification from the Federal Bureau of Investigation. Although they had been perfect gentlemen, they had frightened his wife, Ruth, terribly, and created a bit of conflict in Randy's life.

The FBI men had politely, but firmly, insisted that Randy not preach any further sermons on comets or make any mention of things falling from the sky. When Randy asked the reason for this prohibition, they could not or would not give him a firm answer. They instead called upon his patriotism and said that it was a matter of national security. They could not elaborate further but reassured Randy that it would all be cleared up in a short while. The agents had even presented him with a hand-signed letter from the president himself asking him for restraint and thanking him in advance for his cooperation.

To ensure his compliance, they would speak to the station manager and be at the station to monitor his future programming. Again, they had apologized for the inconvenience and then had gone, secure in the belief that Reverend Randall P. Davis would comply.

He would not.

Normally, it was so simple. He had an acceptable script by FBI standards. All he had to do was to read it into the camcorder and he would be done. Not tonight, however. Not tonight. Randall P. Davis knew exactly what his subject must be tonight, and he also knew that no matter how long he procrastinated, in the end, he would present the message in exactly the way that God wanted him to.

His show last Sunday had been wonderfully well received, judging by the number of calls WVM had gotten and the social-media activity praising it. He wondered. Perhaps if he just spoke honestly from his heart and the depths of his belief, God would help him find the words. At the same time, he feared it might be arrogant of him to believe God had the time to fuss over a simple one-hour TV show by an unknown preacher from West Virginia. *Well, Randy*, he told himself, *there's only one way to find out...*

He rose from the battered old oak desk that had been his father's and stretched the kinks out of his six-foot, two-inch frame. As he moved easily across the tattered carpet in his office to the big double windows that faced the wide back lawn, he prayed, "Lord, show me a sign, and I will follow."

The night sky was crystal clear and freckled with a million bright points of light. *All the stars are there tonight*, Randy thought, *and all of them are exactly where they should be.* Just then, just as had happened last Sunday, a bright streak of light flashed across the sky and flickered out just above the hills to the west. Randy held his breath for a few moments, and there came another streak of light, almost in the same place as the first. Randy had always been a sky watcher and a keen observer. He had often wondered why the shooting stars he so loved to watch came in from all different directions. In a God-created universe of order and predictability, meteors seemed to be the exception. That was unless they were part of a periodic shower, when they all seemed to come out of the constellation for which they were named. The ones that he had observed recently were like that in that they all came from the exact same direction.

*That does it*, he thought. "I will do as God wants me to do."

The Reverend Randall P. Davis went to the weathered desk and sat down. He calmly faced the camcorder, depressed the foot control that Allan Marshall from the station had rigged up for him, and began to read from the script he had prepared using the FBI guidelines. The script worked out perfectly, and he completed the recording just as his stopwatch reached the hour. Randy calmly removed the flash drive and placed a small self-adhesive label on it. He wrote "Sermon for Sunday, March 7."

He then inserted a new flash drive in the camcorder, returned to his desk, and, with a steadily growing assurance that he was correct in his actions, he began, "My friends, this may very well be the last time I will be allowed to speak to you, so please lend an ear and listen well to what I have to say. Last Monday, I was visited by two gentlemen from the Federal Bureau of Investigation. The men politely but strongly suggested my subject matter was not appropriate for public consumption and that I must use a less inflammatory text tonight. I cannot do this, however, as I must follow my heart and my Lord and tell you what is to be, as God gives me the light to see it.

"I am very well aware that many good men who truly believe they are God's messengers have preached falsely about the Mountain striking us and bringing about the end of the world. As you now know, this danger has passed us by. I must tell you tonight, however, that it is not the Mountain that God has sent to bring his straying lambs back into the fold. It is the angels of the Lord that follow it.

"Read your Bible, my friends, and in the Revelation of St. John, you will learn the angels of the Lord are set to hurl down upon the earth fiery missiles and falling stars and to bring forth volcanoes and all manner of natural disasters."

As before, Randy finished his sermon within the sixty-minute time frame and removed the memory stick from the camcorder. This flash drive he labeled simply "The Fifth Angel" and stowed it away in his briefcase.

\* \* \*

Regina Morrisette peeked out from behind the curtains to survey the Saturday-night crowd at the Doll House strip club on River Street in New Orleans. She listened to the hum of the crowd and tapped her feet to the last few bars of Mighty Maxine's finale. She stepped aside as the big-breasted thirty-year-old blonde came bursting through the curtains, hugging her tips tightly to her very ample silicone investments.

"Good crowd for the late show?" Gina asked. Her earlier set had been a disappointment. A lot of gropers and not too many tips.

"I don't think I can retire on it," Maxine said. "Maybe you can do better."

Gina waited as the master of ceremonies gave the crowd time to drink up their five-dollar beers before he sent out his star performer. She danced under the name of Tina Anisette, a clever little parody of her real name she had thought when she picked it. She had been using it for the past eight years, so by this time, she was a pro.

"And now, folks," roared Joey Green, master of ceremonies, "here's what you've all been waiting for.... She's young.... She's beautiful.... She's sweet.... And she packs a wallop! So put your hands together, and let's hear a big reception for our headliner tonight, *Miss Tina Anisette!*" The announcer clapped his hands in a parody of applause and pointed to the stage as the lights dimmed.

Gina waited behind the curtain until the first notes of "La Bamba" began, then threw her arms wide and stepped out. The announcer had not exaggerated one bit. Gina was young-looking at twenty-six years of age, and she was beautiful. She had mid-length auburn hair and a golden glow to her skin, inherited from generations of Cajun ancestors. Her dark brown-and-green eyes could look right through someone, and from the stage, they often did. Her breasts were full and firm, her waist small with a nice flare to well-rounded hips. Her legs were long and well-shaped and went all the way up to her ass, as many customers were fond of saying. She had a large and faithful following at the Doll House.

Gina was wearing her Mexican outfit for this number. It was one of her personal favorites and consisted of a white leather micro miniskirt cut completely up one side and a short white bolero jacket. Both pieces barely covered their assigned territories. They were decorated with black cotton-ball fringe that Gina had sewn on herself. Her fans seemed to like the way the bouncing balls accentuated the motion of her body as she danced. On her head, Gina wore a tiny white sombrero. She moved around the stage on her six-inch high heels with the light-footed natural grace of a ballet dancer, even though she had never had a lesson in her life or even seen a ballet, for that matter.

Gina moved easily around the edge of the long rectangular stage and quickly began to warm up the crowd and get a read on who the spenders might be. She was slightly unnerved when she noticed that Willie Lump Lump was here tonight. She hated the way he stared at her with those flat, gray, dead-looking eyes of his. Willie was a local character who had been in some kind of terrible accident when he was younger and had suffered a brain injury. That was why he stared blankly at the world. There seemed to be nothing going on behind those empty eyes. Still, Gina hated the way he undressed her with them. It gave her the creeps, even though she was going to undress herself for the other customers anyway. She liked to work on her own terms.

Midway through the set, Gina stepped up the erotic pace a notch and stood center stage with her legs set wide apart. She bent over very low to allow a good look at her cleavage, then brought her hands slowly up her legs, caressing her thighs. She ran her hands invitingly across her flat tummy and walked her fingers slowly upward into the middle of her bolero jacket and felt for the clasp hidden there. The crowd sensed what was coming, and some ragged applause began as she moved around the stage to where some inviting prospects were sitting. With a quick twist of the clasp and spin of her body, the jacket was gone and she wore only a tiny string bikini top. There was a small groan from the crowd, who had expected her breasts to be bare. Gina knew she had them.

With a little jog to set her breasts in motion and a slightly lewd bump of her hips, she set up for the first number's finale. A whirl, a dip, and a twist of the clasp on the side of the microminiskirt, and then it was sailing through the air to the back of the stage, leaving Gina attired in a black string bikini exactly when the last note of the music screamed forth.

The lights dimmed as she moved backstage to get ready for the second set. Her next number was a nice vocal rendition of "Spanish Eyes" with a strong and heavily accented back beat. Such a slow song was unusual for a strip act, but it allowed Gina to establish a romantic mood with her audience and to move slowly around the stage. As the music began, she did just that, giving each man in the audience a good look and making him feel that she was dancing just for him. Men all around the stage were elbowing each other, clapping and cheering her on. Gina reached behind her for the tie of her bikini top, and the audience responded loudly. In response, she shook her head and brought both hands in front to cover her breasts. The noise level in the club rose again, so she responded by reaching behind her again. A quick pull on the string to her bikini top set it loose, but Gina kept her hands cupped over her breasts and continued to tease the crowd, so at just the right moment, she spun around and flung her arms in the air, bare-breasted, and the crowd roared. With practiced grace, she set them into motion, bringing more cheers from the crowd as she shook her finger at them as if they were naughty boys.

Now was the time to make some money, so she began to work around the stage to where men were waving bills to be stuffed under the strings of her bikini bottom. Time was a factor, so Gina picked the more prosperous men she had identified earlier, squatted before them, leaned forward, and jiggled her breasts close to them, but not too close. Then she allowed them a few seconds to fit the bills under her bikini string before retreating quickly with a nice smile and a wink to seek another patron. Gina was experienced and stage-wise, so she picked only men who had their bills folded longways, which made them easy to tuck under the strings, and avoided the few who held their money wadded up. She avoided Willie altogether.

As her number neared its end, Gina backed slowly to center stage and did some serious bumps, working always back toward the curtains. When she reached her spot, she set her feet wide apart, pulled the knot in the bikini string, and dropped her bottom altogether. She stood completely naked for a full minute, giving them a last look, then turned around and bent over to look between her legs at the cheering crowd. Then she quickly squatted, gathered her tips in her hands, and gave the guys an enticing quick wink over her shoulder as she left the stage.

"I hope you left some loose change out there for me," Mary said as she prepared to go on next. "That was a great show!"

"Fish eyes is out there tonight," Gina said with a shudder that had nothing to do with being cold. "I hate it when he's here."

"I know what you mean; he gives me the creeps."

Gina gathered up her money and retreated to the dressing room, still feeling Willie Lump Lump's eyes on her. A quick shower to remove the body makeup, and she would be out of here and on her way home. No table dancing for her tonight; to hell with the money.

\* \* \*

Willie "Lump Lump" Seaman felt Gina leaving the stage as a physical thing. *Maybe she'll come out and do some private dancing,* he thought. *Then I can see her some more.* He hated it when the other men got to see her close and talk to her, but they had the money for her, and Willie had none.

When she didn't show up, Willie felt betrayed and even a little angry. He would have to go home now, disappointed again. She hadn't come over to get his grubby and twisted-up dollar bill, even though he had held it up for her to see. One of these days she would see him, he thought to himself, one of these days.

## Sunday, March 7

"Wake up, John. Wake up." Devon was almost shouting at the sleeping form curled up on her sofa while she shook him by the shoulder.

"What?" John asked as Devon continued shaking him out of a deep sleep.

"Look at the papers, sleepyhead."

John's eyes were blurry with lack of sleep, and he had trouble focusing on the newsprint that Devon seemed to be shaking in front of him. He shook his head to clear it and reached out to hold her hand still so he could focus his eyes on what she was showing him.

There, on page three, was an article about a huge brush fire in Western Australia. John's foggy mind refused to understand why Devon saw anything very interesting or even newsworthy about the story. Then he looked down at a picture that accompanied the article and saw several very strange small black men pointing toward the sky. The caption pointed out that several of the aboriginal natives of the area swore the fires were started by spears from the sky. "Fires from the sky," they kept repeating over and over while pointing toward the heavens. John was fully awake now and took the paper from Devon.

"Three sheep stations burned, and thousands of acres of grassland also. That must have been quite a fire," John said.

"Quite a fire is right, and the third report of something falling from the sky in just a few days," Devon said excitedly. "That has to be what they're concerned about."

"Makes a lot of sense," John said. "Is there a library near here?"

"Yes," she answered. "That is quite a turnabout from Australian brush fires."

"I know, but I thought we could look through recent magazine articles to see if anyone else suspects something is going on and has put it into print."

"Wouldn't the government be sitting on them too, keeping such stories out of publication?" Devon asked.

"You're right, of course. Excuse me, I'm only half awake."

"No problem. I think I have a better idea, anyway. I'll call Dr. Schmidt at the university. He's an astronomy professor, and I'm sure he'll be able to help. I'll do it right after I cook us some breakfast."

"Now that really sounds good to me," John answered, noticing a slight rumble in his belly. "Are you sure you don't want to go out to eat?"

"I'm sure."

Over a pleasant breakfast of scrambled eggs and bacon, John Halloran was quiet, which was not unusual for him, and Devon Grant was quiet, which *was* unusual for her. Halfway through the meal, John looked over at her and noticed the lines of concentration that had formed between her eyes.

"Penny for your thoughts," he said, using a worn-out old expression of his mother's.

"At the current rate of inflation, you're going to have to do a lot better than that," Devon said and smiled.

"I was just wondering what you were concentrating on so hard," John said.

"The man I'm going to call is Professor Karl Schmidt. I met him at work while he was doing some cooperative work with Space Environmental Labs. I bet he not only has a clue as to what is happening in space, he probably knows about the cover-up at the lab, too." Devon was positively glowing with pleasure at her discovery. "I wonder why I never thought of him before."

"Combination of working night shifts added to everything else going on, probably," John said, munching on the last of his rye toast. "Why don't you give him a call right now? If he's free, I'll help you with the dishes and we can go right over."

"And if he is not free, then I have to do the dishes myself?" Devon asked with a wry grin.

"No. If he is not free, then I'll do the dishes myself."

"Boy, I sure hope he's busy," Devon said, smiling as she took out the Boulder phone book to look up the number.

An hour later, the dishes were done by both of them, and John and Devon were dressed and headed downstairs for the parking lot. Dr. Karl Schmidt, professor of astronomy at the University of Colorado, said that he would be happy for Devon and her friend to come over and let him speak learnedly on his favorite subject.

\* \* \*

"Good morning, Amos. Sorry to bother you on a Sunday," said the president as Amos Bellinger entered the Oval Office. The president was dressed in slacks and a plaid cotton shirt open at the collar. His feet were in his favorite pair of LL Bean *Wicked Good Slippers*. Amos thought Coleridge looked even wearier than he himself felt after having had only a few hours' sleep.

Coleridge was a strong man, both physically and morally, and he cared deeply and sincerely for the people of the United States. The American people had sensed that caring in him as he campaigned, and that was why they had elected him to the White House. That was precisely why it bothered him so terribly not to be forthright about what was coming. "Have you been briefed on the Siberian incident, Amos?"

"No, sir. I came straight here after your secretary called."

"At approximately 4:30 this morning our time, one of our KH-11C satellites spotted a bright flash in the central Siberian plateau. CIA boys tell me such a flash is consistent with the detonation of a nuclear device. CIA also noted the flash is very close to a soviet nuclear weapons manufacturing facility currently in the process of being dismantled and that there are American technicians and military on-site. So far, I've heard nothing from the Russians."

"This could prove to be interesting," Amos answered.

"The satellite detected no radiation emissions, and only a small tremor was recorded on seismographs in Alaska. CIA also tells me there was a similar flash sighted in the southern Atlantic and western Indian Oceans area way back in 1978. Early speculation was that Israel or South Africa had done a clandestine explosion of a two-kiloton nuclear weapon. There was no gamma radiation, however, and no fallout, so the flash was later classified as a meteor strike. I understand the pieces of Shoemaker-Levy 9 comet exploded in a similar fashion when they struck Jupiter's atmosphere."

"When will we know for sure, sir?"

"Not for several hours, or so I'm told, but there's another problem."

"What's that?"

"At the nuclear weapons plant, there is an electric generating station of the same design as Chernobyl. If it was a meteorite strike that damaged the plant in any way, then this incident will add fuel to Mrs. Coulter's plan to shut down our own nuclear plants."

"I'll have a word with her as soon as we can get some definitive damage reports," Amos said wearily. "Can we depend on the Russians to keep this quiet?"

"They won't say anything," the president answered. "They have more than enough internal problems to deal with.

"I wasn't prepared for meteorites to be coming in so soon, Amos. I was led to believe we still had a few weeks before it would start. I want to know why I'm being surprised."

"Ben Cohen and I talked about this just after the London incident. Apparently, these are a few strays ahead of the main field. Ben says we can expect them to increase slightly also."

"Why wasn't I made aware this could occur, Amos? And why didn't we see them coming?"

"As I understand it, Mr. President, there is no way to spot them inbound. The particles are too small and there's just too much sky up there to be able to spot all of them, not to mention their approach is at too low of an angle."

"I thought we were tracking things as small as an astronaut's glove with the big Spacetrack Radar," the president said.

"Yes, sir, that's true, but we know where those things are and can reacquire them whenever we want to. These meteors come in quick and fast and give us no time to locate or plot them."

"Then light a fire under Ben Cohen's ass and get me some definitive information. I will not keep this under wraps any longer unless I have it."

"We have been able to pretty well keep the few hits we've had so far out of the press, or at least off the front page, sir; and I have to assume we can continue to do so."

"Still, it makes me wonder if Liz has a good point in getting our nuclear units shut down." Jameson Coleridge ran his fingers through his hair and continued, "I've been going over this rather lengthy document sent over by the National

Academy of Sciences. It's entitled 'Nuclear Winter and Its Sociopolitical Consequence.' Quite the Sunday-morning cheery subject, isn't it?"

The president began pacing slowly around the office, idly looking out windows without seeing, and fingering objects in the office without really feeling them. "This study was based on a previous study started back in the eighties by Paul Crutzen, a Dutch meteorologist at the Max Planck Institute. Richard Turco continued and refined the study, which became known as TTAPS for its authors, Toon, Turco, Ackerman, Pollack, and Sagan. Yes, that is the Dr. Carl Sagan of Cornell University. They began by studying the environmental effects of various scenarios of nuclear exchange and discovered that an exchange of only a small portion of the world's nuclear arsenal could cause a nuclear winter in the northern hemisphere. They also found that the worst of these scenarios was the most likely one to be used—that of a counterforce strike against the enemy's hardened ballistic missile force.

"The model they used was one based on smoke from large forest fires and particulate matter rising into the atmosphere and its effect on our weather. As time progressed, their mathematical model improved and they came to the realization that even small cities are candidates for the creation of nuclear winter. Think about it. Cities are merely vast concentrations of flammable material, from stored gasoline and heating fuels to gas mains and flammable materials in buildings, right down to the asphalt with which they coat their rooves and pave their roads. Multiply this a hundred times and you have a month-long worldwide winter. Scary stuff the population has no idea about.

"Over the years, several studies were done both individually and jointly by NOAA, NASA, and the Environmental Protection Agency, among others. Parallel studies were made worldwide and have come to the same conclusions. The effect does not have to be initiated by a nuclear exchange at all but any event that can cause widespread burning, or volcanic activity that can cause an intrusion of dust and ash into the troposphere and stratosphere, causing global cooling on a major scale. Did you know, Amos, that a drop of only one degree globally can trigger widespread crop failures and worldwide famine? I sure didn't," he said, not waiting for an answer before continuing.

"A little history lesson here, Amos. Way back in 1815, a volcano named Mount Tambore erupted in Indonesia. The explosion destroyed most of the island, which the volcano had previously created, and injected millions of tons of ash and sulfur dioxide into the atmosphere to an altitude of over twenty miles. This dust circled the entire globe and caused what meteorologists call the year without summer. There was actually snow in July 1816 in the northern United States. Worldwide temperatures dropped drastically and remained unseasonably low for several years. After Mount Pinatubo erupted in the Philippines in 1991, weather patterns were changed all around the world. Meteorologists believe this eruption was in part responsible for the abysmal weather we suffered in 1992 and 1993, including Hurricane Andrew, a killing nor'easter, and the blizzard of '93.

"The dust and gasses that remain in the troposphere, the part where we live, should be washed clean by rains within a few weeks to a few months, but dust and ash that reach higher elevations can persist for many months and even years.

"NOAA adds to this that a strike by a meteor the size of the one that caused the Barringer Crater in Arizona could set off earthquakes of 7.5 on the Richter scale, or higher, and initiate sufficient volcanic activity to create nuclear winter on a global scale. That's just to add insult to injury, I suppose. But, Amos, just what the hell is a man like me supposed to do with this kind of information coupled with the responsibility for the well-being of three hundred million people?"

"Mr. President, you are doing everything you can do at this time." Fatigue and depression were settling into Amos's bones even as he spoke.

"Then why do I feel like I'm doing nothing? I know in my head I'm doing the best thing, but my heart tells me to let it out and have the chips fall where they may."

"Sir, I can only imagine the terrible pressure you are under, but we simply must wait and pick the most opportune time to make the public announcement, and we absolutely must be completely prepared to give thoughtful instructions to the people on the best course of action for them to take. We must also be prepared to assure the public we have made the proper preparations, and be prepared to prevent mass hysteria. It's a huge undertaking, sir, and it takes time."

"Jesus Christ, Amos, don't preach to me on what we should do. I damn well know that as well as you do. I want to know *when*!"

"I don't know."

"Then find out! Put Ben Cohen on a fire pit and roast his ass if you have to, but get me some answers!" Coleridge was angrier than Amos had ever seen him. "And while you're at it, have that select committee of yours start looking into the long-range problems of nuclear winter and come up with some long-range solutions."

"We will get on it tomorrow."

"*Bullshit*! You'll get on it today!"

Amos was shocked at the depth of the president's concern. He wondered briefly if Coleridge was losing his grip. "Then if you will excuse me, sir, I'll get started calling them right away." Amos bit the words off in anger.

"You're excused."

As Amos turned to leave the room, a strong hand took hold of his shoulder and stopped him. "Amos, I'm sorry. I shouldn't be dumping on you because my problems are getting the best of me," the president said sincerely.

"I understand, sir, and it's alright," Amos answered, still furious.

"Before you go, Amos, please fill me in on the security side."

Amos lowered his head for a moment and stared at the presidential seal emblazoned on the carpet. He managed to fight down his anger and collect his thoughts so he could continue. "Sir, we have things in Boulder well in hand. Dick Morgan has assigned two new men to the surveillance team. They are men who have done freelance work for the CIA before and who will do whatever is necessary or whatever they are told. They can add a little muscle to the equation if necessary."

"No violence, Amos."

"No, sir. The boy in Texas was given a National Science Award and a brand-new high-power telescope as a prize. He is busily studying things he couldn't even dream of seeing with his old junkyard telescope. He seems to be quite content doing that, and neither he nor his mom have questioned how he could win a second contest that he never entered. In any event, he has discontinued staring at the meteorite stream, as we had hoped.

"Good old Reverend Randy has two FBI agents living in his house and two more monitoring his program. He will not go off preaching Revelations any more. And if he does, there are two men at WVM-TV pretending to be doing an FCC audit. They will monitor his broadcasts, and they've got a kill switch for the station if necessary.

"I'll personally talk to Liz Coulter and see that she doesn't do anything rash without clearing with us first."

"Leave Liz alone," the president said resignedly.

"Do you think that is wise, sir?"

"Yes, Amos, I do. Now let's talk about more pleasant things. How is your lovely Lisa doing?"

The conversation was more pleasant through the remainder of breakfast, and then both men parted ways, one to go on reading the impossibly thick report filled with charts, graphs, and enough statistics to boggle the mind of any man, but Jameson Coleridge was no ordinary man. His practiced eye cut through the scientific rhetoric to the beating heart of the matter. *If we do get hit by a big one, then life on Earth will be changed forever, period, end of quote.*

The other man went to his apartment and tried to get in a few hours of much-needed sleep, alone.

\* \* \*

Devon expertly swung the Prius into a parking spot at the front of the Fiske Planetarium and Science Center of the University of Colorado. John stood for a moment and admired the impressive structures.

"Quite something, aren't they?" Devon asked with a touch of pride.

"You've got that right," John answered.

"Wait until you get inside to be impressed," Devon said.

"Let's go, then."

In just a few minutes, Devon and John were entering the second-floor office of Dr. Karl Schmidt, professor of astronomy. Dr. Schmidt's office was spacious and well appointed, with large windows looking west across Broadway toward the mountains. John was quite taken by the beauty of both the campus and the surrounding countryside.

The room had a comfortable, lived-in feeling and was filled to capacity with books, star charts, drawings, and photographs. Papers and computer printouts were piled on every flat surface. Dr. Schmidt was a diminutive man with a rim of snow-white hair surrounding a well-tanned bald spot. He had mischievous blue eyes and a quick grin, but the pleasant exterior did not hide an unmistakable air of authority. This man would make a good power grid operator, John thought.

"Good morning, Miss Grant," Schmidt said as John and Devon entered. "It's nice to see you again, and I'm pleased to see you are continuing with your studies." He extended his hand and shook John's firmly, all the while smiling at Devon and giving her a broad wink.

Devon hesitated slightly, wondering if Professor Schmidt might be a little confused. She had clearly asked for a few moments of his time for a little research assistance and had said nothing at all about continuing studies. And why the big wink?

Taking Devon's hand, Schmidt continued speaking, abruptly cutting off any chance for conversation. "I wish that circumstances had been better for me this morning, because I always enjoy tutoring a beautiful young woman, but unfortunately, some very pressing matters have come up that will require my immediate attention. You understand, I'm sure. This matter may take several days to resolve."

Devon was momentarily shocked by the professor's sudden change in plans, and at a loss for words. "But, Professor," she began questioningly, "my friend, Mr. Halloran, has come out all the way from New York to help me search out some answers to a very strange situation I find myself in. I was sure that you could help." She was obviously upset, and John took her hand and squeezed it gently.

"I would like nothing better than to assist you, Miss Grant, but unfortunately, circumstances have changed for me. I may be able to give you some guidance, however. I have made up a list of study materials for you, and a guide for their use. If you follow my directions, I am sure you will find everything that you need to know."

Dr. Schmidt took Devon's elbow and gently but firmly turned with her toward the door. "Please excuse me; I hate to be rude, but I have many things in progress that demand my immediate attention. I hope very much to see you later." This last comment was spoken very smoothly but was strongly accented by another big wink and a rise of his bushy white eyebrows.

The professor escorted Devon and John out the door and into the hallway, saying, "I'm sure you can find your way out, and be sure to go over those notes thoroughly."

Professor Schmidt's office door closed behind them with a quiet thump, and Devon and John found themselves standing out in the hallway in a state of disbelief. Devon looked down at the sheaf of papers Dr. Schmidt had forced into her hands. Idly, she began to shuffle through them. On top were a few copies of meaningless astronomy notes, but all of the papers in the remainder of the pile were blank, with the exception of one in the middle. It was boldly handwritten and said simply RATS, 10P.

"What in the hell is that supposed to mean?" John asked.

"I don't have a clue, but I think that we'd better go back to the car to think about it," Devon answered with a still-puzzled expression.

Back at the car, Devon said, "That was certainly an unusual interview. I can't understand it, John. He was so nice and accommodating on the phone this morning; I really thought he would help us. Then when we go to see him, we get ushered out like a couple of door-to-door vacuum salesmen."

"Obviously, something happened in the meantime to change his plans. Did you notice his eyes when we were talking?"

"Yes, I did. He winked at me twice." Devon blushed slightly, and John smiled at that.

"When he was shaking my hand," John continued, "he kept shifting his eyes across the office toward a doorway, but when I followed his eyes over in that direction, he squeezed my hand hard and nodded slightly. I noticed the door was slightly ajar, and I had a weird feeling he was trying to signal me there was someone listening in the adjoining office."

"Who could have been in there?"

"Probably someone connected with our recently acquired friends. We're such damned amateurs at this stuff. Neither of us even thought about your home phone being tapped. They must have intercepted your call to Professor Schmidt this morning and simply gotten to him first. We're going to have to get a lot smarter in the future."

"That does account for his sudden change in plans, but what about the note?"

"Let's look at that note again, Dev. Maybe it's a code of some sort."

Devon took out the sheaf of papers to read the handwritten message, RATS 10P. Her mind ran through it several times before her face completely lit up. "I know what it means, John!" she said excitedly.

"Well, let me in on the secret."

"Ratskeller, ten o'clock tonight," came the simple answer. "The Ratskeller Brauhaus is a popular student and faculty hangout over on Pearl Street. They have good food and wonderful beer, and it would be a perfect place to blend in with a crowd for a clandestine meeting." Devon was very proud of her discovery, and beaming with the gratification of it.

"We'll go there tonight to see if you're right, then maybe your little old professor can help us fill in the blanks. In the meantime, we could take a look around this complex and see if the Herr Professor Dr. Schmidt really has company or not."

Devon thought it was a great idea and immediately started the Prius in motion.

\* \* \*

"Very well done, Dr. Schmidt, very well indeed," said Roger Markson as he reentered the professor's office from the anteroom. "But I am just a little curious about one thing."

"And what might that be?"

"Where did the study notes that you gave to Miss Grant come from? I know you didn't have time to prepare any before they arrived."

"I am not like most government employees, Mr. Markson," Professor Schmidt answered with completely unmasked sarcasm. "I started the notes immediately after her call this morning and completed them before you and your friend arrived. I always have prepared lists of reference reading on file for my students to help guide them along the rocky road to scientific literacy."

"Okay, okay, Professor. That sounds feasible," Markson agreed, with his thin lips only. His eyes and his body language said that he was only taking the professor's answer under advisement and would decide its merit in his own good time. "Now if you'll just sit down a moment, we can set a few things straight and I'll be gone."

"Sit," repeated Sal Grizetti right on cue, grasping Dr. Schmidt by the shoulders and pushing him back down into his chair much more roughly than necessary. He held the professor there by digging his blunt and powerful fingers in between the professor's neck and clavicle bone. Grizetti was dumbly pleased by the slight grimace of pain on Dr. Schmidt's face, but it passed quickly.

Dr. Schmidt looked up into Roger Markson's bland blue eyes. He thought that Markson and Grizetti were the perfect team for a low-budget television police show. Bad and good, neat and scruffy, cruel and kind…perfect opposites…epitome of good cop, bad cop. Roger Markson was fair-haired and blue-eyed, with an annoying neat-as-a-pin appearance, while Sal Grizetti was a perfect take off Peter Faulk's Lieutenant Colombo character: wrinkled and slovenly with a scruffy growth of five o'clock shadow, complete with bad breath and an unhealthy desire to do bodily harm. Quite a lineup.

Markson pulled a chair up directly front and center to the desk and sat down, bringing himself directly into the professor's line of sight. He jutted his chin forward in a vaguely threatening manner and repeated the liturgy exactly as he had stated it upon arrival at the office. "It would be greatly appreciated by my superiors in Washington, Professor Schmidt, if you would discontinue any association with Miss Grant and Mr. Halloran immediately and for the foreseeable future. Do you understand what I am saying?"

The corners of Professor Schmidt's mouth turned up slightly at the temptation to look behind him to see if Grizetti had that message written on a cue card. He made no answer but winced in pain again as, right on cue, Sal Grizetti put a strong squeeze on his collarbone. He stubbornly refused to break eye contact with Markson, however, and clamped his jaw tight. His knuckles turned white as he held on to the arms of his desk chair, fighting for control as the pressure on his clavicle increased. With a surprising act of will, Professor Schmidt held eye contact until Grizetti had to let off.

"Very good, Doctor. Now, we all know you are a stubborn and persistent old man, but please remember what I've told you and act accordingly." Markson rose and moved to leave the office, with Grizetti trailing behind him like a scruffy dog. "Do we have an understanding, Doctor Schmidt?"

"You have my permission to leave my office immediately," Dr. Schmidt said through clenched teeth.

"Very well, but please don't give me any excuse to bring my friend Mr. Grizetti back here, Doctor, or the results will not be as pleasant as today's."

"Good day!" Dr. Schmidt growled, his face deeply flushed with anger even though he was secretly pleased with himself for getting in the last word.

\* \* \*

John and Devon cruised slowly through the Kitteridge Complex, carefully looking over all of the parked cars. The last vestiges of winter were still apparent in the piles of snow, and a few assorted snow sculptures outside the dormitory halls. John and Devon found what they were looking for parked at the back of the complex near the tennis courts a plain, tan-colored Ford sedan with US government license plates. They hadn't even bothered to use a rental car.

"Pretty cute, wasn't it, parking way back here, away from the planetarium building?" Devon observed.

"Yes, they're cute, alright. Let's park your car someplace inconspicuous and walk back here so we can keep an eye on it," John suggested.

"Good idea," Devon said, "but you stay here. I'll park the car and be right back."

"Okay."

John got out of the Prius and moved casually over to the bleachers beside the Kitteridge tennis courts. Several students dressed in sweats were getting a little pre-season practice in, and John watched idly. He found a seat in a spot not easily visible from where the tan sedan was parked, but it afforded a good view of the approaches to the car. Devon was back in just a few minutes. "Anything yet?" she asked, a little breathless. "I parked over behind Arnette Hall and ran all the way back."

"No, nothing yet," John answered, not taking his eyes off the tan sedan.

It was only a few moments later that two men walked past the Fleming Law building and across the street to visitor parking. They moved with complete confidence and made no effort to disguise their presence or their purpose. One was rather tall and blonde, with Nordic features and a very determined look. The other was short, dark, and stocky, with a look of unbridled violence that made Devon shiver. "We have seen the enemy, and he is us," John said absently.

"What is that supposed to mean?" Devon asked.

"Just a quote from the very old Pogo Possum comic strip," John answered. "It used to be one of my dad's favorites. For us, it simply means we've seen their faces and know who to look for. That's much better than jumping at shadows and suspecting everyone."

"They both give me the creeps." Devon shuddered again. John slipped his arm around her shoulder, thinking she was chilly, and she snuggled in close to him, finding comfort and warmth.

"You're right especially about the short, squatty guy. He looks downright pug-ugly."

"He's ugly, alright," Devon answered with a slight shiver, "they both really scare me."

\* \* \*

Lt. Colonel Mark Persons listened to the phone ringing on the other end and waited for a response.

"Hello?" came a sleepy feminine response.

"Connie?"

"Yes, Mark. Who did you expect?"

"Of course I expected you, but you sound sleepy, and that's not like you at this hour," Mark answered, wrinkling his brow with curiosity.

"I've been working late and just thought I'd catch a nap. The boys are out."

Mark thought he heard some rustling noises in the background. "I need to talk with you."

"Go ahead."

Mark Persons was perplexed and more than a little concerned with the way the conversation with his wife was going. Connie Persons was not the dutiful Air Force wife who followed her husband's career wherever it went. She hated the frequent changes of station and made no attempt to hide it. Bracing himself, Mark continued. "I'd like it if you would bring the boys up to Boulder for a few days to visit," he posed.

"I thought it would be something like that."

"Well, why not?" he asked. "You are my wife, after all, and they are our sons, and I'd like to see all of you," Mark said a little more vigorously than he had intended.

"That's all true, but we remain here in Houston while you go off playing airborne Boy Scout. Then you have the nerve to expect us to change all our plans at an instant's notice and fly up there to you? It just won't work, Mark."

"Connie, there are things happening that I can't talk about. They make it imperative that you and the boys get out of Houston and come here."

"I'm sorry, Mark, but the boys are in the middle of spring semester, and I've got responsibilities at my school that I can't avoid. It may be fine for you to jump up and go any time the good old Air Force has a whim to send you off, but that doesn't work for us civilians." There was a note of finality in her voice that Mark knew all too well.

"Listen, Connie, if you truly can't get away, then at least send the boys up for a few days." He hated the pleading tone in his voice.

"I'll talk to their teachers and get back to you."

"Connie, what's going on there?" There was an undercurrent in her voice that Mark neither understood nor liked. He realized there had been a lot of anger in his leaving for temporary duty in Boulder, and that, he could understand, as it had happened before, but there was a detachment in her voice tonight that was both strange and disquieting. "If there's a problem, let's talk about it."

"Nothing to talk about right now, Mark. I'll call you after I talk to the boys' teachers."

"Screw the teachers; they're my boys, and I want to see them!" Mark was angrier than he could ever remember being. "Get them on the first available airplane from Houston, and if you're smart, you'll be on it with them." He slammed the phone down in the cradle so hard that the whole desk jolted.

That damned woman was bright and beautiful, but she could be the most frustrating pain in the ass in the world, he thought as he turned from the desk to attend to much more pressing concerns.

* * *

President Coleridge paced back and forth across the presidential seal emblazoned on the carpet in front of his desk in the Oval Office. He was a troubled man, and the stress was beginning to show. "I had a call from Mrs. Elizabeth Coulter just an hour ago. She sent notification to all nuclear plant operators of boiling-water–type reactors to begin a controlled shutdown immediately and to have the units on cold standby at the earliest possible time. The balloon has gone up," he said.

Amos Bellinger rubbed his stubbly chin tiredly and made a huge effort to get his sleep-deprived mind back into working order. "Who the hell would have thought Liz would issue the order on a freaking Sunday, of all days?" he mumbled half to himself.

"She got word of the Siberian strike from a colleague who is at the site," the president grumbled.

"How could that happen?" Amos asked.

"Someone there had a secure satellite uplink and was not afraid to use it without permission. He got Liz the message that the strike was of considerable size and that it caused a jam in the reactor moderator controls. The operators acted quickly and correctly and performed an emergency shutdown, but it upset a lot of the nuclear people at the site."

"So she orders our plants off without checking first."

"It's within her authority to do so, and she did it, but that's not the only thing. She's been busy on the phone with her counterparts around the world and has stirred up a hornet's nest."

"Some people around the world will agree with her," Amos said, his mind reeling at the ramifications.

"The members of the European community are all violently opposed to such an action. They're heavily dependent on nuclear energy, and most of them have no way to replace it. There's going to be hell to pay when the press gets wind of this. I'll handle my end and do what I can to soothe our troubled allies. Damage control on this side of the pond is up to you, Amos."

"There is one other thing to consider, Mr. President," Amos said. "The meteorite struck within ten miles of a Russian nuclear reactor of the graphite-moderator type."

"The same as Chernobyl?"

"Yes, but much smaller. The plant supplied electricity to a soviet nuclear-weapons research and production facility that has been shut down for over a year."

"Yes, Amos, what is your point?"

"Perhaps Liz Coulter is correct in her actions and the rest of the world had better follow suit before we have a dozen Chernobyls spewing forth radioactivity all over Europe or Asia."

"Not an option, Amos. France is positively opposed to any such action on our part, and the Germans and Brits are on the fence. The Japanese are completely torn over it. Fukushima was an event they will never forget, on one hand. On the other hand, they have 130 million people jammed into a space smaller than California, and they just don't have enough generating capacity without the nuclear. If they shut the nuclear down, they will have to shut down more than thirty percent of their country, and that is going to lead to other problems. To be honest, I don't know what I would do if I was in their shoes. Everything we do depends on electricity, dammit, which puts everyone over there squarely in a no-win position. We can shut our plants down and survive with some minor problems simply because after the Three Mile Island incident, our utilities have limited their nuclear capacity. I know that our allies are not in the same position. They can't shut down without eliminating vital services and shutting off consumers for large parts of the day. You cannot deny people their comforts without a damned good explanation. Just what would you suggest we tell them?"

*The president has been doing his homework*, Amos thought, *and all of his points are valid. This one is a real Chinese puzzle.* "I don't know, sir."

"Well, I do," Jameson Coleridge said with more authority and confidence than he knew he had. "I'm going to tell them we are shutting down our reactors as a safety precaution and that they had better seriously consider doing the same. Then I'm going to tell the American people what I am doing and why I am doing it. Whatever happens after that, we will just have to deal with it."

"Mr. President, are you sure you've thought this through completely?" Amos asked, his nerves jumping through his skin.

"Surer than I have ever been of anything."

"Yes, Mr. President."

\* \* \*

Devon and John waited for a half hour on the bleachers, just talking quietly, huddled together against the March chill. They watched as they waited to be sure the two men they had seen drive off in the tan sedan were the only two around.

"Do you really have to go back to New York tomorrow afternoon?" Devon asked a little sadly.

"I'm afraid so," John answered. "I have to be back at work Tuesday morning, and I have some personal business to settle. We can still talk on the phone, and I'll get back here as soon as I can. I've got a few days' vacation time starting next Thursday. If I leave after my shift on Wednesday, we can have a real mini-vacation."

Devon remembered her mother's warning against long-distance relationships but couldn't help believing her relationship with John was rapidly developing into one. "What if my friend from the FBI comes back for a visit?" she asked.

"I'll put some security locks on your apartment door before I leave, and I'll call you every night to remind you to use them." John gave her a nice hug, and she relaxed a little, still not liking the situation.

"Great, but I still wish you could stay longer."

"Next time."

They strolled hand in hand around the Kitteridge Complex, then paused, seeming to admire the buffalo statue in front of the events center while they really checked out the parking along Regent Drive, all the way down to the planetarium. Only when they were sure that all was clear did they drift over to the Prius and drive off, looking for a place for lunch.

"After lunch," John said, "will you drop me off someplace crowded where I can walk to a car-rental agency?"

"Why? Don't you like my little hybrid?" Devon asked.

"It's fine, but it's also well known by our mutual friends."

"True," she conceded.

"I think it's time to go under the radar, into stealth mode."

Four hours later, John parked a wonderfully battered old Ford Taurus station wagon two blocks from Devon's apartment. Then he walked a slow roundabout route back to the Elk Ridge Apartments, always watchful to be certain he wasn't being followed. He entered Devon's building through a little-used side door that she had told him about and had left propped open with a match book upon her return. Fortunately, this door was on the opposite side of the apartments from the Boulder Senior Center and the surveillance team did not notice.

John had to ring the doorbell five times before Devon opened up to let him in. She was fresh out of the shower, wearing a terry-cloth robe with her hair wet and curly. She impulsively treated him to a big, soapy hug and then said, "Where have you been all this time?"

John thoroughly enjoyed her fresh, clean smell and imagining her nakedness beneath the robe. He held on to the embrace for a moment longer.

Devon realized the intimacy of their situation and briefly leaned back in his arms and looked searchingly into his eyes. She held them fixed for a moment, then relaxed and let him hold her, resting her head against his shoulder.

Speaking into her freshly shampooed curls, John said, "I did a little shopping and then took my time getting a car from good old Budget Rent-a-car. Then I rode around just to get the lay of the land."

"So tell me next time when you're going to be away long; I was worried. And what's in the bag, by the way?"

"Yes, dear," John answered with a put-on expression of remorse, which won him a playful slap on the shoulder and then a smile that made it all right. "I picked up two dead bolts for the door, and a chain to back them up."

"Do I really need all that hardware?" Devon asked, moving away from him to close the door. "I already have a lock and a dead bolt."

"I know, but they both have key locks, and locks can be picked. These are manual bolts, and when you close them from inside, they stay closed."

"Alright, if you think that's best," Devon said, feeling more secure already.

"Oh, and I almost forgot this," John said, handing her a perfect red rosebud just on the verge of opening.

"Thank you, John," Devon said, her eyes misting slightly and a warm feeling spreading through her body. "That was so nice." She cocked her head slightly to the side and said, "We don't have to be at the Ratskeller until ten tonight."

"I know."

"I can think of a few things we could do to pass some time."

"Yes?"

"Lock the door, John."

"No problem."

He did, and she stepped into his arms again, this time with a kiss and an embrace that set his senses reeling.

Devon stepped back and began unbuttoning John's shirt as she gently pulled him slowly toward the bedroom. Backing up through the doorway, she said, "You can put up the hardware later, can't you?"

"Absolutely."

\* \* \*

"Ooh, what I wouldn't give to be in his shoes right now," sighed Sal Grizetti, staring intently into the spotting scope. "That is one tender piece of ass, and she's dragging that lucky bastard into the bedroom."

Frank Muller had to bite his lip to keep from biting Sal's head off. The two new agents were an unknown quantity to Frank, and he wanted to be careful to get to know them before pulling rank too hard. New or not, they were unpleasant and irritating and would bear watching. They were a mean pair. "Just stick to the job and can the commentary," he grumbled.

"Got a soft spot for the mark?" Grizetti asked, not really caring, "Or a hard one, maybe."

"That's enough," Frank snapped in a tone that left no room for negotiation.

"Fuck off," Sal said under his breath, but he held on to his tongue and continued to watch the couple until Devon closed the bedroom door, cutting off his view. Things were getting pretty warm over there, Sal thought. Maybe tonight they would get more interesting.

Frank Muller was just glad that Halloran was back. It had upset him when the couple had separated and he and his team had lost track of John for more than two hours. Kim Yamaguci and Chris Demarco had been playing a lazy game of tennis at the Kitteridge Complex and watching John and Devon. The two girls had stayed with them until the couple had gone into the crowds at the Boulder Mall. Kim and Chris were professionals and had picked up Devon again fairly quickly, but Halloran had eluded them, much to their chagrin.

*At least he's back, and all the chickens are back in the nest*, Frank thought, then returned his mind to the two loose cannons he now had on his team and how to handle them. At Frank's request, Angela Freece had been allowed to stay on in Boulder to assist Frank, but he hadn't yet introduced her to the rest of them. *I think I'll use her for a little game of watch the watcher,* Frank thought, *until I can get a better handle on Markson and Grizetti.* Satisfied with this decision, he allowed himself a little doze. Watching Grant and Halloran all day, and Markson and Grizetti all night, was wearing him thin.

\* \* \*

The Ratskeller Brauhaus was nestled quietly in the half basement of an old house on 16th Street off Pearl at the eastern end of the Boulder Mall. If you didn't know it was there, you could almost walk right by and never notice it. Called simply the Rats by students and faculty alike, it was well known and needed no large sign or advertising. It simply had the best food and the coldest beer in town, and all at reasonable prices, a sure key to success in a college town.

John and Devon left all the lights off in the apartment and slipped quietly out. They exited through the side door John had used earlier and walked briskly to the old Taurus. They parked at the west end of the mall and strolled through it, using store windows as mirrors to check their back trail for followers. There were none. When they were sure it was clear, they walked quickly two blocks east, directly to the Rats.

Entering the pub, John and Devon were greeted by a rush of warm air carrying with it the sounds and smells of good food and good company. They stepped inside quickly and then paused a moment at the entrance, waiting for their eyes to adjust to the darkness before surveying the room for a familiar face. All the way in the back of the room, Devon spotted the suntanned dome with its fringe of white hair that indicated Dr. Schmidt's presence. Devon hesitated for a minute when she noticed that there was someone with him, then realized it was Colonel Mark Persons in civilian clothes. This was not unusual, since most of the Air Force people at SWPC dressed in civvies most of the time.

She took John's hand and led him easily through the happy crowd to the back. "Good evening, Dr. Schmidt. We got your message," Devon said, smiling and obviously quite proud of having deciphered his code.

Dr. Karl Schmidt stood up and took Devon in his arms in a great hug. "I'm so glad you understood my little message and came tonight," he said. "I believe you're already acquainted with Colonel Persons."

"Yes, we've met before," Devon said. "Hi, Colonel. I'd like you to meet my friend John Halloran from New York."

Mark Persons took John's hand and shook it well. *No dead-fish handshake there*, thought John. *I like that.*

"Call me Mark," the colonel said, "and please join us." He slid over in the booth to make room for John to sit by him, and Devon slid in next to Dr. Schmidt.

The good doctor signaled the waitress to bring two more beers. Without preamble, Professor Schmidt assumed command of the conversation and got right down to business. "I do not think that it's a good idea for us to be together for too long a time, so I'll get right down to the subject. Devon, you and John have apparently been probing around the periphery of a situation that Washington does not want you or anyone else in the country to know about. The FBI is not sure exactly what you do know, and this makes them paranoid, and they don't like it at all.

"For that reason," he continued, "I was visited today by two very unpleasant gentlemen, supposedly from the FBI but acting more like a couple of goomba's from the Mafia. They made it quite clear that it would be unhealthy for me to talk to you, and that is what necessitated the little play in my office. Mark and I have discussed the situation and have decided that if you will assure us that you will keep the confidence, we will fill in the gaps in your investigation. Can you do this?" He studied Devon and John with his blue eyes, which turned hard and cautious. After a brief glance at Mark Persons, he continued.

"Obviously, you're both well aware of the large comet that is currently making a passage through our solar system. Some call it the Mountain because of its shape, and others call it the Extinctor because of what it could have done if it impacted the earth. Had it done so, we most likely would be as extinct as the dinosaurs. The huge comet is the remains of an ancient long-period comet that has lost its icy mantle through many passages through the inner planets and around the sun over more than a billion years. In this process, millions of 'small' pieces have fallen behind it, forming what is known as the cometary tail. The Mountain has passed by the earth at an uncomfortably close margin, and we are encountering the tail, as witnessed by the increased meteoric activity."

Dr. Schmidt cleared his throat, then took a long sip on his beer mug and continued. "The concern is, the tail is passing close enough that our gravity will pull them in to us, leaving the possibility of untold numbers of impacts of varying size. It is this possibility that Washington is concerned about, and why they are concerned about who else knows, including you two and who you might tell."

Professor Schmidt was surprised at the looks of shock on Devon and John's faces. He took another sip of his beer and said, "Colonel, would you continue?"

Mark looked at the John and Devon and picked up the narrative. "I can see the surprise and sadness in your eyes, so I know you can imagine the reaction of the millions of people here and around the world: first surprise, then disbelief, then fright and fear of the consequences, then anger and panic when the truth sinks in and they find out they were the last to know. The president is well aware of the panic and anger and manic violence he can cause by premature release of the situation. He is busily doing all that needs to be done to help prevent the civil uproar that will follow his announcement; therefore, you must keep your newfound knowledge to yourself and wait for him to do so. He is in an awful position.

"Damages cannot be estimated, but I believe he and his team are more concerned with collateral damage from civil panic and unrest than from the actual meteorite strikes themselves. I am sure that the governments of all countries feel much the same way.

"Please accept the fact that you cannot do anything about this situation; nor can you force the government to take what it considers precipitous action. The only thing we can do is to make arrangements to protect ourselves and our loved ones. If you have any family living along either coastline, I would strongly advise they relocate to higher ground. I would also strongly advise anyone living in or near a large metropolitan area to find a more isolated place to wait out the bombardment," Mark finished.

Dr. Schmidt could see Devon's eyes beginning to well up, and he wanted to comfort her. "This is the second part of why I have asked you here tonight…to offer you an alternative place to be when things here begin to get difficult. Many years ago, I purchased a vacation home up in the mountains beyond Gold Hill. It is a big, comfortable old building in a place with the ignominious name of Jackass Valley. I know that you will ask, so I will tell you. The story goes that many years ago, a miner became lost in a terrible snowstorm and froze to death in the valley. Locals claim that on a clear winter night, you can still hear his jackass braying and looking for him. Anyway, if things get difficult here in Boulder, you are more than welcome to come up and stay with me."

"I don't understand what you mean by difficult," John said. "It seems that if you don't get hit, you're okay."

"You are only partially correct, John. A small percentage of the total casualties will be people killed or injured by the direct effects of meteor strikes. Most of the damage and loss of life will be caused by ancillary events and the terrible social problems that will inevitably follow.

"Since country people are usually prepared for loss of power and the vagaries of weather, they will suffer much less than people in the metropolitan areas. In the short term, a lack of electricity, water, and transportation of food and fuel will cause chaos in cities.

"Highways, bridges, and tunnels will be blocked by masses of people seeking refuge in the countryside. Communications will fail, and people accustomed to turning on the TV, radio, or internet for instructions will now feel lost and betrayed. Fires may burn unabated for days due to the blocked roadways and lack of manpower, water, or equipment to fight them. People will begin to leave the cities on foot, eventually causing problems in the suburbs and countryside.

"Later on, the lack of sanitation and garbage collection, and degradation of the general health due to starvation and exposure will allow diseases to take hold. An explosion in the rat population will facilitate their spread. Implicit in all this are the deaths inflicted on mankind by mankind due to a steadily increasing competition for diminishing resources.

"In the longest term, there may be changed weather patterns. Nuclear winter is a catchphrase for an array of major atmospheric upheavals causing drastically altered weather and climate—the coming ice age, if you will. For all of this, we need to be prepared to act in concert with others for self-preservation."

Quietly, John said, "That is not a pretty picture, Professor."

"Definitely not a pretty sight, John, but a distinct possibility, nonetheless."

Devon was just sitting there silently, with tears streaming down her face. John took her hand and squeezed it and was gifted with a barely noticeable smile, but the tears continued unchanged.

\* \* \*

Reverend Randy stood outside the door of WVM-TV and took several deep breaths in an attempt to calm his trembling nerves. Never in his life had he even contemplated doing anything at all similar to what he had planned for tonight.

Randall P. Davis raised his face to the heavens and spoke of his fears to his final authority. "Please, God, give me the strength to carry out your wishes as you have made me see them. Guide my hand to Thy bidding and strengthen me so that Thy people may be saved."

For the second time, he scanned the parking lot to assure himself there was nothing out of the ordinary there tonight. *Yes,* he thought, *only a few at work tonight, so that will make things easier.* Then, squaring his shoulders, he inserted his magnetic pass card into the security reader and opened the door as the lock clicked open.

Allan Marshall was in the control booth as usual when Randy came into the studio. Reverend Davis smiled and nodded a greeting to Al as he crossed to the control booth door. "Evening, Al. Everything quiet tonight?" he asked.

"Just like church, Reverend."

"That's good, because I need to talk to you for a moment."

"Talk away, Reverend, but don't be too long about it, because this show only runs another ten minutes, then you go on. When it got to be so late, I began wondering if you were going to show up with your show at all. I got out a backup flash drive of one of your old shows just to cover."

"That's excellent, Al. In fact, it's just what I need to talk to you about. Are there any strange people in the station tonight?" he asked.

"Yes. How did you know?" Allan Marshall questioned. "There are two guys here from the FCC checking local program contents for our license renewal application. Routine stuff, but a little strange to be doing it on a Sunday at midnight."

"That's what I thought. Al, I need a favor of you tonight."

"Sure, Reverend, anything you like."

"This may cause you some trouble, Al, so please think about it."

"Don't have to. If you want something, just ask."

"All right, here it is. When you broadcast my show tonight, can you send something different to the monitors that the men from the FCC are watching?"

Allan noticed that Reverend Randy looked a little pale and nervous tonight. He began to regret telling Randy that he would do him any favors without knowing what they might be, but it was too late for that. Besides, Reverend Randy was a good and honest man and would never knowingly do anything wrong.

Reverend Randy had two flash drives in his hands. He held up the left-hand flash drive and said, "This is the one I want you to play for the FCC men." Then the right hand came up. "This is the one to be broadcast normally. Got it?"

"Just take me a minute to set it up, Reverend. Do you want to stay and view the show?"

"Yes I do, Al. I'll sit in the studio, if you don't mind."

"You can watch that monitor right there."

"Thanks for your help."

Reverend Randall Davis went into the darkened studio and sat down quietly at the monitor. Commercials were running now, just before his show was to go on. He looked over at Allan Marshall and got a thumbs-up sign, indicating that everything was going according to plan. He sat back with his heart pounding and closed his eyes, took out his father's tattered old Bible and held it tightly in his hands, and began to pray. "Lord, I pray that what I've done tonight is truly Your will and that I have not misread your desires. Please see me through the difficult days ahead and protect my family from the retribution that surely is about to come. I love You, Lord, and I always have, and I only seek to be Your obedient servant."

"Good evening, ladies and gentlemen. This is Reverend Randall P. Davis, coming to you with a heavy heart from beautiful downtown Wheeling, West Virginia. Tonight, my friends, I have been forced to use subterfuge and deception in order to circumvent the direct orders of the Federal Bureau of Investigation to bring my message to you. Please listen carefully to what I have to say, as this will be my last broadcast."

Randall Davis refused to look into the control booth, where he was certain Allan Marshall would be staring at him in disbelief. His only regret for the evening was the necessity of involving Al in his plan and quite possibly getting him in trouble with the federal law.

"Last Sunday, I spoke to you of the hand of the Lord that guided me through the Bible to the Revelation of Saint John the Divine and bade me to give you warning to put your houses in order in preparation for terrible things to come. While preparing for tonight's broadcast, I was given to know that the seven angels are assembled and that the end time is come upon us." On the show, the Reverend began to read from his Bible.

"Seven angels of the Lord God will we see, and their trumpets will sound, and they will be terrible.

"The first angel shall come, and there will be hail and fire from the sky, and the trees and green things will be burned up. And a third part of the Earth shall perish in blood.

"The second angel shall come, and there will be a burning mountain, and fire will be cast upon the seas. Great volcanos will erupt and turn the seas to blood and blacken the skies with their smoke. And a third part of the creatures of the seas and the ships that sail thereon shall perish.

"The third angel shall come, and there will be a great star falling from the heaven, burning as if it were a lamp upon the mountains and rivers. And the rivers and fountains shall become poison as bitter as wormwood and thousands shall perish thereof."

Reverend Randy's heart was pounding in his chest, and he could feel it like thunder throughout his body. *Please let the show continue until the message is out*, he prayed silently.

"And the fourth angel shall come and a third part of the sun shall be smitten and a third part of the moon and stars shall disappear. And the sun shall leave the heavens and the stars shall leave the skies, and the days shall be as night. And an angel shall move through the skies crying woe, woe to mankind for the voices of the angels yet to come.

"The fifth angel shall come and a star shall fall from heaven unto the earth, and from this shall open the bottomless pit. And from this pit shall rise smoke that will darken the skies yet three days more.

"And the sixth angel shall come and release the four horsemen of apocalypse bringing forth fire, flood, famine, and pestilence upon all of mankind. And by these shall a third of the men be killed."

*Almost done,* Reverend Randy thought as he watched the broadcast. *Just a few moments more, and the people will know what manner of wrath is surely upon them.*

"And last shall come the seventh angel, bearing a small book in his hand, and in this book shall be named all those who have taken Jesus Christ as their Savior, and have followed his commandments...and they shall be saved. Hallelujah, Hallelujah.

"My loyal friends"

The broadcast was cut off at that point, and the monitor went blank. Although he could not bring himself to look, Reverend Randy knew that Al Marshall was fumbling quickly with his controls. Suddenly, a message appeared on the screen, stating that technical difficulties were being encountered and that viewers should please stand by for the regular broadcast programming.

Reverend Randy looked finally into the control booth and saw one man gesturing angrily at Al Marshall and another wearing a furious expression on his face, holding an iPad in one hand and a gun in the other. The men were now coming for him.

Reverend Randy never returned to WVM-TV.

## Monday, March 8

John Halloran awoke to one of the most beautiful sights he had ever seen. Devon was standing at the bedroom window. The pale blue glow of the Mercury vapor lights in the parking lot was shining through her sheer nightgown. She was half turned away from him, and the light accentuated the swell of her breast and the fine curve of her hip. He was totally captivated and waited silently for a few moments, simply enjoying her unconscious beauty, before speaking.

"Come back to bed, Dev. You'll get cold out there."

"Oh, I thought you were sound asleep."

"I was, but something woke me up. I must have missed you in bed with me."

Devon rewarded his gallantry with a smile and returned to bed. As she slid over close and wrapped herself around him, she said quietly, "I know we really haven't known each other for very long, but I don't want you to leave me, John."

"Dev, you know I have to go back east for a while. My job and my life is back there, so I have no choice. You just have to believe that I don't have to know you for a long time to love you, and know that we're right together. After this trip, I promise I'll never leave you again."

Warm tears were flowing from Devon's eyes again, and he bent to kiss them away. "Don't cry, Dev. I'll be back so soon, you'll never realize I was gone. When this mess is finally over, we can talk more about the future together."

She smiled at that little lie and cuddled even closer. She kissed him resoundingly and said, "Enough of the sad talk, let's make the best use of the time we have left."

They did.

A little while later, they decided to get something to eat. "Are your folks still living on the Jersey Shore?" John asked.

"My folks have been divorced for years. My dad travels a lot on his job and I rarely ever see him. But then, I rarely saw him before the divorce, either, and when he was home, he was either drunk or fighting with my mother. If I think back, I do remember some good times, but they were few and far between. When I was little, my dad would sometimes take me on the ferry over to Lewes, Delaware, and then down to Rehoboth Beach or Ocean City, Maryland. We would spend the day swimming or walking the boardwalk and stuff ourselves with carnival food. They were some of the good days. One year, he took me to Dover Air Force Base for an air show. That was wonderful, and I'll never forget it. Mom always seemed to have other things to do on those days, and that made me sad. The fights were terrible.

"My mother is remarried to a very wealthy man, and I see them even less than my father. It was a really ugly divorce. Dad drank too much, and Mom ran around. They aired all the dirty laundry in public during the proceedings, and I was just old enough to be humiliated by it all.

"They fought like cats and dogs over me in court, and my mother, naturally, won. I've often wondered since then just why she fought so hard for me, because almost immediately after the divorce was final, she married Paulie, the greaseball, shipped me off to a boarding school, and disappeared from my life. I sometimes think having a teenage daughter made her feel or seem older than she wanted to be, so I went from school to school, and rarely was there a holiday I could come home. When I got older and was in college, I would see them on some holidays, but Paulie began to get overly handy, and Mom and I agreed it would stop. Paulie has more money than breeding, and they travel all the time. Right at this moment, I really wouldn't know where to call either one of them."

"My God, Dev, that's a horribly sad story."

"That's life, I guess," she said, but her cavalier words were belied by the look of deep sadness in her blue eyes. This told John how strong a person she really was to turn out as well as she had, coming from where she did.

They were enjoying the time together at the Boulder Café on Pearl Street, before going back to the airport for John's flight home. It was the first time either one of them had shared anything significant of their family or private life.

"I don't have any real strings, either," John said. "My parents were killed five years ago in a car accident on I-95 near Lumberton, North Carolina. They were on their way to Florida just after my dad retired. A damned drunk driver fell asleep at the wheel and barreled straight across the median and hit them head-on. The Carolina State Police said that they never saw him coming. He had forgotten to put his lights on, and it was just at sunset. They were both killed instantly, and the damned drunk just walked away without a scratch." It was John's turn to wear a look of deep sadness and loss.

"Let's change the subject; this is a sad enough day as it is," Devon said, soft tears puddling in her eyes. "What will we do if this whole crazy scene is just a big bust and nothing happens?" Devon asked.

"Then I'll thank the powers to be for sparing us, and bring you back to New York to see my nice little house in the hills."

"I'd like that, John. Tell me about it."

"It's just a small place that was originally built as a grandma house on a large family farm. I guess that over the years, the family farm could not compete with the big corporate farms that were forming, and the place ran down quite a bit. After the main house burned years ago, the land was broken up and sold off in parcels. My little house sat empty for several years until my parents were killed. I used some of the estate money to buy it. Sally, she's the girl from the diner, put me up to it, and I have loved it ever since."

"I think I'm going to like her."

"You will." John smiled.

"Where did you grow up, John?"

"In a little town in the Adirondacks called Star Lake, which is not too far from Lake Placid. My dad was the resident operator at a small hydroelectric plant. He worked for the old Niagara Mohawk Power Company, and they owned the plant and the house. Dad maintained the place, and the system operator would call with the schedule for the units to come on and off the line, and Dad would relay the water elevations.

"Dad taught Mom and I both to roll the units and phase them on the line so that if the system operator called for an emergency startup when he wasn't home, then we could do it. The system operators used to joke that they always knew when Mom put a unit on the line because she did it so smoothly.

"It was a great place for a boy to grow up. There were ponds and rivers to fish and swim in, and you could hunt and trap or just play wild Indians in the woods. I built huts and tree houses wherever I wanted. I learned to hunt deer and trap fox and raccoon in those woods. It got lonely sometimes, but it was worth it.

"After the company automated all the generators and eliminated resident operators, Mom and Dad moved into town and rented a house. Mom just loved it; it was then I realized how lonely it must have been for her living out at the plant. Dad worked as a traveling operator, going from station to station as needed, but I don't think he ever liked it as much as he did living at the plant."

"It sounds like a wonderful life. I can see you loved it, too, just by the look on your face when you talk about it."

"You're right, Dev, but we had better think about going."

The joy left her face as she said, "You're right; let's get it over with."

They took the fifty-minute trip from Boulder to Denver without talking a great deal.

Devon pulled directly up to the American Airlines curbside check-in. "I'm not going to stay and see you leave," she said. "I don't think I could stand it."

"I understand, Dev. It's alright."

John set down his travel case and took Devon in his arms in a fierce embrace. "I'll miss you, Devon, and I will be back as soon as I can."

"You had better, if you know what's good for you." She gave him a long and passionate kiss, then spun around to ease back into her trusty Prius. Tears were coursing down her cheeks as she mouthed the words "I love you" and pulled away from the curb. And she was gone.

John stood watching until the car was completely out of sight, then turned to enter the terminal.

* * *

For Devon, it was a long and lonely ride home. Her mind was filled with all the new things she had learned about John and with thoughts about how quickly she had come to love him. He had turned out to be all the things she admired and wanted in a man and had never thought she would find.

Her mind was filled with thoughts of John when she parked in the Elk Hills lot and locked up the car. She went directly up to her apartment, never looking back to notice that a tan Ford sedan was idling at the 9th Street entrance with two men sitting and waiting.

\* \* \*

"That's one classy little piece," Sal Grizetti said.

"Don't even think about it. She's way out of your league," Roger Markson said with some vigor.

"And you're not?" Sal bristled as he put the Ford in gear and headed back to the stakeout at the senior center.

\* \* \*

Patsy Cox just loved tooling her classic bright-red Mustang T-top down the old US Route 50 from the sleepy little farming community of Parsonsburg, Maryland, into Salisbury, where she worked. It was just a flat, old two-lane tar road across the sandy soil of Maryland's Eastern Shore, but she knew every bump and curve, and she loved it anyway.

She drove the car too fast, played the radio too loud, and kept her arm out of the window even in the winter. The wind blowing through her short, light brown hair and the countryside whizzing by were sheer heaven.

Patsy drove this road five afternoons a week to her job as the pediatric charge nurse on the three-to-eleven shift at Peninsula General Hospital. She never tired of watching the seasons change over the flat fields of corn or wheat or soybeans, or of the long, low houses full of chickens just waiting for a visit from Frank Perdue and company.

Patsy loved her car, her job, and all the children in her ward. They were her own kids, at least when she was on shift. Everything else in life, she accepted as it came. Life wasn't so bad for a thirty-five-year-old spinster nurse. She and the Peninsula Savings Bank were partners in a nice little home. She had money in the bank, and she had her church, plenty of good friends, and her kids in the ward. What more could she ask for? Usually at this point in her ramblings, Patsy would change the subject. In the back of her mind, she was afraid one day she would finally have to admit to herself that there was something she lacked.

Coming into Salisbury, she raised her spirits a bit by beating out a kid in a red pickup for the left turn arrow onto US Route 13. She downshifted neatly and squealed her wheels in the turn. Only minutes later, she was parked under the light in the center of the staff parking lot of Peninsula General. Patsy liked to have plenty of light when she came out of work near midnight.

"Hi, Andrea," Patsy said cheerily as she put her bags down at the nurses' station. "How'd your day go?"

"Short and slow, just the way I like it," Andrea Kincaid, the day shift charge nurse, answered.

The next half hour was hectic with all the business of the shift change to take care of: admissions, discharges, medications, special orders, staffing problems, parent and doctor problems, and a review of the logged notes that Andrea had made during her eight-hour day shift. When all this was completed to both women's satisfaction, the shift changed and Patsy took over.

Patsy spent the next half hour with her RNs, LPNs and nurses' aids. She listened to their problems without making any unnecessary suggestions or criticisms, and then she nicely but firmly laid out their duties for the night. Feeding time was fast approaching, then it would be medications, then bedtime, the best part of the day.

In the next hour, she visited all her little patients, talked and kidded with them, and, in the course of her gentle and loving attentions, found out all the things about them she needed to know that the charts did not tell.

Toward the middle of her shift, just as things were quieting down, Patsy was deeply engrossed in her paperwork when the outside phone rang, startling her. "Two B, Pediatrics. Patsy Cox speaking."

"Hi, Em," came a deep voice from straight out of the past and into the pit of her stomach.

"Tommy?" she asked, although she knew perfectly well it was him. Nobody else but Tommy Brooks had ever called her that, and most people didn't even know that her middle name was Emily, after her mother.

"Yes, Em, it's me."

"Stop calling me that! And what are you doing calling me at work after all these years?" She was getting more than a little pissed.

"Don't hang up on me, Patsy. I've got so many things going bad in my life that I needed a friendly voice to talk to."

"I'm a person, not a voice."

"Come on, Patsy…you know what I mean."

For the first time in thirty years, Patricia Emily Cox was speechless. She just sat chewing on her lip while in her mind, old memories came tumbling down like a mountain stream in springtime. Tommy Brooks had been her first and only love, but that had been many years ago, when she had been a junior nursing student at Salisbury State and he had been a junior transfer from another school. There among the wide green lawns and red brick buildings, she had given her one and all to him, and then he had just up and disappeared. No word, just gone.

Tommy had been a handsome boy from a good family in western Maryland. He'd had a really nice car and was fun to be with. He'd had quite a reputation with the female undergraduates at Salisbury. But then he had met Patsy. It was the first time his irresistible force had met her immovable object, and in his pursuit of her conquest, they had fallen in love.

Tommy had been nothing if not persistent, and he had kept at it until he had worn her down with his charm. Patsy had finally agreed to go out with him, but only with stern admonition. "I'm not just another notch in your belt, Brooks. Either be serious or be history."

In the course of time, they had become lovers and he had confided in her that he was in trouble at home. His father had been terribly angry with Tommy's lackluster grades and had been threatening to cut him off if he didn't concentrate on the three R's—reading, 'riting, 'rithmatic and forget the three B's—beer, broads, and bullshit. Patsy had a simple solution for him: "Cut the shit, Brooks, and get to work."

This had been easy for Patsy to say because she had grown up rough and had known all there was to know about hard work. She also knew what it was like to have two brothers who played slap and tickle with her way too much, and a father who might have done worse himself when he was drunk, which was most of the time. Patsy had learned young how to stay out of sight. Her poor mouse of a mother couldn't do a thing for her.

Things had been difficult, but tolerable, at home, until Patsy had matured physically and had to put up with her father's rough jokes and her brothers' pinching and probing—that is, until the day she had found out that her brothers had drilled a peephole in the boards of the bathroom wall and were enjoying her baths more than she was. When she had complained about this to her father, he had just shrugged and said, "Boys will be boys." Her mother had finally stood up for her, and this had led to a screaming fight. Her father had stormed out of the house to get good and drunk. He had come home and beat her mother senseless. And that had been the last straw.

Then finally, good fortune had smiled on Patsy in the unlikely person of her seventh-grade teacher, Mrs. Michelle Mullaly, who had saved her life. Finding Patsy crying in the girl's bathroom at school, Mrs. Mullaly had gently pried the story out of her, then escorted Patsy home. She'd had Patsy remain in her car while she had gone into the house alone, with her prominent jaw set and her shoulders back. Mrs. Mullaly had worn a look that afternoon that would have befitted General George Patton, and Louie Cox never stood a chance.

In the short and decidedly one-sided battle that followed, the tall and twig-thin Mrs. Mullaly had reduced the hulking, red-cheeked part-time farmer to rubble. In a scant few minutes, she had put the fear of God and Sheriff Seeley into Louie Cox and extorted from him permission for Patsy to come and stay with her any time the girl wished. Although Patsy hadn't been able to hear most of what had gone on, she'd gotten the message that if her father didn't straighten up, Mrs. Mullaly would see his lazy ass in jail and let the whole county know what a good-for-nothing drunk he really was.

From that day on, Daddy and the boys had given Patsy a wide berth, and even though life at home had become tolerable, Patsy had stayed with Mrs. Mullaly and her family more and more often until she had finally stayed there full time, with her mother's approval.

Life became better, for Patsy…until that spring break when Tommy had gone home and never come back. Until now, that is.

"I haven't got much time, Patsy, so let me tell it quick and straight and finally get it off my conscience. When I went home for spring break, I got drunk one night and smacked up my car. The sheriff's patrol said I had resisted arrest, and threw me in jail.

"My dad had been unhappy with my behavior and disgusted with my grades at school, so he decided to straighten me out and teach me some responsibility. He talked to his good friend the judge, and I was quickly found guilty. Judge gave me a choice of either going into the Air Force for four years or going to jail for two. I chose the Air Force. I tried to call you, Pats, I really did, but they kept me in jail until it was time for me to leave for boot camp. They took me right from jail to the airport and walked me to the plane.

"I felt horrible about leaving you like that, but I was too ashamed of myself and too full of self-pity to do anything about it. Aside from missing you every day, the Air Force has been one of the best decisions I ever made. Except for hurting you, I have never regretted it. I wanted to call you, but I never managed to get up the guts to do it. I wrote a hundred letters to you, but I tore them all up. They all made me sound so small and weak. It took me a long time to realize that I was weak.

"At first, I didn't know what to say to you, and the more time that slipped by, the harder it got. Then I got drunk one night and got a girl pregnant. I had to marry her, and then I surely couldn't call you. So after that, I just never bothered, but I never stopped loving you, Patsy."

"And I never forgot you, Tommy, and I really hated you for a long time."

"I deserved that."

"But why now, after all these years?"

"As I said, there are several things going on at work and in my life that are out of my control, and I have to make some hard decisions. I need someone steady to talk to. Someone that I care about and can trust."

"You're talking around in circles, Tommy. There must be more to it than that."

"Yes, there is so much, I can't even explain it all now. Can I call you again sometime so we can talk longer?" he pleaded shamelessly.

"Yes, take my cell number." She rattled off the numbers.

"Thanks, Patsy, but I have to go. I'll call you soon. Bye."

Then he was gone. Again. And Patsy was left with a phone hanging limply in her hand and with her mind a riot of memories and questions she would have preferred to leave buried.

*   *   *

Jameson Coleridge stood at his bedroom window in the presidential quarters in the East Wing of the White House and stared solemnly out at the night sky. He was watching the lights of a commercial jet winging its way east and just skirting around the air traffic exclusion area over Washington, DC. The president was sleepless this night because he was deeply troubled and could find no way out of this new dilemma. The first lady had admonished him repeatedly that it was undignified for the president of the United States to be standing around the house in his skivvies. Jameson had reminded her that because he was the president and leader of the free world, he could stand around his bedroom any damned way he chose.

As Jameson stared up into the great night sky, a bright streak appeared, traveling from west to east and flashing out just seconds afterward. *Point riders of the Apocalypse,* he thought absently. If only that damned rebel preacher had kept his mouth shut, Jameson may have been able to get a full night's sleep. He felt somewhat renewed after deciding to go to the people with news of the asteroid debris and letting them make their personal preparations as they saw fit. At least they would have been informed by their president. Now this damned Reverend Randy was forcing him to advance his schedule.

His problem was the same one that had troubled leaders in positions of authority all through the centuries: how to care for the well-being of his people while knowing that what he had to do was putting them at risk. Certainly, he would go public with the asteroid menace, but only after having put in place the appropriate security measures. To prevent a mass exodus, he had already conferred secretly with the mayors of many large metropolitan areas and with the National Guard. They had assured him that stability could be maintained. But then how would he care for the people who would inevitably escape from the cities? No matter what security restraints were in place, the countryside would have no real means of support. If these refugees formed into groups, they could easily forage through the countryside in search of shelter and sustenance. Local people would see this as an invasion and seek to protect their families and property in whatever means they deemed necessary. If this were allowed to happen, then both city and country people would suffer, and many would probably die. The first people killed by the meteorites would actually be neighbor killing neighbor.

When was the optimum time to make this announcement so that the rights and security of all his people could be guarded without sacrificing one group for another? To hold off announcing the impending doom long enough to protect the cities would thereby not give the country people adequate time to make preparations for their comfort and survival that were readily available to them otherwise. It was a terrible choice no person or government should ever have to make.

To postpone the announcement meant he was risking American taxpayers' lives. He was sure this was not what he had been elected for.

Jameson Coleridge had read somewhere that Dwight Eisenhower had suffered these same pangs of conscience on the night before the Normandy landing on D-Day. So many lives at risk, so many variables to consider, so many damned things that could go wrong.

He shrugged the dismal thoughts away with a shake of his head and slowly turned from the window, returning to his bed. So much to do and so little time to do it in. He briefly wondered if his longtime friend Amos was still awake and pondering the same troubling thoughts as well.

## Tuesday, March 9

John Halloran arrived at Albany International Airport ten minutes late, at 4:50 a.m.. On this cold and breezy morning, the sun hid behind a ridgeline of the Berkshire Mountains to the east.

By the time he had retrieved his old pickup truck from long-term parking, paid his bill, and gotten on the road, it was a quarter past five, and he had to be at work at six thirty. It was going to be close. He felt grimy after a night on airplanes and suffering through the unavoidable airport security delays. John wanted nothing more than to go home and grab a quick shower. He decided this would be as good a day as any for his first tardy relief, and he headed home, already feeling a little better. Let Bud Flynn wait for him for a change.

There was little traffic in the early morning hours on Route 155, and less on Route 20, so he made it home from the airport in record time, grabbed a quick, stinging-hot shower, and was back on the road with time to spare for a quick cup of coffee at the diner.

"Oh dear, Johnny boy, you look like the devil dragged you through a keyhole," was his greeting from Sally Prentiss as he walked into the Duanesburg Diner.

"Hi yourself, and yes, it is good to be home," John came back.

"That little girl out west had better start taking better care of you, Johnny boy, or you'll never survive."

"Not her fault," John said. "Just airline schedules and having to work day shift with just a couple hours' sleep on the red-eye and a mild case of jet lag."

Sally had already poured him a cup of coffee and was leaning over the counter in his favorite position. "Get some of this into you and you'll feel better," she said, smiling as she noticed her position was having its usual remedial effect on John and he was perking up already. "How did your trip go?" she asked, fixing him with her serious green eyes.

"I found out all that I wanted to, and a lot more that I didn't."

"Good or bad?"

"Not good."

"What now?"

"How would you like to take a nice trip out west?" John asked, suddenly getting serious.

"Can't do it, I've got commitments right here."

"What if I said it might become too dangerous for you to stay here. And that it may be soon."

"I can't imagine what could be dangerous in this little town, and there's always old Duke to consider."

"Screw Duke; he's not invited to go."

Duke Duncan was Sally's long-term, sometimes live-in lover but most times, a thrown-out drunk. John hated Duke because he himself cared about Sally in a special way and it bothered him to see her misused. He never could understand why Sally even bothered with Duke.

"Well since you're so feisty this morning, we'll have to discuss it another time."

John clamped down on both his jaw and his temper when he saw the look in her eyes. When Sally Prentice looked like that, you didn't mess around.

Sally walked off into the kitchen in a huff, and John dropped his head and sipped the scalding-hot black coffee, feeling better and worse at the same time.

"You had better get your shit together, or you're never going to make it to work, Johnny boy." Sally was grinning and leaning again, and she had a brown bag in her hand that John knew contained some lunch for him.

John looked deep into her eyes and said as firmly as he could manage, "I can't tell you any more about it now, but I may be leaving to go back out west on short notice. I think you should come. I know this is your town and normally you don't have anything to worry about here, but that situation might change quickly, and I want you to have thought about it. You're a good friend; that's all."

"You're really serious, aren't you?" Sally asked, handing him a large container of coffee to go. Her expression had turned suddenly serious.

"Yes, you're damned right I am."

"I can't make any decision unless I know what it is that I have to be frightened of, John. I can't just go running off because a friend of mine thinks it might be a fun thing to do."

"You're right as usual, and I'm saying this all wrong, but I'm out of time. Will you be free this evening?"

"Why?"

"I thought we might get together and maybe I can do a better job of explaining what's going on."

"Stop by later; I'll be here."

"Wonderful. Either tonight or tomorrow night, I will let you know. See you, Sally."

"Bye, John."

After John left, Sally looked out after the fading taillights of his Chevy pickup and thought this had to be the strangest conversation they had ever had, and they'd had some beauties. Still, John had been a lot more serious than usual, and it wouldn't do her any harm to think about it.

\* \* \*

"Hey, Willie. How's it going? I thought Flynny was on," John said as he put his tote bag on the shift supervisor's desk. "What's new on our mighty system?"

"He called in sick, so I got the dreaded call to cover; pisses me off to no end. As far as the system goes, it is not as mighty as it once was, and getting less so by the day," answered Willie Davis. Willie was a pessimist in the best of times, but he ran a fine system and gave a big damn about how he turned it over to his relief. Willie was sixty-five years old and still resisting retirement. His wife had passed away a few years ago, and since then, his job, his two black Labrador retrievers, Jeet and Mo, and Yankees baseball were his whole life—and Willie Davis took life seriously.

"How's that?" John asked.

"I just got a call from LIPA; Northport 3 has a super-heater tube leak and is on the way down and off. Our load is covered for today without him, but you'll probably be running a lot of gas turbines over the peak. You've been off for a couple of days, haven't you?"

"Yes."

"Well, there's a batch of new memos in the book, and operations engineering have completed the system part of the study you started on the world without nukes. They have lowered all of our transmission interface stability limits in case the big guys come down. No big stable machines to take up voltage swings. Damned limits are getting to be just like a yo-yo."

"Anything else?"

"No. Otherwise, it has been fairly quiet."

"Okay, then go on home and get some sleep. You look worse than I feel."

"See you tonight, John."

"See ya."

John settled into the comfortably familiar day-shift routine quickly. He made calls to get the slow-responding generators moving to pick up the morning load, put capacitor banks in service to keep the transmission voltages up, and generally fine-tune the bulk power system of New York to his liking. He had a baker's dozen of new memos to read in the bargain.

It was only 8:15 in the morning when *the* call came in. "NYISO, Halloran," John answered the call from National Grid Company.

"Hey, Johnny. I just got some news you're not going to like any more than I do," said the system operator.

"Break it to me gently."

"We just got a call from Nine Mile Point. They have orders from the Nuclear Regulatory Commission to begin shutdown of both units. They are to be off the line in eight hours and are then to begin defueling and storing fuel bundles. Both units, believe it or not, are going into cold standby."

"Holy shit. I knew the NRC was looking at it, but I never thought they would really do it."

"Wow. Remember, recorded lines, John, and they done it, my friend. I gotta go," said the member system operator. "I've got to see what I can do about getting the Hudson unit back on. We're sure as hell going to need her."

"Call back everything you own, Pete. Is there any chance of getting Oswego 5 back on? I don't think this is going to end with you."

"Same as a snowball in hell, John. They've been scavenging her for parts to keep number six running."

"Keep me up on whatever progress you make."

"Right you are, buddy. Keep smiling."

John was just turning around in his chair to signal Roger Adamski of trouble brewing when his phone rang again. He turned to the console to find the New York Power Authority phone ringing.

"Hey, John, what the hell's going on here?" came the voice of Bill Wilkens before John even had a chance to say hello.

"I'll bet you got a call from NRC to shut Fitzpatrick down."

"How the hell did you know? I only just heard it myself. Add Indian Point to your list as well."

"I just got off with National G; they have to shut down Nine Mile points 1 and 2."

"I'm gonna be deficient in meeting my delivery schedules when they start bringing Fitzpatrick down and off."

John's anxiety was building, but he never let it show. "We'll see if we can buy some emergency power from Ontario or Quebec to replace what we have to shut down; otherwise, we'll just have to run everything we own and use voltage reduction for reserve. I'll get back to you as soon as I know."

John hung up again and turned to see Roger heading for his desk with a worried look. "I can see from your face you've already got the news," John said.

"Yes, I got it. So how will it be fixed?" Roger asked.

"Hell, I don't know yet. I just got the word myself. The rest of our nuclear units are pressurized-water reactors, and maybe they'll stay on a while longer. Let us work it out here, and I'll get back to you."

"Will do." Roger shrugged. "But hurry it up! I've got every asshole in the state plus their entire staffs calling me."

"That's what you get the big money for." John couldn't pass up the chance for a cheap shot. "You'll get what I've got when I get it," John answered, turning to give instructions to his crew to start calling around to purchase power to cover any shortages for today and get generators called back on the line for tomorrow. This was going to be an absolutely shitty freaking day, John thought.

\* \* \*

"No need to have a hissy fit, old girl. I was just inquiring as to his health," said Priscilla Jameson with a pretty pout.

"That's plain bullshit, Priss, and you know it! The last boy of mine that you inquired as to his health wound up in your bed within the week," replied Meave McCormak testily. "The only part of his health you're concerned about is his tallywhacker!"

"No need to be gross about it."

"Gross or not, it's all of the truth, and the worst part is that when you threw Stanley out of your bed, the bastard wanted to get back into mine. Just you stay away from my Billy."

The object of the young women's attention was William J. Appleby, also known variously as Billy Appleton, Wilhelm Appledoorn, Bill Applegate and several other Apple aliases—the same William Appleby who had witnessed the meteorite crashing into Foyles Charing Cross Road Bookstore and had also carefully observed the crowd's reaction at the time.

"I hear he has a sweet little scam going for him," Priss said as she perched on the corner of the desk.

"Scam? I don't think so, he's been selling meteor insurance, against possible damages caused by meteors, you know similar to the meteor that hit Foyles," Meave replied.

"Seems a lot of folks are getting nervous about them shootin' stars," Priscilla said. "I'm sure he's doing just fine." She took a mirrored powder compact from her purse and began checking her makeup, causing her to miss Billy Appleton when he arrived at work.

William J. Appleby had responded to this unexpected disaster by quickly renting this small office and establishing the Appleby Insurance Group, specialists in fire, life, and casualty protection. He had wasted no time to appoint Meave as his administrative assistant. The glass door to the new office was lettered in gold leaf, and William's business cards and bogus insurance forms were imprinted with a large logo emblazoned with a comet shooting across the London skyline. Billy had these printed by the hundred. He had then emptied his meager savings account and flooded the media with advertisements complete with the shooting-star logo, calling on people to prepare for the worst and to cover their possible losses with first-rate insurance from the Appleby Group, to which he already had many inquiries and sales. Billy was quite confident that Scotland Yard would have too many other problems on their blotters to be concerned with a little insurance scam. He was quite correct.

Meave jumped up quickly and flung herself into Billy's arms, delivering a resounding kiss and pressing herself close so that he could have no doubt as to how little she had on under her form-fitting dress. Always good to keep them aroused, her mum always said. Keep their minds below the belt, and men were no problem at all.

Priss had recovered quickly, and as Billy looked over Meave's shoulder, she swung around to face him. From where she was sitting on the edge of the lone desk, she allowed Billy a good look at her long, stocking-clad legs. When she was sure she had his full attention, she slowly crossed them, in a perfect imitation of Sharon Stone in *Basic Instinct*, and Billy was rewarded with a view of a half acre of creamy thigh and just a glimpse of something dark and vastly more tantalizing. Billy caught his breath at the sight, and Meave misinterpreted its meaning completely and wiggled happily against him.

"Hear the insurance business is going great guns, Billy," Priss said, arching her eyebrows.

"Just super, since you ask," Billy said. "The papers and the telly are playing it up real proper, and that's free advertising for me. That old gal in Australia who burned to death on her own front porch was worth a few thousand pounds. All them little black fellers shouting and pointing their spears at the stars are worth another. People have been watching the sky and seeing lots of shooting stars at night. Now they're only too happy to come and see Uncle Billy and lay down a few pounds for complete protection."

Priscilla slid slowly from the desk and proceeded to smooth her dress down over her perfect hips, giving a slight tug at the waist with seeming innocence while in reality tightening her bodice to accentuate her full and unencumbered breasts. "Maybe you'll show me some of them 'shooters' one night," she said suggestively.

If looks could truly kill, the one Meave McCormak gave Priss would have done the deed twice over.

\* \* \*

Devon Grant's phone rang at 11:30 that Tuesday morning and roused her from her funk. "Hello?"

"Miss Grant?" came a nice, deep masculine voice. "This is Master Sergeant Tom Brooks. I work for Colonel Persons."

"Yes, what can I do for you?" Devon was curious.

"The colonel and I are taking a ride out to a place called Jackass Valley, pardon the expressionand he thought that you might like to come along."

Devon decided instantly this might be just the thing to help get her out of the funk she'd been in since John's departure. "That sounds wonderful," she said. "Where can I meet you?"

"Are you familiar with the visitors' parking at the Boulder Reservoir?"

"Yes, I was out there once."

"We'll meet you there at 1 p.m."

"I'll be there," Devon said, already feeling better at the anticipation of a trip, no matter where or how short.

The taxi dropped Devon off at the reservoir parking at 12:45. She paid the driver, then strolled over to the low wooden railing at the slope of the reservoir bank and sat on it, looking out at the blue water. *It's starting to fill up already*, she thought. *The runoff must be starting.*

In just a few moments, she heard the sounds of a vehicle crunching on gravel in the parking area. She looked around and saw a battered blue Chevy SUV with more than a few years under its belted tires. The SUV seemed to be running well enough, though it was dusty and mud-splattered and carrying a load of bundles tied to the luggage rack. Devon recognized Mark Persons in the passenger seat and a handsome, dark-haired man driving, whom she assumed must be Master Sergeant Brooks.

"Hi, Devon," Mark Persons said. "Where's your car?"

"I took a cab today just to mix things up. I'm quite sure that I wasn't followed."

"If I would have known that, I would have picked a place closer."

"No problem," Devon said as Mark opened the door on the passenger side and pulled the seat forward. Devon realized she barely had room to get in with the way the car was loaded. Whoever had packed the vehicle had left her barely enough space to squeeze in and settle on the edge of the backseat in the middle. "You've got quite a load here."

"No time to go up empty-handed. Devon, this is Tommy Brooks, my good right hand, and sometimes my left one too," Mark Persons said, nodding his head toward the driver.

Tom Brooks smiled and shook Devon's hand, and she thought again that he was a good-looking man, but she noticed that his impossibly blue eyes seemed to be troubled.

"Nice to meet you, Tom."

"Same here, Devon."

Tommy put the SUV in gear and gunned off, flinging gravel behind as he left the parking area and headed out Boulder Canyon Road toward Gold Hill.

The ride up to Jackass Valley was beautiful. Leaving the park lands surrounding Boulder, a short ride took them into the foothills of the Rockies, clothed in aspen, tag alder, and some mixed coniferous forest. Steep-sided canyons abounded, most with streams at their bottoms rapidly flowing with runoff from the melting winter snows.

Route 119 wound up into the mountains headed for Nederland, but they turned off onto an improved gravel road toward Salina and Gold Hill. The road continued past Gold Hill, and a few miles out of town, Tom put the SUV in a hard right-hand turn into a tiny dirt track Devon would never have noticed if they hadn't been riding on it. Tom stopped just after turning off onto the track, and Mark Persons got out with him. They quickly unloaded some green-painted five-gallon cans from the back of the Chevy, which they quickly concealed in the brush beside the dirt track, then returned to the car.

"What kind of driveway is this?" Devon asked.

"It started out as a mule track up to some gold diggings until they ran out in the 1870s. Later, it was used as a logging road to haul out timber for the railroad and building material for the local towns. After that, it went unused again for many years until the lodge was built. Even then, the owners and guests were the only ones to use it regularly. After the lodge went out of business almost twenty years ago, only a few hunters and fishermen ever came up this way. When Professor Schmidt purchased the lodge, he had to spend a good deal of his time during the spring and summer just cutting the brush back to keep it clear. Now I think that he should let it grow up again."

"Why do that?" Devon asked.

"The less people know about the lodge or the old road, the better off we'll be," Tom Brooks answered.

Devon's puzzled look prompted Colonel Persons to continue, "Devon, when we do get hit by some of the asteroid debris, and by we, I mean America, people living in urban areas will have a very difficult time for a while."

Devon noticed that Mark Persons had said *when* we are hit, not *if,* and a shiver of fear ran down her spine.

"America is a country that depends on a constant supply of electric power to provide our basic needs and comforts and conveniences. We rely on our transportation system for supplies of consumable goods, and any disruption, no matter for how short a time, will cause shortages. I read once that there is no place in America that is more than seven days away from starvation if the transportation system shuts down. A good Mormon housewife keeps a year's supply of food in the house for just that reason. The Mormons greatly fear starvation.

"If we are here at the lodge and we have adequate food stored, then we will be the haves. When living in urban areas nearby becomes difficult and competition for available food becomes severe, people will leave and try to live in the surrounding countryside. They may come by here and want to share what we have or take it from us by force. Later on, evacuees from other cities in the west may pass through here also. We cannot possibly feed them all, and we don't want to fight them, so being hidden away is a good idea for the foreseeable future."

That was by far the longest speech Devon had heard Mark Persons give, and although she didn't like the content, she had to accept the basic truth in it. "Is that what we're doing today, stockpiling?" she asked.

"Yes, we are making a start at putting away some things that will help to assure our survival."

Devon subsided into silence as she thought over what had just been told to her. Until now, the meteorite threat had just been sort of a puzzle or a game that she and John had been trying to unravel. Now it was becoming all too real, frighteningly real, and she didn't like that at all. The specter of starving hordes leaving the surrounding metropolitan areas and heading up into the mountains to forage was terrifying, and the fact that these were military men intending to hold on to what they had, by whatever means, was equally frightening.

A short while later, they pulled in to a clearing and up to a large rustic building. It was of unpainted clapboard construction, two stories high, with cedar shingle roofing. The upper floor consisted of four gables extending out from the center like the arms of a cross. Each had a steeply pitched roof and a double window at the end. She would later learn that each arm of the cross was a large bedroom accessed from a central stairwell and that there was a small attic above.

The main floor consisted of a huge living room area in front, with a kitchen and dining room at the back. A deep covered porch ran all around the front and sides, and large fireplaces back to back faced the living room and the dining room. In the kitchen was a huge old black monster of a wood-burning cookstove. The walls were plastered above oak wainscoting and were decorated with many pictures of hunting scenes, dead deer hanging on meat poles, or men holding up strings of fish. It seemed to be a good place to live off the land.

The lodge was furnished with rustic, masculine furniture of oak and leather, with a few overstuffed pieces of undeterminable vintage. An adirondack chair and several wooden rockers completed the scene. The dining room table was made of massive oak planks and was surrounded with assorted chairs and benches. Elk horns and two bearskin rugs added to the rugged appeal of the place. The lodge had a feeling of great strength and security, along with a homey charm that Devon took to immediately. If you had to hole up in a place, she thought, this one would be better than most.

The four bedrooms were large but had no closets. A big wardrobe stood in each room, along with a double bed, a small desk, and bedside tables. The double windows at the end of each room provided sufficient light, and the rooms offered different views of the surrounding woods and park lands. In the distance appeared to be a lake, and a small stream ran across the land in back of the house. Behind the lodge, of all things, was a double outhouse complete with sickle moons carved into the doors.

Exploring the attic, Devon found it to be small and stuffed with the usual array of cast-off items from earlier times. She decided this would be a good place to explore later, as there appeared to be a number of things that might prove to be valuable if the power went off and they needed to fend for themselves. There was also a fairly large steel tank built into the chimney, for what purpose she could not say.

While Devon had been investigating the house, Mark Persons and Tom Brooks had been busily unloading the SUV, storing many bulky items in a small barn at the rear of the lodge. What caught her eye, however, were six obviously new military rifles and several boxes of ammunition stacked against the side of the car. *Welcome to Fort Jackass*, she thought as she walked toward the barn.

Inside, Tom Brooks was pouring gasoline from five jerry cans into a new 275-gallon fuel tank painted red and fitted with four pipe legs and a bright new brass valve. "For the car?" she asked as she walked over to him.

"No. For chainsaws and a log splitter in case we need to add to the firewood supply or make log structures. I don't expect we'll use the old Chevy much for a while; no fuel economy."

Devon noticed that Tom had said log structures, not cabins or buildings, but she let it pass and continued exploring the barn.

"What's in there?" asked Devon, pointing to a blue-painted tank standing alongside the barn.

"Kerosene for the lamps and heaters," Tom answered. "It's just a start, but we should be pretty well set up before things get bad. As long as we don't waste time doing it."

"We could use your help making up a supply list, Devon," Mark Persons said.

"What sort of list?" Devon asked.

"Long shelf-life food items, foul-weather clothing, medical supplies, cooking and preserving supplies; the list goes on endlessly. Start thinking along those lines, would you?"

Devon spent the rest of the day cleaning up the kitchen area and tidying downstairs. As she worked along happily, she made a mental review of what would be needed and jotted notes down on a pad. It was an altogether pleasant day.

After a quick sandwich break, Mark and Tom disappeared for a few hours, taking a shovel down the road toward Gold Hill. When they returned, they were all dirty and muddy. It was getting dark and time to leave. On their drive out, they stopped just past the pull-off for the main road, and Devon discovered what the men had been doing all afternoon. They had potted several small pines in ten-gallon buckets, which they pulled across the logging road to the lodge, effectively camouflaging the road's existence to anyone who didn't already know that it was there. They dragged an old rotten log and some brush across the tire ruts at the road's edge, and then, once they were satisfied with their work, it was time to head home.

"Here's that list you asked me for," Devon said, handing Mark Persons two pages of note paper.

"Wow," he said, looking at them, "you really took me seriously."

"I'm always serious about eating," she joked.

Mark scanned the list, and his impression of Devon Grant escalated by several notches. This was not just a girl with a pretty face; there was actually a brain in there and it worked quite well. She had even noted at the top that the list of items was in order of importance. Impressive.

She had listed under food such staples as rice, pasta (spaghetti, preferably, for compactness), cooking oil, Bisquick (complete, and thus more versatile than flour), oatmeal, cornmeal, dried beans and legumes, sugar, salt, spices, syrup, and pepper.

The list was full with such items as peanut butter and jelly, vitamin pills, canned goods, coffee, tea, and canned or powdered milk. There was also an extensive list of over-the-counter medicines and first-aid supplies.

"This should keep us going for quite a while," Mark said. "It's an excellent list, Devon, really excellent. Thanks."

Mark and Tom dropped Devon off a few blocks from the Elk Ridge Apartments. Colonel Persons had wanted to take her directly to her door, but she had refused, reminding him that she was being watched and didn't want her tails to know about any of her new contacts. That made good sense, but Mark was still uneasy about leaving her. Devon assured him she would be all right, and walked the few blocks home easily.

She entered the apartment building by the side entrance and went upstairs to her apartment. She unlocked the door and went inside quickly.

As Devon reached for the light switch beside the door, a strong hand grabbed her wrist and twisted it, spinning her around and pinning her arm behind her back in a vicious hammerlock, then jamming it up further just to inflict pain and immobilize her. Another hand had clamped across her mouth, successfully stifling any chance for a scream. The hand in her back pressed upward as the hand at her mouth pulled back, arching her body and propelling her forward at the same time. The thought that her attacker had done this before foolishly entered Devon's mind as she was forced inexorably toward the bedroom.

"Hello, sweet cheeks," the man whispered gruffly in her ear. "Now that we've been formally introduced, let's see if we can get to know each other better, with our clothes off."

\* \* \*

The ladies of the Boston Tea Party were gathered in Paula Patowski's apartment this evening, not to play cards but to make plans. Paula had called the girls together after watching Reverend Randy's program and seeing the frightened determination and absolute belief in his eyes. She had gone to her window after his sermon was cut off and watched the skies over Boston. Sure as you are born, there had been several shooting stars in the course of just a short while, and Paula had become convinced of the truth in what he had said.

Even at the late hour after his show, she had gone down to the recreation room and shuffled through the magazines piled there until she had found what she was looking for. It was a very old *Popular Science* magazine left by Gary Melby the handsome handyman. There was a picture on the cover of a comet burning through the air before smashing into a helpless city. Inside was an article that explained all of the terrible consequences of such a strike and the doom-and-gloom results for the people of Earth. It was purely terrifying. She had decided then and there that Boston was not the place to be should this occur. It was simply too close to the ocean.

Paula set the bottle of Southern Comfort down in the middle of her kitchen table, four juice glasses with it. "Girls, I think we may need something stronger than tea tonight," she said. "Did you all watch Reverend Randy?"

All the ladies nodded in the affirmative, and their expressions changed slowly from the anticipation of imbibing a little liquor to real concern over what they had heard and seen. "He frightened me," Annie Phillips said, which was unusual, as she was more often seen and not heard. "I almost peed myself."

"That's nothing new," grumbled Paula "You're always doing that."

"He frightened me too," said Burtha Kurtz. "I wonder why the government would want to shut him down?"

"They don't want him scaring all the people, I guess," said Wilma Krauss, taking a glass and splashing it half full of Southern Comfort and then taking a good stiff swallow. "People can treat each other badly enough in normal times, without the scare of the world ending for an excuse."

"Well, he scared the bejesus out of me," Paula said, "and I'm going to do something about it." She put the very old *Popular Science* issue on the table, and eight eyeballs focused on the cover with the big comet crashing into Manhattan.

Burtha firmly grasped the bottle and filled all the glasses just for something to do. "Drink up, ladies," she said.

"I read the article inside here," Paula said, pointing to the magazine. "They say there are a lot of things out in space…meteoroids, pieces that broke off asteroids, old pieces of burned-out comets, all sorts of space junk. If one of them falls down on the earth and lands in the Atlantic Ocean, it can cause a tidal wave, they call them tsunamis now-a-days and they can roll over the whole East Coast, as far inland as the mountains. They showed one as high as the Empire State Building. I don't want to be in Boston if one comes. The article says a meteor or a comet is what caused the dinosaurs to go extinct. If one of them hits us, I don't want to be a dinosaur just yet."

Paula had a head of steam up by now, and she continued without interruption. "I've been planning to go out to Nevada to visit my grandson Stanley for a while now, and I think this may be a good time to do it. I hope you all will come with me."

The atmosphere around Paula's kitchen changed radically with the decision made, by Paula, as usual, and all the girls cheered up, drinking and talking rapidly, making plans for the big trip.

Burtha had a friend whose husband worked at the Hare family car dealership, so she would rent a full-sized van for two weeks so they could all pile in together and drive west. The gloom of being bombarded with meteorites changed into the excitement of taking a trip, and they all talked at once. Each widow had a little money put back, and they had their kitty from the card games. They could make it alright with maybe a little extra for some gambling in Reno. They would leave tomorrow to beat the weekend traffic, Thursday at the latest.

\* \* \*

Rita Morgenstern put the finishing touch by taking the cut-glass stopper from her bottle of Chanel No 5 and touching it down deep in the cleavage between her breasts. She surveyed her handiwork with satisfaction. Her blue-black hair was long and brushed to a lustrous sheen. Her makeup was perfect, and her mauve silk blouse was just barely tight enough to accentuate her full chest. Her long skirt fit well over her quite ample hips and flowed well with her movements. She may be Big-assed Rita to the rest of the world, and then only behind her back, but she would show that little punk, Jeff Ryder, what he might be getting. That is, if his story proved to be as good as he had promised when he called earlier that evening.

Rita was an up-and-coming investigative reporter on NBC4-TV, the NBC affiliate in Washington, DC, and she was hungry for an anchor spot there as a final step before moving up the network to New York. Rita was absolutely sure she would get there, and she was willing to do whatever it took to do it.

She was not averse to sleeping with a man to get a good story or to gain some advantage at the station and had done so on several occasions, so tonight would be nothing new. The only difference was that she hadn't had any strong feelings one way or the other for the previous men she had slept with but she hated Jeff Ryder's guts with an unrelenting passion.

The doorbell chimed, and Rita gave the wine bottle a final twirl in the ice bucket on the way to answering the door. She paused for a moment at the door to take a deep breath and get herself together. *Let him wait*, she thought as she patted her hips and composed her face before opening the door.

Jeff was slightly shorter than average, but well built. He had a mousy look, despite the well groomed dark blonde hair and blue eyes. His only problem was that he believed he was God's gift to women, and he let it show.

*What an arrogant ass*, Rita seethed.

He said, "Hello," and handed her a bottle of Montrachet as he entered. Rita was grudgingly surprised and briefly hid her eyes behind her long lashes as she moved aside to let him in. She checked the label—1974, not a bad year, either. She was both irritated and impressed. Perhaps there was some hope for tonight, after all.

The good impression lasted only until she closed and locked the door and turned to face Jeff. His eyes roamed slowly over her until they fastened themselves on the front of her blouse and he began, "I see you are all ready to begin negotiations," while licking his somewhat thick lips.

"Negotiations, my ass," she said with a little more gusto than she had intended. "You can see what I have. But, I want to see what you have, and if it's as good as you claim, then off to bed and no bullshit. If it's not, you can shove your expensive bottle up your tight ass on the way out the door."

With a confident half smile, Jeff slowly lowered his eyes to the chilling wine and said, "Can we at least have a drink first while I tell you my story? Then you can apologize for being so rude and put the chain on the door."

Rita's movements had become somewhat stiff and jerky from the supreme effort of holding her anger in check. She marveled at his arrogance as she moved to the wine bucket and poured two glasses for them. She was proud that her self-control had kicked in and her hand hadn't trembled as she poured. She took an unlady-like gulp just to brace herself and slowly settled onto the sofa. "So let's hear it."

"Here it is," he began, his wine untouched.

Rita could have appreciated his directness, if not for the fact of his obvious anxiety to have the bargain consummated, in the biblical sense, of course.

"Senator Braxton has been acting very strangely for the past week and a half."

"So what's new about that? He's always strange."

"No, I mean really strange. He's been locking up files in his desk, which he has never done before, and taking calls on his cell phone. Then he goes running out for unscheduled meetings and won't tell anyone in the office where he's going. This is so totally out of character, it raised my curiosity to the point where I bugged his phone."

"You put a bug in your boss's phone?"

"Yes, I did. He's usually so transparent and predictable that it's laughable. So I took a chance, and the bug hit pay dirt. This morning after he called a sporting goods outfitter and arranged for enough camping gear and freeze-dried food to feed the cavalry for a month, I decided it was time to look further into this new and unpredictable behavior."

"After he left the office tonight, I picked the lock on his desk and went through his papers."

"You've got more balls than brains," Rita said with some amazement, "Going through his desk like that? What if someone had come in?"

"Well, they didn't, and the little search paid off. It appears the danger of the Mountain passing by the earth is not over as everyone thinks. There is a huge tail of debris behind it. There is a very likely chance the earth's gravitational pull will cause this tail to go right through the earth, causing lots of strikes. Now the president is on the fence with the dilemma about whether or not to announce to the public the obvious danger of being struck by this debris and risk public panic, strikes, absenteeism and riots, totally tanking the economy, or to hold off until all his civil-defense preparations are in place and thereby leave the American public with little time to make their own personal preparations.

"Good old Senator Barry Braxton became privy to this information because he chairs the Air and Space Appropriations Committee, and the Air Force and NASA are rushing preparations for a shuttle launch to put some new armored satellites into geo-orbit. At the same time, he's been making preparations to get his fat old ass up into the mountains of his home state of North Carolina, with enough food, booze, and guns to live like a little king for a year, all of this while his loyal constituents stand at risk of drowning in a tsunami, getting smashed by meteorites, or just plain murdered by their neighbors for a little food or a blanket."

Jeff let his eyes trail slowly down Rita's body to her ample hips and said, "If you get that magnificent ass of yours in gear, you can corroborate this information and beat the president to the draw by making your own public announcement and get yourself the big scoop that you've always wanted. You've got a chance to roast his ass real good."

Rita's pulse was pounding in her temples, and she was sure the flush that she felt in her face and neck had extended itself all the way down to her breasts. Jeff had not failed to notice this or the erect nipples that were making themselves incredibly obvious through the fine silk of her blouse. She couldn't help it if a thrilling opportunity like this, affected her in a sexual way. The punk had really come with his guns loaded, in more ways than one. "Of course, I'll need some corroborating evidence to show my producer before she'll let me air anything like this," Rita said to give herself some time to get her hormones under control and her mind in gear.

Jeff reached inside his suit jacket and withdrew a small pack of papers. "These are copies, of course. I had to put the originals back in the file, but I think this should be enough to convince him."

"Her," Rita said absently as she scanned the typewritten pages. It was all there, and in spades. She knew in her gut this would be a blockbuster story. *New York, here I come*, she thought.

She reached over and took Jeff's hand. She traced slow circles on the back of it, then turned it palm up, brought it up to her lips for a kiss, then caressed it slowly for a moment with the tip of her tongue. Rita held his hand in both of hers for a moment before bringing it slowly down to cup her breast. A warm glow began to spread through her body as he caressed her. "You've made your case, Jeff. Now let's see if you can make mine."

An hour later, Rita stretched herself like a well-fed cat and enjoyed the sensuous feel of the satin sheets sliding against her naked skin. Jeff Ryder may have been a puke as a person, but he was not half bad between the sheets, she thought lazily. *This may be a promising and enjoyable new source of information.*

Her mind was reeling with the thought of all the work she needed to do to get corroboration of the story to sell it to her producer, the bitch, so she could beat the president's march. She slid slowly from the bed and enjoyed the chill of the cool air on her naked skin. Jeff merely grunted and rolled over, resuming his soft snore. Smiling slightly, she quickly headed for the shower.

\* \* \*

The pain in Devon's shoulder increased hugely as her assailant increased the pressure on her wrist and she was helplessly propelled across the room. At the same time, she was being lifted onto her tiptoes by the relentless pressure on her arm in the hammerlock. "I wondered where you were all day, sweet buns," a smooth voice whispered into her ear as she was guided into the bedroom. "Maybe now I'll find out, and we'll have a little fun in the process."

As she was thrown down onto the bed, Devon Grant knew she was definitely not having any fun.

Her attacker was on her in a split second. He didn't waste time by struggling to unbutton her jacket or blouse but merely ripped them open down the front, scattering buttons across the floor. Then he pulled them both back behind her shoulders, effectively pinning her arms to her sides. He first grabbed one of her breasts roughly, then began to fumble with the button at the waist of her jeans as Devon recovered from her shocked silence. She screamed at the top of her lungs and tried to sit up. She then began to struggle silently, fighting to regain some freedom, and using her feet and teeth to good effect. Her assailant pulled back with a growl and struck her with a short, vicious underhand chop to the solar plexus that drove the wind and the fight out of her. She was fading off into a fuzzy black void when his weight suddenly flew away. "What the fuck?" Devon heard him say at the sound of a hard object striking flesh, and then she heard a grunt.

"Not so tough when you're up against a man, are you?" said a slightly familiar voice, then another few quick blows followed.

Devon sat up and reached for the bedside lamp, but a strong hand caught her wrist and restrained her. "No, leave the lights off." She blinked her eyes and in the dim light recognized Frank Muller, FBI man and break-in artist, crouched over the prostrate form of the blonde-haired man she and John had seen leaving Professor Schmidt's office at the planetarium. She relaxed and slid off the bed, landing on her tush.

"I'm sorry about this, Miss Grant," Frank Muller said. "It shames me to have one of the men in my command do something like this. He and his partner were newly assigned to me, and I never quite trusted them. I have tried to keep an eye on their activities as much as I could. Tonight, he and his partner took it on themselves to come over here after we hadn't seen you all day. They played it cool and waited until I was out for some supper to make their move. I don't know where you were all day, but I know how you eluded us. It was a dangerous thing to do on your part." Muller was breathing heavily and talking rapidly between breaths, trying to explain and not condone the misbehavior of one of his agents, but his eyes were calm and steady, and somehow reassuring.

"Are you all right, Miss Grant?" he asked as he helped Devon up from the floor where she had fallen.

"Yes, I think so, and thank you for showing up when you did," she said as she clumsily rearranged her clothes with trembling hands and fingers.

"I came over as soon as I realized this creep and his partner were missing. It didn't take a genius to figure out where they had gone."

"Where is his partner, the short, tough-looking man?"

"He's not nearly as tough as he thought he was. He's downstairs, wearing my handcuffs, with my handkerchief stuffed in his mouth. I was waiting in the back of the parking lot, watching him, when I saw you come in the side door. We thought the side door was locked at all times and for emergency use only; that's why we didn't bother to cover it. That's also probably how you slipped out on us. It was no problem to put him away for a short nap."

Devon was simply standing beside the bed, holding the tattered parts of her blouse together and looking deep into Frank Muller's sort of sad-looking gray eyes. Her soft sobs were subsiding as she realized she was safe and that she could trust this man.

"I'm Frank Muller, Special Agent for the FBI, and this animal and his partner were sent to help my team with your surveillance. I don't know where the hell he's from, but he's a cowboy, definitely not from the bureau."

Devon watched silently as Frank Muller moved swiftly and surely, with no wasted motions. He removed Markson's necktie and stuffed it into the unconscious man's mouth. Then Frank took two electrical ties from his pocket and used one to bind Markson's feet before he rolled him over onto his belly to use the other one to bind his hands behind his back. "Do you have another place to stay tonight?" he asked gently as he admired his handiwork.

"No, I don't," Devon answered, unable to question his authority.

"Then put a few things together, and I'll put you in a motel until tomorrow morning."

"Why are you doing this?" Devon asked. "You already have these two as your prisoners. What else could be a danger to me?"

"My job is to watch you and report any unusual activities, not to harm you or restrain you. If you want to remain here, I can't stop you, but if I put you into a motel, then I'll know where you are and I'm doing my job, and maybe I can catch a few hours' sleep in the bargain."

Devon thought about that a moment. "How did he get in here?"

"Those new locks on your door are no problem for anyone with a little knowledge and the right tools," Frank said absently.

"I'll take your offer of a motel room for tonight," she said with finality. "Tomorrow, you can replace the locks with something better."

"That's a done deal." Frank smiled at her for the first time. "You can come back here in the morning, but please be visible for part of the time during the day so my people don't get nervous."

"I have to go to work tomorrow morning."

While they were talking, Devon had gotten over her shock and begun moving carefully around the bedroom. She quickly pulled on a floppy sweater and stuffed some night things into a small bag. She then followed Frank Muller as he unceremoniously grabbed Markson's feet and dragged him through the open apartment door and down the stairs with Markson's head bouncing on every step.

Grunting with the effort, Muller deposited the unconscious man into the trunk of the gray Impala, alongside his swarthy partner, and slammed the lid down. "Let's go," was all he said.

"Will they be all right in there?" Devon asked.

"They won't be in there long; we have a stop to make on the way to the motel."

\* \* \*

Angela Freece came out of sleep quickly, and automatically checked her surroundings. She was in her room at the Holiday Inn across from the university, and someone was knocking at the door. She slipped out of bed and retrieved her revolver from the night table beside the bed. Without wasted motion, she went to the door, visually checking the security bolt in place. Squinting her eye, she looked through the peephole and saw a middle-aged man with a day-old salt-and-pepper growth of beard, dressed in a rumpled gray suit, standing there and knocking. She opened the door quickly and said, "Frank, what's up? You should have called me. I would have dressed for the occasion," she joked.

Frank smiled. Angela was dressed in a short, sheer silk nightgown of some creamy color, and matching big-legged shorts, and she was holding a .38-caliber Colt Combat Masterpiece in her hands. He scrubbed the nearly two-day growth of beard on his chin and smiled slowly, saying, "I guess you're dressed just about perfect right now."

She looked down at herself and smiled quickly, then retreated back into the room to collect her robe. "Come on in, Frank. Don't just stand there in the hallway. To what do I owe the honor of this visit, business or pleasure?"

"Business, I'm afraid," Frank answered.

"That's too bad."

"Angie, I've got Markson and Grizetti trussed up like Thanksgiving turkeys stored in the trunk of my car. Dommy is coming to get the car and take them back to Denver. He has some friends there who will baby-sit them for a couple of days until I decide what to do with them."

"I gotta say, Frank, you sure know how to get a girl's attention. How did this all come about?"

Frank slumped down into the chair and rubbed his stubbly cheek again tiredly. "It's like I explained to you when I asked you to stay on out here. I've had bad feelings about them ever since they reported in. I've been working days and splitting nights with Dommy so we could keep tabs on them. They just didn't seem like bureau people to me."

"Here, Frank, try some of this. You'll feel better," Angie said, handing him a glass of bourbon on the rocks.

"Devon Grant hadn't been around all day," Frank continued. "We were concerned about where she was and how she slipped our surveillance. When I went out to get some supper, these two reported in, then decided to pay her apartment a visit and check for other exits, is what they told Chris DeMarco. Anyway, when I came back from supper and found out they'd left, I went right over to the apartment. It didn't take a rocket scientist to figure out where they'd be. They've been making suggestive comments all week. I found the spaghetti bender downstairs keeping watch, and maybe waiting for his turn, and I just saw red. I put him down, cuffed him, and went upstairs. It's surprising how easy these tough-looking cruds go down.

"Markson was upstairs, already assaulting the girl when I got there, so I put him down too. Then I put them both in my trunk and decided to put Miss Grant up here for the rest of the night since I knew you were here to keep an eye on her. She's in 242."

"Have you got a thing for the girl, Frank?"

"Jesus no, Angie. She's just a kid, but she does sorta remind me of Cathy sometimes, and it's my job to watch her, and watch out for her."

"Just checking, Frank. Now why don't you go in there and catch a hot shower and a shave. My razor's in the tub."

"I didn't mean to impose on you, Angie. I can get a room of my own. I just wanted you to know she's here."

"You're not imposing, and she is a big girl. She doesn't need a baby-sitter, but you sure as hell need some rest. Now get in there like a good boy," Angie said, gently shoving him toward the bathroom.

"You're the boss," he said, wearily slumping across the room. "I've been on short sleep for the past week."

When she heard the shower start running, Angela quickly undressed and threw on some street clothes. She listened at the door for the sound of Frank getting into the shower, then quietly opened the bathroom door and hung her white terry-cloth robe behind it. She could see his outline through the translucent shower curtain and thought briefly to herself that he didn't have a bad body for an older gentleman.

She always had something of a soft spot for Frank, ever since she first met him as an instructor to her class at the academy, then later on several assignments. Only a few years ago, they had been working on a drug case out of the Albany, New York, office when his wife was killed in a terrible car accident. Frank and Lori had been a close couple, married for twenty years, and her loss had been a terrible blow. His daughter Cathy had taken it even worse than Frank, and Frank hadn't had a clue how to cope with a teenage girl's grief or how it could appear as anger directed at him. He had been totally lost.

Cathy had grown up very close to her mother because of Frank's frequent case-related absences, and at times, the pair seemed more like sisters than mother and daughter. Even though Frank had been in town when Lori had been killed, Cathy somehow blamed him for the accident, and it created a wedge between them that existed to this day. Frank had come to Angie in desperation, and she spent many hours with Cathy, first slowly gaining her trust and then her friendship and in the process helping the girl deal with the grief.

Angie and Frank had gotten drunk together once or twice after that, and she had spent hours listening unselfishly to Frank's problems. He confided in her many things about his wife and daughter and his marriage, and through this process, a strong friendship and trust had developed between them. Angela had never betrayed that trust and always liked him for being a kind and caring man. It was nice to find a man who could be a little sentimental and old-fashioned in a cynical world. She liked him.

After his shower, Frank sat on the bed and numbly took the bourbon on the rocks that Angie made him, drinking thirstily. "Damn, that's good," he said, tugging idly at the bathrobe, which was much too small for him and barely covered his waist. "I considered putting this damned thing on backwards," he said, "but then my ass would be out."

"Your ass is already out, with two federal agents trussed up in the trunk of your car," Angela said.

"Dommy will take care of them. They may be uncomfortable, but they'll survive."

"Your call, Frank. Crawl under the covers and get some sleep. I'll take a little walk and check on your girl."

"She's not my girl," he grumbled.

"Yeah, yeah," Angela said, getting a jacket out of the closet.

Frank drained his glass and rolled over into bed with the robe still on. He pulled the covers up over his shoulders, and in a few seconds, was soundly asleep.

Angela crossed over to the bed and looked down at the sleeping man with a small, sad smile. She hated times like this because they made her retrospective, and she did not always like what she saw when she looked back. She had always wanted to be a special agent for the FBI, and worked terribly hard to be a good one. She had fully expected the need to prove herself every day while functioning in a man's world. She simply underestimated the toll it would take on her personal life.

Over the past ten years, Angela had accepted only two men into her life, and neither one stood the test of time. It was nearly impossible for anyone to meet her standards and fulfill her needs. She was drifting toward forty with no prospects for a permanent relationship and no noticeable lessening of her standards. She had nearly resigned herself to the single-life when this assignment had suddenly come up and thrown her together with Frank Muller again. Now she was thinking about more than just her temporary assignment.

\* \* \*

It was 11:30 p.m. when Jameson Coleridge finally folded the papers before him and picked up the phone to get his press secretary. He rubbed his sleep-deprived eyes, feeling fatigue like burning lead sinking deep into his bones. Never in his life had he felt this level of exhaustion. The White River Scandal, a couple of poor choices in his cabinet nominations, the national health care disaster, and the endless and acrimonious budget battles had all taken their toll on him.

Madge Sinclair answered somewhat sleepily on the second ring.

"Sorry to bother you this late, Madge, but I need you to arrange air time for me at seven tomorrow night on all networks. Tell them I have an announcement of the greatest urgency. Please get on it immediately."

"Yes, sir," Madge Sinclair said still a little sleepily. "I'll have full arrangements for you in the morning."

"Thanks, Madge, good night."

He strolled over to the window and looked out at the night sky. As he did, a small blue-white streak flashed across the heavens. "Bastards won't let me alone at all," he groaned and turned to go to bed, hoping for some much-needed sleep. *The makeup people will have their work cut out for them tomorrow*, he thought.

## Wednesday, March 10

"Morning, Willie. How was your night?" John said, setting his bag down on the console, as always.

"Damned long."

"How's the system?"

"All screwed up. Nine Mile points one and two are off, and Fitzpatrick is down to one hundred megawatts. He's due off shortly. Thank God the rest of our atom crushers are pressurized reactors. PJM and New England are in the hurt bag, too, but Ontario and Quebec are helping out a lot. They're both running their hydro wide open and supplying us up to the tie line limits. I hear MISO is doing their best also but occasionally relying on their Canadian friends from Manitoba pretty heavily too. Damned blue-eyed Arabs up north are going to get rich on this one. The warm weather they've had up there is helping start the spring runoff, but their hydro ponds are not full yet, and they're using this coming summer's water allocations to help us out. We'll have to pay them back big time on all the diversity contracts after things settle out. Any extra megawatts we have, we are exporting to PJM and they are wheeling it south and west of their system to help out SOCO and TVA. I told them we would keep our units wide open and sell them the excess on the ties as long as our fuel stocks hold out. Looks like the whole damned Eastern Interconnection is short.

"Operations engineers have been here all night, God love 'em, 'cause I don't. Those poor buggers are just not cut out for working night shifts, they looked like shit when they left. They did, however, come up with new stability limits that will allow us to import 2,400 megawatts from Quebec and also withstand the coincident loss of New England's tie with Quebec loaded at 2,000. I'll be damned if I can see how we can do it without the voltage collapsing all over the state, and I sure as hell don't want to be on if it happens. Seems like we just have no choice. It's just like your mom used to say when you didn't want to eat your spinach, 'You don't have to like it, you just have to eat it.'" Willie Davis just shook his head.

"I'm getting too old for this. These damned big flows south out of Canada remind me of the training simulation we had recreating how things were just before the big blackout of 1965. I think these limits are full of shit, and that makes me nervous, because I've been around long enough to know that figures don't lie but liars figure.

"Ralph has finally convinced the member companies that they have no alternative but to run their gas turbines at full capacity around the clock and to let the steam units follow the system load. The gas turbines are running on natural gas, and that seems to be the only fuel that's not in short supply. We're not exactly running the most cost-effective system, but we're not the only ones doing it. If we have to run this way for any length of time, it's the only sensible way to go. Our friendly non-utility generators are getting nervous as hell because they're rapidly using up their gas allotments, but their public-relations people still manage to get their names in the papers by telling the world how they're saving our asses. Ralph had a hell of a fight to get them to agree to continue running their units at full load no matter the gas supply, so we have over 4,000 megawatts of cogeneration online. Wind generation is obviously giving us what the good Lord decides to give to them, but lately, it has been working out well. The Gilboa pump storage pond is pumped up as full as we can get it, and that's about all that's new."

"That is quite enough," John said, his head spinning with the changes in the system overnight. "You're an old hand, Willie. How do you think we are going to make out?"

"We're on the ragged edge, John. We'll be alright if nothing breaks, but if it does, then someone's lights will go out, no other way about it. The old seventy-two-hour rule still applies."

"What's that?"

"No matter how bad things get on the system, you can usually hold out for three days; after that, things will begin to break and then all bets are off."

\* \* \*

Jamaal Kaleel watched as the blue and white Denver city police car cruised slowly by. He studied it for a minute, his dark eyes taking in every detail. He thought about it for a minute and then nudged his first lieutenant Bobby Simms, also known as Mustafa Kahn to the boys in the hood, "You see them pig wagons go by, brother?"

"Yeah, I seed 'em."

"You notice anything different?"

"Nope."

"Dumbass, didn't you notice all the cars we seen has two pigs in the front and two damn soldiers in the back?"

"No."

"Then you prob'ly didn't notice that them big long hard things they was holdin' up between they legs wasn't der' cocks, either."

"Nope."

"Then what the hell you been lookin' at fer the past hour?"

"That sweet-ass little Lila Mendez over there. Damn it, man, she could make my day."

"Well supposing you had a brain, and supposing you could use it to think of something besides gettin' laid, what would you think of cops and soldiers carryin' rifles 'n' ridin' in the same cars?"

"I'd think they suspect something big goin' down and wants to be able to stop it quick and hard."

"There now, it ain't so hard when you starts to thinkin' with your brain and not your dick, is it?"

"Nope."

Jamaal Kaleel looked over at his friend and saw that his eyes had strayed across the street again to where Lila Mendez was talking with some of her friends on the corner. Bobby's eyes had a glassy, faraway look. He was all done thinking for today.

Lila was a classy-looking little piece with nice regular features and dark curly hair cut short. She had a great ass and a nice pair of tits, but she was also trouble. Jamaal elbowed Bobby hard in the ribs to get his attention and said, "First off, that pussy is on the 49ers' turf and you better forget about it, and we has got to go back to the house 'cause I want to think about this pigmobile business some more. Second, I may have to do a deal with that asshole Santos, and I don't want him pissed at us for you messin' 'round with one of his bitches. You see what I sayin'?"

"Yep."

Jamaal just shook his head and started for the house. He knew even though Bobby's eyes were finally off Lila's backside, his mind was still not on business. On the way back to the Blues' house, Jamaal remained deep in thought about the future. Strange things were happening in town that made the cops nervous, and this nervous feeling caused them to put on extra forces in the neighborhoods. Jamaal had no clue what might be causing this nervous condition, but whatever it was, it might be just the thing he needed to put his plan into action; the only problem being that for the plan to work, he needed cooperation from another gang.

This was the main reason he had decided he should make contact with Ricky "the Rickster" Santos from the 49ers. This might be a good time to declare a truce and examine the possibility of some mutually profitable joint action.

Bobby Simms was still lost in his thoughts, not bothering the always-thinking visionary Jamaal Kaleel.

Jamaal continued to think.

\* \* \*

Frank Muller came awake slowly and began to take account of his surroundings. He recalled that he had come to Angie's room last night to enlist her aid, and realized he must have fallen asleep in her bed at the Holiday Inn. What he couldn't quite place was the cause of the tickling sensation on his nose. With a start, he realized that he was snuggled up close to someone very soft and warm who smelled wonderful, and that the tickling sensation was her hair. He also realized that the warm, soft, wonderful-smelling someone was Angela Freece and that his arm was around her and his hand was cupping her breast. When he tried to move his hand away, he also found that her hand was on his and was holding him firmly in place.

Frank had not awakened like this since long before Lori had been killed, and he had not been this nervous about a woman or this aroused since high school. Angela

Freece was a coworker and a good friend, and Frank did not want anything to compromise this. He had to admit, however, that he did have some very conflicting feelings about her and that he was becoming less and less aware of the differences in their ages.

"Are you going to lay there all morning, Frank Muller, or are you going to make the best of a good situation?" Angie asked as she snuggled back against him. "I already know that you're glad to be here."

Frank thought about that for a second and realized it was obvious he was truly happy. Happier, in fact, than he had thought he was capable of being. Happier, in fact, than he had been in many years. Angie rolled over in his arms and cuddled up to him. "Good morning, boss," she said, kissing him on the lips. "I'm glad that you had a good rest."

Before he could protest, she covered his mouth with a deep kiss and he responded. "Angie, I haven't done anything like this in such a long time," Frank said after their lips had parted.

"Then it's about time you started." Angela sat up in bed and knelt next to Frank, completely naked and beautiful. She slowly untied the white terry robe that was twisted around him and, with some help from Frank, removed it. She allowed him plenty of time to look things over before she stretched herself out on top of him. From here on, Angie was in complete control, and Frank did not mind it one bit.

* * *

Rita Morgenstern watched the director count the seconds down on his fingers as she prepared to present her special report at the beginning of the noon news. Rita was fairly glowing at getting the prime spot. A few discreet calls had assured her producer that the network would be carrying her bulletin nationwide. She would finally get the national recognition she deserved. Rita didn't even mind the butterflies that were fluttering in her belly. She was ready. Her story had been corroborated by two separate and entirely reliable sources, and approved by her producer, the bitch. Her copy had been written and also approved by the same bitch. She was ready. It was her story to run with, and Rita intended to do just that.

As the last finger folded in, making a fist, and the red light came alive on camera, Rita put on her serious face and began. "Good afternoon. I am Rita Morgenstern, investigative reporter, and I have some very grave news for America and the world. From a confirmed source close to the president, this reporter has learned that at this very moment, our planet is in grave danger.

"I have learned that all the while we were watching the huge asteroid which has been called the Mountain as it passed by the earth, there has been another deeper and more sinister danger lurking right behind it. All the while our government has been busily supplying us with wonderful video footage and dazzling text on the huge asteroid passing us by at a safe distance, the real danger was yet to come.

"What we have been led to believe is a solid, monolithic asteroid passing us by is in reality an ancient comet that has probably passed us by many times before. For the unknown millions of years that this comet has been visiting and revisiting our solar system, it has had some of its volatile gases burned off on each pass, and as these gases burn off, they release a trail of debris behind to follow along in the comet's orbit. It is this meteorite stream, as astronomers call it, that poses a threat to mankind. The meteorite stream is as extensive as the comet is large and contains an area in which the debris is considerably more dense and of considerable size, and the earth will pass directly through it.

"Confirmed expert sources state that within the next week, the earth will be exposed to the likelihood of being struck by meteorites of many sizes, and some of them, as I have previously stated, could be very large indeed.

"I have also learned that the government has known about the mass of meteoroids for weeks and has not seen fit to make this information public. This reporter wonders what would make our own government deny us the information that would allow us as a people to make our own personal preparations for the possibility of impending disaster. Especially a government that was elected on a platform of truth and honesty." She paused here for dramatic effect and to let the news sink in. Rita was silently hoping that people all around the nation would take a moment to call a friend and alert them to watch the rest of her report. Her heart drummed at the thought of how her ratings would soar. Rita cared not at all what the effect of her announcement would be on the American public, the stock market, the inner cities, or anything else. Rita cared only that she had gotten her big scoop and that she was live on the network. Everything and everyone else would have to look out for themselves.

"I understand that the president has requested air time on all major television networks for this evening and presumably is prepared to finally make the announcement to the nation that should have been made a week or more ago. On prime time this evening, President Jameson Coleridge will tell us what we should already know. I wonder at the audacity of a government that promises truth and honesty, then covers up an event of this magnitude and denies its people the time to prepare for it."

The producer shifted Rita to blue screen and broadcast her in the foreground of a series of animated scenes depicting the earth being subjected to strikes by various extraterrestrial objects, and file footage on all types of disasters that might come about as a result of meteorite strikes, from earthquakes and floods to volcanic eruptions.

Speaking calmly and learnedly as the scenes of disaster played in the background, Rita provided the nation's viewers with enough sensationalism to, quite frankly, scare the hell out of them. Her staff had done their jobs well and had gathered together footage of the pockmarked surface of the moon and various impact craters on Earth to demonstrate the effect of a meteorite strike. They had cleverly dovetailed in both old and recent footage of devastation caused by fire, flood storms, and other natural disasters. All of this had been gleaned from the network archives this morning and assembled into a truly frightening package. Even the working crew in the studio was strangely silent.

Rita had done her own homework and was able to speak with considerable authority on the subject of disaster. Her producer had not been idle and had quickly called in several so-called experts on disaster and coached them thoroughly so they could embellish Rita's story with details of death and extinction of entire species, up to and including the dinosaurs, and prove that such extinction had been caused by objects falling from the skies. All in all, it was a chilling quarter hour.

\* \* \*

"That *fucking* self-serving fucking whore! *Fuck!* Where did she get that from?" Amos Bellinger roared as he jumped up from his desk, spilling a stack of papers and the half-eaten remains of a roast beef on pumpernickel swirl bread onto the floor. Whenever he did not have an engagement, Amos was in the habit of eating lunch at his desk and watching the local news at noon. It was a convenient way to keep abreast of current events in DC. The noon news also touched lightly on world news and foreign affairs from a strictly Washingtonian point of view and occasionally had a special report as part of the show. The show was usually very well done, and Amos found it to be a profitable way to spend his lunch hour. Today was quite different. Rita Morgenstern's exposé was the last thing he had expected to hear, and for the full fifteen minutes, Amos had sat as if mesmerized. For the station to have given her a full quarter hour was unprecedented.

Lisa Howard turned pale under her fashionably done makeup and shuddered slightly at the look of raw fury on Amos's face. She was glad she was not involved in any part of the security breach, and sorry for whoever was.

Amos slammed a button down on his phone console and waited for the Secret Service supervisor on shift to pick up.

"Maloy," came the brisk answer.

"Mike, Amos here. Get some men over to NBC and pick up Rita Morgenstern and the whole crew from the noon news. Get their asses over here ASAP, and no need to be gentle about it. Call in all available people, and double presidential and White House security immediately. I'll be with the president if you need me for anything."

"What should I do with the TV people?"

"Let them sit here and damned well cool their heels until I can think of something bad enough to do to them!" Amos roared while his heart was thumping hard and his stomach was turning over.

Amos slammed down the phone receiver before he could hear Malloy's cautious "Yes, sir."

"I'll make that bitch sweat, and I'll find out her source before we go on the air tonight if I have to choke it out of her. Damn it, if she had only contacted me first, we could have made an arrangement to delay her show until tomorrow. I would have given her enough good stuff to make up for her holding off until after the president had spoken to the people. Now she's made her scoop and made the president look like an ass. And he's going to bite a big chunk out of mine. Dammit!" Amos was thinking out loud, which Lisa Howard had never known him to do. He was normally completely controlled, even under the most stressful of situations, and she had never before seen him wearing the look of deep concern he had on his face right now.

\* \* \*

Willie "Lump Lump" Seaman stared hard at the pretty brunette reporter on the television. She was sweet, for sure, but it was what she was saying that had Willie excited. The show was a Bulletin…Bulletin…Bulletin…and Willie knew that meant something important was cutting in on the regular show. Cognitive thinking was never easy for Willie, and when he was excited, sometimes the effort to bring his thoughts together was just too great for his damaged brain to manage, but today, he was able to make the extra effort needed to make a connection. Way back in the dim recesses of his mind, he vaguely remembered a magazine article he had looked at when he was pretending to read in the barber's chair. It had been a short while ago. To Willie, everything was a short while ago.

These red-hot things fell out of the sky and smashed into the earth. Willie understood what the earth was. When these hot rocks hit in cities, there were fires, and big buildings fell down, and the police got very busy keeping people from running around and breaking windows and stealing televisions and computers and such stuff. That meant that the police would be too busy to care about Willie or what Willie did. Maybe Willie didn't have to wait any longer. Maybe the lights would go out in New Orleans, too, from those hot rocks in the sky. That would be perfect, because Willie knew every street and alley on the New Orleans waterfront, and every place to hide, and every place to grab a pretty lady and drag her into an alley and have his way with her. Yes, Old Willie knew all about that, and he didn't need any lights to do it, either. No, sir…not Willie.

Willie's mind wandered to the girl who danced at the Doll House, and he became embarrassingly erect. He smiled to himself because he already knew the alley where he would wait for her, and it was perfect, just perfect. He left his room immediately to go to the animal shelter where he cleaned cages occasionally to earn an extra few dollars. Public assistance didn't pay him very much, and he needed dollars to go to The Doll House. He felt his bowels suddenly get loose from the excitement of the thoughts he was having, but with an effort of sheer will power, he regained control and didn't mess himself. He would not live up to his nickname today.

\* \* \*

"My fellow Americans," Jameson Coleridge said, beginning his speech smoothly, even though he hated the circumstances of his prime-time address to the people of America. He was an excellent speaker, and under normal circumstances, he enjoyed speaking to the nation. This was not at all the case tonight. Coleridge had briefly considered the idea of presenting the situation to a joint session of Congress with full television coverage but had decided against it. Too many damned interruptions. Instead, he was speaking quietly to the nation from his desk in the Oval Office. Rita Morgenstern had made an ass out of him, and he had a lot of damage control to do.

"I am sure that by now you have heard many versions of the story first broken by Ms. Morgenstern on the NBC news at noon today and thereafter picked up by all the news media around this great nation of ours. What she had to say today was partly true but, for the most part, heavily overstated for dramatic effect. I am here tonight to tell you the truth." Jameson Coleridge sincerely wished that he could.

"You elected me last November on a plank of truth and honesty in government, and I am sure you are asking yourselves how an open and honest president could keep this kind of information from you. Here is the answer.

"While the story that Ms. Morgenstern reported this noontime was substantially correct, much of it was over sensationalized for effect. It is completely true that most of the world's people have been watching closely the progress of the large asteroid that the media have been calling the Mountain. I have been doing so myself, and why not? It is one of the most exciting astronomical events of our generation. This focus on the Mountain is and has been your individual choice because it is interesting. It is patently untrue that your government has been slanting the news and press releases to focus your attention upon it. Our national news media have a history of printing or broadcasting whatever they perceive to be the story that will garner the larger audience without any great regard for its merit or validity." White lie, with a good shot at the press corps.

"Ms. Morgenstern went to great length to describe the meteorite stream, which follows behind the asteroid as a huge mass of deadly debris approaching the earth which will undoubtedly and heavily bombard it in the process. This is not a certified fact at all. Yes, there is a meteorite stream, and yes, the earth will pass very close to part of it, but exactly which part has not yet been accurately predicted. The size and density of meteoroids in the contact area has not been determined." Monster white lie.

"Astronomers around the world have been studying the meteorite stream with earthbound optics, radar, and the most technologically advanced telescopes but still are unable to say for certain the extent to which Earth itself will be exposed." Huge white lie.

"Calculations have been made with the largest, fastest computers available to modern science, and with all of this technology, no one can predict the degree of our involvement." Monster white lie.

"I'm sure you are still asking yourselves, why the delay in sharing this information with us? We are all well-educated people and we can understand complex situations and handle difficult decisions; we do it every day, don't we? And you are quite correct in this, but the United States is not the only nation involved in this situation. As difficult as the decision was, I had to cooperate with leaders of all nations around the world in timing a joint message to be given when astronomical calculations were complete enough to accurately predict the degree of involvement and time of contact, but not so early that panic and public demonstrations caused more damage than the meteorites themselves." Complete crock of shit.

"Your government has been hard at work improving our nation's existing civil-defense system and preparing for all possible contingencies by utilizing both the American Red Cross and Salvation Army for local preparations in full cooperation with the United States military establishment who are responsible for national civil-defense preparations. We have also had the complete cooperation of, and are working in close coordination with, both state and local governments." Substantially true.

"I have terminated all exports of foodstuffs and of all strategic materials, including petroleum products, and have directed the military and Department of Agriculture to arrange for its relocation and safe storage in diverse staging areas." Substantially true, but grossly overstated.

"I, as your president, had to make the difficult decision as to the optimum time to release this information to you, the American public, and toward that end, and over the vehement protests of many of our allies overseas, I scheduled this speech several days ago." First part true, last a complete fabrication.

"At this moment, supplies of emergency equipment, food, medical supplies, and highly trained emergency personnel are in place all around the country, prepared to go into action in the event that they are needed. National Guard and regular service military personnel are on full alert and ready to react. Local police forces have been reinforced with National Guard troops to maintain law and order. My friends, that is all we can do at the present time. Until we see the situation develop, we must simply wait and pray." Partly true, mostly overstated.

"Please be assured that your government has done all that can be done to prepare for this and that you will be completely and accurately informed of the facts in this ever-changing situation. Our world is now in the hands of God." Huge overstatement for man, totally true for God.

"I implore you, as your president, to remain calm and to continue with your normal daily activities. Wait out the next several days along with me. It will be that long before the earth will reach the vicinity of the meteorite stream, and the possibility still exists that it may pass us by altogether." Wishful thinking, but it sounded good.

"Please continue to cooperate with your local civil authorities, and have patience with any inconvenience forced upon you by these circumstances. I will remain in the White House for the duration and will report daily to keep you informed of any new developments and your government's response to them. It is imperative that you remain calm and follow your local authority's directions." More totally wishful thinking.

"In the meantime, updates and instructions will be available through all media, including internet, television, and National Public Radio. You can rest assured that everything possible has been done and will be done to see to your safety and our national preparedness. My staff will issue regular press releases and informational updates as they become available." *People will be watching all right, but they'll be watching the sky, not the media.*

"Following this program, Dr. Benjamin Cohen, noted astronomer, will address you from the National Academy of Sciences building to explain, in much greater detail, the chronology of events leading up to today and explain as much as is possible what can be done as individuals to protect yourselves and your nation." True, as far as it went.

"I realize you have seen many frightening things on your televisions and on the internet today, with flaming mountains falling from the sky and all life on Earth being annihilated and mankind going the way of the dinosaurs. This will not happen, I assure you. But if you feel more comfortable having extra food or milk in the house, or need an excuse to buy new tools or camping equipment, then by all means, do so. I will certainly welcome the boost in our economy." Sick joke. "But please do it in an orderly manner. America is a wealthy nation, and there is more than enough to go around." True for the supply, untrue for the distribution.

"In closing, I ask for your understanding of my delay in reporting this discovery until now. The decision to delay was mine, and mine alone, and I accept the full responsibility for it. It has weighed heavily on my conscience to not be completely candid and forthcoming with the people who put me in this office, but my decision was made in what I perceived to be the best interest of you, my fellow Americans, and of people all around the world. At this very moment, leaders of nations great and small are speaking to their people just as I am doing now." Frosting on the cake.

"Again, I will ask you, the American people, to act calmly and courageously and to set the example for all nations of the world. Please stay abreast of events as they occur through your television, internet, and public radio stations. Watch for reports from your local authorities on regional conditions. As I have previously stated, this time slot will be reserved for me by all major television and radio networks, and I will speak to you daily until we are through these difficult times. I have arranged to have NASA and the National Academy of Sciences keep the media completely informed of any changes in the situation. This is the time to act responsibly, to remain composed, and to help your neighbors. If you know of a shut-in or of any special-needs person, please take the time to check on them and see that they are aware of this situation and prepared to face any problems. If they are not, please contact local authorities and they will respond immediately." More of the same.

"I am reminded of the quiet courage of Londoners during the Blitz of October 1940. Through several terrible weeks, they accepted daily bombings, terrible fires, and the lack of human services. Through all this, they went about their daily routine with calm and courage. They shared what they had, assisted and supported one another, and grieved together over their losses. In short, they acted like decent, civilized people, and I am certain that Americans today will do no less. America became the great nation that it is today because neighbor helped neighbor and all citizens pulled together for the common good. It is just that same spirit that will see us through the coming weeks. Now is the time for all Americans to take strength from each other and be the good neighbors that we know how to be.

"Thank you. God bless us all, and good night."

\* \* \*

Sally Prentiss stood calmly on the porch of the ramshackle farmhouse that had been in her family since it was built. It looked as if it hadn't seen a coat of paint or been otherwise improved very much since then. She held her jacket close to ward off the chilly March wind as John Halloran climbed down from a shiny new Jeep Grand Cherokee and waved to her. She smiled back at him as he came up to the porch. "Where's the old rust bucket?" she asked.

"Traded her in on this one. Like it?" John asked.

"Yes, but how'd you get it so fast?"

"Old friends with the Lacy family dealership in Catskill and no problem with credit. Did most of the paperwork online and on the phone while I was at work, and picked it up before stopping here. Just sign on the line and here she is. I had to pay an egregious price, though, because it seems like everyone wants one."

"I don't doubt that after Mr. Frosty made his little confession on national TV tonight. She's almost too pretty to drive on these muddy roads. What is that red thing you've mounted on the front bumper?" Sally asked, seeming quite interested.

"It's a Honda generator. You don't expect a power grid operator to be without power, do you? That's an electric winch next to it in case we get stuck."

"Taking a lot for granted, aren't you?"

"No, I don't think so. You did say that you caught the president on TV tonight?"

"You don't think one of those things is going to hit us and put all the lights out, do you?" Sally had assumed a defensive stance on the porch, and John noticed that she hadn't invited him inside. Her body language said very plainly, "Show me."

"I think that Washington knows a damned sight more than they are telling us and there's a good chance one of them is damned well going to hit us. I also think that if one or more does, then the power will definitely go off, at least in many places. I want you to believe that too and agree to come west with me."

"Why, John? You've got no commitment to me. You've got a nice girl out west to go to. My life is here." Sally riveted his eyes with a direct stare. "I serve you some breakfast, listen to your troubles now and then, and let you look down my dress once in a while, but that's no reason for you to ask me to uproot my life here and move to Colorado."

"You mean a lot more than that to me, Sally, and you damned well know it." It was John's turn to hold Sally's attention with his impassioned speech. "You are my best friend, Sally, and friends do not run out on friends when there's going to be trouble. Every time my life turned to shit, you were always there for me. It was you who convinced me to buy my house. You've always taken the time to listen to me cry in my coffee when my love life went sour, or complain about my job until you probably know enough about power grid operations to be able to do it as well as I do. You've guided and supported me through too many tough times for you not to know how much it meant to me. You're just too damned aloof and elusive to be more than friends, but you are still my best friend."

John's impassioned speech brought the shadow of a smile to Sally's lips.

"There is going to be trouble, Sally. The president didn't tell even half of what could or will happen when we get hit by a meteorite, and nobody that followed him told any more of the truth. It's a Washington, DC, snow job."

"Just how the hell do you know all this?" Sally asked, getting just a little angry. She tried for control, but her emotions seemed to be on a roller coaster. She wanted to hit him and hug him at the same time but wouldn't do either one, or let him know that she wanted to.

"Devon introduced me to a professor of astronomy from Colorado University, there in Boulder, and it was he who laid the whole scenario out for us. It wasn't pretty.

Let me tell you what I believe to be true, and then make up your own mind. You will anyway."

John spent the next half hour explaining to Sally, in as lurid detail as he could muster, the scenario Professor Schmidt had laid out for them at the Ratskeller in Boulder. Sally did not flinch at the description of the meteorite strikes or the tsunamis, and not too badly on the weather changes. When he talked about food shortages and transportation breakdowns and of the competition of people for the dwindling supplies, her eyes grew dark and brooding and he knew that he had struck a nerve. He pressed the point until he saw a fat tear begin to trickle from the corner of her eye. He felt a twinge of guilt at causing her pain, but his need to have her understand the situation and come to safety with him overcame it. He pressed on firmly.

"All I'm asking you to do is to close up this place so you can come to Colorado and visit with Devon and me for a few weeks. If the president is telling the truth and nothing happens, then I'll put you on a plane back here and nothing is lost except a little time. If we do get hit and Professor Schmidt is correct, then you'll be on high ground and among friends."

"When you put it that way, it's hard to say no, but I won't be ready to go until morning. Is that okay?"

John was a little taken aback by her sudden change of mind but gathered his wits about him quickly and said, "I have to work my last day shift tomorrow, but we can leave immediately after. They're pretty pissed at me for taking time off, but I have it coming to me and I forced the issue. Do you want me to pick you up?"

"No, I'll come over to your place. Should I bring anything special?" Sally's answer left no room for negotiation.

"Rough clothes, blankets or sleeping bags, and any personal items that you think you'll need. Really, anything that you think might come in handy in a situation like the one I just described."

"Alright, I'll be at your place tomorrow afternoon, around five." It was Sally's closing statement, and with it, she turned and went into the house without another word. John just stood there staring at the door, curious that he'd never been asked inside. Sally was a strange and silent girl sometimes. He shrugged it off and returned to the Jeep. He ran his hand over the beautiful dark red paint job and thought that he might get to like the Jeep as well as his old Chevy. Before he was out of her driveway, John was already thinking of several more preparations he could do before work in the morning.

* * *

Patsy Cox opened the door of her small house in Parsonsburg, Maryland to the sound of a jangling phone. It was a bad omen to have her phone ringing as soon as she arrived home after working her usual afternoon shift. Her heart was in her throat at the thought that something had gone wrong with one of her kids at the hospital. Patsy's mind raced back over the past eight hours. She had two post-op kids in the unit, but they had been doing well when she left. Her mind was so filled with these thoughts and concerns that it took her a second to realize she had picked up the phone and Tom Brooks was on the line.

"Patsy...Patsy...are you there?" Tom said with some concern obvious in his voice.

"I'm here, Tom. You just surprised me, calling right as I was getting home. I've got a couple of very sick kids in the unit, and I was worried one of them had gone bad."

"I'm sorry, Patsy."

"No matter. What do you want?"

"Did you hear the president's speech on the news tonight, Pats?"

"Yes, parts of it. I don't think I thoroughly understood it. I was at work, and I could only watch odd bits of it on the patients' TVs."

"We have known about some of it out here for a couple of days and haven't understood why Coleridge has been sitting on it. That's part of the reason why I called you the other night."

"Because some space junk is coming close to the earth, you decide to call an old girlfriend? You're going to have to do better than that, Tom."

"No, that's just part of it. They are going to hit us, Patsy, and probably hit us hard. Because of this situation, I've been so busy at work, I'm neglecting my family. My wife isn't well and can't help much."

"Well what can I do for you, Tom? I'm two thousand miles away."

"It's not that you can help so much as I got to thinking about you with Holly sick so much and that I don't like the idea of you being on the Eastern Shore if one of those meteorites should hit in the Atlantic. The tsunami would roll right over you. Then I got to thinking if I could talk you into coming west for a few weeks, you would be safe. I know it just sounds like crazy thinking now, but it made good sense to me at the time." Tom had a full head of steam up and was talking fast.

"Slow down, Tom, I can't understand you. What's a tsunami have to do with a meteorite strike?"

"Tsunami's just a Japanese name for a tidal wave. Around here, they call them seismic sea waves. A meteorite strike at sea can cause one, and they can be hundreds of feet high. That would be high enough to roll right over the Eastern Shore. It's not safe there, Patsy, and crazy or not, I want you to be safe."

"Crazy or not, you want me to be safe, wow, thanks Tommy," she said sarcastically.

"Patsy, I'm just lonely as hell all the time. I'm scared of what will happen to my children if something happens to Holly when I'm away working. I'm scared for you living on that overgrown sandbar. I'm just running on overload and need a friendly face."

"But why would I go there?"

"Because the coastlines are dangerous and we're on a mile-high plateau out here, and geologically, this is reasonably stable ground. You'd be safer here than anywhere else I can think of, and I'm here."

"How long will it take me to drive out there?"

"You could do it in two days."

"You said your wife was sick, Tommy. What's the problem?"

"She's made me promise not to tell you anything about her condition, Patsy. She wants to talk to you when you get out here."

Patsy was both surprised and curious about this but was sure this was a sick woman, very sick. "She knows you've been calling me, Tommy?"

"She asked me to call you, Patsy. She wants you to come out here, and she wants to talk to you."

"Oh, my God," Patsy said, the words coming out with a rush of air, sounding as if someone had hit her in the pit of the stomach. Her hand, holding the phone, trembled. "How long has she got, Tommy?"

"Not long now."

"I'll leave sometime tomorrow," she rushed, surprising herself at having made and communicated the decision without any conscious thought.

"Leave tonight."

"I just got home from work, Tommy. I'm tired. I'm not packed. I have to work tomorrow. I have people I have to see."

"Leave now, Patsy."

"But, I can't."

"Call work and tell them. Pack up the car and just leave. Everything else will take care of itself."

"You don't know what you're saying. For God's sake, Tommy, I can't just uproot my life and go running off to Colorado on a whim and not think of another thing. I just can't."

"Please, Patsy, don't argue with me. Just leave now."

There was a click and a buzz as Tommy Brooks hung up the phone, effectively cutting off any chance of further argument. Patsy stood there dumbfounded, staring at the receiver, with a million thoughts racing through her mind. *Why not do one wild and crazy thing in your life, girl? Go out and see him, just to see him, and let the rest take care of itself.* Patsy Cox hesitated for one more minute, then dialed the hospital.

Patsy's practical mind was already running down a list of things that she should do before leaving the only life she had known for more years than she cared to admit. Even so, her runaway mind was already driving down US Route 13 south toward Norfolk and then west across Virginia, and beyond that, half the continent. Patsy hated conflicts and found herself squarely in the middle of one, a big one: what to take and what to leave.

With a violent shake of her head, she began to toss away all the nonessentials and cut her packing to the bone. She went to her bedroom closet and took down her luggage. With an absolute minimum of wasted motion, she packed her clothing and toiletries. She then grabbed a square, heavy black nylon zipper bag and began packing up all the medical supplies she had accumulated at home for any type of emergencies. These supplies were quite significant. When this was done, she quickly packed the car.

Patsy was in high gear, and she had the good sense to go with it and let her instincts guide her actions. She emptied the refrigerator into the garbage, and then took the garbage outside. Then she locked up her home, looked back wistfully for a moment, and left in a spray of pea gravel from the driveway.

Now that the decision was made, Patsy wanted nothing more than to be on the road, but she knew she had several stops to make before she could. First, she needed to gas up the car and stop at a pharmacy. Then, she thought that she might just pay a last visit to Peninsula General. It would be nice to check on her kids quickly before she left. Those matters settled in her mind, she gripped the wheel tightly and blasted through the early spring night.

## Thursday, March 11

Angela Freece could not contain a small grin as she toyed with her scrambled eggs and watched Frank Muller apply himself studiously to the Big Breakfast Special at the Holiday Inn coffee shop.

"What's that smile all about?" Frank asked, still eating.

"I'll never tell," Angie said. "But you of all people should have a pretty good idea." It was Frank's turn to grin.

"What happens now, Frank?" she asked.

"Devon Grant checked out early and took a cab back to her apartment. I assume she's at work," Frank answered, chasing the last piece of sausage around his plate. "My car is gone, so I also assume Dommy has taken our friends to Denver. I told him to deposit them as he saw fit, so I imagine they're not too comfortable. Dommy never liked them any more than I did. What do you say about us taking a ride up there in your rental, just to check?"

"Works for me," Angie answered, still smiling. "Is Dommy staying up in Denver?"

"Yes, I told him to hang loose for a couple of days. He needed to check on his family and take care of a few errands for me. Maria gets nervous if he's away too long."

"You know, Frank Muller, you try very hard to come across as some sort of a bureau hard-ass, but you're really an old softy."

"Not always." Frank treated her with a rare mischievous grin.

"No argument there, but what remains of this surveillance for us?"

"I assume our subjects had some knowledge of the meteorite situation that NBC broke yesterday and that Coleridge quickly followed up. What a case of obvious damage control that was. I'm glad the leak didn't come from here, but since the cat is out of the bag now, I assume our assignment is pretty well done."

"What's next, then?" Angela asked over the rim of her coffee cup.

"I've got a call in for Vito, and when he calls back, we should have some new instructions. Meanwhile, let's take a nice slow ride back to Denver. I told him that I needed you to stay out here a while longer, and I do. He agreed."

"Sounds like a plan to me." Angela was smiling foolishly again and hoping that Frank didn't notice."

He did, but he didn't give a damn; he felt the same way.

\* \* \*

Devon Grant was far too busy at work this morning to be watching the depressing news on television. The monitor she was looking at had a listing of her priority-one customers, and she was busily running down the list and notifying them of an impending severe solar storm. No time to think about Jackass Valley, or meteorites, or strangers in her room, or anything but wading through the list.

This storm had begun appearing on the edge of the sun's visible disc two days before, while she was off. Everyone at Space Environmental Labs was excited about it because it exhibited all of the characteristics of a major storm and quite possibly one of the largest solar storms on record. Devon had saved the New York ISO call until last.

"NYISO, Halloran," came the voice over the phone, and Devon felt both flooded with relief at hearing John's voice and anger that he was still there.

"This is the Space Weather Prediction Center, and I have an SMD alert for you." Devon was very cool and efficient.

"Yes, go ahead."

"An SMD of K-8 intensity was observed from 11:00 to 14:00 universal time on March tenth. Additional SMDs of K-9 intensity are expected over the next twenty-four to forty-eight hours. I already know your initials."

"Devon, it's great to hear from you. I tried calling you all day yesterday, and last night, too, but you weren't home. I've been worried out of my skin."

"I was out with a sky guy, if you know what I mean."

"All night?"

"No, that's not what I mean, but I'm glad you noticed. Too much happened yesterday to talk about on this phone. Why haven't you left yet?"

John was not about to be put off by the anger in her voice; there was too much he wanted to tell her and too much he wanted to know about what she had been doing. He maintained a steadfast calm and said, "I'm leaving right after my shift ends this afternoon." He wondered briefly why he hadn't told her about bringing Sally out with him. He had fully intended to and had even rehearsed the message in his mind, but when the time had come to do so, he choked and simply glossed over it. Oh well, time enough to worry about that later.

"Hurry, John! I love you, and I miss you, and I want you out here."

"I know, and I will, and I love you too," he said, concerned by her obvious stress. "Just tell me if you're alright?"

"I'm fine, John; it's just that things got a little crazy around here for a while." She wanted badly to tell him about almost being raped.

"And you're really okay?" John persisted. "I have to know."

"Yes, John, I'm fine. Just hurry up, and remember I love you." The sadness in her voice made John long to hold her and keep her safe.

"Same here, only double. I'll see you in a couple of days, Devon."

"The sooner the better."

"Devon, have all priority ones been notified?" asked Art Capiletti from the solar forecaster's desk.

"Yes, I just finished the last one," Devon replied.

The sly grin on Art's face told Devon he had heard the conversation and knew she had notified New York out of order. She almost blushed.

"I know, just finish up the priority twos and threes as quickly as you can," Art said. "This is the biggest storm we've ever seen, and we're going to be busy."

"Yes, boss." she grinned over at him.

Art's warm brown eyes smiled at her from under his half glasses, and he gave her a big wink, then turned back to his work. Art was a warm and good-hearted man, and Devon enjoyed working with him. He had been very patient during her training and orientation and had taught her a lot. She knew with this new storm, he would be terribly busy, and she felt a little guilty about not helping more. She took the report Art had prepared, and went over to the fax machine. She selected the automatic send feature for priority-two customers and sent it off.

Active Region 7045 had been recognized by the Space Environment Lab as a significant event even before it had rotated into view. Significant solar flare activity had been noted in the region behind the sun's visible disc for the past three days, and forecasters at SWPC had been anxiously awaiting its appearance.

When 7045 had finally rotated into view this morning, it had revealed a huge area of large sunspots arranged in a very compact configuration. This was a true indication of a major storm in the making. The sunspots in 7045 had also been quickly classified as having the highest degree of magnetic complexity, using the Mount Wilson magnetic classification system.

Two separate solar flares were in progress from the region, both of them sending huge amounts of energy looping outward from the sun's surface into space and returning to the solar surface in fiery ellipses. The energy being expelled from them was huge and would be affecting Earth very soon.

A sunspot appears to earthbound observers as simply a darkened area on the surface of the sun. In reality, it is an area of transient and highly concentrated magnetic fields that writhe and coil like a basket of snakes. A moderate-sized sunspot can cover an area as large as the earth and may form and dissipate several times over a period of weeks. The darkened appearance on the surface of the sun of these concentrated magnetic fields actually indicates a cooling of the sun's surface temperature from a normal temperature of 6000 C down to 4200 C.

Active regions of sunspot activity frequently produce solar flares such as the ones that were appearing today. Flares are intense but temporary and have been known to release energy equivalent to forty billion atomic bombs the size of the one that dropped on Hiroshima. Their source seems to be the tearing apart and reconnection of the strong magnetic fields writhing within the active sunspot regions. The resultant flares of visible light also release huge amounts of magnetic energy. Area 7045 was producing all of these activities in abundance. It was very intense.

One to four days after a flare or an eruptive event appears on the solar surface, a cloud of solar material and magnetic energy travels approximately ninety-three million miles and reaches the earth to buffet the earth's own magnetic field and cause a geomagnetic storm. These storms produce extraordinary variations in the earth's magnetic field both at the earth's surface and in the area in space surrounding Earth known as the magnetosphere. These variations are known to cause widespread communications disruptions, problems with electronic and satellite navigation systems, disruptions in railroad communications, and a number of unpleasant reactions on electric power systems.

The solar energy itself is intense enough to cause increased drag on orbiting satellites and would be extremely hazardous to astronauts in orbit. The energy expelled from the sun in the form of protons and electrons is what excites atoms of gas in the earth's atmosphere and causes the vivid and colorful auroral displays in both north and south polar regions. The colors and intensity of these displays can give observers on Earth an indication of the intensity of the storm.

Forecasters at the Space Weather Prediction Center had been tracking 7045 with interest, and it was proving to be larger and more intense than area 5395, which had caused considerable damage to terrestrial communications equipment and satellites and caused a province-wide blackout in Quebec, Canada in March 1989.

Things were definitely heating up and getting tense.

\* \* \*

Amos Bellinger usually enjoyed the occasional breakfast meeting at the White House. The coffee was excellent, and the kitchen provided an interesting, well-prepared, and beautifully presented menu. Unfortunately, this morning, Amos was in no mood to enjoy the cuisine or the ambiance. The president sat, dark and brooding, across the small table, eating his meal without really tasting it. "You can begin whenever you want, Amos," was all he said to start. This was not going to be any fun.

"Sir, I might as well start with Ms. Morgenstern and NBC. It can only get better from there."

The president's scowl indicated this was not his favorite subject. After yesterday's broadcast, the president had wanted to deport the entire staff to a far northern Gulag Prison camp in Siberia. After the press reviews of his speech to the nation the night before, he had revised this to the death penalty: slow strangulation with a silken cord.

"Ms. Morgenstern has a fifteen-minute time slot reserved on the noon news today, and another spot at seven p.m. After much discussion, she has agreed not to stir up any more trouble and to severely curb the sensational pictures and dialogue. She has promised to continue to play it straight so long as we keep feeding her the newest situation updates. Well ahead of all the other networks. I think we should consider doing this in order to keep her in line, and possibly, after we gain some confidence in her performance, we can use her for our own purposes."

"How exactly do you propose we do this?"

"As you know, we have been forced to use the National Guard to reinforce roadblocks controlling egress from several cities. We have given her this information in a form that subtly attempts to make the evacuees appear to be cowardly and traitors to the nation in time of national stress and the National Guard look like loyal Americans who are just doing their job as ordered by their president. The last thing we need is to have the media digging up footage of Kent State." Amos continued with as much conviction as he could muster. "If she handles this well, then we may be able to use her to pass on some other disinformation."

"You can give it a try, Amos, but remember she's hard to fool. I think she'll spot your subtitles in a second and throw them back in your face."

"She gave up her source with surprisingly little fight, and we have taken Mr. Ryder and that asshole Braxton under the protective custody of the Secret Service, and none too gently. I told Agent Maloy to use that huge beast, Agent Somervold, the one you used to joke around with on the South Lawn."

This news brought the semblance of a small grin to the president's troubled features. "What about Braxton's staff?"

"Apparently, only Ryder was privy to any information, and only because he put a bug in Braxton's phone."

"He did what?" the president asked in amazement.

"He bugged his boss's phone."

"Don't put that bastard in jail, Amos; give him a job with the CIA. But seriously, keep them under wraps. Can we arrange to have someone on hand to put a foot in Ms. Morgenstern's mouth if she should get out of line later today?" Coleridge asked, looking up from his food.

"I don't think so, sir. The station has a battery of reporters and lawyers standing by to make sure her First Amendment rights are not impinged. I'll look into it personally and try to get a couple of bureau people in there just in case."

"What about some unavoidable technical difficulties?"

"That is being looked into."

"Good," the president said halfheartedly.

"General Gates's report is a lot more encouraging. His national civil-defense plan is progressing nicely, and his zone headquarters have been established and their communications tested. The troops are in place and have already responded to a few local problems. The Canadians and Mexicans are also cooperating well. According to his first report, there appears to be surprisingly little civil unrest, and in general, the people seem to be adopting a sort of wait-and-see attitude. Those families that are leaving are the ones who own property or have relatives in the country. They have a legal place to go, so the Guard is letting them through."

"I am surprised at that," the president said. "I expected the shit to hit the fan right away."

"I feel the same way, sir, but I'm happy for any respite we can get. Cohen and Van Patten have been doing a masterful job of supplying the public with just enough information to keep them satisfied without scaring the hell out of them. They have effectively been playing down the very real possibility of communications and transportation breakdowns, and shortages of consumables. General Gates has reported a little panic buying. There have been numerous incidences of runs on food stores, and also on hardware and sporting goods stores, but no real disturbances. People have been busily emptying their bank accounts, and a lot of buying is on credit cards. Treasury is a little worried about the economy whether or not we receive any meteorite hits."

Amos paused so the president could take all of this in, and then he continued, "In a few days, there will begin to be shortages in some food items and there won't be an ax or a blanket or a battery to be had anywhere. This may very well be when some problems start to show up. Lastly, we've had a few incidences of store or warehouse robberies, and of all things, a few truck hijackings. Nothing too serious, however, and General Gates has it under control. All in all, it appears that people are cautiously preparing for the worst while hoping for the best. There have been a few incidences of violence, but nothing out of hand. No large-scale looting or civil unrest in the inner cities at all. The quiet is making the local police uneasy."

The president remained quiet, reserved, and very attentive.

Amos followed up with, "Ben Cohen has an unusual theory about this. He's of the opinion that people are so glutted on science-fiction and mass-mayhem movies that they are viewing this situation more like a story or video game than reality and might continue to do so until something really sensational happens to shake them out of their current lethargy. God grant us some time, or a nice clean miss."

Jameson Coleridge shook his head and said, "It's not the same overseas. Europe seems to be having an unusual amount of civil unrest. I have reports from London and Paris of numerous incidences of ethnic confrontation and some near riots. CIA reported severe fighting in Dresden, Hamburg, and especially in Munich. There have been over a hundred killed so far in Germany, with a considerable amount of looting and arson. It seems like some unemployed Germans are bound on taking back what they feel was lost to the imported foreign labor.

"The Serbs have taken the opportunity to go on the offensive against the Bosnians and Muslims again. Fortunately for us, we have just pulled the last of our peacekeepers out. They now have a free hand to continue their ethnic cleansing. The only bright side is we left some very good equipment behind for the Bosnians, and I hope they kick the Serbs' asses with it. Either way, that poor country is going to be a mess, even before any meteorites can get here."

It was Amos's turn to look dejected at the sad state of world affairs.

"The Japanese are currently experiencing a number of mass demonstrations against nuclear power. The Fukushima event is still far too fresh in their minds. The people are demanding the government to force the shutdown of all their nuclear power plants. They're understandably sensitive about radiation threats. Premier Sanjomoto is trying every way possible to calm their fears, apparently to no avail. It appears that older Japanese are remaining calm but the younger people are taking to the streets. When the Japanese media picked up on our nuclear-unit shutdown and went to press with it, the entire nation started demanding their government do the same. Unfortunately for the government, the economy is based on production, and production requires huge amounts of electricity. They are in a catch-22. They can't shut down their nuclear generation without shutting down major parts of their heavy industry or blacking out residential customers. There is so much red tape built into the Japanese bureaucracy that I don't think either alternative will ever be used. Sanjomoto's got a real mess on his hands."

At that, Amos responded, "On the same subject, Liz Coulter has been watching TV and has ordered our remaining nuclear generating plants off the line. The pressurized-water reactors are starting to come off-line today. I called her on this, but she is obstinate and says doing this may cause some local brown-outs but that the industry as a whole can withstand the loss. I really believe she'd shut them down even if we had to shut down the whole country."

"Liz is a tough customer, but I think she has the right idea in this case," Jameson Coleridge said thoughtfully. "I have told Premier Givorsky the same thing and urged him to do the same with his nuclear units. Unfortunately, I had to suffer through a long lecture on how Russian technology has improved since Chernobyl and how all safety precautions have been instituted. Immediately after this tirade was finished, I got a complete stonewall as usual, and no assurance he would even consider this alternative. It's their funeral, I guess.

"All in all, I think things are a lot more stable than I had envisioned for the first day after the announcement. I hope this trend continues for a few more days so the military can get completely set up and in control of their civil-defense zones.

"Well, Amos, anything else?"

"There is one other thing I think you should take under advisement, Mr. President."

"And what might that be?"

"You're leaving Washington for Cheyenne Mountain and keeping the vice president here until you are established."

"Absolutely not!" Jameson Coleridge roared. "I told the people that I would be here in Washington at the helm, and here I will be."

"Yes, sir, I understand that, but I think it more important that you survive this mess and preserve the continuity of your administration than play the hero and allow the country to be run by men far less qualified than yourself."

"That sounds flattering, Amos, but I lied to them once, and I will not do that again." The look on the president's face was enough to convince Amos that any further argument would be futile.

"Will you at least let me make preparations for relocating the federal government to a safer place in the event that Washington, DC, becomes unsafe or unusable as the nation's capital?" Amos was praying silently as he finished his request.

"You can make your contingency plans, Amos, but that will be as far as it goes."

"Yes, sir, and thank you."

\* \* \*

"Lisa," Amos said as he entered his office and began gathering papers, "Institute plan B immediately. Call Andrews and get yourself a hop out to Cheyenne Mountain. Call me on a secure line when you get there and get things in motion. Before you leave, make absolutely sure that Kingpin is in motion to join you there, understand?"

"Yes, completely."

"Hop to it. I'll arrange the necessary clearances."

"What about the president?"

"He'll stay until Washington, DC, becomes uninhabitable; then we'll helicopter out and catch our ride to Cheyenne. It's all arranged."

"Good. I'll see you there?"

"Yes, Lisa, I'll be there."

"Be sure, Amos, because I think I love you."

Amos Bellinger's look of amazement was not unnoticed as Lisa Howard came forward into his arms and hugged him tightly for a fleeting moment before leaving the room. He watched her shapely figure with smiling appreciation as she went quickly down the carpeted hallway. His look turned to one of concern as he turned to his desk and began making arrangements.

\* \* \*

"Persons residence," came the boyish voice through the phone.

Mark Persons's heart rate began to decelerate toward normal at the sound of his son's voice on the line. "Clint, this is Dad. It's great to hear your voice."

"Hi, Dad. How are things out in the Rockies? Is there much snow left out there? Are you going to be there long?" The questions came shotgun fashion, the next one coming before Mark had a chance to answer the first.

"Whoa, slow down, Clint."

"Sorry, Dad. I just got a little excited. Mom said we may be coming out to see you."

"That's great, son. That is what I was calling about. Is Mom there?"

The phone line went silent, and the silence stretched on for a seemingly endless time. "Clint, are you still there?" Mark asked.

"Mom's not here, Dad," the youthful voice said, hushed and tentative.

"Where is she, son? I have to speak to her."

"I don't know, Dad."

"What do you mean, you don't know?" Mark was beginning to get frazzled with the way the conversation was going, and more than a little upset. Mark realized from his younger son's almost frightened tone that he would get nowhere with him. "Is your brother there?"

"Hold on, Dad."

Mark could hear Clint calling in the background, "Eric, Eric, come to the phone! Dad wants to talk to you."

Mark Persons waited for a minute or so. He could hear the boys talking animatedly in the background, but no one came on the line until his elder son, Eric, picked up and said, "Hello, Dad?"

"Yes, it's me. What the hell is going on out there?" Mark could not help venting some of his frustration.

"Jeez, I'm sorry, Dad, but Mom ain't here. She went away with a friend the day before yesterday, and she hasn't come back yet." Eric's voice was also showing the sharp edge of fear.

"Do you mean to tell me that she has left you two boys alone for two days?"

"No, Dad, Elisa is here with us, and after all, I'm fourteen and old enough to take care of us. I told Mom that before she left."

"Who the heck is Elisa?" Alarm bells were sounding in Mark's head, and his temper was on the loose.

"She's a girl mom hired to cook and clean up and stay with us when she has to be away for school stuff."

"What do you mean, school stuff? What kind of school stuff?"

"I don't know, just college stuff she's doing."

"Who did she go with?"

"Professor Morton."

"Andrew Morton?"

"Yes."

Mark's mind went reeling wildly at this news. Erotic pictures of Connie and Andy Morton kept playing in his head as he tried to think and reason out what to do. Andy Morton was a professor of American Indian anthropology. Native American, Andy would always remind you, was the politically correct term, but it all meant the same to Mark.

Andy and his wife, June, had been friends with Mark and Connie before their split-up over a year ago. June Morton had long been upset over Andy's philandering around among the undergraduate females at Texas Tech College in Houston, and the final break had come after she walked into his office one day unexpectedly and found him in a compromising position with a half-naked eighteen-year-old blonde student. This was not Native American study.

The Mortons and the Personses had drifted apart after that, with Connie and June remaining good friends while Andy's visits became less and less frequent. Mark wondered how good of friends they'd be after June found out about these little field trips. Andy was a good-looking bastard and had always had a way with the ladies, and now Connie was going on field trips with him, without the boys. Mark did not like the sound of this at all.

"Eric," Mark said as calmly as he could, "what did your mom say about you and Clint coming out to Boulder for a visit?"

"She said you had asked for us to come and that she was thinking about it."

"This was before she went off with Professor Morton?"

"Yes, Dad."

Mark made his decision instantly. "Eric, I want you to listen to me very carefully."

"Okay, Dad."

"I want you to go and look in the top drawer of my dresser. See if there's a Bank of Houston Visa card there. Go now." Mark's tone left no room for argument. Mark and Connie had always kept this credit card in the dresser so it would be handy in case of emergency but not to be used casually.

Eric was back in a few moments. "Yes, Dad, the credit card is here."

"Great. Now listen carefully. I want you to call Anytime Travel and book a flight for you and your brother from Houston to Denver, Colorado, on the very first available flight. Give the person at the travel agency the Visa card number and make sure they confirm the reservation. Do you understand me so far?"

"Yes, Dad."

"Then pack your outdoor clothing. Be sure to bring warm clothes; it's still pretty cold here in Boulder. I want you to write your mother a note explaining what you have done, and why, and leave it with Elisa. Then call me on my cell phone. Do you have something to write with?"

"Yes." The answers were getting more crisp and less frightened.

"I may not be able to answer when you call, but leave a message as to what airline you are flying and your ETA. I will be at the airport to meet you. Take a taxi to the airport, and ask Elisa to loan you some money to pay for it. Mom can pay her back when she gets home. Do you understand all of this?"

Eric Persons related back to his father all of his instructions with crisp military precision. "Wonderful," Mark said. "Now get to it, son, and I'll be seeing you in Denver. Remember to call me with the flight and ETA."

"Dad, are you sure this will be all right with Mom?"

"Don't worry, Eric. I'll straighten your mom out when I speak to her."

Eric simply said, "Yes, Dad," and hung up.

Mark Persons's mind was ablaze with anxiety over his wife's strange behavior, his sons' safety, and how to sandwich a trip to Denver to pick them up into his busy schedule. The new solar magnetic disturbance was raising hell with his satellites, and now the Air Force wanted to put up some specially armored communications birds on an emergency schedule. They were bugging him to bypass flight safety rules for a shuttle crew during a solar event. A man should never be posed with two impossible tasks at the same time, he thought as he bent to his work, hoping Eric was already making the plans.

\* \* \*

Rita Morgenstern kept her jaw clamped tightly shut and took several long deep breaths, inhaling through her nose and exhaling through her mouth slowly. This was an old and longstanding relaxation exercise that she could do without anyone noticing. As she was breathing, she kept her eye on the director as he counted the time down from the commercial break to her cue. Fingers closing down into a fist, he ticked off five…four…three…two…one…and she was back on the air. "Good afternoon, ladies and gentlemen. This is Rita Morgenstern, bringing you an update on the meteorite-storm situation."

Rita had to keep her eyes slightly to the left of center on the camera to keep the left-hand window of the control room in the periphery of her vision. She knew two Secret Service agents were standing by in the control room of NBC4-TV, and she knew that they were fully prepared to take whatever action necessary to prevent her from further terrorizing the American people with career-building sensationalism. She also knew they were terrified of what Amos Bellinger would do if they failed to keep her in line and that they fully intended to make sure that this would not happen. Unfortunately for the agents, Rita had other plans.

She began her segment smoothly and followed exactly along the lines that had been agreed upon before air time. Rita could see the agents began to relax as her silky-smooth voice repeated the government's wait-and-see theme. It began to appear to the agents that this would not be quite the hair-raising assignment it first appeared to be. They were dead wrong.

It was time. From the broadcast desk, Rita could see Kimberly Salisbury slowly rise from her seat and give a conspiratorial wink. The statuesque blonde girl slowly stretched across the console as if reaching for something in front of her on the window ledge. This simple movement caused her tight white miniskirt to stretch across her shapely young buttocks and rise up alarmingly, exposing the lacy tops of her stockings and a small expanse of naked thigh above them. A barely noticeable nod told Rita the Secret Service agents had not failed to notice. Men were so disgustingly predictable.

As smoothly as a well-oiled piece of equipment, Rita shifted from the accepted text and flipped the switch on an already open phone line to Reverend Randall P. Davis at his home in Wheeling, West Virginia. The two Secret Service agents were still talking quietly together, contemplating the well rounded and perfect ass of the young blonde production assistant. Rita was pretty sure they were speculating on how Kimberly could bend over in that tight skirt and show no panty lines. It was a subject worthy of consideration.

By the time the men realized what was happening in the studio, the trap had closed on them and the phone interview had already begun. Now they could not cut it off without raising serious questions of government interference by both the station management and the television audience, but if they let it run, Amos Bellinger would have their collective ass. They stood there for a few moments, paralyzed with indecision until Kimberly Salisbury slowly turned around to them and smiled a very slow, very sexy grin. They'd been had.

"Reverend Davis, we have both had our First Amendment rights to free speech impinged upon by the government. I know very well how I feel about that, and I and my viewers would like to know how you feel."

"Miss Morgenstern, I have been at war with myself for several days. I believe I am a good and loyal American, and I have always supported my country both in my personal life and from my pulpit. Now I am faced with the terrible choice of maintaining the loyalty to my country which I was taught as a child or the belief in the guidance of my God which I believe in with all my heart."

The screen showed some publicity footage provided obligingly by WVM-TV of Reverend Davis's modest parsonage and his family, and some excellent footage of him preaching in his small church in West Virginia. Truth and sincerity glowed in his eyes as he spoke to his small congregation. Rita was inset in a window on the screen, speaking into a dummy telephone handset. "Reverend Davis, our time may be short, so I will ask only for your heartfelt word to the American people."

"My good friends," Randy began sincerely, "listen to your hearts. I have nothing to gain from speaking falsely and bringing fear into your lives. In truth, I may lose my own freedom for speaking to you today. I have told you that I fully believe the angels of God are descending upon the earth and woe is he who does not believe, repent, and prepare for that day. I also firmly believe that God has given me the task of bringing this message to you, and I will follow His will as I always have, no matter the personal cost to me or my family. You must have faith in yourselves. Help yourselves, help your neighbors, and always follow the word of God, and you will be saved from these terrible times."

"Thank you, sir. That was Reverend Randall P. Davis speaking to you by phone from his home in Wheeling, West Virginia, where he is being held a veritable hostage by the FBI for speaking the word of his God to his flock. There is nothing more I can add to these words, so I will simply say good luck and Godspeed to you all." Rita signed off with the angelic look of a choir girl.

"We've been had." the Secret Service men said almost simultaneously. They were quite correct.

"What the hell are we going to do?" the younger agent asked.

"Cuff her and take her in. After that, we report to Amos Bellinger, and if we survive that, we can pack our bags and accept our new assignments, probably monitoring the migration of imperial penguins in the Bering Strait."

\* \* \*

The sun was already quite low in the western sky as John Halloran stood leaning against the side of his brand-new Grand Cherokee and watching Sally Prentiss's battered Toyota pull up the drive from Lone Pine Road. The car appeared to be loaded to the hilt, and there also seemed to be an extra passenger. John was more than a little curious. Sally stopped alongside the brand-new Jeep and got out of the car with a determined expression on her face. She looked John directly in the eye, almost daring him to comment as she glanced back into the car at her boy who was ten years of age. The boy wore a sullen expression below a shock of red hair, and he had a scattering of freckles and two ears that would take him a while to grow into. She said proudly, "John Halloran, I'd like you to meet my son, Paul."

John stood as if rooted to the spot, his mouth hanging open in surprise. As long as he had known Sally, she never once mentioned having a son. Now that he took time to think about it, she had never said very much about her own personal life at all, while at the same time managing to pump out of him everything about his own. She was pretty crafty.

"Well don't just stand there catching flies, John. You'd better help me load this stuff if you want to get started today."

John snapped out of his contemplation and found his voice. "Hi, Paul, how are you?"

"I'm fine, call me Butch," was the boy's brief reply as he got out of the car. He treated John to a long, accusing look that spoke volumes of how he felt about being taken from his father, and then he bent to retrieve a knapsack off the floor. His hair was red from his mother, but not as bright. His deep voice and large, gangly frame obviously came from Duke Duncan.

"Duke never liked the name Paul and has always called him Butch," Sally said with a resigned shrug. "I guess he likes it better too."

The Cherokee was fairly well loaded already, and John had left only a small space on the back seat for Sally's gear. Sally had thought to purchase a rooftop carrier from Sears Roebuck, and after the carrier had been strapped onto the Jeep's roof rack, it provided ample room for her things and some room for Butch. Sally had two nylon duffel bags with clothing and sundries, and several boxes that were obviously from food vendors of some sort. "What's in here?" John asked, surprised at how light one of the boxes was in relation to its size.

"Spices. They'll be worth their weight in gold one day, if this mess of yours comes off."

It was only a matter of a few minutes for them to load up the Cherokee and mount up. After loading Sally's stuff, there was very little room for Butch in the back seat, but he sat quietly with his jaw set and didn't complain. Then they were off down the road. At the intersection of New York Routes 7 and 20, John put on his turn signal to turn east on Route 20. "Just where the hell do you think you're going, Halloran?" Sally asked briskly.

"I thought I'd drop by work to see how things are, then swing up and onto the I-90."

"Not in this lifetime, Halloran. If it's so damned important to be heading west, then we're going west. The NYISO got along without you before you came, and they'll get along without you now. Let's go."

Sally's voice was firm, and her logic made sense, as usual. John changed the turn signal direction and, when the light changed, swung west on NY Route 20, headed for Boulder. Neither of them noticed the massive bank of dark clouds building to the south and they would have no clue as to the cause until later—much later.

\* \* \*

"How about another beer, Frank?" Vito Pianese said as he muted the sound of the CNN commentators giving Americans their personal analysis of the president's speech, what they should have heard and learned from it.

"No thanks, I'm one over my limit now."

"What did you think of the old man's speech last night?" Vito asked.

"I only caught part of it while I was having dinner, but from what I did see, and from what the networks are telling me I should have seen, I think he covered the subject admirably but that he covered it with bullshit."

"Nicely put, and about the way I felt about it." Vito shrugged.

"Can you tell me what our surveillance subjects knew about this meteorite mess and why Washington had us sitting on them?"

"Our friends in Washington didn't really have any clear idea of what they knew, or what they would do with the information if they did discover anything. We were here to make sure these individuals did not go public with a meteorite scare before Washington was ready to come clean." Vito's expression said more than words about how he felt on the subject. "What are you going to do Frank, now that the surveillance is over here in Boulder?"

"I think I'll take a few weeks of my leave and just kick back for a while. How about you?" Frank knew his boss well enough to know when something was bothering him, and this was one of these times.

"Well, now that you ask, I was planning to take Florence and the children back east for a while. She wants to be with her family in case something really is happening out there, and Tony is at Georgetown. I was going to ask you to take over the office while I'm away, but if you've got other plans…" Vito hesitated.

"You know damned well I'll watch the store for you but, maybe you can do something for me when you're back east."

"What's that?" Vito asked, obviously pleased.

"Go and see Cathy for me. She's staffing for Senator Dave Drahman. I'd like you to talk to her and see if you can convince her to come out here for a week or so, just to visit the old man. We've grown apart some since Lori died, and watching Devon Grant and some of the things she did made me think a lot about Cathy. I'd sure like to see her. Maybe have a chance to put things right between us. You know?"

"Yes, I know, but why don't you call her and ask her yourself?"

"I have. Several times, in fact, but she just puts me off gently and says that she will come out someday, when she can get the time off. Only I have the feeling that someday will never come."

"It's a deal. You watch the store, and I'll go and see Cathy. Uncle Vito will use all of his Mediterranean charm on her; she can't resist that."

The two old friends shook on it and went back to nursing their beers and watching the silent TV scenes of disaster.

\* \* \*

Willie Seaman was crouched down between two garbage cans about halfway down an alley in the middle of St. Charles Street. It was dark and damp there, and more than a little scary, but Willie didn't mind. He was holding a small kitten in his lap, and it was purring gently as he gently stroked its head, while another slept quietly in the sack at his feet. He knew what he was going to do, and to pass the time and calm his fears, he was trying to keep his mind focused on what Gina was doing in her last dance number at the Doll House. He thought about her all naked up on the stage, or all naked in the shower after she was done for the night and getting ready to walk home. Willie knew that Gina always walked home from work. Willie knew this because he had followed her, many times, right past this alley. And she never even knew that he was there.

Willie Seaman knew very well who he was, and what he was, and what the police would do to him if they caught him. The police had caught him peeking through some windows at girls who would undress in their apartments without closing their blinds. The girls had thought they couldn't be seen because they were up high enough, or off a remote alley, or in the back of a building, but they couldn't fool old Willie. The police had beaten him and thrown him in a jail cell with some men who had done worse things to him than just beat him up. Willie did not want this to happen again, no sir, not again, but his feeble mind kept repeating that those hot rocks would be falling from the sky and that the police would be busy with other things and let poor old Willie alone.

Willie had been born to an alcoholic prostitute of a mother and a missing father, and he had always been a little slow in the head. He had never been able to keep up with the other kids in school, and because of an unfortunate lack of bowel control in times of stress, he had always been teased unmercifully.

But Willie had grown up tough and street-smart and had managed to survive all his problems, until that night. That terrible, awful night so long ago. He tried not to think about that night, but it kept coming back in his dreams, his wake-up screaming dreams. "Here comes Willie," the kids in the neighborhood would shout when he came out to play. "Ya got any lumps in yer drawers today, Willie?" No matter how many times he heard it, it still hurt him. "Ya shit yourself today, Willie?" It never ended. "You got your diapers on today, Willie?"

Because of these taunts and because he could never think of an adequate response to them, he had retreated within himself and become a loner. Willie had prowled the neighborhood and the riverside dock area day and night, learning all the places he could hide away or could while away a few hours spying on people and making up stories in his head. That was better than school or reading, which only served to make his head all woozy.

The only happy times in his young life had been the rare occasions his mother would take him into her bed on a Sunday morning and hold his head to her chest. She would often cry silently and croon softly to him, rubbing his hair and telling him things would be all right when their ship came in. Willie had no idea what kind of ship she was referring to, but he would often go down to the riverside and closely watch all the ships on the river, just to see if one of them might be his. It never came.

Life was not perfect, but Willie had gotten along all right until that night. It was a horrible night which left him with no mother and no mind to use either; he was left with only the wake-up crying dreams. Willie had been twelve years old, and he had known what his mama had to do so they could live. She had made him understand that if the bedroom shade was down, he was not to come into the apartment for any reason because mama was working.

That night, Willie had had to go real bad and had not wanted to mess up his pants and start getting called Lump Lump again. He had thought he could sneak in quietly to use the bathroom and no one would know. That had been his first mistake.

As soon as he had sneaked in through the back door, he had known something was wrong—terribly wrong. The bright coppery smell of blood had been in in the air, and he could hear Mama making a funny sound through her nose. The bedsprings had been squeaking something awful, and Willie could not help but to take a peek into the bedroom. That had been his second mistake.

There had been a man on the bed with Mama, and they had been rolling around and making noises. This was nothing new to Willie, as he had watched his Mama roll around the bed with a veritable parade of "uncles" and "friends" over the years and was vaguely aware he shouldn't be watching, but this had been different, very different. There had been blood.

Looking closer in the semi-dark, he could see that Mama's step-ins had been stuffed into her mouth, her hands had been tied to the bedposts, and she was bleeding in several places. The man had been on top of her and doing it to her, but he had also been cutting her with a knife that he had in his hand and mumbling incoherently. Mama's legs had been wrapped around him. The man had made a finish as Willie had heard his mama try to say something, and as she did, she had reared up and groaned in pain, then the man had plunged the long knife down into her chest. Mama had bucked a couple of times real hard and then lain very, very still.

Willie had been so frightened, he had lost all control of his bowels right there and messed himself. He had also started to scream and cry in panic and humiliation. That had been his third mistake.

The man had looked up and seen him with eyes that were wild and bloodshot and terrible. Willie could never get them out of his head. He had been riveted to the floor with fear and had just watched as the man had calmly reached down and tugged on the knife in Mama's chest. It wouldn't budge, so he had tugged on it harder, and then he'd said a curse word and tugged at it even harder, but Willie had just stood there mewing in shame and panic like a wounded kitten. The man had tugged at the knife unsuccessfully once more, then had jumped up off the bed, screaming in rage, and come at Willie with his fists clenched.

"You spying little bastard, did you see enough?" he had roared as he'd come barefoot across the old linoleum floor. His hands had been all bloody and balled into fists, and his big thing had just been hanging there.

The first blow had caught Willie on the temple and knocked him half senseless, sprawling to the floor on all fours. It was then that Willie had finally realized, if only in some dull and visceral way, that if he didn't move now, he might never move again, so, on hands and knees, he had begun to scramble for the front door. The man had been amazingly quick, however, and he'd grabbed Willie by the hair and slammed his forehead into the floor. Willie had continued his blind retreat, his hands and feet wind-milling in the air as the man simply picked him up like a rag doll and slammed his head into the massive front doorjamb, chanting in rhythm, "You will forget me, you will forget me." He kept chanting those words and slamming Willie's head into the doorpost until Willie had gone completely limp.

After that night, Willie really had forgotten. In fact, he could not remember much of anything at all about that night, ever.

Willie Seaman had spent the rest of his youth at the Louisiana State Home for Mentally Disabled Children. He had awakened from this nightmare screaming in a hospital, screaming about blood and knives, and he had done so almost every night since. His dreams were vivid, but his waking hours were a haze where he was only vaguely conscious of what was going on around him. Brain damage, they had said, no one will ever adopt a kid like that. Put him in the home, they said. And they had done just that. He had been there for ten years.

\* \* \*

"Did you hear the boss pig in the White House on TV last night, Ricky? He was talking about meteors falling down on Earth sometime soon." Jamaal felt the light sheen of perspiration growing around his collar and hated it. It made him nervous, being in the 49ers' crib, and more so because Ricardo Santos was such a temperamental and vicious character.

"Nah, I didn't watch him, but I heard about it. So what?" Ricky was paying more attention to Bobby Simms, who was lolling near the entrance and paying more attention than necessary to Lila Mendez, than to Jamaal.

"If this really happens, then we have a golden opportunity," Jamaal continued, trying to get Ricky to focus on his plan.

"How is that?"

"I been noticin' that lately there has been two soldiers ridin' in the back of all the pig wagons that patrol the hood. I began to think that this meant somethin' big was happenin'. I rapped some with a bro who is in the guards, and he was tellin' me that there are people from all over the state stayin' at the armory and patrollin' with the Denveeer Powlice. He agrees that somethin' is happenin'. Now that I heard the president's speech, I know what it is. The man thinks that when one of these meteors falls, then the brothers will rise up just like when we did in East LA after 'em pigs got off from beatin' up on dat Rodney King way back when. They're afraid of riots in the hood and lootin' of stores and such. That's why the extra guns are in the wagons. The man is nervous, and he's plannin' ahead on how to stop trouble before it gets a chance to start. I have a plan to outsmart his plans and make them work against him and for us."

The leader of the 49ers was a tall, muscular, and swarthy Hispanic boy with an angry look. His name was Ricardo Montoya Santos, and he was known variously as Ricky, Rick or the Rickster to his faithful followers. Jamaal knew Ricky's only qualifications for leadership were a big mouth, a big dick, and a mean streak as wide as the Grand Canyon. Rick was tough and street-smart but not overly bright, and that combination made him very dangerous. He was not getting the drift of the deal that Jamaal was offering him, and he didn't like that. He wanted very badly to confer with Benny "the Brain" Munoz, his second in command, but couldn't do this because it would let Jamaal know that he didn't understand. He had also foolishly agreed to confer with Jamaal alone tonight. He didn't like the way Jamaal's boy Bobby Simms was leering at Lila Mendez. All of these feelings combined to make the Rickster as mean as a snake, and doubly dangerous, but in Bobby's actions, he thought he could see a way to save face and maybe put that smartass nigger back in his place a little.

"You see what I'm saying, don't you? If what the old fart in the big white house says is true, then when them meteors hits anywhere near here, the pigs will be so busy cleaning up, there will be lots of time for us to grab off anything we want. If we cooperate with each other and coordinate our actions, we can make them more confused and spread out even thinner. We can maybe double our take." Jamaal looked to Rick for approval or understanding but saw nothing more than a clenched jaw and angry eyes. He cursed Bobby Simms in his mind for so openly leering at one of the 49ers' women.

Jamaal reached over and touched Ricky's shoulder to get his attention. "You see what I'm saying, don't you?"

"I see your boy over there making hot eyes at one of our women," Rickey growled. "That's what I see. If you can't keep one brother in line, how the hell can I trust you to do your part of any agreement? I see your point about the pigs, but I have a problem working with you when we're out of our turf. Also, you gotta respect where we live."

"That's cool, man. I don't want to get in your space; I just want to coordinate what we do, so's we can keep the pigs goin' back and forth chasin' us, and that way we can keep the heat off each other."

"First, I gotta trust you'll do what you say and not let the pigs come down on us so you can do your thing on our turf. Like your boy Bobby, he's got some hot eyes for Lila, and she's ours," Ricky said with authority. "I don't like that."

"Might be a good idea to let the brothers and sisters get together a little to show that we have cooperation," Jamaal said.

"Might be a better idea to tell him to keep it in his fuckin' pants." Rick was letting his anger show in order to cut off conversation until he could confer with Benny Munoz. "I've got to think this over and talk to my people, so until then, he'd better cool his jets." The look on Santos's face left no room for comment, and Jamaal again mentally cursed Bobby for his indiscretion. "Lila, gits your ass over here," Ricky said in a low, rumbling voice that was quiet yet heard by all, including Bobby Simms, whose dreamy look turned angry.

Jamaal was deeply disappointed at not getting an unqualified agreement from Santos, but he tried desperately not to show it. Things were getting tense, and he needed it to be calm. His fine mind had envisioned a grand-scale cooperation between the two neighboring gangs so each could hit and loot successively selected and widely separated targets in such a way as to keep the police chasing themselves back and forth between reported trouble spots. Let the other brothers and sisters run around the streets, breaking windows and taking whatever came to hand; Jamaal wanted to do things right and make the big score. He didn't want no funky TV set or computer; he wanted cash, diamonds, jewelry, and other kinds of small valuable stuff that was transported easily and readily turned into cash or kind. His mind raced, looking for a way to distract Santos and regain the initiative.

Lila Mendez came quickly over to Ricky's side, wearing a look on her face that alternated between anger and sheer terror. "You want me, Ricky?"

Rick Santos continued to glare at Bobby Simms as he roughly grabbed Lila's wrist and pulled her down on the arm of his chair. "I always want you, bitch. Now sit here and shut up," he ordered. Lila's look remained one of fear. She glanced quickly at Jamaal, her eyes begging him to do something. Ricky's hand began to slowly rotate across her jeans-clad buttocks.

Jamaal took a deep breath, fighting for calm. He was concerned about the effect that Ricky's caressing Lila's bottom would have on Bobby and knew this was a test of his control over his people. He was desperate and had to play his trump card, even though he was unsure of its validity. "We got a line on a bitch who used to live over on our turf who I hear you might be a little interested in," Jamaal said with a calm he did not feel. Ricky's eyes remained hooded and glaring at Bobby.

"Her name is Selena Escobedo, and she is one fine looker. We tried many times, but she would never be a gang banger with us. I thought you might want to try her." Jamaal had purposely left the statement wide open to interpretation, and he could see the change in Ricky's eyes. He was already "trying her" in his mind.

It was an old story in the Blues that Santos had always had the hots for Selena but she had dumped on him badly. Selena was a beautiful, intelligent, and independent girl who had joined no gang, and she had gotten out of the neighborhood as soon as she could manage it. She was currently enrolled in several classes, including astronomy, at the University of Colorado. It was evident that Ricky had not forgotten her. The Rickster had tried everything he could to recruit her and finally, in frustration, had threatened that if she would not be a 49er, she would be an outcast and would not be protected by any gang in any neighborhood. She was fair game, and Jamaal had an idea on how to get her over to Ricky's turf. After that, it was up to Ricky.

"Well, brother, do we have an accommodation?" Jamaal asked, pushing the issue. Jamaal had a plan, and he knew now that the Rickster would join it. But the plan had a price—a big one.

"I'm not your damn brother, and we don't have nothin' until I have time to think it over. Get lost for a minute, and I'll talk to my man."

Jamaal held his temper in check, even though he wanted nothing more than to smash this slick-haired beaner's face in. Struggling to keep his features composed, he slowly rose from his seat and sauntered over to where Bobby Simms was standing with his jaws clamped shut, watching Ricky caress Lila.

"Put it back in your pants, asshole, and quit messing up my deal. You promised to leave the bitch alone if I brought you over here."

Bobby knew in an instant that Jamaal was really pissed and backed off. "Aww, man…. Chill a minute." Bobby tore his eyes from Lila and asked, "You not getting anywhere with these assholes?"

"No, and I never will if you keep this shit up. Now listen to me good. Is it true that Selena Escobedo has a grandmother who lives on this turf?"

"Yeah, I already told you she did, and I told you that Ricky's had a thing for Selena ever since grade school. Grandma's name is Ortiz, and she lives in the Belcher Project."

"Good. We may need to do Grandma a little hurt in order to get Selena to come down here when we want her to."

"No problem, bro. I can have the old bag screaming so loud the Escobedo bitch will hear her all the way over home. You gonna use her for bait?"

"If I have to."

"Good deal. That Santos will go all the way for that one if you play it right."

"Good. Now you wait outside while Santos talks to his brains, then we can go."

"Only way he can talk to his brains is if he sticks his head up in his ass," Bobby said, not daring to look at what Santos was doing. He grudgingly made his way across the 49ers' clubhouse area and up the stairs to the street, being careful all the while not to look back.

Jamaal walked slowly back to where Rick was conferring with his second in command. Benny Munoz was looking at both of them in a strange way, and Jamaal hesitated for a second before returning to push his plan. Ricky looked up and noticed Jamaal waiting.

"My man here says that you have a good plan and that it can be profitable for both of us. I like it because it will drive the pigs wild. We want to do a dry run just to test the plan out. Benny will come over to your turf to coordinate plans with you when he is ready. Now, how are you going to get Selena Escobedo over here to my turf?"

Jamaal was shocked almost to silence by Ricky's complete capitulation and the ease with which he changed moods. He recovered quickly and said with a confidence that he did not really feel, "That is already in the works, and I'll tell Benny the plan when he comes over, but now how about letting Bobby see Lila?" He had the first down and wanted another ten yards.

Jamaal felt a chill of fear course through him at the look of hate that took over Rick Santos's face. "You think I'm stupid, don't you, nigger? Well, I'm not, and you're getting your way just because the plan is good and profitable for us. As far as Lila is concerned, she's 49ers property until I say not, and right now, I don't say." He pulled the frightened girl down on his lap and slowly began to caress her small breasts through her shirt. "Tonight we're going to see if she can score a ten on the Rickster scale. When I'm done with her, then it may be okay for Bobby, but not until after we have Selena down here. Then we can both celebrate together and I can give Selena a ten too." Ricky Santos gave a huge ugly laugh at that, then slapped Lila across the face and said, "Get in the back and get ready, bitch."

Benny Munoz laughed as was expected of him when his leader cracked a joke, but Jamaal noticed he laughed with his mouth only. Benny's eyes remained fixated on Jamaal.

The two leaders shook hands on the deal, and Jamaal started for the door, his body and mind alive with conflicting emotions. He held his body rigidly erect so as not to show the worry he had over Bobby's reaction to Lila staying with Ricky tonight. That was going to be a bad scene, and Jamaal wanted to be back on their own turf before he broke the news. He was also very curious about the strange, angry looks he kept getting from Benny the Brain. Why should he care if the two gangs made a profitable deal? Selena Escobedo would be the only loser in that equation. Or maybe that was the key.

"Why don't you stay around and celebrate a little," Ricky said to Jamaal's departing back. "Cleo over there seems to have an eye for some black meat tonight. Why don't you give her some?"

"No time," Jamaal said, though the offer was tempting; damn, did she have a body to kill for. "I've got to get things rolling on my end."

"Okay then, but you're missing some good pussy. Benny will have to keep her happy."

Jamaal looked quickly back at Munoz and received a look that made his blood run cold.

\* \* \*

Paula Patowski closed the back door of the big Ford Club Van that Burtha had rented from her friend's husband. It was only one year old and had less than ten thousand miles on it, so it was perfect for their purpose. The dealer had told Burtha this was the best vehicle for their trip, and he was right. It was roomy inside, nicely appointed, and comfortable. It had ample baggage room and a rooftop carrier that could hold their luggage if necessary. The front-wheel drive was perfect should they hit any bad weather in the mountains, and with all this, the van was still economical. Paula had wanted a full-sized van because she was a big woman and wanted to have a vehicle that was comfortable to drive and would give her no trouble moving around inside. She had to admit that Burtha had done a good job. This was a nice car and would suit them just fine. They were all packed and were ready to leave early next morning.

Paula went around front and double-checked that her AAA TripTik was in the door pocket, along with her other maps. All was in order, and she closed and locked the door. Little Annie Phillips said, "Paula, are you sleepy?"

"No, I'm too excited to be sleepy. Are you?"

"No, and I'll bet the other girls are not sleepy, either. What would you say to leaving now? We can be well gone before the commuter traffic starts tomorrow morning. If you get too tired, one of us can drive for a while and you can take a nap."

Paula was surprised at this lengthy speech from Annie, who rarely said more than a few words. Annie had been getting downright gabby since they'd started planning this trip.

"Getting a little anxious, are you?"

"Yes. I don't know what it is, but I have a feeling we should be out of here as soon as possible."

"Me too. Let's get the others and get on the road."

The ladies of the Boston Tea Party entered Interstate 90, the Mass Turnpike, at the very first interchange directly off Kneeland Street at exactly 11:01 p.m. Thursday, March 11, and proceeded west toward Albany, New York. None of them had the least idea of the adventure that lay ahead of them.

\* \* \*

Lieutenant Barry Shannahan, USN, was shivering in his boots on the catwalk surrounding the Doppler radar tower at the United States Navy weather station in Point Barrow, Alaska. He glanced at his watch and noted that it was 18:01, one minute after six pm.

Barry had a three-man crew working inside the radar dome on the main worm gear drive that kept the huge antenna circling around and around to monitor cloud cover and precipitation movement in this sector of the Arctic Circle. It was dark, as it was for almost twenty hours of the day at this time of year, and the aurora borealis was unusually brilliant this evening. It was showing huge sheets of yellow-green light occasionally filling with flashes of red. *There must be a pretty active solar magnetic disturbance going on to cause such a show*, he thought as he fought back another shiver. He absolutely hated the cold.

Machinist Mate First Class Andrew Gigante stuck his head and shoulders out of the hatch and motioned for Barry to come over. "Sir, we should have her rotating in about five minutes. We had to put a couple of shims in the worm gear thrust bearing, but she's within tolerance now and should run just—What the hell was that, sir?"

A brilliant streak like a small blue-white sun had just flashed across the sky over the weather station and sunk itself down behind the horizon in the direction of Wrangel Island far to the north in the Chukchi Sea. A moment later, the steel latticework of the tower reverberated to a series of shockwaves similar to an earthquake.

"What the flipping hell was that, Lieutenant?" Gigante asked again in an awed voice, unusual for this bombastic red-haired Italian.

"Meteorite, I would suspect, and a fairly big one."

"One of them angels Reverend Randy has been talking about?"

"Forget about the damned preacher and get this radar working, quick time. If that meteorite landed in the sea as I believe it did, it could brew us up some nasty weather. I'm going down to the radio shack to report." Barry had purposely left out the worst part. No need in upsetting the men he needed to get the work done. He would keep the worry to himself.

"Right you are, sir." Gigante's answer was muffled as he ducked back inside the radar dome to hustle up his work gang and get the big antenna rotating.

Barry had already started down the stairs from the dome tower, descending as quickly as possible while hampered by heavy arctic boots and gloves. He was already working out some rough coordinates for the strike in his mind and composing his report. He had a strong feeling that things might get busy here for a while.

A half hour later, Lt. Barry Shannahan had completed his second report and handed it to the radio operator to transmit to the Office of Naval Operations in Washington. He used his fingernail to scrape the frost off the inside of the window and watched his work gang descend the spiderweb-thin ladder from the now-rotating radar antenna. He had set the output of the radar to go simultaneously to both the Navy department and the NOAA weather services. From what he could see of the suddenly violent cloud movements to the northeast, a huge low-pressure ridge was forming in the area of the supposed strike.

"Sparks, will you call in the off-duty watch for me, please?" Barry said.

"But, sir, they're all sacked out. They had a rough watch working on that damned tower."

"I know, Sparks, but I've got to speak to all of you together."

Shaking his head at the crazy behavior of all officers, the RO went through the door into the enlisted men's quarters to rouse the off-duty watch. When the men were all gathered, grumbling in their coffee cups as might be expected, Barry opened the seabag he had brought from his quarters and took out two bottles of twelve-year-old single-malt Scotch whiskey. He opened both bottles and set them down on the table alongside a stack of paper cups. "Help yourselves to a drink, please. I think you'll need it for what I'm about to tell you."

Without the usual glee reserved for being allowed to drink on Navy time, and drinking excellent Scotch into the bargain, the men filled paper cups and returned to their seats. Barry Shannahan filled his glass and held it up in salute to them. They were all sitting erect, waiting for the bad news. Good news in the Navy was never preceded with a drink of good Scotch.

"That flash across the sky earlier this evening has been confirmed as a meteorite strike off Wrangel Island. A strike of the size indicated by the seismographic reports will generate a sea wave of considerable size. Since there is no high ground in the area for us to retreat to, we might as well toast our fate in good style. I want you all to know it has been a pleasure to work with each of you, and if you have any booze stashed away, now would be a good time to break it out."

Eighteen men and two women sat in their seats and stared at each other silently for nearly a full minute, all absorbing the unbelievable news in their own way, then machinist mate Andrew Gigante stood up. "Erasers!" he belted out the drink name that has the effect of wiping away any memory. "I've got a quart of Grey Goose in my locker, and I'm damned well going to finish it before that wave comes." With the ice broken, the group all scattered to gather the ingredients for one hell of a going-away party.

In his quarters, Lt. Barry Shannahan completed a brief note to his fiancée and closed it up in a watertight strongbox. He hoped vainly that in a few thousand years, some archaeologist would study the rubble left on the Point Barrow shore by the huge tsunami and find a metal box with a note to a young lady who lived in a place called Baldwin, Long Island, New York, that said her man loved her to the end. He placed the box on the corner of his desk and again scraped the ice off the window. He could see the waters of the Bering Sea beginning to recede from the shingle beach only a few hundred yards away. Barry shrugged and went out to join his people in their *celebration*.

Seven hundred sixty-five kilometers to the northwest, the icy waters of the Chukchi Sea were boiling and a huge cloud of superheated steam was rising with unbelievable speed into the upper atmosphere. This steam would affect weather over Siberia and the North American continent for months to come.

## Friday, March 12

Regina Morrisette stood for a few moments under the stinging hot needles of the shower and enjoyed the tingly, warming sensation on her back. It was one thirty in the morning, and she was finished with her night's work at the Doll House strip club. She had counted up her tips, packed away her costumes, and showered off her stage makeup. She was enjoying one of the very few luxuries of working here. The club was old, and the dancers' dressing room had no amenities. Two walls were cinder block and were always cold and clammy to the touch, even in summer. The other two walls were badly cracked plaster stained yellow from cigarette smoke and almost completely devoid of paint. The makeup mirrors were cracked and dull and the lighting was abysmal, but the girls kept the shower clean and the water was stinging hot and felt good.

When she stepped out of the shower, Gina quickly donned her oversized thick terry-cloth bathrobe and used it to blot off the water. She had often thought it strange that she could go on stage and dance naked for a room full of strange drunk men but afterward prize her privacy and resent the men who would frequently find an excuse to sneak in the dressing room in hopes of catching one of the girls getting dressed or in the shower. As she wrapped a towel around her hair, she saw Joey Green, master of ceremonies, come into the dressing room. Joey liked to pop in like that, without knocking, of course. Gina shook her head and thought him strange, because he saw all of them in the buff on stage two or three times a night. It was his little game, and Joey was a good guy, so no one really minded, too much. All the girls trusted him.

"Hey, Gina, good show tonight," he said as he saw her emerge from the shower. "They were really hoppin'."

Gina smiled as she turned away to gather up her street clothes. "They may have been hopping as you say, but they didn't hop into their wallets too quickly," Gina answered.

"Oh well, there's better nights ahead, I'm sure."

"Say Joey, did you notice if old fish-eye Willie was here tonight?" Gina asked, a shadow of concern crossing her face.

"No, I didn't see him tonight."

"Neither did I." Gina shuddered slightly. "That guy just gives me the creeps."

"You're not alone."

Gina shuddered again at the thought, and Joey stood there a moment and studied her. He knew she was waiting for him to leave so she could get dressed in private, and he liked to tease a little by hanging around. Tonight, he could feel her tension and said, "Say, Gina, if you're feeling jumpy, I can give you a lift home. It's not out of my way at all."

Gina did not give the offer a second thought before saying, "Thanks, Joe. I think I'll take you up on that. Just give me a minute to throw some clothes on." She looked him in the eye and gave him a slow, knowing smile, and Joey got the message.

"Okay, Gina, I'll wait out back by the car."

\* \* \*

"What did you and Cathy do last night," asked Ken Becker the copilot of the Lockheed WC-130J Hurricane Hunter aircraft.

"We watched a couple of episodes of Breaking Bad on NetFlix, I am telling you that show is great. You've got to start watching it," answered Bob Bertelli, pilot and aircraft commander on this early morning routine training mission with a full crew in the back of the plane.

"Yeah I know, you keep mentioning it, I will get.."

"Hunter one-four, Hunter one-four, this is Miami Center. Over."

"Center, this is Hunter one-four. Go ahead," Bob answered.

"One-four, say your location and fuel situation. Over."

"Two hundred eighty-five miles east-southeast of San Juan, heading 090, fuel is good, cruising on two. Over."

"Roger that. Stand by."

"What the hell is that all about, I thought this was a routine training exercise?" asked Ken.

"Not sure, Ken, guess will find out shortly," Bob responded.

"Roger that, partner."

Hunter 14 and her crew were outbound on a routine mission to satisfy the *new and improved* compliance requirements someone at the United States Department of Commerce dreamed up, and then handed down on NOAA's pilots and crews this year.

Somewhere below them on the endless blue waters was the *Mary A. Goddard*, a US-owned, Panamanian-flagged collier outbound from Charleston to Rabat Morocco. The *Goddard* had been one of many to report a massive fireball with blinding light leading a long smoky or vapor like trail from the sky down to the ocean.

A number of seismographs of the World-Wide Standard Seismograph Network had coincidentally reported light to moderate tremors in the vicinity. A NOAA weather satellite had recorded a large area low pressure forming, and an expanding area of dense cloud cover. All of this information had been sufficient to have NOAA contact Hunter 14 to break from their routine mission. Satellite coverage is good and helpful, as are local surface reports, but there is no substitute for a manned aircraft observing and transmitting on-site information.

"Hunter one-four, this is Miami. We have received multiple reports of a possible meteorite sighting. Thought while you're up there it's worthwhile to send you that way to gather some data; we are sending the coordinates now."

Ken Becker groaned aloud. He had plans later this afternoon to play in his club's tennis finals. Over the past year he had risen to a rating of 4.0 since mastering the slice serve. He knew he had a good shot at taking the title this year. *Hope I don't have to forfeit*, he thought to himself.

There was a long silence on the radio as Miami Center waited for a response. "Miami this is Hunter one-four, we have the coordinates now, and will light up all sensors and cameras and run complete diagnostics on all equipment. Then we'll establish a secure uplink and send everything to you ASAP. Over." Bob replied.

"Approach the area with caution and go only as close as you deem advisable. You have a much better sense of what is happening out there than we do at this time, but we need everything that you can send us. Be careful, Bob. Over."

"Roger that, Manny; we're going in, talk to you soon. Over."

Bob Bertelli turned to look out his side cockpit window as Ken Becker punched the start switch for the left outboard engine. Two outboard engines had been shut down after reaching their twenty-five-thousand-foot cruising altitude to conserve fuel. As the big turboprop fired up and began running, Kenny monitored the #4 engine startup while Bob pressed his intercom button. "OK, folks, it's time to earn your keep. Light up all equipment, run a full-scale diagnostic, and establish a secure uplink to Miami for all data. Our training exercise just got upgraded, we're going to go hunt for a space rock that fell in the Atlantic."

With all four turboprops fired up, Kenny Becker slowly applied pitch to the outboard props to increase power, and as Hunter 14 accelerated, Bob Bertelli banked easily to starboard and brought her nose around to point directly to the coordinates given. "Here we go," he said. Ken Becker just nodded and stared ahead.

* * *

"Jesus Christ, Ben, where the hell are these things coming from?" Amos Bellinger sat back and waited while the white-haired astronomer finished studying the report from Point Barrow on the strike in the Arctic Ocean.

"People seem to be starting sentences with that particular gentleman's name quite often these days. I repeat, I don't subscribe to his existence, and I am as surprised as you are that we are sustaining moderately large meteorite strikes at this early date. As you well know, I have been kept quite busy playing the part of a television star and repeating our government's wait-and see policy to the people. I will have to speak with the people who are monitoring the field to answer your question accurately. As a first guess, I would say we miscalculated somewhat the speed of expansion of the debris field. It is equally likely that since we discovered the field, we were unable to see small objects that were outside the main field. This to me is the more likely scenario. Whichever case is correct, we must expect to be receiving more frequent strikes in the very near future, but before the full meteorite shower is upon us."

Amos took a moment to study the astronomer and noticed how the dark circles under his eyes had deepened and expanded, and the way he was cradling one hand in the other as if his joints were made of glass. As much as he knew Ben Cohen to be an honest man, Amos could not help feeling he was hiding something or had a secret agenda of his own. The very thought of his government's top advisor keeping secrets made Amos shudder inside. He deeply regretted having to keep Dr. Cohen working so many hours, but the president wanted Amos's report as soon as possible, and he needed Ben Cohen's expertise to complete it. It was obvious that the stress and the heavy work schedule were beginning to tell on Dr. Benjamin Cohen; they were beginning to take a toll on Amos also.

"Amos, we realized from the time of the original discovery that some of the particles of comet debris were traveling directly toward the earth and would be the first to reach us. We also concluded that later on in time, others would be pulled in toward Earth by our gravitational field. Several mathematical models were developed to calculate the speed of approach of the direct-line particles, but they were all based on sketchy information. This problem was compounded by the degree of difficulty in measuring the movement of objects coming almost directly at the measuring device. It's like seeing the movement of a bullet aimed between your eyes."

"I understand that you and your fellow astronomers are doing your very best, Ben, but I have to meet with the president soon, and he's going to want some hard answers. You well know that he delayed making his announcement based on your estimated time of arrival, and it seems he waited too long. He's eating his liver out over it and making my life a living hell."

"I can sympathize with your problem, Amos, but I can offer very little more at this time. Possibly when David gets here, he can let us know if NASA has any significant new data. If you like, I'll go with you to talk to the president. Possibly, I can explain myself better to him and take some heat off of you."

"That would be wonderful, Ben, and I appreciate the offer, but it's my heat to take, not yours. David is on his way and should be here any second. You are welcome to stay if you like, but you've done enough, and you look bone-tired. Just please get me an update as soon as you can." Again, Amos could not put his finger on the cause of his disquiet, but he did not want Ben Cohen talking to the president until he was certain of the astronomer's motives.

Amos's thoughts were interrupted by a soft knock on the door, and David walked in, asking, "When did you last hear from Point Barrow?"

"It has been quite some time now. Why?"

"Because if the strike was as large as the seismographs seem to indicate and the resulting tsunami travels approximately five hundred miles an hour in open sea, then you won't be hearing anything from them again. I assume that tidal-wave warnings have gone out for eastern Alaska and the Bering Strait and St. Lawrence Island."

"The Navy has taken care of that, but do you think that it will be that powerful?"

"Judging from the seismographic reports from WWSN, and we have gotten them from as far south as San Diego, the wave was probably fifty feet high or more. Point Barrow is at sea level, with no high ground nearby to retreat to, so we must assume it was swamped; there's no getting around that. Evacuation to high ground should be under way all around the eastern Alaska coastline, and the Russians should be notified, even though they probably already know. Any fishing boats in the area, and especially the oil-field workers at Prudhoe Bay, should be warned."

"And this is just the beginning, David?"

"I am sorry to say, yes, just the very beginning."

Amos shook his head as if to clear cobwebs and asked, "Ben, I know we've been over this before, but will you tell me about what we can expect if we get hit? I have to be able to brief the president. I'm sorry now that I skipped out on most of the disaster-preparedness meetings and missed this information."

Ben Cohen stared at the president's chief advisor for a moment and then lapsed into his lecture-hall mode of speech. "Well, Amos, this is a weighty subject, but I will attempt to condense it for you. Astronomers have known for years that the earth is much like the little ducks in a shooting gallery. The moon and all of the planets in our solar system are heavily cratered, the inner planets in particular. This evidence provides us with a living record of cosmic violence. There are no such things as friendly skies anymore, but we used to be supremely arrogant and believed that our Earth would be spared this violence just because we are here. Unfortunately, that is exactly what we did believe until we began to look at our planet from another perspective.

"Ever since we began looking down at our home planet from satellites, we have been discovering new impact craters on Earth, and not just a few. We have located over 140 such craters, and we discover five or six new ones each year. And you must realize that these are just the ones that have not been obliterated by erosion or tectonic-plate movements on Earth. Remember also, Amos, the earth is three-fourths covered by water and impacts there leave no easily discernible trace.

"NASA has actively studied this situation and has estimated there are thousands of asteroids which cross Earth's orbit. NASA works closely with the International Astronomical Union Minor Planet Center who is in charge of organizing all of the data. Collectively we have discovered nearly 1,500 PHA's which are potentially hazardous asteroids. Some of them pass closer to the earth than the moon.

"We currently have a much larger, twofold problem. First, the meteorite stream through which we will pass has regions which are denser than others, and we are in an orbit for a close encounter with one of these. The tale will be told on that in a few weeks' time. Currently, we are unable to locate and track the meteoroids that are striking us. I can only assume they are debris from the Mountain. By coming at us from that direction, they blindside us since they are in an area of the sky in which we cannot observe them. We can only assume that there are more of them approaching and that some of them will strike us. Then after we pass this current encounter with the Mountain's meteorite stream, it will likely not return for thousands of years.

"I will attempt to put into plain language for you the effect of an impact. Judging from the reports of impacts we have received, the meteorites are coming in at an angle and a speed that expose them to minimum atmospheric burn-off. The report from the collier in the Atlantic described the entry as a flashbulb-like flash. Examination of the Australian strike indicates the meteorites are of nickel-iron composition. With these two facts known, we only have to deal with the size, and I will attempt to put this in ordinary terms.

"Any pieces the size of a pickup truck or smaller will probably explode upon entry or mostly burn up before impacting the surface. We have witnessed a number of these recently, and they provide a burst of light or heat but no other danger."

Ben was so full of information that he tried to slow himself down. "If a chunk the size of a building, say a diameter of ten to fifty meters, comes in, it will burn through the atmosphere and strike the surface and causes some damage, a great example would be the recent event in Chelyabinsk Russia. The size of that one is estimated to be 20 meters in diameter and it caused hundreds of injuries and significant property damage to thousands of buildings throughout the region. But if one the size of the Canyon Diablo meteorite, which fell about 50,000 years ago, struck in the center of one of our world's major cities, the impact and explosion, would create a shock wave that could flatten buildings for several miles, it would kill millions. In a seismic zone, it could trigger earthquakes of 7.5 Richter or more.

"Many authors have suggested in various reports throughout history, enormous tsunami like waves can be created by relatively small asteroids that strike in the ocean. The asteroid size they refer to in these reports are categorized as greater than one hundred meters in diameter. However, if it makes you feel better, a more recent study called the Van Dorn Report scientifically contradicts these reports. But just imagine what it would do to a civilization such as ours, where the major portion of the population lives on the coastal plains if two hundred foot oceanic waves roll over our coastlines. This would be the greatest catastrophe in human history. The cloud of dust thrown up into the upper ionosphere as a result would block sufficient sunlight to eliminate the possibility for any crops to be grown for at least a year.

"A huge asteroid hit, thought to be approximately six miles in diameter, is believed to be the cause of the extinction of the dinosaurs and would surely be the same for mankind. If the Van Dorn report is inaccurate the dust created from the tsunami would be taken so high up in the stratosphere that agriculture would be impossible for countless years. Mankind would probably go the way of the trilobites."

With that, Ben concluded, "I'm sorry, it's not a very pleasant picture, is it?"

"That is the understatement of the century." It was Amos Bellinger's turn to look as worried as Ben Cohen did. "Can you estimate the size of the asteroid debris that is coming?"

"My guess is that most of it is on the smaller side, but there is a considerable amount of it, so we may expect multiple smaller strikes. It is the larger pieces that we use for sightings to track the field, and there are a number of those. Fortunately for us, the odds against them hitting are very large sufficiently so to be discounted."

"We have to be concerned about the buckshot and not the slug," Amos stated to demonstrate that he understood completely.

"Simply stated, but quite correct," David added.

Amos Bellinger rose and extended his hand to Ben. "Thank you for being candid with me, Ben. I will try to be the same with the president. I'm sorry to have kept you up so late. Why don't you sleep in tomorrow morning, and I'll arrange for someone to cover for you. You really need the rest. I will get back to you later on tomorrow, and we can continue my education on meteorites."

"Be honest with him, Amos," Ben said, slowly rising to collect his overcoat and scarf. "The man cannot make proper decisions unless he has proper information."

Amos nodded as Ben turned to leave. Something about Ben just didn't seem right. *Yes he is tired, but it is more than that* he thought. He decided to question David Van Patten after Ben was out the door to see if he still had the same concerns about Cohen that he had brought up a while back.

\* \* \*

Regina Morrisette was walking briskly down River Street toward her apartment in the damp, chilly late-night/early-morning March air. Her hair was still a bit damp from the shower, and she couldn't seem to shake off a deep-seated sense of foreboding that was making her skin tingle as if an electric current were passing over it. The fine hairs on her arms seemed to be standing up on end. Under her breath, she vehemently cursed Joey Green for his slovenly maintenance on the battered blue Toyota, which had prevented the car from starting back at the club. Even though she was forced to walk home, she derived some small satisfaction from the fact that he was still back there, scratching his head and staring at the oily, dead engine. Gina lived close to the club, and she was too practical to call a taxi.

She had a funny, fluttery feeling in the pit of her stomach that was urging her to hurry, and as she walked, her eyes roved from side to side of the street. It was quiet here just before three a.m., even in New Orleans. The hookers were mostly off the street by now, and tourists had all gone to bed. She sincerely wished there was someone around.

As she passed a dark alley in the middle of the block, she heard the unmistakable sound of a kitten squealing. Without a second thought, Gina stopped and looked down the alley. As her eyes adjusted to the more intense darkness in the alley, she saw that it was a typical scene. Garbage cans were strewn haphazardly around two battered dumpsters, and many years' accumulation of waste lay in-between. It only took a minute to spot the kitten. It was stuck between two garbage cans, where it squealed again and feebly struggled to get free. Instinctively, Gina went to help, and then stopped suddenly just as she reached it. The kitten suddenly came free and skittered away down the alley. A movement behind one of the cans caught Gina's eye, and she froze in terror. There was Willie Seaman, leering at her with his awful, flat gray eyes.

He had exposed himself and was standing there in the dark shadows, staring at her with a foolish, leering grin on his face. He held a second kitten, identical to the first, in his hand and was slowly rubbing it up and down himself. Warm, bitter bile rose in her throat.

Gina wanted to scream, smash his leering face, and grab the poor misused kitten and run away, all at the same time, but unfortunately, she did none of them. She simply stood frozen and unbelieving, staring at the grotesque sight. Her mind was unable to compute the situation and direct any remedial action.

Willie Seaman was not troubled by any sort of paralysis. He had planned this night for too long, and as long as he didn't have to think, he could act. All that planning had cost him too much effort to allow himself to fail. Quick as a snake striking, his hand shot out and grabbed the front of Gina's light windbreaker and pulled her toward him.

The sight and smell of him made Gina's stomach roll. Her knees went weak with fear and collapsed under her, scraping along the rough concrete as he drew her closer.

Until now, Willie's plan had been working perfectly. The only thing he had miscalculated was the reaction of the furry little feline in his other hand. Frightened by his sudden move and Gina's squeal and her body collapsing toward it, the kitten recoiled. Hissing in terror, the kitten wriggled and writhed and, in desperation, clawed Willie in the part of his anatomy that was closest to it. Now it was Willie Seaman's turn to call out in surprise and agony.

The sudden intense pain distracted Willie just long enough for Gina to regain some of her senses and draw in a deep breath. She screamed and began to fight back. Uncaring of the pain in her scored knees, Gina screamed again and went for Willie's eyes with clawed fingers. She refused to be raped... *again*, she thought.

Still maintaining his grip on Gina's jacket, Willie grunted in pain and hurled the kitten in anger across the alley, where it bounced off the brick wall like a furry tennis ball then bounded away. Gina screamed again and continued to claw at Willie's eyes in an instinctive self-defense effort. Ignoring the pain and the violence of her counterattack, Willie easily batted her hands away with a swat of one powerful arm, all the while making a strange, low sound that Gina found completely disconcerting.

Now free of the kitten, one amazingly powerful hand grabbed Gina's throat between thumb and forefinger and pushed her upper body away from Willie's. At the same time, the hand on the front of her jacket gripped more tightly and ripped down with such force that her blouse and jacket were torn open to her waist. Gina flew backward away from him, landing painfully on the rough concrete. As Gina landed, Willie drove forward with his lowered head and butted her in the solar plexus, driving all the air out of her lungs and stopping the screams completely. With an evil lopsided grin, Willie drew her up and then again flung her backward like a rag doll onto the rough pavement, scraping her ass through the tough fabric of her jeans. He knew he was going to have his way with her.

Willie was on top of her, and into his program. He was fully erect and so excited, he could barely slow himself down. He was moving without conscious thought but with deceptive speed. His hands scrambled down to the top button on Gina's jeans and tugged them open, exposing the white lace panties beneath. Just then, a voice rang out, "Hey, what the hell's going on down there?"

The sound of a man's voice revived Gina's senses a little, and she managed to draw enough air into her lungs to emit a weak "Help!" while sending an off-balance kick at Willie's crotch. It missed the mark, and Willie simply grunted and ignored it.

Willie's hands left her jeans then, and one clamped quickly over her nose and mouth while the other went to his jacket pocket. Footsteps were thudding down the alley, and Gina felt a quick ray of hope, but then suddenly, the equation changed again. With a slippery, metallic sound, a switchblade suddenly opened in Willie's hand, and he half rose to meet his assailant. Gina kicked again and missed the intended target again but managed to land a painful blow on his thigh.

Gina's field of vision was restricted to an area only twelve inches off the ground as the next few seconds flashed by her in a blur. A pair of well-worn work boots appeared, with tan work pants above. "Jesus Christ!" shouted the unseen stranger as Willie's arm slashed out with the knife. The boots jumped back and caught their heels on a garbage can cover, tripping their owner, who fell flat on his back. Willie Seaman scrabbled quickly off Gina and moved after him. The work boots kicked out quickly, partially deflecting Willie, but not quite enough, and the knife slashed through the side of his blue chambray work shirt, causing an immediate red stain to appear. "Aaagh," was the only sound Gina heard as the man's hands shot up defensively and grabbed Willie's arm.

Suddenly, Gina realized she was free. She sat up quickly, looking about the alley for any sort of weapon to help the wounded stranger. Her hand was blindly feeling through a pile of rubbish and found a thin, wiry piece of steel, which she realized was the handle of a paint can. Picking it up, she was pleased to find the can was still half full and heavy enough to do some damage. Without hesitation, she gripped the handle with two hands and swung the can in a savage arc that caught Willie on the back of his head, driving him forward and deflecting his second attempt to stab her rescuer. She was drawing the can back, preparing to deliver a second blow, when one of the well-worn boots finally found its target and drove itself into Willie's crotch, doing vastly more damage and sending Willie crawling up the alley on all fours, slobbering and retching as he went. Neither Gina nor her rescuer was in any condition or had any desire to follow his retreat.

Gina crawled over to the stranger, who was lying on the ground, holding his side and grinning foolishly at her. "Are you all right?" she asked breathlessly.

"Yeah, I'm okay," he said, still grinning.

"Just what the hell are you grinning at?" Gina asked, beginning to get angry at his strange behavior, and then she looked down at herself and began to see some of the humor in the otherwise sordid situation. She was kneeling in the alley with her jacket and shirt hanging open, her jeans half pulled down, and the cheek of her left buttock beginning to bleed through her white cotton panties. She was holding her paint can high as if ready to strike, and she was asking him if he was all right.

"I don't think this is too serious," he said, nodding toward where his hand was clamped to his side and bright blood was beginning to show through. "Doesn't hurt much, anyway."

Gina rose quickly and tugged up her jeans, then pulled her jacket closed and reached down to help him up. "Not a hell of a lot of help, was I?" he asked with a sheepish grin.

"You just saved my life. My name is Regina Morrisette, and I live over there," she said, pointing to a building just a few doors down. "Let me help you up to my place, and we'll have a look at that cut on your side."

"Bruce McCartan, and I think I'd better move my truck first. I left it running in the middle of the road."

"Let me look at that first," Gina said, gently lifting his fingers from where they were pressing on his side. She pulled the bloodsoaked shirt away and nodded sagely. "Have you got a handkerchief?"

Bruce took a blue bandanna from his back pocket, and Gina pressed it firmly against the wound. "Hold that down hard," she said with authority. "Can you move the truck one-handed?"

"I think so."

"Alright, then pull it into the alley there beside my building and come right on upstairs through the side door."

Bruce McCartan moved as quickly as the steadily increasing pain in his side allowed and parked the old Chevy Suburban in the alley Gina had indicated. He locked it up and allowed Gina to help him up the stairs. He was immediately impressed. The apartment was small but very tidy, and immaculately clean. It contained just one small bedroom with two single beds, a bathroom, and a living-dining-kitchen area. "Take off your shirt while I get some things to fix you up," Gina said, heading for the bathroom.

Bruce took off his work shirt and then replaced the handkerchief, pressing it firmly against the four-inch wound in his side. The cut was clean and did not appear to be too deep but was bleeding profusely, so Bruce maintained the direct pressure.

When Gina returned, her hands were full of first-aid supplies. She wore a look of intense concentration as she saturated a pad with a dark brown solution, then gently removed Bruce's hand holding the handkerchief from the wound. "This may smart a little," she said as she clucked her tongue unconsciously and swabbed the area with the gauze pad saturated in Bio-dyne solution.

"Ow, that hurts like hell," Bruce exclaimed as the antiseptic solution hit his nerve endings. He tried to pull away from the burning sensation, but Gina's hand held the pad firmly in place.

"Don't be a baby; I know what I'm doing."

"I didn't say you don't know what you were doing. I said it hurts."

Gina removed the antiseptic pad and quickly replaced it with a clean one. "Press on this hard for a minute," she said in deep concentration, completely ignoring his complaints.

She expertly stripped off a two-inch piece of adhesive tape, then spun the roll around and around until the tape became a tight string, then she stripped off another two-inch strip. She repeated this procedure until she had six nice, neat, handmade butterfly closures stuck in a line at the edge of the table.

When she was ready, Gina looked up at him and smiled. "Ready?" she asked.

"As I'll ever be, I guess."

With that, Gina removed his hand and, with quick, sure motions, closed the wound with the fingers of her left hand while placing one butterfly firmly across the wound with her right. Quick as a wink, she repeated the procedure five more times, until the wound was neatly closed and barely bleeding. "I learned this from a friend whose boyfriend had a bad habit of getting into knife fights," Gina said, not losing her focus as she neatly blotted the wound, dusted the area with antibiotic powder, and applied a Telfa pad. In another moment, Bruce was wrapped around the torso with a gauze bandage, and, after adding a few more strips of tape, Gina was standing up, admiring her handiwork. "Pretty neat, if I do say so myself."

"Yes, you make a pretty good nurse, Gina."

She smiled up at him again, and Bruce realized how stunning she really was. Her hair was wavy, of medium length, and dark chestnut in color. Her eyes were a deep green and large, with abundant dark lashes. Her smile made him lose his train of thought completely.

"I haven't thanked you yet for saving me from Willie Lump Lump," Gina said in a low voice.

"Willie who?" Bruce exploded, laughing out loud and hurting his side.

"Willie Lump Lump.... It's just a nickname, and I never knew where he got it. I never knew what his proper last name was, but he sometimes hangs around the club where I work. Most of the girls thought he was harmless, but he always gave me the creeps."

"Waitress?" Bruce asked thoughtlessly.

"Dancer," Gina answered without hesitation as she moved off into the small bathroom and partially closed the door.

"Near here?" Bruce asked, just for something to say to the beautiful young woman.

"Just down the street, the Doll House. Maybe you've seen it?"

"Don't think so."

"It's not much of a place anyways," Gina said through the bathroom door. "If you've got a few moments, I'll make us a cup of coffee and thank you properly for rescuing me."

Bruce's mind was telling him that he should be getting back on the road, but he ignored it, and without any hesitation, his mouth said, "Okay."

"Damn!" Gina exclaimed from the bathroom.

"What's wrong?"

"Will you come in here for a minute, but don't get any wrong ideas?"

Bruce opened the bathroom door. Gina was standing there in a slightly tattered but immaculately white cotton bra and panties. "Not very sexy, but very comfortable," she said, smiling at him.

Her left foot was resting on the toilet bowl lid, and she was trying without much success to reach around behind her to clean up the scrapes on her backside. With a sort of shy little grin, she handed him the gauze pad and poured on some more peroxide. "Just clean the dirt off, please."

Gina rolled down the side of her panties from the waist, easing it back to expose the area, and Bruce turned scarlet as he began to gently scrub the abrasion clean. Gina said with a little giggle, "Don't be embarrassed for me, Bruce. Where I work, this is considered overdressed."

"That's going to be a tough place to put a bandage on," Bruce said, finally finding his tongue.

"It's not bleeding much," Gina answered, slipping a Telfa pad inside her panties. "Just a couple of small tapes will do," she said, handing him the roll. He finished quickly, and then she rolled the panties back up. After she had retrieved her fluffy white chenille robe from the hook behind the door and slid into it, she noticed that Bruce relaxed slightly. Gina smiled at him and instinctively reached up with both hands, holding his cheeks between them while she planted a long, firm kiss on his lips. "Thank you for being my hero down there, Bruce. There aren't many of you around anymore."

"Was that creep in the club tonight?" Bruce asked.

"No, he wasn't, but that's not unusual. He must have been stalking me and followed me home another night to have known where I live and that I love cats. He used kittens to bait me into the alley, but I never let mine out. I guess that means he was somehow watching me inside the apartment." The thought made Gina shiver inside. "Would you like that coffee now?" she said quickly to cover the upset she was feeling.

"Coffee would be nice, but a little touch of whiskey would go down real easy right now."

"Bourbon okay?"

"Works for me."

Gina giggled and bent over to fetch a nearly full bottle of Jim Beam from under the kitchen cabinet, then took some ice cubes out of the freezer. "On the rocks?" she asked, arching her eyebrow seductively.

"Still works for me," Bruce answered, and they both laughed.

"Where were you going, riding around at three o'clock in the morning, if I may ask?" Gina asked. "Not that I'm complaining."

"I was leaving town," Bruce answered seriously, his mind being forcibly brought back to the real reason for his rapid exodus. "I've been living in a trailer out back of the old Royal Sanesta Hotel down on Bourbon Street, so this is the best route to the interstate."

Her nose crinkled up at the thought of that neighborhood, and she asked, "Not just one step ahead of the sheriff, I hope?"

"No, not at all."

"Then why so early in the morning?"

"As good a time as any, I guess, and a good time to beat the morning commuter traffic."

"Where were you headed?"

"Boulder, Colorado."

"Just going on vacation, I guess. I'm jealous, but why so far?"

"I've always wanted to see the Rocky Mountains, and I'm meeting my kids there, but basically just anywhere out of New Orleans."

"I knew it, one step ahead of the law," Gina said firmly.

"Not so. It's just a long story to try to explain."

"I'm not sleepy."

That was how Bruce McCartan got to give a very brief outline of his recent life to a beautiful young exotic dancer who kept her eyes fixed on his face through the whole story. Had he not been so busy trying to figure out why he was doing this, he would have noticed that she was reading every expression displayed there and falling attentively on his every word. She seemed to understand his reasoning better than he did himself, and had he watched her face instead of his drink as he talked, he would have seen that all his hurt and pain were understood completely and mirrored in her own features. When he had finished a much abbreviated version of his life for the past several days, Gina simply looked into his eyes and said, "Want some company going west?"

Bruce was completely taken aback by the sudden offer and stammered, "Don't you have anything to keep you here?"

"Nothing that's not portable, and I surely don't want to dance in that club again after tonight. I don't want to walk home alone anymore, either. I know he was watching me, maybe right here in the apartment. I never expected this, and it makes me feel violated, even more than what he tried to do to me back in the alley. There are a lot more out there just like him. I just don't feel safe here anymore, and I don't want to spend my life with the shades pulled down tight."

There was more, and Bruce sensed that, but he didn't press the issue. "Are you serious about just going off with me, Gina? You don't even know me."

"I know enough, Bruce, and my Cajun intuition tells me the rest. I can be packed and ready to go in just a few minutes, and I promise that I won't be a burden to you. I just have to make two quick calls first."

Without even taking the time to make a conscious decision, Bruce said, "Okay, Gina, I'll bring the truck around the front of the building. You come down when you're ready."

With complete trust that he wasn't running out on her, Gina turned and began to pack up her few things into a huge nylon zipper bag. Bruce watched her move around the tiny apartment with an unconscious grace and economy of movement that he admired. He hesitated only a few seconds more and then surrendered to his fate and went on downstairs, hoping that she wouldn't try to fit the refrigerator in the bag too.

By the time Bruce had turned the truck around, parked out front at the curb, and listened to the song *Some Nights* by the band Fun on WMOZ radio, Gina was coming out the door with two bulging bags and a big grin. "We have to make one little tiny stop on the way. Is that all right?" she asked with a beautiful smile.

"Climb aboard, and let's get going."

\* \* \*

"Ham and Swiss or roast beef on rye?" Sally asked to make sure John was still alert.

Sally's question snapped John out of his concentration. They had been making fairly good time down Interstate 88 south to Binghamton and then on Interstate 81 south past Scranton when the snow began, first as big, fat scattered flakes and now in a driving white wall that had them down to 50 miles per hour. As if the snow itself wasn't bad enough, it seemed to be filled with little balls of ice that streaked and tried to stick to the windshield on contact. Only the constant use of the defrosters and windshield wipers made visibility tolerable.

The snow had been increasing steadily since they had turned west onto Interstate 80, and the road surface was churned into a rutted mass of slush in the driving lane and a smooth layer of four inches of very wet snow in the passing lane, where John Halloran was doing most of his driving. No need to battle the slushy ruts when a clear lane was available. Amazing too, that so few people thought of it.

The local and national radio weather reports spoke of an unusual upper-atmospheric disturbance in the Arctic causing a perturbation. John liked that word. A perturbation of the jet stream was pouring bitter-cold arctic air down onto the contiguous forty-eight states and causing an ungodly amount of snow and freezing rain. They would not attempt to forecast when this unpleasant condition might end.

"Roast beef please," John answered, appreciating Sally's forethought in providing abundant hot coffee and sandwiches for the road. Thin-sliced roast beef on good hearty rye bread was just what he needed. Sally had also taken her turn at driving for an hour and a half earlier in the evening. It had been a nice rest, but John had taken over driving again after he had noticed that she was being unusually quiet. He had studied her for a moment and seen her intense focus and how white her knuckles were from gripping the wheel. He had been doing the driving ever since, with no argument.

Sally had proven to be an excellent traveling partner in other ways. She had followed their progress carefully on the Magellan Roadmate GPS system until it had given out. She had then used the road atlas John had packed in fear the GPS would not work because a meteorite might hit the satellite. She was always ready with directions or road information when he needed it. She talked just enough to keep John alert but demanded no constant chatter from him in return. She kept an eye on the gas gauge and the map and suggested where they could find places to fuel up, always trying to keep the tank no less than half full. Butch merely sat in the back and watched the wintry landscape go by with little comment or complaint. John was not sure if he was the reason for the frequent gas stops or not, but he refrained from asking in case Sally had a good and purely practical reason for the stops that he hadn't thought of.

"Bloomsburg exit is coming up shortly, John," Sally said. "It might be a good spot to gas up and stretch our legs a bit. Should be coming up about two miles ahead."

"Sounds good to me," John answered, flexing the aching muscles in his hands and scooting his butt around on the seat, looking for a sweet spot to settle in. They had been going up and downhill for hours through the endless mountains of Pennsylvania, and had many more miles through the Appalachians almost to Pittsburgh before the land would flatten out. "Bloomsburg, next stop."

\* \* \*

While John and Sally were toiling through the mountains of northwestern Pennsylvania, Bruce McCartan was pushing the aging Chevrolet Suburban he had "borrowed" from the Pritchard Construction Company through sleety rain in northwest Louisiana. Bruce had wondered at first why the windshield wipers were having such a hard time cleaning off his windshield, and he had used the windshield washers repeatedly. They had seemed to have little effect, so he had rolled down the window and put his hand out into the rain. Lord God, but it was cold out there all of a sudden, and that's when he had realized it was not the wipers' fault at all, because the tiny snowballs were coming down mixed in the rain itself. His only recourse had been to slow to a speed where the wipers worked efficiently and to crank up the defrosters. As he rolled the Suburban down Interstate 49, headed for Shreveport, where he could pick up I-20 into Texas, he allowed his mind to wander back to the unusual events of the evening and what had to have been the most unusual day of his life. And he'd had a few of those.

The "little stop" Gina had casually mentioned when she'd gotten into his truck had turned out to be quite a surprise, which Gina seemed to be full of. Somehow, Bruce didn't seem to mind. While he had brought the truck around to the front of the apartment, she had quickly changed into a pair of cotton Dockers and a white oxford shirt and a brightly colored windbreaker. Her clothes were obviously worn and comfortable, and also admirably filled out. When he had pulled up out front, she had come out grinning like a schoolgirl going for a joyride and tossed her nylon zipper bags into the back of the truck. Climbing into the passenger seat, she had given Bruce directions. "Go down to the corner," she had said sweetly. "Take a right on King Street, please, then a left on St. Louis."

When they had pulled up in front of the big old house on St. Louis Street, lights had already been shining inside, and Gina was out of the truck in a flash. "I'll only be a minute," she'd called over her shoulder as she'd sped up the walk to the steps of the high porch.

The first surprise had come when Gina had walked out of the house carrying a large flowered pillow and a hot pink suitcase in one arm, and a sleeping young girl of seven or eight years in the other. Gina had deftly slid the suitcase onto the floor in the back behind the driver's seat, plumped the pillow, and plunked the young girl down safely in the seat. Buckling up the girl's safety belt, she had looked directly into Bruce's eyes and said, "I'd like you to meet my daughter, Ashley." Her look had said much more clearly than words could "If you've got a problem with this, get it out now; if not, then let it go."

When no complaint had been forthcoming, Gina had smiled and said, "Ashley, this is mama's friend Mr. McCartan. He's a nice man, and we'll be traveling with him for a few days."

"Yes, Mama," had come the very sleepy reply from young Miss Ashley Morrisette as she had lain her head down on the pillow and fallen instantly back to sleep.

"Quite a little surprise," Bruce had said, turning to Gina.

"She's my pride and joy, Bruce. You don't really mind, do you?" Gina had asked with a mischievous little grin.

Just looking into those dark brownish-green Cajun eyes, Bruce had felt that any small chance of resistance he might have had was simply melting away, and at that moment, he could not have denied Gina anything—which was a good thing, because suddenly, the passenger-side back door had opened and a crackly voice said, "Wait up just one damned minute here. You all doesn't think youse leaving without old Evvie Bascom, does ya?"

Evangeline Bascom had wasted no time installing her threadbare suitcase behind the back seat and sliding in right beside the already-sleeping Ashley. "I's ready, Mr. Bruce; we can go whenever you's a mind to." Her black skin was loose and wrinkled, but her eyes had flashed with intelligent good humor, and as her grin had spread wide, her teeth had glowed in the night. She looked for all the world like an ancient Whoopie Goldberg. Her flowered cotton dress was well worn but scrupulously clean and pressed, and her floppy straw hat had the front brim pinned firmly up with a pink silk posy. She had sat up very erect in the back seat, placed a work-hardened and bony hand protectively on Ashley's shoulder, and then favored Bruce with a wink. He had been done for. What Bruce hadn't noticed was the pair of golden eyes that were steadily appraising him from the red-striped head sticking out of the top of Evvie Bascom's small zipper bag. Tabatha the cat had also been weighing his attributes carefully.

He couldn't believe how quickly his well-laid plans had changed. He had started out the evening prepared to leave New Orleans alone to drive to Boulder, Colorado, and pick up his children. Now, quite suddenly, he was tooling down the road with three strange females in his truck.

Shortly after leaving St. Louis Street for Interstate 10, he had been surprised by the appearance of an old red tabby cat on the back of his seat. She had taken her time and slowly sniffed across the back of his neck and then, reading the mood of acceptance of the other three ladies, calmly dropped down beside him on the front seat and curled up against his leg. She had immediately fallen asleep, rubbing her cheek against his leg. He had no clue at all as to where she had come from, but she appeared to have taken a liking to him. He guessed that made it four females.

"Tabatha seems to be as taken with you as the rest of us are." Gina had smiled at Bruce, picking the cat off the seat and settling her on her own lap. Tabatha had promptly stood up, stretched hugely, arching her back, then moved back over to Bruce and gone to sleep, curled up against his leg. Bruce had simply grinned in resignation, dropped his hand to the cat's head, and scratched, receiving a soft purr as reward. He had shaken his head, smiling, and continued down the highway. After all, hadn't this whole trip started out just as strangely? His plans for a quick, solitary trip to Colorado had suddenly been altered to include two women, a young girl, and a red cat of indeterminate age who all seemed to have taken an instant liking to him. He thought that he would have preferred it if Gina was cuddled up against his leg and the damned cat over by the door. Oh well, all in good time.

A short while later, Bruce became aware of the silence in the truck and stole a glance over at Gina to discover that she was sound asleep with her head rested against the window, snoring just slightly. He smiled and looked back further into the open and alert eyes of Evangeline Bascom. She smiled and said, "Jus' you go ahead and drive, Mister Bruce. Old Evvie will keep an eye on you to make sure you don't fall asleep."

Bruce did just that as the rain began to increase in intensity, but it seemed to be cleaner, if cleaner rain is a possible thing.

Just west of Shreveport, Louisiana, after making the big swing onto Interstate 20, Bruce felt a hand on his arm and realized with alarm that he had been nodding off to sleep. A quick glance into the back seat told him Evvie Bascom had nodded off herself, but Gina had awakened without his noticing and had been watching him. She turned in the seat to face him and said, "Maybe if you talk, you'll stay awake better. I know it helps me."

"What should I talk about?"

"Why don't you tell me some more about yourself? We really didn't have much time back in town to get to know about each other."

"That will only take a couple of miles."

"Well, why don't you start out slowly and see how it goes?" Gina insisted.

"Well, I'm thirty-eight years old, divorced, two kids both living in California with their mom, and I'm going to Colorado. That didn't take long, did it?"

"No, it didn't, but you also didn't tell me anything."

"Anything, like what?"

"Like where were you born?"

"Gulfport, Mississippi."

"Where did you meet your wife? What did she look like?"

"We met when we were both attending Mississippi State. She was tall and slender and beautiful and had long blonde hair, and all the boys wanted her, but I got her. I sure did get her. What I got her was very pregnant, and because of that, she never finished her senior year and never let me forget it. I was able to finish the year and got my degree in civil engineering, but I had to take on two extra part time jobs to do it.

"Neither of our parents took it too well, but Bonnie's parents never forgave me for it. I'm sure they had much higher aspirations for their Bonnie Anne than to be married to a struggling civil engineer working for a construction company. We settled down in New Orleans, mainly because that was where the work was, and secondarily because Bonnie liked the excitement of the big city. My son, Keith, was born in our first summer in New Orleans."

"What about your other child?"

"Kaitlin was born almost two years later. Keith coming along was a surprise to me, and I know that Kaitlin was a much bigger surprise to Bonnie. That's my ex's name, Bonnie, in case you haven't already guessed." When he said her name, Bruce's voice got raspy and it was obviously painful for him to continue.

Bruce continued without any more of Gina's gentle prodding this time, but he sounded to Gina as if he were chewing on ground glass slivers just to get the words out. "We settled down in a little housing tract north of the city, and things were going very well, at least I thought they were. When Keith was three, Bonnie got it into her head that we needed a bigger, better home, but money was tight, so I decided to build my own. I laid out a plan and bought the property. It took me about two years of working every spare moment that I had just to finish it. By then, Bonnie was already deciding it was too small and in the wrong neighborhood, so I had to do it all again.

"After the second house was completed and decorated to her satisfaction, it had to be furnished up to the standard of the neighborhood. After that, it was clothes for her and the children, quality cars, more furniture, and finally, a membership in the country club. It seemed like all I was doing was working and taking care of the children and all she was doing was playing golf or tennis or working on her suntan. The maid was more company to me and more of a mother to the children than Bonnie ever was.

"I have worked for the Pritchard Construction Company ever since I got out of school and have been project engineer for them on several big jobs. That's where the trouble really started."

"What kind of trouble?"

"Well, Bonnie was spending every dime I made, and a few more I didn't, on herself and the kids, and always wanting more. I began to wear out, just got plain tired of keeping up with whomever. In order to keep up with her and not have to work eighty hours a week, I began to skim a little off of the petty cash accounts, between paychecks. Then sometimes it wouldn't get back and I'd have to skim a little in another place to cover it. I sometimes think that juggling the books was harder than getting another job.

"About this time, we began to argue a lot. I would complain about her spending too much money and not enough time with the children. When I told her the maid was a better mother to them, she accused me of making the maid a better wife than she was. She would always end up throwing back at me that I had gotten her 'in trouble' back in college and that it was all my fault that she didn't finish and have a career. That's when I would cry bullshit and storm out. Over the years, I've become more and more certain her getting pregnant was just an excuse to avoid making her grades to graduate and get a job. I wonder how much she helped the pregnancy process along, too. As it is, she never worked a day in her life. Either way, nothing ever got settled or got any better.

"Two years ago, I came home from work one day in the early afternoon because I had forgotten some blueprints, and I found her in bed with Lonny, the golf pro from the country club—the one she had insisted we join but we plainly could not afford. Then, instead of being contrite at being caught in bed with another man, she got angry with me for coming home and blurted out that she was getting a divorce and moving to California with her lover and my children. After that, things just seemed to come apart and all my willpower just left me. I got tired and just gave up the fight.

"I was forced to move out of the house, and as time went by, it became apparent that Bonnie was entertaining a prominent attorney who was also a member at the country club—guy's last name was Pickering, I think. Can't remember his first name; it could have easily been Ruthless. He was bright, powerful, and extremely well connected in family court, because without much effort on his part, he tore my life apart. Bonnie got the children, the house, the car, the savings, such as they were, and sixty percent of anything I earned for the rest of my natural life. I got to visit the children every other weekend, and she even managed to screw me out of that whenever she could."

Bruce was staring ahead at the rain-slicked highway as he rattled on. Gina said nothing but was absorbing every word. "She must have been sleeping with the judge and the lawyer, because the final settlement she got left me destitute. It took most of my pay just for the alimony and child support. I became so damned depressed that I began to hit the bottle, and from there on, my life just went from bad to awful. I had to give Bonnie most of my share of the house. Then I had to pay off what I had skimmed from the company's petty cash accounts.

"The only place I could afford to live was a broken-down trailer in back of the Royal Sanesta down by the water. They let me have the trailer for a few dollars' rent, and I worked the rest out in maintenance and repairs on the motel. The place itself was not too bad, but they got more than their money's worth of labor out of me. The condition of the place really didn't matter much anyway, because most of the business was short-stay stuff—very short-stay."

Bruce blinked his eyes slowly to lubricate them and again stared straight ahead into the night. "As soon as she could, Bonnie took the children and moved to California with her golf pro, who supposedly had a very good job offer out there, and I couldn't do a damned thing to stop her. I was so poor, I often couldn't afford to call the kids long-distance and could only e-mail them from the company computer. When I asked them to meet me in Colorado, I had to call them collect and couldn't even send them funds to travel on.

"Then about three days ago, I woke up in the morning with a horrendous hangover, and a young black hooker named Bitsie was in my bedroom, shaking me awake and begging me to help her start her broken-down old car."

Bruce noticed the immediate change of expression on Gina's face and added, "She was not in there doing business, Gina. She had a room out front for that."

Gina's smile told him he could continue.

"I asked her what the hell was all the rush about, and she said some man on TV had said that there were shooting stars falling all around and if one of them hit in Lake Ponchitrain, then the city was done for, and she didn't want to be here when all that water came down and drowned the city. Bitsie had been through Hurricane Katrina and knew all too well what that was about.

"She and her good friend, Birdie, who also worked out front, had immediately packed all their belongings and gathered their money and were leaving town immediately, but they couldn't get the car started. They had simply flooded it in their anxiety to get started, so I gave the battery a jump and got them started, and they left in a spray of stones."

"You seem to be inundated with damsels in distress lately," Gina said with a smile.

"Seems that way, doesn't it?"

"Go on, Bruce."

"Well, after my head cleared a little, I got to thinking about what Bitsie had said, so I switched on the TV and watched a while. It seemed like every station had something on about meteorites falling in the Atlantic and the Bering Sea, and more could be expected. They replayed clips from a Washington correspondent who had apparently first reported the story, and from the president's speech that same night, both of which I had missed. I remembered a book that I had read in college called *The Great Extinction* about the end of the dinosaurs being caused by a large meteorite or comet's head, and a *National Geographic* article I had read on the same subject. I realized the delta might not be a good place to be if any of these things came true.

"After that, I went to the library and read some recent newspaper and magazine articles by a guy named Neil deGrasse Tyson who is supposedly one of the smartest guys around on the subject, and that was enough for me. On the spur of the moment, I decided to get the hell off the delta."

"I decided to 'borrow' the company truck I've been using because it's tough and dependable and I'm used to it. I put it in the shop for a quick checkup and oil change and went shopping. I took the money I needed out of good old petty cash and bought supplies like some food and blankets, some camping stuff, and first-aid equipment. I added some booze at the last minute, picked the truck up from the shop, and called the ex to meet me at the Super 8 Motel in Boulder, Colorado, simply because it seemed to me to be the gateway to the Rockies. It was late afternoon by then, so I laid down to catch a short nap and let the commuter rush dissipate before leaving. I slept a little later than I had planned to, and that's how I happened along in front of your place last night."

"Why Colorado?" Gina asked.

"I've got an old dog-eared Rand-McNally travel atlas I used to look at often when I needed to daydream about getting away from all my problems. On the cover is a picture of a beautiful mountain lake, and I used to fantasize about living there. I would build a log cabin and live the frontier life. Boulder, Colorado, seemed like the gateway to my dream, so I just decided to go, and here I am; I'm on my way."

Bruce seemed to be relieved after telling his story, and Gina was more than pleased at getting an insight into his past. His words seemed to confirm her opinion that he was really a good man who was down on his luck and trying to start again. That was an honorable way to be. "Thank you for being honest with me and all that, Bruce. I know how difficult it is to relive the past."

"How do you know that I wasn't just making it all up as I went along?" Bruce asked.

"I watched your face," was her only answer.

"Actually, I feel a little better having talked about it. It seems to give me a clearer picture of where I'm going." He smiled at Gina, liking her a lot, and she sent a smile back to him that made the entire episode worthwhile.

\* \* \*

Manny Cruz-Lebron placed the receiver down on the cradle and rubbed his eyes for the thousandth time. He wanted a cigarette so badly that his head ached, but he could not leave the group of hastily gathered students and technicians in the National Hurricane Center. Many of them had friends or acquaintances aboard Hunter 14, and she was late returning from the search—very, very late. Manny shrugged his shoulders and shook his head to try to clear off some of the weariness and sadness as he turned around to face the group.

"My friends, I am afraid we have held on to our vain hopes as long as we possibly can. Hunter 14 is missing. We have had no contact with the crew since they made their last pass to try obtaining some readings from the eye of the storm itself. Had they started for Miami after that pass when we lost contact, they would have arrived hours ago. By this time, there is no possibility of their having any fuel left, so they have been declared missing and assumed down. The Air Force and Coast Guard will begin a search as soon as conditions permit. I know how deeply saddened you all are by this situation; we all had friends on 14. Let's take this time to finish our work and make what they did out there count.

"On a positive note, there is a ship very close to the storm area, and her captain has agreed to put his ship and crew in harm's way to patrol the area in search of 14. Let's hope he is successful."

Manny then rose from his desk and began to herd all the staff back to their workstations and to gently encourage, cajole, or prod them into action. When this was done, he returned to his desk and took a small telephone book from his wallet, punching in the number he did not want to dial.

"Amos, this is Manuel Cruz-Lebron from the National Hurricane Center." He listened for a moment. "No, they have not yet returned and are assumed to be down and missing. The data they transmitted just before we lost all contact confirms my theory that what we have is a red-hot meatball sitting on the bottom of the Atlantic. Preliminary reports from our aircraft indicate that it is probably a pretty good-sized meteorite that can generate enough heat to create a large low-pressure system and probably spin off one or more tropical storms. We'll have to track them and warn residents throughout the Caribbean and up the East Coast."

Manny's jaw tightened in frustration as he listened for a few minutes. "No, sir, I will not do that. Hurricane warnings will go out as usual. I will, however, try to find a plausible reason for tropical storms in this season."

Manny listened for another few minutes. "I understand your position fully, sir, but I must do my job. There is something else you must consider."

The voice coming from the other end of the phone line was audible in the room. Manny's tone became more defiant. "Yes, sir, but a strike of any significant size can cause tsunamis large enough to threaten coastal areas. Residents must be warned."

More discussion followed. "Yes, sir, I can do that. The captain of the collier is in the area, but Sir, we have to assume this will probably generate tsunami waves. We'll still have to warn coastal areas to be prepared for a tidal surge of several feet." Manny listened to the phone for another few minutes, his sensitive features mirroring both the sadness of losing his crew and the anger derived from the pressure being put on him by uncaring politicians.

"Yes, sir," he concluded, "I will definitely keep you informed."

Manny held the phone off the hook for a few moments as he fought to control his anger and disgust, then he motioned over to Maggie Ravalli, his secretary.

"What can I do, Manny?" she asked quietly.

"Start tracking down all our staff, wherever they are, and get them in here to work. You can get hold of the lead people, then let them gather up their staffs. Don't take any shit from them Maggie; just tell them that I want them in here now because the Atlantic hurricane season is starting early this year."

\* \* \*

Collier *Mary A. Goddard* wallowed slowly in an angry six-foot swell, maintaining just enough turns on her huge propeller to hold her seaway in the heavy weather. Loaded to the top plimsoll mark as she was with West Virginia "topsoil," it was extremely difficult for her captain to maintain her position as her whaleboat brought in the survivors. There had appeared to be several people in the round, bright-orange life raft that they had spotted after responding to the distress call and Coast Guard report of an aircraft down nearby.

Captain Konrad Kitzke had immediately reversed his course and begun steaming back through increasingly bad weather toward the area where he had observed the bright flash several hours ago. The report they had received had been clear and left no room to consider personal or financial losses. The Coast Guard had notified him that Hunter 14, a Lockheed WC-130J hurricane-hunter aircraft with a crew of fourteen aboard, had been dispatched to investigate the flash he had reported, which might have been the cause of the rapidly expanding tropical depression. Hunter 14 was currently overdue back in Miami and was presumed missing. She had not responded to repeated calls for status since making a close approach to the storm center earlier that day. The reason for this lapse was quite obvious.

Captain Kitzke worked his boat carefully as his crew of black and mixed Asian origin chattered excitedly and crowded around the gangway ladder helping as the survivors were brought aboard. The captain's blue eyes were deeply set in his tanned, leathery face, and they studied the rescue effort carefully. There appeared to be some wounded among the survivors, and he silently thanked God that his first officer had some medical training and that one of the Chinese in the black gang was excellent at first aid. On Kitzke's orders, they had already established a sick bay in the officer's wardroom.

The captain watched carefully as one of the survivors, obviously an officer, separated himself from the others and came limping slowly toward the companionway to the bridge with his own third officer's assistance. When they arrived on the bridge, he said simply, "Welcome aboard, sir. I am Captain Konrad Kitzke, master of the Mary Goddard. I hope that I can be of assistance to you and your crew."

"Thank you, Captain Kitzke, but you already have been. I'm Captain Bob Bertelli of NOAA hurricane research aircraft Hunter 14. I understand from Mr. Lee that you turned your ship back and came to our rescue, and I also understand some of what that is costing you and your company in time and money, and I thank you on my crew's behalf and mine." Even given the unusual circumstances, the conversation sounded stiff and stilted to Bob. Captain Kitzke was a dour and standoffish man, and Bob had to restrain himself from embracing him in joy and thanks for his rescue. "Captain," Bob said, covering his discomfort, "I was reporting some critical information to the NOAA hurricane center when my aircraft got into trouble. I wonder if I might use your radio to get a radio message back to them."

"Certainly, Captain Bertelli. We have already notified the Coast Guard of your rescue, and we will be pleased to make all the resources of this vessel available to you, but first, we must speak privately. Will you come to my cabin for a moment?" Without waiting for an assent, Captain Kitzke turned and entered his sea cabin, immediately off the bridge.

The cabin was Spartan and small, containing only a small desk, a cot, and the equipment necessary to work the ship at sea. One amenity that it did have was a small bar, and Captain Kitzke poured two stiff glasses of brandy without asking, handing the larger one to Bob. "Captain Bertelli, I must ask you to confer with me in a difficult decision."

Bob Bertelli's stomach sank with the words. He knew what the *Mary A. Goddard's* captain was about to say, because he had already thought about it himself. Nonetheless, he did not want to deal with the reality.

Captain Kitzke got right to the heart of the matter. "Captain Bertelli, how many of your crew remains unaccounted for?"

"Five are still missing, including my copilot."

Captain Kitzke nodded. "I understand it has been many hours since your aircraft went into the sea. Is that correct, Captain?" Konrad Kitzke's eyes bored into Bob's.

"That is correct, sir," absolutely hating the direction of this conversation.

"And in that time, you were not able to locate or contact any other survivors of your crew?" Captain Kitzke's stilted English might have been humorous under different circumstances.

"That is also correct."

Captain Kitzke nodded sadly and continued. "Since that is the case, Captain Bertelli, I must secure from this search and put my vessel under way and clear this weather area as quickly as possible. She is heavy laden and not riding well in these seas, and the glass is still falling. I am sorry for your loss, Captain Bertelli, and if I could, I would remain in the area to search for bodies, but I must consider the safety of my crew and my vessel." Konrad Kitzke's blue eyes looked sadly into Bob's, but the set of his jaw showed that there would be no change in his decision.

"I understand, Captain. I sincerely appreciate your efforts, and the danger you have already accepted to help us."

Konrad Kitzke simply nodded his head very slightly and stepped to the cabin door. "Come in, Mr. Lee, please," he said in a conversational tone, and Sammy Lee came into the cabin immediately. Nodding to his third officer, the Captain continued. "Sammy, please take Captain Bertelli to the radio shack so that he can get his message off to Miami Center. Then see to the remaining survivors. If the raft is not onboard, then set it adrift; we have to begin to make some headway immediately."

"Yes, sir," Third Officer Samuel Lee snapped off, then proceeded to lead Bob Bertelli off the bridge and into the narrow companionway that led to the tiny radio shack. Bob was pleased to see that although, on the exterior, the collier was not a new ship, her keel having been laid in 1969, she was immaculately maintained for a coal carrier, and the ship's electronic equipment seemed to be both modern and in good condition.

"I need to contact the National Hurricane Center in Miami on"

The radio operator cut him off with a hand chop and handed him the radiophone handset. He had apparently overheard Bob's request of Captain Kitzke through the companionway that connected the radio shack to the bridge and had already made the connection.

"Bob, is that you? This is Manny in Miami Center."

"Yes, Manny, it's me."

"What the hell happened out there? I need to know everything."

"It all happened so fast, Manny, that it's hard to make a clear word picture of it. We were making one last close pass of the cloud bank, when we were caught in a wind shear or gust, or something close to that. I've never experienced anything like it. One minute, we were in control, and the next, we were being sucked right into it. Kenny and I both had the controls, and between us, we could not level off the aircraft. It was simply impossible to stay airborne." Bob Bertelli hesitated here to regain his composure.

"No sooner than we had cleared the clouds, the turbulence became unmanageable and we were slammed upward by a monster updraft. Manny, if 14 hadn't been an ex-Navy P3C aircraft with the beefed-up wings for armaments, that updraft would have torn both wings right off."

Bob Bertelli scrubbed his hand back through his short-cut hair and shook his head clear so he could continue. "We were spun around like a top, then we flipped over on our back as we were spit out of the turbulence before we had much chance to understand what we were dealing with. Kenny and I fought the controls, but we were nose-down and diving and couldn't seem to hold anything like a stable altitude. It took all of our strength just to level off before the tail section slammed into the sea and we just pancaked in. After that, she just came apart. There were nine of us in the raft, Manny; that's all I can find. Kenny's one of the missing."

Bob Bertelli dropped down into a vacant chair in front of the radio console and hung his head. Ken Becker had been a longtime friend and frequent crew member, and the shock of his loss was just settling in.

"I know this is a bad time, Bobby, but I need to know what your impression of the cloud column's internals were. Can you do that for me?"

"Hot and turbulent, with a vicious updraft. I had a brief impression of a steam bath, and we couldn't find an eye. It appeared to be all storm with no center, but I can't be sure of that. It was just hot and bumpy and more violent than anything I've ever flown into." Bob hung his head again, near exhaustion.

Sammy Lee took the radiophone from Bob's hand, and the captain's arm just flopped lifelessly down into his lap. "Miami, this is Third Officer Lee of the Mary A. Goddard. Captain Bertelli is in no condition to continue this conversation. We are preparing to make way and must terminate the search operation. Thank you. Out."

Sam set down the radiophone and put his arm around Bob Bertelli's back. "Captain, I'll get you over to sick bay, and they can check you over, then we had better get you some rest; you're about done in. After you are well rested, you can call Miami back." The words were more of an order than a request, and in any case, Bob was not in any condition to argue the point. Sam Lee raised him up as if he were a child and shortly had him settled into a comfortable bunk in his own cabin. A quick, almost perfunctory, checkup by the first officer had shown no medical problems, and a double shot of medicinal brandy had been all it had taken to put Bob out for an extended rest.

\* \* \*

At the National Hurricane Center, Dr. Emmanuel Cruz-Lebron turned to Catherine Bertelli and said with a huge grin, "He's okay, Cathy. It just took that old tub of a collier a long time to come about and steam back into the area."

Cathy Bertelli burst into joyous tears and collapsed into Manny's arms. He held her tenderly, understanding the release of her pent-up fears and emotion as if they were his own. All around the large room, technicians and forecasters looked up from their monitors that showed satellite views of the huge depression and lists of regional weather stations to be notified. They all smiled. Bob and Cathy Bertelli were a popular couple.

Cathy stayed still for a few moments, then leaned back and asked, "Any word on Kenny or the rest?"

"Nine have been recovered; five are missing. I'm sorry to say Kenny has not been found yet."

Tears again began to flow from Cathy Bertelli's eyes as she thought of Kenny's wife and family, and the strong possibility of their great loss. *I'll go right over and sit with Kaleigh until some further word comes,* she thought. *At least then she'll have some company.*

Cathy Bertelli had no idea that in a few hours, all of her own sorrow and that of Kaleigh Becker would become academic when the great tsunami that was even now beginning to build off the continental shelf arrived in Miami and along the East Coast with devastating effect. Additional meteorites further north in the Atlantic would soon add to the tsunami's strength and size.

\* \* \*

Patsy Cox shifted her body into a more comfortable position in the seat as she tooled her Mustang down US Route 13 southbound. After leaving Salisbury in a spray of half-frozen slush, she had rolled quickly through the sleeping villages of Princess Anne and Pokomoke City and was traveling deep into the agriculturally rich area of Virginia's eastern shore. The night was a velvety pitch black that was relieved only by the occasional night-light in a long, low chicken house, or an outside light in a farmyard to show her that civilization really existed. It was an eerie feeling, and she shivered slightly in response to a sudden chill that ran up her spine. She instinctively reached for the dashboard and raised the heater setting a notch.

The rain-and-snow mixture was just intense enough to force Patsy to moderate her speed, even on this very familiar stretch of road, and this annoyed her greatly. Now that she had made the decision to leave her comfortable and familiar life and travel two thousand miles to see Tom Brooks, she wanted to race right through the night. And she couldn't.

To keep herself awake and alert, Patsy was playing a movie in her mind. She was the director, and she ran the film back through the evening's activities, going through them scene by scene. Her movie was like the last chapter in a romance novel that is at once difficult to believe but nonetheless completely true.

After carefully considering Tom's phone call, and after her difficult decision to go west had finally been made, Patsy had moved swiftly. With her usual decisiveness and economy of motion, she had quickly sorted through her clothes, selecting the ones that were practical and fit her mission, rejecting the rest. Her toiletries and personal items had been quickly added, along with a few things from her little home that she did not want to be without no matter what the outcome of this little trip might be.

An album of photos had been added to the small pile of very personal items, along with a leather-bound diary. At the last minute, she had added her framed degree in nursing from Salisbury State and her Maryland nursing certificate. Patsy regretted not being able to complete the course work in nurse practitioner studies that she had nearly finished, but there was no other way for her. On an impulse, she had added the texts and workbooks for the last semester, bowing to her need for closure, and she vowed to herself to finish it on her own.

Last, but certainly not least, Patsy had added her portable pharmacopia, the name given to her travel bag of drugs and medical supplies by Hilda Bastenbeck. More than a first-aid kit, the square nylon bag contained everything necessary to administer aid to an accident victim or to deliver a baby. A brief inspection of the contents had convinced her that she needed to make a few critical additions, for which she would have to go back to Peninsula General. In her heart, she was not really sure if this wasn't just a good excuse to say good-bye, but it really didn't matter. She wanted to make the stop, and it was right on her way.

After quickly loading her bags into the Mustang, Patsy had emptied the refrigerator and taken out the garbage. These mundane chores seemed to calm her heart and give her a sense of returning. Lastly, she had taken one final walk around her home, storing it all in her memory and taking a moment to touch the treasures she had to leave behind. Then she had turned out the lights, locked the house, and stored the key behind the "Welcome Friends" door topper sign, as usual, and left the only home she had ever loved. She never looked back.

Her first stop had been at the all-night pharmacy in Salisbury, where she purchased eighty dollars' worth of first-aid supplies and some over-the-counter medications, which she packed in her pharmacopia. Her second stop had been at Peninsula General Hospital, where Richie Madden had been on duty at the pharmacy. "Hey there, Patsy. What you doin' workin' so late tonight?" had been his cheery greeting at two thirty a.m.

"Just working a little overtime to help out," Patsy had lied. "Can you fill this out for me?" She'd handed him a neatly printed list of the items she needed. "It's for the unit," she'd lied, again.

"Sure thing," Richie had assented, not batting an eye. He was a nice young man who greatly resembled one of Frank Perdue's prized chickens. From the side, Richie's nose, chin, and Adam's apple lined up, and when he walked, he bobbed his head forward just like a chicken. At times, Patsy had a hard time not chuckling at the analogy.

"I'll be back in a minute, Richie," Patsy had said, smiling.

"Sure enough, Pats. It'll be ready when you get back."

Patsy had watched him move back into the room before she'd turned and gone down the hall to the emergency admitting area. It was a quiet night there, and the nurses had been taking their ease at the station. Patsy had slid in quietly and gone into the first empty room, #10. With quick intentional movements, she had gathered up bottles of xilocane and syringes. She'd added two small surgical kits and some assorted sutures, bandages, tapes, and dressings. Then, satisfied that she had pretty well cleaned the room out, she had stepped to the door, lightly gripping the knob.

At that instant, a shadow had appeared on the door and she'd heard a familiar voice say, "What I wanted to show you is right in here, Miss DeWitt." Patsy's heart had sunk, and her mind had raced. The voice belonged to Dr. Krasney, a young resident with a reputation for luring young and pretty nurses into empty rooms for a quick game of slap and tickle, and anything else that might develop. Through the frosted glass, she could see the shadow of an arm reaching for the doorknob that she was still holding. She had bolted.

Four quick steps had taken her to the door of the adjoining room, and with a quick twist of the knob, she had been through the door. "What the hell?" had come a startled voice.

In an instant, Patsy had realized what was happening. There had been a scattering of clothes on the floor, and a pair of intertwined bodies on the examination table. *Oops,* she'd thought foolishly, *out of the frying pan and into the fornicating fire.*

She'd never broken stride on her way to the door and had even managed to mumble a brief, "Don't mind me," as she had gone out into the lighted corridor just as the door to room 10 closed. The duty nurses had still been occupied with their coffee and gossip, so she had quickly stepped out of the emergency area. Shaking her head, she'd thought briefly, *What have I been missing by working afternoon shift all these years?*

Back at the pharmacy, Richie had filled her order and had it packed neatly in a blue plastic basket. Patsy had smiled her sweetest smile as she had accepted the requisition form he'd handed her and signed without batting an eye: Patricia E. Cox, RN. "Thanks, Richie. You're a sweetheart." A quick conspiratorial wink, and she'd been gone.

Her heart was heavy at the need for this small felony, but Patsy had firmly drawn the line against taking any controlled substances under false pretenses, and this made her feel just a little better. She'd made a stop at the supervisor of nursing office and there penned a quick note for her boss, requesting two weeks of emergency leave for personal reasons and promising to be in contact about a return date. Patsy was also pleased she had taken the few minutes necessary to go through the pediatrics ward and say a quick good-bye to her friends on shift and to look in on her kids one last time before leaving. After this, she'd had only one more stop to make.

"Goin on a trip, Pats?" Nate Holloway had asked as he pumped her gas and thoroughly checked out the luggage, food, and things that she had packed inside the car. Nate had been night man at the Wawa Food and Gas-Mart in Salisbury for as long as there had been one, and Patsy often stopped in after work for gas or coffee, or just to chat. Nate was a good man and honest as the day was long. In fact, he had only one minor fault—he was an insatiable gossip. Nate was always polite and responsible, and he knew every bit of news around the town and for most of Wicomico County. He could tell you who was sick, who was pregnant, and, usually, who the father was. He always knew what fish were biting in the bay or in the ocean, day or night, and what bait or lure they were hitting, and even though he rarely left the store, he could tell you exactly how to fish them. He always knew what the weather was for the town, the county, and the Delmarva Peninsula, and usually for the entire eastern United States.

"Yes, I'll be gone for a couple of weeks, Nate. Will you stop in and check my place for me once in a while? You know where the key is."

"Sure will, Pats. I figured you'd be gone for a right-smart time, from all that stuff in the back seat. Anything else I can do?"

"That's all, Nate. Just see my place stays okay, will you?"

"Be glad to, Patsy. You know that."

Nate had been boiling with curiosity, but he also knew Patsy well enough not to try to wheedle it out of her. Nate thought that Patsy was a great girl, and he liked her a lot, but she could be tight as a clam's ass at high tide when she wanted to be. He had finished topping off the tank, watching through the window as she had filled a sixteen-ounce coffee cup and selected some snacks for the road. He would have one last attempt to ask her when she paid up.

"Thanks, Pats. See you in a couple weeks, then?" At least he'd have something to tell if he knew when she was coming back.

"You bet, Nate, couple of weeks."

"You be careful in this rain," Nate had said, getting really serious. "This is one damn strange storm…can't seem to make up its mind if it wants to rain, snow, sleet, or all three at the same time. I'll bet those meteorites they keep talking about on TV are what's screwing up the weather. Going south, are ya?" Nate hadn't been able to resist trying to glean a little more information for the gossip mill.

"See you, Nate. Take care of yourself."

"You do the same Patsy." It was almost as if he'd known he'd never see her again.

Patsy choked back sudden tears, mashed the accelerator, and spun her wheels a little when skidding away from the pumps and out onto Route 13 southbound. She had to smile a little, though, because she knew Nate was watching and wondering who it was she knew in Virginia. She also made a mental note to take it a little easier until she had a better feel for the road. It wouldn't do her any good to wreck her nice car before she even got out of town.

A gust of wind shook the Mustang and carried with it sleet that rattled on the roof and windshield. Patsy shivered involuntarily and edged the temperature up a little more on the heater. It was going to be a long night, but if she could get through the bridge tunnel and onto I-64 in Norfolk, she felt that she would be well started. She could catch some sleep in a motel where I-64 and I-81 crossed in Staunton, Virginia. *Yes*, she thought, *that will be a really good start.*

Traffic was no problem at this hour of the morning. Farmers were all sound asleep, preparing themselves for another busy day. No more were the flat fields filled with watermelons and cantaloupes for the northeastern markets. Interstate 95 had opened these markets to the growers in the Carolinas and Georgia and had put the economy of the Delmarva into a tailspin until Frank Perdue and his chickens had come along. He had been a man with an idea, and the time had been right.

Frank had said to the failing truck farmers something along the line of "You build the chicken houses, and I'll put in the chickens. I'll give you the feed, and you raise the birds. You grow the grain, and I'll buy it to make the feed. When the chickens are raised, then I'll take them to market and sell them, take out the cost of the birds and the feed, and keep twenty-five percent of the profit. You get seventy-five percent." It worked wonderfully, and it had saved Delmarva.

Since then, the area's economy had blossomed around the poultry and freezer-plant industries and was self-contained and self-sufficient. In the rich, sandy soil and gentle climate, a farmer could grow grain and soybeans on the same acreage in the same season, and these provided the feed for the poultry industry. Potatoes and vegetables were also grown to fill out the trays for TV dinners at the Swanson's and Bird's Eye freezer plants, and the agro-economy blossomed.

This morning, the weather was proving to be more of an impediment to Patsy's progress than traffic or her lack of rest was. All morning long, it had alternated between rain and sleet and snow, all the way down US 13 to the bridge tunnel. Going across the Chesapeake Bay, gusts of wind that buffeted the car on the bridges and from time to unpredictable time helped to keep her tense and alert, along with a steady stream of caffeine coursing through her system, Patsy took the long, sweeping concrete ramp onto Interstate 64 in Norfolk, Virginia, around four thirty a.m. as it turned north toward the Hampton Roads Bridge Tunnel to the mainland. As she passed the US Naval base at Norfolk, she was surprised to see it was ablaze with lights and was a beehive of activity. It seemed to her that every ship at the base was preparing to go to sea this morning. Patsy felt sorry for the poor sailors who had to work their ships and make ready for sea in this awful weather.

As she crossed the high arch of the Hampton Roads Bridge, she noticed that several large naval ships were already outbound from Norfolk. Patsy was no expert on military affairs, but this seemed to her to be a lot of activity for this weather and time of morning.

She promptly forgot about naval affairs as she fought her own battle against the wet snow and slushy roads, all the way from Williamsburg to Richmond, and blowing, heavy wet snow from the west. It was ungodly bad weather for this time of year.

It had taken much longer than Patsy had predicted to reach Staunton, Virginia, and she was emotionally and physically exhausted. Patsy selected the Comfort Inn, which was just before the entrance to Interstate 81, and pulled in, praying silently that they had a room available. They did.

She never even bothered to remove her clothes before collapsing onto the queen-sized bed and falling almost immediately into a deep sleep. Outside, the wind continued to howl and the mixed precipitation continued to rattle unheard against her windowpane.

\* \* \*

The sun was just beginning to brighten the heavy, snow-laden clouds in the eastern sky as Amos Bellinger knocked on the door to the president's private study in the East Wing of the White House. It had been a long and difficult day and night yesterday, and this early-morning call did not indicate that things would be getting better. Even though Amos had managed to catch a few hours of sleep in bits and pieces through the night, it had done little to relieve the deep bone-weariness he felt. He was actually a little jealous of the Marine guard at the entrance to the presidential quarters because the Marine would be relieved shortly and could return to his quarters and catch a full day's sleep.

"Come in, Amos," Jameson Coleridge said through the door.

The president of the United States was sitting in his bathrobe with his feet propped up to a crackling fire in the study. His face was pale and unshaven, and his eyes showed dark circles under them. Amos went first to the sideboard and got himself a cup of black coffee before joining the president fireside. "Horrible weather today, sir," Amos began hopefully.

"I hope you've got that bitch Morgenstern staked out naked in the Rose Garden so she can enjoy it along with us."

"No such luck, sir, but she's securely tucked away at Bethesda, suffering from nervous collapse and needing constant sedation."

"With dull needles, I hope."

"She is not getting the VIP treatment, sir. That is for sure. I told you Agent Somervold is in charge of that."

"Whatever she is getting is more than she deserves. Do you see this pile of messages?" the president said, picking up and shaking a stack of yellow sheets from the communications room downstairs. "These are from General Gates's headquarters, and every one is a new trouble spot erupting. The bitch hasn't the faintest conception of the terrible cost to the country her last broadcast created. She got her notoriety and national coverage, but at what personal cost for the people?"

"Seriously? All of those?"

"Yes, all of them. These are mostly small incidents, some looting and some uncontrolled fires, and a lot of pushing and shoving outside stores by ordinary people who just want to make up for lost time and stock up on consumables and hardware. Not surprisingly, traffic backups are becoming a problem. Long lines and gridlocks are hampering firefighting and emergency services. People are getting pretty pissed, and I don't blame them, either. Ms. Morgenstern's last broadcast opened the floodgates, and now all the networks have dropped all restraint and are blasting the airwaves with end-of-the-world stories. Our official informational broadcasts are getting lower ratings than *Miami Vice* reruns.

"I spoke to Tailspin Tommy just an hour ago, and he believes he can contain all the trouble spots as long as the power stays on. The utilities on the East Coast have done a magnificent job of restoring power wherever they have sufficient equipment left operational to do so. General Gates claims that his worst problem areas are those without power. Darkness seems to be the catalyst that removes inhibitions and allows normal people to go out and raise hell."

"Do they miss Ben Cohen and David Van Patten? I really had to pull them off for other things." Amos said as he studied Jameson Coleridge's face, trying to read the mood behind it.

"No, that doesn't seem to be the problem. We could have Alicia Keys sing the news acapella, and people would still switch over to a cable station and watch a bunch of geologists picking through an old crater and speaking learnedly about how many times we have been impacted before and how many species have been made extinct by these very impacts. You know, Amos, I really had no idea of how many times the earth has been struck by extraterrestrial objects in the past, not only by small stuff, but big craters like the Barringer hit in Arizona, or Wolfe Creek in Australia, or Manicouagan in Quebec. Did you know they found a sixty-ton meteorite in Namibia named Hoba, I think sixty tons…imagine. It still weighed sixty tons after all the atmospheric burn-off. They said on CNN yesterday that a meteorite the size of a couple of railroad cars created the Barringer crater, which is almost a mile wide and flung up 175 million metric tons of debris into the air. The sheer magnitude of it boggles my mind."

"Yes, sir, those kinds of numbers would boggle anyone's mind."

Jameson Coleridge shot Amos a look that said in no uncertain terms, "Stop placating me and give me some good news for a change." Unfortunately, there was not much of that.

"The Navy has been doing a good job of getting their major units out into open seas, sir. They've been working miracles."

"Now that is a positive note. Are they fully loaded?"

"Some units are loaded to safe capacity, sir, and any spare spaces on them are being filled in with bulk grain. My last report from the Navy was late yesterday, and they were concerned with the tsunami. They were planning to put all units out to sea, no matter what stage of loading they were in."

"Good, good," the president said, rubbing the salt-and-pepper stubble on his chin.

"The news from north and south of us is not so good."

"I know."

"The North Slope of Alaska took a pounding, and we haven't had any reports from up there in several hours. The Caribbean and Florida took a pounding from the wave caused by the south Atlantic hit. Atlantic coastal cities in Florida are a mess, and Cape Canaveral is out of commission for the foreseeable future. The damned tidal wave is running its way up the East Coast. Brunswick, Savannah, Charleston, Myrtle

Beach, and Wilmington are all badly hit, and the damned thing may be running up the Chesapeake Bay and the Potomac River soon. Won't you reconsider relocating to a safer place, sir?"

"No," the president said definitively. "What kind of relief effort is being mounted for the Eastern Seaboard, Amos?"

"Currently just reconnaissance by radio, sir. There are few, if any, local reports. Our best source of information has been the ham radio operators in the area. Most of them seem to have thought of a backup power supply and are staying online. The FCC is trying to establish them into a network for emergency information and coordination.

"The weather has been too bad for any visual flights over the area. We'll have to wait and see if the Navy can get anything close enough to the coast to get us an accurate report."

"Jesus Christ. How far north will it go, Amos?"

"It's pretty well petered out, sir, but New York and New Jersey coasts will see a tidal surgemuch worse than Hurricane Sandy gave them. The Delmarva Peninsula will also take some significant flooding."

"Keep me informed."

"Yes, sir."

"What else? I know there's more."

"Cuba took a pounding from the tidal wave," Amos continued, "and things are in a state of chaos down there. We have had no reports from Guantanamo Bay in the past several hours. Fortunately, we had evacuated the base down to a skeleton staff and battened down the hatches, but it's impossible to say what the state of affairs is down there. Castro's a miserable old bastard, but at least he was better than his brother. This is not the way I would have chosen to get rid of him."

The president nodded in agreement and let Amos continue.

"Both of these impacts are messing up our continental weather patterns significantly, and I'm told by NOAA and the Weather Service that this disruption will probably continue for quite a while." Amos hesitated. When he got no response from the president, he continued. "Airline schedules are in a shambles. Between the horrible weather, absenteeism, and scattered power outages, the air traffic control system is barely functioning. They're being pretty creative in finding ways to network and overlap control areas. Fortunately, there don't seem to be a lot of people who are interested in flying right now anyway. Agriculture department is making noises about poor to no crops this summer and the possibility of extreme shortages if much of our stored food stocks are destroyed by the weather or man-made intervention. This is another case where, in responding to budgetary constraints, we allowed grain stocks in storage to dwindle. We'll have to be willing to accept civilian casualties in order to maintain security on what remains." Amos glanced at the president to gauge his reaction and saw only a slight tightening of the muscles around Coleridge's mouth.

"Do what you have to do, Amos. We're going to be in this for the long haul."

"Yes, sir, I'll take care of it."

"What else is bothering you, Amos? You look like a kid who has to tell his father about a bad report card."

"There is something about Ben Cohen, sir." Amos hesitated.

"Well, what about him? Spit it out."

"I've been getting suspicious about all the meteorite strikes we're getting a full week or more ahead of their predicted arrival, so I had David Van Patten checking back on Ben's calculations, and it appears that Ben has either made a huge mistake or has purposely changed his original figures so that we would be looking in the wrong direction." Amos looked ashen.

Jameson Coleridge looked worse. "This can't be," the president stammered, the blood slowly returning to his face. "If this is true, he will be responsible for the unnecessary deaths of millions of people worldwide, and unimaginable and unnecessary suffering. Why would he do that? What could have been his motivation?"

"I wish I knew, sir, but I understand your reaction. In principle, it seems to be true, sir. David is waiting for a second independent confirmation from the Hayden Planetarium, but he feels his calculations are correct. He told me in confidence that Ben has been quite depressed lately and has even stated several times that he did not believe we should tell the American people anything at all about the meteorite showers."

"Depressed my ass, nobody could be depressed enough to purposely do something of this magnitude."

"Well, Mr. President, it seems that he could."

Both men were silent for a few minutes, just sitting there, staring into the crackling fire. Finally, Amos broke the silence and said softly, "Sir, I have a few things to clear up, then I'll get back to you. Will that be alright?"

"Certainly, Amos. See me as soon as you get organized for the day."

As Amos left the office, the Marine sergeant stopped him. "Sir, there is an important message for you."

"Thank you, Sergeant."

Amos took the message and slowly read it, then folded it carefully and put it in his pocket without comment. He would save this for later.

\* \* \*

Patsy Cox slept peacefully in her bed at the Comfort Inn in Staunton, Virginia, blissfully unaware that the lights she had seen blazing at the Norfolk Naval Station were all out and would not blaze again, or that she had just missed the arrival of the worst tidal wave in American history by the smallest of margins.

\* \* \*

The electronic sounds of her phone roused Devon Grant from a deep, exhausted sleep at exactly 5:30 a.m. by her bedside clock. She picked up the receiver, dropped it on her pillow, and mumbled into it, "Hello?"

"Devon, this is Art Capiletti. Are you awake?"

"No."

"Good. Get dressed and come in as soon as you can. We're up to our collective asses in wildcats around here and need your help."

"But this is my day off," Devon said foggily.

"Tell somebody who cares. Just get dressed and come in."

"How can I get dressed and come in if I'm not awake?"

"Find a way." His last statement was followed by the dial tone.

"Can't argue with a dial tone," she said to herself. She almost fell back to sleep before she regained her senses and sat up in bed, blinking away her lethargy. *Unreal; it's still dark outside.*

Forty minutes later, Devon was pulling into the Space Weather Prediction Center parking lot with a hot cup of Starbucks coffee, a piece of banana bread in a bag, and a steadily mounting curiosity as to just what was so damned important to get her out of bed this early on her day off.

The Space Environment Lab was a beehive of activity this morning. The staff was all running about wearing hushed and serious looks of determination. As Devon entered the SWPC operations room, she spotted Art Capiletti and went directly to him. "What's up, boss?"

"Devon, I'm glad you're here. We've got several things going on at once, and not enough hands on board to keep up with the workload. AR7045 is still putting out at record levels, and so we have a K-9 plus to deal with. Satellite operators, the electric utilities, communications, and the railroads are all experiencing some major problems with this one. We have reports of some spotty blackouts in the East and Midwest. Apparently, some of the utilities are in a pissing match over whether or not they are SMD-related, and they're trying to get us in the middle of it. This is not a good thing.

"As if we don't already have enough to do, NASA has put up a shuttle flight on an emergency mission right into the middle of this solar storm, completely against our recommendation. They launched from Canaveral just minutes before it was hit by a seismic sea wave, and the facility has been trashed. The shuttle will have to adjust orbit to land at the Air Force Base at Edwards. Colonel Persons is working out a maximum time in orbit based on current levels of proton and x-ray exposure levels. Since they're already up, we can't do anything about that, but we need to monitor and report their exposure and forecasted accumulations so they can calculate an optimum landing site."

"What was that about a tsunami striking the Florida east coast?" Devon asked, suddenly alert and processing the Canaveral information.

"There was a meteorite strike in the southeast Atlantic of a fairly considerable size. It has apparently caused a tsunami large enough to raise hell with the entire East Coast. From all accounts, and they're admittedly sporadic, it's just terrible back there." Art noticed the immediate look of anxiety cloud her face but couldn't respond to it. "I wish I knew enough to give you encouraging news, Dev, but I don't. I do know that it's the coastal areas that are hardest hit, but if your guy is near Albany, New York, it's a seaport and not much above mean sea level. If the wave went roaring up the Hudson River, then he could be in trouble. I wish I could be more reassuring." Art's face was rumpled with lines of concern.

"What can I do?" Devon asked, suddenly needing desperately to be busy and involved.

"That's my girl," Art said, mistaking her need to be busy with feeling better. "Would you take over the tech desk from Joe? He has more experience with forecasting, and I need him to help me. He'll fill you in on the notifications."

"Sure thing, boss."

Devon moved quickly to the solar technician's desk and tapped Joe Florents on the shoulder. "Fill me in quickly, then go help Art with some studies he needs yesterday." Devon smiled at Joe's exited look.

"I just got off with New York ISO. Dev, they're all right so far, but things seem to be a mess back there." Joe smiled at the relief that blossomed on Devon's face. Apparently, her relationship with John wasn't such a well-kept secret after all. "Priority-one customers that have been called are checked off on the list," Joe continued. "I haven't had time to make up the fax report for priority twos and threes yet, so you'll have to do that. We're at K-9 plus, and a lot of major GIC activity has been reported. We've been getting a lot of information from the Sunburst system GIC recorders, and it's amazing. Recorders in the auroral zone are off the chart. In the sub-auroral zone from Labrador through Quebec and Ontario, the charts are bouncing around like crazy. In the United States, the same thing is showing up from Maine to Pennsylvania. I can understand why the utilities are having problems. Beyond that, there's nothing to report except that Shellcroft's little memos are all canceled and we play it square now. Got it?"

"Got it. Go ahead and help Art." Devon sat down and immediately hit the speed dial for NYISO operations center.

"ISO. Flynn speaking," came the quick, nervous answer.

"Hi, this is Devon Grant calling from SWPC. I'm looking for John Halloran."

"Then you'll have to look out around Ohio, because he left on vacation yesterday afternoon."

"He's gone?" Devon's feeling of relief was huge.

"Completely."

"What's your situation there?" Devon asked, trying to get a line on conditions that John might be driving through.

"All of southern New York and Long Island are blacked out along with New England, most of New Jersey, and eastern Pennsylvania. They got hit by the big ocean wave. Quite a lot of damage and loss of life. Never thought I would live long enough to see something worse than Hurricane Sandy up here, but I did. I understand there are a lot of small power outages in the rest of the Eastern Interconnection, but no really good information on them since communications are a mess. That's all I know, except that the weather is horrible back here, with heavy snow and high winds hampering our restoration plan. The rest of the state is holding on."

"Exactly what does the Eastern Interconnection mean?"

The often-repeated answer was delivered. "The Eastern Interconnection is made up of all the interconnected electric utilities from the Rocky Mountains east to the

Atlantic ocean and from Mexico north including all of Canada, but excluding Texas, which is its own operating area."

"All of the utilities in that whole area?"

"Yes, all of them."

"Then there could be problems in the Midwest?"

"That's correct. I'm told MISO operators are dealing with voltage swings larger than anyone has studied in simulations. Your SMD is raising hell with the high-voltage direct-current ties from the western systems across the mountains. There have been several trip-outs and power swings around the mountains, and a number of localized blackouts occurred. I believe they're pretty well cleared up by now, but with communications as bad as they are, no one can be sure." Bud Flynn was beginning to sound anxious to get off the line.

"Thanks, New York. I'll probably be talking to you later." She felt a bit overwhelmed, not understanding most of what he'd said.

"Call me anytime, but make it good news when you call."

She quickly checked the list of notifications Joe had started and continued where he had left off. She noticed Colonel Persons crossing the room with a concerned expression that was becoming familiar, but she was far too busy to stop and ask him about the situation back east. He began conferring with Art Capiletti, and they both were shaking their heads. A few minutes later, Joe Florents crossed the room, and Devon arched an eyebrow at him. He swung over past her desk and said, "Canaveral is a complete washout from the tsunami. They're going to have to change orbits and extend the flight so that the crew can land at Edwards. Colonel Persons is not at all happy about it, but it's too late now. I think he's pissed because he believes NASA knew about the tsunami and launched anyway. Gotta go!"

Devon turned to her console and got back to work. As she began to compose the fax to be sent to lower-priority customers, she noticed Mr. Shellcroft's crazy memos in the recycling basket. *Best place for them*, she thought and continued working.

\* \* \*

Buried deep beneath the rich alluvial soils of southern Louisiana in an area called WOTAB, which stands for West of the Atchafalaya Basin, there is a small area where the southwest corner of Evangeline Parish and the northwest corner of Acadia Parish meet. In this area lies one of the heaviest concentrations of natural gas pipelines in America. Hundreds of miles of accumulation lines run from numerous wellheads to compressor stations, where the gas pressure is raised to distribution levels. From there, the gas flows into distribution mains, which carry it to the next-stage compressor station. Here, the gas pressure is raised to transmission pressures of several hundred pounds per square inch. Billions of cubic feet of natural gas then flow into any one of the six thirty-inch transmission mains for delivery to bulk gas customers to the north and east areas of the United States.

Three of these huge arteries carry the bulk of the natural gas consumed by the energy-hungry northeastern states, and three others carry the gas due north to supply all of the mid-western states.

Located just north of the sleepy village of Basile, Louisiana, is the TransCo Basile pumping station. The station contains three gigantic Ingersoll Rand four-stage water-cooled, turbo compressors rated at 1200 cubic feet per second capacity at 725 pounds discharge pressure. All three compressors have been running at full capacity for more than a full day since the weather has been a bit colder than normal for March, but mostly due to the nuclear generation being shut down. This gas is supplying the fuel for many of the electric generators that are supplying electricity throughout the Midwest and Northeast.

Powered by the natural gas that they compress, the gas turbine compressors are powerful yet very delicately balanced precision machines. Today, the #3 compressor at Basile was beginning to run a little rough as its finely machined turbine blades spun thousands of revolutions per minute. The fourth bearing that supported the compressor shaft just past the intermediate-stage turbine wheels was wearing unevenly and beginning to heat up. Expansion of the bearing metal caused by this heating was bowing the turbine shaft a few thousandths of an inch and causing the shaft to shudder slightly. This vibration in and of itself was not a problem, but it was sufficient to set up a sympathetic vibration in the cooling-water supply line to the third-stage intercooler, and over time, this could be trouble.

The cooling-water supply line was connected to the third-stage cooling jacket by a rubber flex connection reinforced with internal braided stainless-steel mesh. The constant vibration of the coolant line opposed to the vibration of the compressor itself had caused the internal stainless-steel wires to begin to fray, and they in turn were beginning to cut deep into the rubber jacket of the flex connection. Already, there was a steady drip of cooling water weeping out of the rubber and onto the floor of the Basile pumping station. The puddle was growing.

\* \* \*

Paula Patowski and her Boston Tea Party had made fairly good time, considering road conditions on this dark and snowy night. They had left Boston shortly after midnight and were approaching Syracuse, New York. They could have made better time, of course, but Little Annie Phillips had needed three pit stops, a fact that was not making Paula very happy. She loved to drive, and this big van drove well in the snow, making the challenge of winter driving a pleasure for her.

"I wonder what's left of home now that the big wave hit Boston?" Burtha Kurtz remarked to no one in particular.

"I'm sure it's a mess, and I'm so glad you girls talked me into leaving early as we did," Wilma Krauss answered wholeheartedly.

"Thank Paula. She was the one who remembered that article in *Popular Science*," Burtha said.

"Stop talking about water, or I'll have to pee again," Annie Phillips answered.

*Please, Lord, not again*, thought Paula. "We only stopped a few minutes ago in Johnstown." The New York State Thruway is a well-maintained road, and the snowplows had been busy spreading salt and plowing, but still, the highway was partially covered with a thin gray slush. Paula appreciated that fact because she could keep them cruising along at a steady, road-eating sixty miles per hour. Lake-effect moisture had been making the snowfall much heavier since they'd passed Utica about sixty miles back, however, and the driving had been getting proportionately more difficult.

Suddenly, Paula's heart leaped into her throat. Just ahead of them was an ocean of brake lights. Paula's foot immediately came off the accelerator pedal and lightly touched the brakes.

Both lanes of the thruway were blocked with stopped cars from what appeared to be a huge chain-reaction accident ahead involving a great many vehicles. Trucks and cars were spread out across both driving lanes and on the shoulders too. It looked like a war zone.

Paula assessed the situation quickly, and her decision was instantaneous. Her eyes scanned left, then right, then rear. "Hold on, girls," she said in her usual commanding voice. "We're going to have to do some maneuvering here."

Handling the controls with a delicacy that was belied by her bulk, Paula darted to the left and onto the shoulder, then cut the wheel hard left. The big van began to tip sickeningly, but Paula held on a few seconds. When she was nearly lined up with the opening in the guardrail, she braked hard until she felt the rear wheels begin to lose the road, then gunned the engine and shot the van through, almost taking down the NO U-TURN sign. She then swung the van into a hard right turn and skidded again until she was driving westbound on the eastbound lanes of the thruway. Paula silently thanked God that the eastbound lanes were strangely empty.

"That sign said no U-turn," Wilma cried in a frightened voice. "We're going the wrong way."

"I thought the sign said no, you turn, so I did, and we're going in the only lanes available to us," Paula answered with more confidence than she felt.

"Where the hell do you think you're going?" asked Wilma Krauss, who was navigating on this leg of the trip, between Annie's pee stops.

"What did that last sign say?" asked Paula, ignoring Wilma's rhetorical question completely.

"Carrier Circle," Wilma answered.

"Where is Interstate 81 from Carrier Circle?" Paula demanded, watching a row of large motels whiz by from the corner of her eye.

"Next exit," Wilma came back.

"Good," Paula said and immediately eased the van across the two empty eastbound lanes to ride on the shoulder. "We can take 81 south and then find a road to head west. We are not going to get much further on the thruway."

"We'll still be driving in the wrong lanes!" Wilma moaned.

"We don't have any damned choice." Paula answered through gritted teeth.

Wilma looked ahead and saw just what Paula meant. Her heart stopped beating as the van careened toward a multiple-car and -truck accident completely blocking the eastbound lanes just ahead. People were milling around in the snow, and some were running toward them, waving their hands foolishly, trying to get the van to stop. Wilma closed her eyes and began to pray as Paula mashed down on the gas pedal and, in a split second, swung the van to the left, skidded sideways across a snow-covered grassy area, and then, at the last second, gunned the accelerator, causing the van to leap onto the exit ramp from northbound Interstate 81. The big van plunged down the hill, and Paula eased it to the left slightly and continued driving on the shoulder of the road, still facing into the oncoming traffic.

Horns were blaring, headlights were flashing, and profanities too numerous to mention were being mouthed through closed windows as Paula picked a soft-looking spot in the traffic and bulled her way across the two oncoming lanes and onto the inside shoulder. Then, again with perfect timing and a great shower of slush, she executed the same maneuver she had when leaving the thruway and cut a diagonal path through an unplowed U-turn path onto the southbound lanes of Interstate 81.

Slowly releasing her white-knuckled hold on the door handle, Wilma Krauss looked over at Paula. "My God Almighty! That was some piece of driving, Paula," she said reverently.

"Never mind that," Paula said grimly. "Just look for a service area, I think I peed myself."

"Me too, and I'm glad to see I'm not the only one," chimed in Little Annie from the back seat, where she was trying to unscramble some luggage that had been thrown about by the violent maneuvering.

Ignoring Annie as usual, Wilma said, "We can stay on 81 South past Binghamton, then take the Pennsylvania Turnpike, which is Interstate 70 West from there."

"Sounds good to me," Paula said, finally able to loosen her grip on the wheel and flex her fingers for a moment. "Now all we have to find is a bathroom."

The next big event would be life changing for all of them. It wouldn't be long from now, a day or two maybe. It would be then that the members of the Boston Tea Party would find the most unlikely, wonderful surprise coincidences of any of their long lives. Unfortunately, it would quickly be followed by overwhelming sadness.

\* \* \*

At NOAA's National Weather Service, several forecasters were standing around a bank of television screens, watching replays of satellite films that showed nothing more than almost complete and unrelieved cloud cover over the North American continent and most of the northern hemisphere. Other men and women were reviewing abbreviated stacks of local weather reports and were plugging available data into the Weather Service computer system. The picture they were seeing was like nothing they had ever seen before, and it actually defied all of the tried-and-true weather patterns for the northern hemisphere.

There were two known large meteorite strikes, one in the southeast Atlantic Ocean and one in the Chukchi Sea. Thousands of tons of water vapor were riding into the earth's upper atmosphere on superheated air rising from their core, and this had created two huge low-pressure areas.

The huge lows were intensifying, and the Coriolis effect of the earth's rotation was creating two huge cyclic low-pressure areas that were spinning off secondary low-pressure fronts, many of which were intensifying into storms of hurricane force.

Intensely cold arctic air was being pumped from the Arctic strike area, down and across North America. It was colliding in the midlands with warm and humid air pumping from the south Atlantic strike. Where the fronts occluded, the vast difference in pressures was creating huge thunderstorms and numerous small tornadoes. It was the most active front any of them had ever seen.

The forecasters didn't even know what to call these huge storm fronts, or how they would react to each other, so it was impossible to predict their course or intensity. What they did know was that the situation was grim and would continue until the meteorites cooled down enough to allow traditional weather patterns to resume. Until then, there would be a relentless parade of storms across the continent, mixed in with intense cold, flooding, and high winds.

Forecasters were trying to send out the information they had through normal communication channels, but without much success. They were concerned about warning people of potential dangers in this weather situation, but they were also aware that it might all be academic. The power had been off in the forecast center for two hours, and they were running whatever equipment they could on their emergency generator, but even this was acting erratically and might soon be gone. Even that might not matter, because if the power was off over a large area, then no one could watch TV or listen to a radio to find out about the weather anyway.

* * *

Kenny Smith was watching his little portable TV and shaving in the kitchen sink, getting ready to go to work when the lights went out. Just like that. The lights dimmed, and the TV picture got small, then they came back on and flickered a few times and then dipped once more before going out for good. Kenny wondered if it was one of those meteorites that he had watched reports about on the CNN special last night. It seemed like all the stations had shows about them. It was getting just a little scary.

Other people must be getting scared, too, he thought, because there had been a big crowd at the grocery store last night when he'd come in, and the same at the Wal-Mart store. The crowds outside had not been rowdy or even angry; they had seemed to be simply waiting to get inside. He had watched out his front window as the parade of shoppers had gone into PJ Jackson's Sporting Goods shop across the road. PJ ran the shop out of his garage behind his house, and all evening, people had been standing there in a line waiting to go in. They had just been talking and waving their arms until it had come their turn. Then they'd come out of there carrying guns and boxes of ammunition and an assortment of camping gear. Knowing PJ as well as he did,

Kenny was sure that he wasn't taking any credit cards or checks, just good old-fashioned cash money.

All of this strange activity was making Kenny restless this morning, and he decided to go down to the Speedway early to get some coffee and see Becky. That would brighten up his day. He never considered for a minute that that there was no power to make the coffee with. On his way downstairs, Kenny got to thinking that if so many people were buying guns, it might be a good idea for him to get one too. On an impulse, he walked across the street and up PJ's driveway to the shop, and then he stopped in his tracks. The shop door was open, and there appeared to be something that resembled a foot sticking out of it. Kenny approached with caution, as there were just too many men walking around with loaded weapons to do otherwise. Staying close to the wall, Kenny looked around the backyard carefully to be sure that no one was around and then moved forward. At the shop door, he saw that it really was a foot sticking out and that it was connected to PJ Petrullo's dead body. He just had to be dead, because there was a big knife sticking out of his back and a huge pool of blood on the shop floor. The shop also looked as if it had been stripped of anything of value and the rest was strewn all over the floor. Kenny backed up quickly and decided he needed to see if PJ's wife was alright. He hurried across the backyard and noticed immediately that the kitchen door was open wide.

A few quick steps brought Kenny to the back steps. He looked around the doorframe carefully, and his worst fears were confirmed. PJ's wife, Nina, was lying on the kitchen floor. She had been beaten terribly, her clothes were torn, and there was a lot of blood. She was not moving at all. Kenny did not want to look at Nina the way she was, but he knew he had to.

He crossed the kitchen in a bound and bent to her side. What he uncovered was worse. Nina's face was bruised, and another big knife protruded from her stomach. She was quite dead. Big salty tears began to course down Kenny's cheeks as a crushing sadness overcame him.

Both PJ and Nina had been good friends to him ever since he had come to town and moved in across the street. Kenny had often helped PJ with odd jobs around the place, and Nina had always rewarded him with some of her fine home cooking. Kenny felt deeply sad and angry at seeing her like this. It was a good thing little Nita couldn't see her like this, Kenny thought. *Nita!*

Suddenly, a weight hit him from the back, nearly driving him across Nina's prostrate body. He managed to brace himself against the force as he was being pummeled about the head and back. Kenny shifted himself around and saw Anita Petrullo, still dressed in pajamas and wearing a wild look on her tiny face. She was trying to get her clawed hands at his eyes. He grabbed her quickly in a bear hug and began speaking softly to her. "Nita, Nita, calm down. It's just Kenny Smith from across the street. Nita, calm down.... I'm not going to hurt you."

Slowly, the young girl relaxed in his arms and began emitting a sound that was somewhere between a cry and a groan but came out as a wail that sawed at the edges of his soul. She grabbed on around his neck and held on so tightly, she nearly cut off his breathing. Kenny held her close for a few minutes, just speaking softly to her, until she relaxed and quieted some, then he realized that he needed to see Becky even more than ever. Still carrying little Nita, he took her coat and scarf from the peg rack by the kitchen door and hurried across the road to his truck. He slid her lightly across the seat and jumped in. As he started up, Nita came over to lie down across the seat with her tiny head on his leg. Kenny kicked the Power Wagon over and roared off down the street, rubbing Nita lightly across her back all the while.

When Kenny got to the Speedway, he knew immediately that his day was not going to improve at all. He noticed right away that something unusual was happening here, and his adrenaline began to pump. There were four 4x4's, all hand-painted in camouflage, parked at the gas pumps, blocking them so no one else could get in there. *But there's no power to pump any gas*, Kenny thought.

He pulled his bright pink Happy Tyme Frozen Food Company truck up in his usual spot and noticed immediately that Becky was not behind the counter as usual. The man who was standing at the gas pumps eyed him nervously while two others were busily unloading what looked like some kind of portable pump from the back of a Jeep. "Nita, you stay here and watch out for Kenny's truck. Can you do that for me?"

She responded with a teary but trusting nod.

Kenny's belly did a nervous flip-flop as he jumped down from the cab and headed straight for the door. One of the camouflage-dressed men came over from the pumps and said in a loud voice, "Store's closed, mister; no power," but Kenny ignored him and brushed right by.

There were few men in the entire county who could have stopped Kenny from doing exactly what he had set in his mind to do. His six-foot, two-inch frame was lean and covered with long, work-hardened muscles. He could throw heavy cases of frozen foods around all day long and never tire, and his hands were big and powerful. The stranger in the camouflage coveralls appraised the situation in one quick glance and, with a shrug of his shoulders, quickly retired to the gas pumps.

Once inside, Kenny glanced around the store and saw that Becky was in the back corner with another man who was also dressed in camouflage and that she looked funny. Her face was drawn, and there was not the usual good-morning smile for Kenny. "What can I do for you, sir?" she said in a strange, flat voice. Nobody had ever called Kenny Smith "sir" before.

Surprising himself, Kenny caught on to Becky's drift immediately and came back, "Is the coffee still hot, sweet cheeks?" he said, trying to sound like one of the good old boys did. "And I need some butts, too."

"Coffee should still be alright; the power's not been off that long. What kind of cigarettes do you want?" Becky asked, moving quickly away from the dark man in camouflage and toward the counter.

"Pack uh Marlboro," Kenny said, fixing his coffee and watching the man in camo from the corner of his eye. The man did not look happy at all.

As Kenny came up to the counter, he saw the hint of a smile of greeting curl the corners of Becky's mouth, but it was her eyes that caught his attention. She was raising her eyebrows up and down very slightly and swinging her eyes toward the back of the store. Without moving his head in that direction, Kenny looked out of the corner of his eye and noticed that the door to the storeroom was ajar. It was plainly marked "Employees Only," and Becky had told him a while back that Speedway had very strict rules about this. That door was never open in all the times Kenny had been there. He caught her eye and nodded to her.

"That'll be $9.86," Becky said, smiling and handing him the cigarettes.

"Thanks," he answered, handing her the money.

Becky squeezed his hand a little as she handed him the change, and then turned toward the window to watch Kenny walk out to his truck. He got in, cranked it up immediately, and pulled out of the lot onto US Highway 36. For a second, Becky thought that she saw a young girl in pink pajamas sitting in Kenny's truck, then she put the thought aside as ridiculous.

"What the hell was that all about?" the man in the camouflage fatigues asked gruffly. He was dark and swarthy with a two-day growth of black beard and seemed to be a man not to be messed with—especially with that pistol on his belt and the big knife tied to his boot.

"Oh, nothing," Becky answered as casually as she could. "Just a guy that stops in here once in a while on his route. Nothing special."

The dark man placed his hand on the butt of the pistol on his hip and nodded his head toward the back of the store. "About time you showed me the storeroom, isn't it, blondie?"

"I don't think that's a good idea," Becky said, "It's strictly against company policy."

"Is it against company policy to get your blood all over the floor?" he asked with an ugly grin as he bent forward and started to draw the deadly looking black 9 mm automatic from the holster.

"Okay, okay," Becky said. "Don't get crazy on me."

"I'll get something on you all right," he said with an ugly leer. "Get back there.... *Move!*"

Becky moved as slowly as she dared toward the storeroom and pushed open the door. The dark man was as anxious as she had hoped he would be, and finally, he grabbed her arm in frustration and pushed her roughly into the back room. She reeled across the floor, pretending to trip, and caught her balance on the brass bar that opened the rear exit, undoing the latch in the process.

What came next was just as bad as she had expected, but only not so soon. The man grabbed the collar of her Speedway blouse and, with terrible strength, ripped it down, popping off all the buttons on the front of her shirt and leaving Becky with her arms immobilized behind her in the remnants of the blouse. "No more fucking around, cookie. I ain't got all day."

"Why are you doing this?" Becky gasped as he grabbed her by the throat and pushed her back onto some packing cases while fumbling the vicious-looking knife from the holster on his boot.

"Because I can, sweetie…because I want to and I can. The lights are out, the comets are falling out of the sky, and the cops are too busy with other things. So I can. And I will."

The knife blade was long, thin, and razor-sharp, and it sent a trail of chills through her as he held her by the throat, her arms behind her, still trapped in the tattered blouse. The man brought the knife up slowly, flat across her rib cage, and, with a quick flick of his wrist, slit the front of her bra, allowing her breasts to fall free. He took a moment to feast his eyes upon them before he said, "The skirt is next, girl, and if you fight me, then I'll have to cut it off, and I won't be so gentle about it. Do you understand?" His breath in her face smelled of whiskey, tobacco, and bad teeth, and it made her stomach uneasy.

Becky turned her face away as he leaned closer and unbuttoned her skirt. His body smelled of old sweat and too little washing, and his beard was black and rough against her cheek. His hands were adept, however, and too soon, her skirt and half slip were puddled around her feet.

The knife had nicked her skin slightly when the man had cut her bra loose, and a drop of blood from between her breasts was making a trail that led down past her belly button and onto the front of her white French-cut bikini panties. She finally managed to free her hands from the tattered blouse behind her, and quick as a snake, the man had the knife blade pressed against her cheek. "One funny move, little girl, and you will cease being the prettiest gal in town. Now drop them panties for me. *Now!*" He fumbled with the front of his fatigue pants.

From the pressure of the blade on her cheek, Becky knew he meant business, and so she slowly ran her thumbs down her sides and inside the waistband of her panties. It was at this instant that Kenny came crashing through the back door, a look of outrage in his eyes and a tire iron in his hand.

The dark man was so concentrated on the beauty of the young woman who was totally at his mercy, so much enjoying the look of sheer terror in her eyes and what he was going to do to her, that when he finished undoing the zipper of his pants, he reacted just a little too slowly. As he began to spin around to face whoever was coming through the door, the tire iron smashed into the side of his head, splitting his skull and sending him crashing to the floor. Kenny was on him in an instant. He had seen the stream of blood down Becky's belly and her initial efforts at taking her panties off, and he was outraged. He hit the man a second solid blow, then a third and a fourth.

"Kenny, stop, stop!" Becky shouted into his ear. She grabbed and held his arm to her bare chest, trying to restrain another blow, and Kenny could feel the heat of her through his shirt. His senses began to return. "Stop, Kenny, or you'll kill him."

"Would be no more than he deserves," Kenny said grimly.

"He's not worth it. Kenny, stop! I'm alright; he never got a chance to touch me."

"He cut off your clothes, didn't he? And you're bleeding, too. I'd call that touching quite a bit."

"He didn't hurt me where it counts, Kenny, so stop now!"

Becky's insistence finally got through to him. He relaxed slightly, lowered his arm, and allowed her to pull him away. The dark man's head was a mass of blood, and he didn't move at all. "I think he's already dead, Kenny."

He knelt and felt for a pulse below the man's jaw and found none. He repeated this on the other side and then at the wrists, All to no avail. The man was dead. "He's done-for, I guess." Kenny said.

"Oh, my God, Kenny! what are we going to do?"

He stood for a moment thinking, then noticed again the blood streaming down Becky's belly. With amazing calm, Kenny took a clean white handkerchief from his pants pocket and began wiping off the blood, starting at her panties and moving upward. When he got to her breasts he hesitated momentarily and Becky took the handkerchief from his hand and she cleaned upward the rest of the way.

Kenny stood for a moment as he got his thoughts in order, then asked firmly, "Have you got some other clothes around here?"

"Yes, I have some in my locker."

"Good. Get dressed, and get your things together. Grab some food and some of that Sterno canned-heat stuff and put it in the truck. We gotta get out of here."

"Can't we just stay and explain what happened?"

"I'd still go into jail, and I couldn't stand to be locked up in there. I've had people telling me what to do and think for most of my life, and I ain't gonna have it no more."

Becky threw her ruined bra and shirt away, using them to wipe away the remaining blood off her belly. She quickly pulled on her skirt and retrieved a clean Speedway shirt and jacket from her locker and pulled them on. Then on impulse, she threw a whole pile of uniforms into a big bag.

She moved quickly, gathering the things Kenny had asked for and adding a few others she thought would be handy. She had finished packing the bags and was halfway to the truck before she realized Kenny was missing. Turning around, she started to go back when he burst out of the back door at a dead run. He was carrying an odd assortment of military-looking guns and packs, and when he got to the truck, he opened a big freezer door and threw them inside. "Come on, Becky, get in!" he shouted, and she did just that.

Kenny cranked up the Power Wagon and realized that Nita Petrullo was still sitting on the wide front seat between them.

"Who is this?" Becky asked.

"Becky, this is Nita Petrullo. Her mother and father were both killed by some thieves this morning at PJ's gun shop, so I guess she'll just have to come with us," Kenny said as he revved the pink delivery truck and pulled out onto US 36 westbound and gunned down the road into the thickening sleet and rain.

Becky's eyes filled with tears at the sight of the big-eyed girl just sitting there on the seat, staring at her. "Nita," Kenny said, "this is Becky. She's a good friend of mine, and she'll be traveling with us. Is that okay?"

Nita just stared at Becky for a moment, then drew her knees up onto the seat, put her arms around Becky, laid her head in Becky's lap, and began to cry quietly.

Kenny began to get upset at the crying and looked at Becky, who just nodded to say that it was alright. He then felt a bit better and continued down the highway. It was very strange driving with no streetlights on a dark day, and no stoplights at the intersections, but Kenny was careful and they got out of town quickly, three pioneers heading west.

\* \* \*

Frank Muller and Angela Freece were sitting in a restaurant in Denver, holding hands across the table like young lovers. His feelings for Angie had grown so big and so quickly that it had never occurred to him to be self-conscious about it. It just felt natural, like his feeling so pleased at seeing the sparkle in her eyes when she teased him. "What is Dommy going to do with our friends Markson and Grizetti?" Angie asked, still holding his hand.

"He's going to leave them with some young friends of his who don't hold the rest of the bureau in such high esteem."

"They won't kill them, will they?"

"No, just make them as uncomfortable as possible for as long as possible."

"Nice," Angie said with a mischievous grin.

The waiter brought their food, and Frank and Angie reluctantly let go of each other to allow him room to set the food down. They both realized how hungry they were and addressed the meal with vigor. In between huge bites of his bacon cheeseburger, Frank said, "If you'll drop me at the office, I'll see if I can close up affairs there, and you can pick up some of the things on my shopping list, plus anything else you think might come in handy. The camp is pretty rustic, so you'd better include some warm clothes and shoes. Just use your judgment and pick up everything we might need out there."

Angie had left Albany on extremely short notice, and there were a lot of things she could think of that she needed, especially because they would be at Frank's camp until things settled down in town. She couldn't suppress a mischievous little grin as she thought about putting all her stuff on the bureau purchase order Frank had given her. *It will serve them right and cost them big*, she thought.

"What's that little grin for?" Frank asked.

"Oh, nothing," she said, "just a private little joke on the company."

"Dommy is gathering up his family, and he might be going out to the camp ahead of us," Frank said, still munching. "I'll have to stick around the office until I'm sure things are shut down. I promised Vito I'd take care of things here for him."

Frank's face took on a brief concerned look that Angie had begun to recognize. She had seen it several times, but only for a fleeting moment when his guard let down. "Worried about Cathy, aren't you?"

"Yes," Frank said, not at all surprised by her perception. "Vito was going to try to see her when he got to Washington and ask her to come out to camp for a visit. Now I just pray that DC didn't get hit too badly from that tidal wave. I just hate not knowing." He put down his burger and gladly took the hand she extended across the table, comforted by the reassuring squeeze she gave him.

"Things will work out, Frank. Just trust and have patience."

"I'll try, but it's never been one of my strong points."

"I'll help."

A little while later, Frank and Angie were quiet on the ride over to the Denver Federal Building. Their eyes were constantly roving, taking in the mood and movement of the people on the streets. There were surprisingly few people out and about for a weekday, and those who were out seemed to be clinging together in groups. On street corners, the talking was agitated. There was a restless and nervous mood in town, and it infected Frank. "Come up to the office with me, and then we'll shop together later," he said, not taking his eyes off a suspicious group of young men on the next corner. They all had blue bandannas either on their heads or tied around their upper arms. Some of the girls used them to tie back their hair. There was a lot of talking and gesticulating going on.

"Really, Frank? I'm a trained agent and I'm armed. I think I should be able to handle a department store by myself." She put on a small frown but was secretly pleased at his concern for her.

"Okay, but be careful and keep your wits about you. I don't like the look of things."

Grudgingly, Frank watched as Angie drove off, and then he entered the lobby of the Denver Federal Building. He was immediately taken a back by what he saw there, or didn't see. The first thing he noticed was the absence of any security personnel in the lobby. The security desk was unmanned, and the metal detector also. Ever since the Oklahoma City bombing, security at federal buildings had been annoyingly severe.

Frank took the elevator to the seventh floor and continued down the empty hallway to the Federal Bureau of Investigation offices. Peggy Callagin was at the reception desk, which was extremely unusual, because she was Vito Pianese's private secretary.

"Afternoon, Peg. What the hell's going on here?"

"Nothing much, Frank. Nobody's here to do much."

"I can see that. Do we have a sudden flu epidemic?"

"Meteorite flu, maybe. Most of the special agents are on duty but scattered out all over hell's half acre. Unfortunately, most of the support staff are not at work. I'm manning all the posts I can from here. Not much going on, however, which is fortunate. The whole damned country seems to be on hold."

Frank was very impressed with her report, not so much that it was gloomy and accurate, but because it was the most words that he had ever heard Peggy string together at one time. She was normally very economical with words. "What do you hear from Washington?" he asked.

"Nothing since 08:10 this morning."

"Anything from Vito?"

"Nothing."

"Anything else for me?"

"Nothing."

"Have you got any pressing duties here other than manning the whole damned office?"

"No."

"Then why don't you take the rest of the day off? Get home before the roads get too bad from this storm."

"Could I have the rest of the week? I'd like to drive down to Pueblo to visit my daughter."

"Sure, Peggy, go and enjoy your trip. I'll be here to watch the store."

Peggy puddled up in tears, which, frankly, shocked the hell out of him, then came around the desk and took him in her arms and hugged him, which shocked him even more. Frank didn't know what to say, so Peggy said it for him. "Frank, thank you. You always were a good man to work for, and Frank, don't stay here too long."

With that, she was gone, leaving behind a faint trace of perfume and a disturbing feeling of foreboding. Frank had never been in an FBI field office that was not alive with a hum of activity and a sense of purpose. This one in Denver was now stark, stone quiet. For something to do and in the faint hope of finding out about Cathy, he dialed up the headquarters number and listened to the phone ring, and ring, and ring, and ring, and ring until finally, a soft feminine voice answered, "Federal Bureau of Investigation. Kendra Jill speaking."

"Hello, this is Frank Muller. I'm temporarily in charge here in Denver. Can you tell me just what the hell is going on back east?"

"I'm sorry sir, but I can't. I'm from electronic surveillance, and I was just pulled out to answer the phones here and take numbers. When there is any information or instructions, you will be called. I have recorded that an inquiry has come from the Denver office, and you will be contacted for a status report in due course." The line cut off, and Frank stood listening to a dial tone.

He stood quietly for a moment, then sat down at Vito Pianese's desk and began sorting through the in-box and preparing a list of things that had to be done just as soon as communications with headquarters were restored.

\* \* \*

While Frank was trying to unravel the mystery of just what the state of the nation was, his partner, Dominic Ortiz was trying to unravel the mystery of exactly where his favorite niece, Selena Escobedo, had gone.

"I think she went down to your mother's apartment to bring her here," Dominic's wife Maria Ortiz said. "I called her this morning and told her to come here by taxi because you were getting ready to leave town for a while, but she refused to come. Grandma thinks that all this fuss about meteorites is nonsense and won't leave her apartment and all her possessions. I'm sure Selena thought she might be able to talk her out of this."

"You know the escape plan; just pack up and meet me behind McDonalds."

"I'll go with you," she said in a scared voice.

"Dammit, Maria! The neighborhoods are the worst place to be. This town is getting very nervous. I'll have to go down there and get the both of them." Dommy Ortiz was not a happy man. He stormed out of the house, mouthing obscenities under his breath as he went, slammed the car door with a resounding bang, and squealed the tires as he went down the street.

*I feel sorry for anyone who gets in his way today*, Maria thought in an uneasy way as she continued packing.

\* \* \*

Jamaal Kaleel was extremely pleased with the way this morning's exercise had gone. The Blues had gone uptown and pulled a job in broad daylight, busting a family-owned jewelry store on 16th Street for a whole bag of gold and diamonds. Everyone who had passed by on the street had been so distracted by the gangbangers standing out front of the store, talking loudly and arguing, that they never noticed that he and Bobby Simms were inside cleaning out the place. The plan had worked just like it was supposed to. Now it was time for the 49ers to pull their raid across town. Jamaal was not pleased that the phone kept ringing at the 49ers house and no one was answering. Finally, someone picked up and answered, "Yeah."

"This is Jamaal. Tell Ricky it's time to go."

"Ricky ain't here."

"Who is this?"

"Benny."

"Where the fuck is he? He's supposed to be ready to do a job."

"He's busy. I'll do the job."

"Don't fuck this up, Benny."

"Yeah." The phone was hung up.

"Shit!" was Jamaal's only comment. He was concerned all of his plans to keep the police running back and forth across town would be ruined if the Rickster didn't keep up his end. He looked up from his phone to see several police cars pulling up outside the jewelry store with their lights flashing. He had done his part; now it was up to Benny the Brain to do his.

\* \* \*

Selena Escobedo stood just inside the door to her grandmother's apartment with her mouth hanging open in surprise. She shook her head, tossing her glossy black curls because her mind was refusing to accept the scene her eyes were recording.

Her grandmother was bound and gagged in a chair directly across the room from the door, and Ricky Santos was standing behind her with a wicked-looking knife held close to the old woman's throat. "Sele-e-ena," he said in a soft, slurred voice, "so good to see you in the old neighborhood again. We thought you were getting too upity for the boys in the hood."

Her senses returned along with her anger, and she said, "I can't say the same for seeing you. You're apparently still the oily-tongued shit you always were, and what the hell are you doing with my grandmother?"

"Just keeping her company, and waiting for you."

"How did you know I'd be here?"

"We been watching and listening to Grandma. We heard her talking to you on the phone about not leaving her place. I know you too well, and I knew you'd come down and try again. That's the way you are, Selena; you don't give up. That's how you got into that nice school and out of the neighborhood, that's how you got away from me before I could have you, and that's how you came back to me again."

"This has nothing to do with you."

"Oh yes, it does, because if you don't be a nice cooperative girl, then she can become a nice dead grandma."

"You wouldn't dare."

Ricky smiled and turned the knife blade a tiny bit inward, then, with a flick of his wrist, cut a tiny slit in grandma's chin."

The old lady only flinched slightly at the quick-burning pain, and she completely ignored the warm blood that began dripping from her chin onto the front of her dress. Her words were muffled behind the red bandanna that was tied across her mouth.

Selena took a step forward. "You bastard!" she exclaimed.

The Rickster turned the knife slightly again and pressed it against the soft skin of the old woman's neck. "Easy now, or the old gal gets it."

Selena held herself back with a pure effort of will and said softly, "What do you want?"

"You."

"Just like that?"

"Yeah…just like that."

"Where?"

"Right here where the old lady can watch me fuck her granddaughter. She can see how I get you up to ten on the good old Rickster scale."

"Not in my lifetime or yours!"

"Your choice." With a quick flick of his wrist, Ricky put another tiny slice in Grandma Ortiz's chin, a tiny bit deeper this time.

"Wait a minute," Selena said, playing for time while her brain searched desperately for a way out of this situation.

"Yes?" Ricky asked with a confident sneer that Selena hated.

"OK, but not here. I can't do it in front of Grandma." Selena was seething inside and held control of her temper only with the greatest of effort. She moved slowly, sidestepping across to the sofa, rolling on her feet as if walking on eggshells.

Ricky's ice-cold obsidian eyes followed her every step, and the knife blade moved slowly away from the old woman's neck, inversely matching Selena's proximity to the sofa. Selena fixed her eyes on Ricky's and said, "Turn the chair around."

"Yeah, then she'll only hear you scream." Ricky watched lasciviously as Selena slid slowly out of her jacket, then holding the jacket on her fingertip, extended her arm out fully before tossing it onto the floor. Never taking her eyes off his, she raised her long, slim fingers to the first button on her blouse. She opened it slowly then moved to the second and the third and the fourth, praying silently all the while for God to provide some means of escape.

Ricky's eyes were mesmerized by the long, slender fingers that were working their way slowly down the front of Selena's blouse and the glow of the golden skin that was being exposed. The fact that there was no bra in sight to diminish the view only deepened his concentration. "Move the chair around," Selena said again firmly as her hands stopped moving at the last button.

Ricky stepped back slightly and began to turn the chair, never once taking his eyes off Selena. His concentration was so complete that he never heard the door open, or the report of the silenced 9 mm Browning that created a third eye exactly in the middle of his forehead.

Ricky's head snapped, and he flew backward against the wall as the smell of gunpowder filled the room. Selena spun around and cried, "Uncle Dommy, how did you get here?"

"Never mind that," he snapped. "Just cut Grandma loose and get something to bandage her chin."

Dommy Ortiz stepped back quickly and peered up and down the hallway. He caught a fleeting glimpse of someone scuttling away down the stairs and snapped off another quick round, missing completely. Turning, he said, "Move it, Selena. We've got to get out of here now!"

With Grandma in tow holding a handkerchief to her chin with one hand and her pillowcase full of treasures in the other, they made their way quickly to Dommy's car. "Get in!" Dommy shouted as Selena's hand scrambled for the door handle. The car was starting to get covered with dirty snow and sleet.

As he pulled open the driver's side door, Dommy heard two sharp popping sounds behind him to his right and instinctively dropped to one knee. He pivoted on that knee and let off three quick unaimed shots in the general direction of the noise. Looking over quickly, he noticed there were two neat stars in his windshield. His mother was standing by the car, crying.

Two more shots rang out, this time from the left and from a larger-caliber gun, maybe a .38 or a .357 Magnum. His mother buckled and dropped to the sidewalk like a bundle of rags. Dom again returned fire blindly and shouted to Selena, "Take the car and go, girl! Maria knows what to do! Find her behind McDonald's."

"No, Uncle Dommy; they'll kill you!"

"Just go now, girl! I'm not that easy to kill. *Just go!*"

With that said, Dommy moved away from the car quickly, keeping low and taking a few random shots at doorways and windows, just to keep the gangbangers' heads down. He rolled quickly between two cars and popped the clip from his gun. He quickly reloaded and saw with satisfaction that Selena was moving. She was keeping her head low as she floored the accelerator and left two stripes in the slush in the process. Dommy was checking in his jacket pocket for his last clip when something struck him. A huge blow between his shoulder blades forced the wind right out of his lungs. A burst of pain followed, as his vision began to fade to shades of gray. Numbness radiated outward down his arms, and he wondered dumbly why his hands didn't want to work, when a hoarse voice behind him began to shout, "I got him, I got him! I shot the motherfucker right in the fucking back. I got him!"

Rough hands took hold of Dommy and threw him down on the pavement. A circle of angry black faces surrounded him, all babbling at one time. He was shocked to realize that none of them could have been more than twenty years old. Several shots rang out, and his body bucked in rhythm.

Selena parked behind a McDonald's several blocks away and sat trembling like a leaf. Grandma was dead, Uncle Dommy was probably dead, and here she was. She was safe and sound and completely surprised at the ease of her escape, and more than a little curious as to the whereabouts of Benny Munoz and the red-scarfed 49ers. She would have expected them to be around the neighborhood in force, covering their leader's back, especially with all this gunfire going on.

She had no idea that while she was sitting behind McDonald's, trying to regain control of her trembling body, Benny the Brain had the 49ers uptown cleaning out a Dick's Sporting Goods store of all of its camping equipment and preserved food. Jamaal could steal all of the diamonds and gold he wanted; Benny would steal things his people could live on.

Maria Ortiz waited nervously for the painfully long two hours that Dommy had instructed her to, then, with deep sadness, she gathered her family together. "We're going on a little trip," she told the children as she loaded them into the already overburdened minivan. For the first time in her married life, Maria Ortiz was going to disobey her husband.

Dommy had drilled her repeatedly on the backup plan he wanted her to take if anything should happen to him. She knew the way to Frank Muller's camp, and she knew her family would all be welcome there, but the remote mountain valley was not what she needed, so she would not go there.

Maria backed the car out of the driveway and drove out to Interstate 25, taking the southbound entrance. She would go south through Colorado Springs and Pueblo to the little town of San Isabel, tucked away in the national forest of the same name. There she would be with family, and if Dommy survived today, he would know where to find her.

Maria Ortiz nodded her head firmly as if to reinforce the correctness of her decision as she roughly brushed away the stinging tears starting to form and offered a quick prayer for her dead husband.

\* \* \*

Reverend Randall P. Davis gathered his small family into his study to discuss their current situation. They were virtually prisoners in their own home, and Randy felt personally responsible and a little guilty for imposing this situation on them. He wanted very badly to ease their concern and to do what he could to reduce the stress of the situation. In the dim light of an oil lamp, he was staring thoughtfully at his two sons, Eli and Noah, who were both unusually quiet and showing some signs of restlessness from their partial imprisonment. They had all been growing more restless since the power had gone off.

Noah asked, "When do you think the lights will come back on, Dad?"

"I can't say, son," Randy replied. "I guess that we'll have to wait until this ice storm ends and the power crews can put the lines back up." He smiled up at his wife, Ruth, when she brought in some refreshments and set them on his old desk. "Thank you, darlin', that looks wonderful," he had just said in his deep but quiet voice when there came a sound of breaking glass from the front of the house.

They were all startled by the noise, and Ruth Randall dropped one of her treasured heirloom teacups. "Darn it!" she exclaimed and might have said considerably more had her husband not motioned to them sharply to stay sitting and be quiet. When his family were settled, Randy rose and went out to investigate.

His study was on the first floor in the rear of the house, and Randy moved out and down the hall as quietly as possible on the squeaky old hardwood floors. All was quiet in the dining room, so he continued to the arch leading to the parlor. The first thing Randy noticed when he entered the living room was an array of shattered glass on the carpet and a round, fist-sized stone lying in the middle of it. Thinking quickly, he crouched and moved around the wall so he could look out from behind the closed drapes. What he saw astounded him.

There was a crowd of twenty or thirty people gathered in front of the parsonage, standing in the awful weather. Some of them, Randy recognized as his own parishioners. One of them had apparently thrown the stone through the front window. The crowd was shouting and shaking their fists at the house. Randy could hear them saying, "Take back your damned shooting stars," and "Let us live our lives," and "Tell God we don't need no meteors." Randy could not understand why they were there attacking him, but they were his people and he had to talk to them.

He moved quickly to the front door and was just turning the knob to go outside when Special Agent Jacob Williams' strong hand grabbed his wrist and held it viselike. "That's not a good idea, Reverend Randall," he said in a tone that left no room for negotiation. "They're not a happy group." He was holding the rock in his other hand.

Randy leaned closer to the door to listen to the crowd shouting, "Take your meteors back and let us live our lives! Come out here, and we'll show you what a flying rock is." Someone threw another stone, which broke the glass in the front door. Reverend Randy and Jacob Williams ducked the flying glass and retreated.

"Why are they blaming me?" Randy asked of Agent Williams.

"Who else have they got to blame? Before the lights went out, the TV was filled with reports of meteorites hitting all around. Now they're in the dark and they're frightened. People are always frightened in the dark. If they were in Washington, they would probably be throwing stones through the windows at the White House, but since they aren't, you are the closest target. It's just human nature."

"What do you think, Jacob?" Agent Dan Daker, who was more commonly known as Double D, asked nervously while holding the second thrown rock in his hand.

"We'll just stay still for a while and hope they get tired and go away. If they get too rowdy, I hate to say it Double D, but we'll have to go out and calm them down," answered Jacob Williams grimly.

Special Agent Williams took Randy by the shoulders and firmly turned him toward the study. "It's our job to handle the crowd, Reverend, and we will do just that. They are frightened and dangerous. You can make our work a lot easier if you will return to the study and stay out of sight."

Another stone came through the front window, and both agents turned toward it. Suddenly, Reverend Randall knew exactly what he must do. Without another conscious thought, every detail of his plan had sprung, crystal clear, into his mind. He hurried back to the study and found his family still huddled in the pool of light from the oil lamp. "God has provided a plan for our deliverance," he said simply. "There are some very frightened and confused people out in front of our house. They seem to be blaming me for the meteorites and are throwing stones. The FBI men will have to go outside to deal with them, and when they do, God has made it clear to me that we must leave."

Ignoring the looks of apprehension on his family's faces, he continued. "Eli and Noah, go to your rooms and pack up whatever clothing you can fit in one zippered bag. Take warm stuff, and wear your rain gear. You can bring some personal items, but remember that we have to travel light. Quickly, now!"

Eli Davis responded instantly to the tone of his voice.

"Ruth, would you please do the same thing with our clothing and get back down here as soon as possible. I know you're frightened, but everything will be alright."

Ruth Davis departed with an unconvinced look.

"Where are we going, Dad?" Noah asked, more than a little frightened.

"West. More than that, I don't know, son, but west, away from here. God will provide, son. Now go!"

When everyone had left on their appointed chores, Randy hurried out to the kitchen and began to pack up food to carry with them. From a narrow cupboard, he took out paper bags and carefully inserted them into doubled plastic store bags and began to fill them with canned and dry goods from the pantry shelves. When they were filled, he placed the bags by the back door and repeated the process with the refrigerator. By the time he was done, the Davis family was all gathered in the kitchen. "Wait here," Randy said. "I'll be right back."

Again, Randy crept quietly through the dark hallway to the front of his house. Agents Williams and Daker were huddled at the front door, peeking out the sidelight. The crowd was still ranting in front of the house, and if anything, they were a little more aggressive than before. Suddenly, a man in the crowd noticed Jacob Williams peeking out at them. He shouted, and several stones flew toward the house, breaking another window and bouncing off the front door.

"Well, Double D, I guess we'd better go out and defuse this situation," Agent Williams said. Now they would be earning their keep.

Randy hurried back to the kitchen, issuing orders quickly. "Noah, get these bags out to the car, and be quick about it. Eli, go pull some wires off the FBI cars' engines. Throw them as far away as you can."

"OK, Dad, I understand." Eli Davis was already headed out the door.

"Ruth, please take all the food you can carry, and get into the car. I'll bring the rest. We're getting out of here." Reverend Davis's voice was full of confidence.

Randy made one more check to reassure himself the agents were occupied. The front door was wide open, and he could see Jacob Williams standing out on the front porch. Dan Daker was standing just inside, next to the open door, with his weapon drawn and ready. Randy silently prayed there would be no use for it. With both agents preoccupied by the angry crowd out front, Randy knew it was now or never. He sprinted to the back of the house and out the back door, jumped into his car, checked his family, and left his home, never to see it again. It didn't even occur to him to think about why he could see agent Jacob Williams so clearly on this dark night.

"We'll go over to Ben Goodman's house. I know he'll let us borrow his van. We'll put our old car in his garage. That way, the FBI or the police will be looking for the wrong car and we'll have much more time to put some miles behind us before they catch on." Randy was so calm and assured, and his plan was such a good one, that both his sons were impressed.

A short while later, the Davis family was heading down Interstate 70, west toward Cambridge, Ohio, with the faint glow of several uncontrolled fires raging behind them in Wheeling. The world as they knew it was changed forever.

\* \* \*

Sheriff Conrad J. "Connie" Hawkings of the Hendricks County, Indiana, Sheriff's Department sat with his feet up on the desk and listened to his deputy's story, as unbelievable as it might be.

"Would you back up ten, and then run that one by me again, Pete? Something in there just don't compute."

"I know it sounds strange, chief, but that's just how we found things."

"OK, take this old man through the story one more time from the beginning. And make it a bit slower, please."

"Old Tracey Bishop came running into the office earlier claiming there was a bunch of dead folks laying all around the Speedway gas station in Danville. When she calmed down a little, it came out that there were three injured, so I put her in the cruiser and we went right over to investigate. When we arrived, we found four four-wheel-drive vehicles loaded with all sorts of survival gear. They were all parked at the gas pumps so no one else could get to them, and two men had apparently been trying to rig up a gas-powered pump to fill up their tanks. They were both unconscious from severe head trauma.

"Inside the store, we found a third man, who was apparently in the process of emptying the shelves of canned goods when he too had received a severe head trauma. I determined these three were alive, so I got on the radio and called for the emergency squad to take them to the hospital. Then I continued to investigate. Are you with me so far?"

"Yes, continue."

"In the storeroom in back of the Speedway was a fourth man Tracey had not seen. He was just lying there with a nasty-looking knife in one hand and his dork in the other. He was dead from massive head trauma. Nearby, we found a size 34B front-opening bra, which had apparently been cut off, and a Speedway blouse with all the buttons ripped off. Both garments had traces of blood on them."

"I take it you're some sort of expert on size 34B front-opening bras?" Sheriff Hawkings asked somewhat smugly, but with a sharp look in his eyes.

Deputy Sheriff Peter Dawkes blushed slightly and said, "I'm not totally unfamiliar with this type of garment. They're a lot easier to open than the ones that hook in back." He watched Sheriff Hawkings closely for a reaction to this avowed knowledge, as Peter had dated his youngest daughter a few times.

"And yet you're sure this one was cut off?"

"Yes, sir, I am. The hook for it was found beside the body, and there were some elastic threads from the bra stuck on the blade of the knife. They both had blood on them."

"Okay."

"We took samples from all around the store, but I guess the lab won't be doing much with them until the power comes back on.

"Tracey says the morning clerk on duty was Becky Crawford. She's a pretty little blonde girl who's somewhat new in town, only been here a year or so. She's missing."

"And I assume she's also missing one size 34B front-opening bra?" Connie Hawkings asked with a grin.

"That would be purely speculation on my part."

"Continue."

"I radioed the Indiana State Police and asked them to check the license plates on the four-wheelers. Apparently, they are all from Indianapolis. The state boys will get the details to us as soon as they can. They're pretty busy over there with this crappy weather. They also put out a bulletin on the big pink truck."

"What the hell pink truck are you talking about? I never heard you mention any pink truck."

"Sorry, Sheriff, I skipped that part."

"Well, fill it in, then."

"Tracey saw this big pink delivery truck parked out front of the store this morning. She says it's there every day, early. It's from the Happy Tyme Frozen Food Company in town, so I checked with the owner, but he wouldn't give me much time. He's about going crazy trying to find a portable generator to keep his stock from going over. The driver's name is Kenny Smith, but he is out on his route and will be gone all day. His boss says he's a good and steady man who's worked for him for three years and never been in any trouble. Real dependable, never any trouble, but a little on the quiet side."

"We'll check him out later. Go on. Anything on the Crawford girl?"

"Like I said, she's only been in town for a year or so. She hails from some little town in New England—Connecticut or Vermont, or someplace like that. I'll check on her as soon as the power gets back on and the phones are working again."

"You're the big bad man about town, aren't you, Peetie? How come you don't have the book on this good-looking little blondie?"

"Like I said, Sheriff," Peter repeated, "she's only been in town for a year or so. We went out once, but she didn't have much to say about her past. She went out some and liked to have a little fun, but that is about all. If she was a bad girl, I'd already know all there is to know about her." Peter Dawkes was not blushing at all now.

Sheriff Hawkings sat back in his chair and took a pack of smokes out of the desk drawer, popped one out and lit it, taking in a big lung full of smoke, and then started coughing.

"I thought you gave them things up," Pete observed.

"No, that's not the case at all. What I said is that I don't smoke no more. I don't smoke no less; I just don't smoke no more." Connie Hawkings took another puff and said, "Continue."

"There were tracks from the Happy Tyme truck in front of the store, then he backed up and pulled around back to the service door."

"Speculation or fact?" the sherriff asked.

"Well, I ain't an Indian scout, but I can read truck tracks in the snow," Pete said a bit sarcastically.

"Keep going."

"Well, sir, my best guess would be that those four were headed west, out for Libertyville or one of those survivalist communes out there like it. I have to assume they stopped here to gas up and found the power off, so while the others rigged the pump for gas, the dark guy decided to have a little fun with Becky in the back room. I have to assume that the others decided to add to their food stocks while they waited their turn, but I don't know where the hell they planned to put it. The vehicles were fully loaded already. Apparently, an unknown assailant came in the back door and took a major exception to the aggravated sexual battery in progress and did him in. We'll have to wait to talk to Kenny Smith when he gets back from his route to see who else was around at that time."

"What's to say that Smith didn't do him in?"

"Nothing, I guess, but his boss gives him a clean bill."

Sheriff Hawkings took one last puff and tapped the cigarette out in the ashtray he kept hidden in the desk drawer. "What we've got here is an enigma, and I don't have time for one of those right now. Notify the state boys and let them handle it. Did you secure the crime scene?"

"Yes, I did, and notified the state police also."

"Did you get the four-wheelers running?"

"Yes."

"Good. Then get some boys to run them over to Jason Patrick's hardware store and let him add the vehicles and their contents to our civil-defense supplies."

"What if somebody wants them?"

"Impounded for evidence. Now get on it."

Before Deputy Dawkes could turn around, the radio squealed so loudly they both jumped a little. Connie Hawkings picked it up, listened for a minute, then cursed loudly. "Dammit, Alma, are you sure you got that right?"

Pete Dawkes could hear Alma Simson's excited voice coming through the set without the speaker even being turned on. "Yes, I'm damned sure. One of them meteors just hit square in the middle of Clayton and busted the place all up. Pieces of it scattered all over town, and several buildings are on fire. They're calling for all the help we can give 'em since the lights are out over there too."

Sherriff Hawkings was just stuffing the dog-eared pack of Marlboros in his shirt pocket and preparing to leave when his daughter burst into the office. "Daddy, you've gotta do something!"

"Slow down a minute, Sissy, and tell me just what it is that's wrong."

"There's a big crowd of people over at PJ Petrullo's Gun Shop, and they're saying he and his wife have been stabbed! They're dead, Daddy!"

"What in the hell is going on?" Connie exclaimed. "I've been sheriff of this county for twenty years and have only had two murders in all that time. Now I've got two in one day, and some damned meteor from outer space to boot?"

Without hesitation, Sherriff Hawkings marshaled his forces and gave out his orders. Sissy, I want you to calm down and stay right here. You know how to use the radio, so you have to be my communicator. Can you do that? The batteries are up and should last out the day. Don't waste them with silly gossip."

"Yes, Dad," Sissy said, giving Peter Dawkes a sly wink behind her dad's back. Connie continued, purposely not noticing. Peter had shown Sissy how to use all the equipment in the office while giving her a few lessons of a more personal nature at the same time.

"Well, Peter, my boy, we've just been handed two jobs with a lot higher priorities than chasing down some pink frozen-food truck. Get on over to PJ's shop and see what the hell went on over there. I'll stop over to Jason Patrick's store on my way to Clayton to tell him to get his ass over to the Speedway to collect the new civil-defense supplies himself, and then he can follow me over to Clayton with them. They may just need some supplies over there."

"Won't we need that civil-defense stuff here in Danville, Sheriff?" Peter Dawkes asked.

"We might well need it here, Pete, but I have a feeling Clayton might just need it a little more. I think it's time we started following what that Reverend Randy said on TV the other day. Time we started acting like the good and decent Americans we always claim to be and begin sharing and helping out our neighbors. Now get along with you."

Sheriff Hawkings stepped out of his office, thinking he might just stop off at the Speedway on his way to Clayton to inspect the crime scene himself. Might just pick up a pack or two of Marlboros while he was at it, too. Out of habit, he looked up to check the dark leaden sky and was hit in the eye by a big, fat snowflake. He brushed it away with his hand and came away with a streak of mud across the back of his hand. "Don't that just beat all?" he said out loud, with no one to hear. "Two murders, a damned meteor in Clayton, and the snow is full of mud. Can't get no worse than this."

While the Hendricks County Sheriff's Department dealt with their more pressing problems, Kenny Smith and Becky Crawford drove over 400 miles in both driving snow and torrential rain straight west on US Highway 36, and they never saw a police officer or anyone else for that matter who paid them the least bit of attention. What they did see was abandoned cars occasionally alongside the road, evidently out of gas.

\* \* \*

Colonel Mark Persons flopped into a soft plastic chair in the SWPC employee lounge and leaned back, resting his head on the high back. He was very close to complete exhaustion from more than two days without sleep and the stress of trying to locate his sons. "Here, try some of this. I just made a new pot," Devon Grant said as she set a cup of black coffee on a table, a safe distance from his elbow.

"Thanks, Devon. That looks good."

"Have you heard anything from the airlines yet?"

"No, nothing at all. From the reports I've gotten, things are pretty messed up; that's probably why."

"How bad is it?" Devon asked.

"Damage to coastal cities has been severe with great loss of life. Inland, we just have this terrible weather to contend with so far. I know we've taken a few major strikes from meteorites, but I simply haven't had the time to check on the details."

"What about the shuttle?"

"NASA has them prepared to set down at Edwards in California. I haven't heard of any meteorites striking in the Pacific, so I assume they will be alright. I don't like the amount of radiation exposure they got from this solar magnetic disturbance, but that's all history. No one wanted to listen to me anyway."

"I don't understand what was so important for them to go up in those conditions," Devon said with conviction.

"They put two specially armored communications satellites up in geo-orbit. When the shower is over and we're ready to use them, we can blow off their protective shields and fire them up. They'll replace the birds that are getting sandblasted up there right now, and the ones that the SMD will push out of place or out of orbit and don't have enough fuel left onboard to be corrected. Cape Canaveral will not be useable for years, if ever, so this was our last good chance to put them up. I was very much against the mission for the human cost, but I understand the need."

"Why don't you go up to the ladies' lounge and catch a few hours' sleep? Just prop the door open and use the sofa in there. There are no other women here working, and you won't be much help to the boys or anyone else in your present condition," Devon suggested. "I'll keep calling until Art Capiletti is ready to go. I'm giving him a ride home."

"Is his car broken down?"

"His wife drove him in. She needed his car today."

"Okay, Devon, keep trying for the boys."

As Mark Persons was leaving, he stopped for a moment and turned to Devon. "When you get home, it would be a good idea to take a few minutes and pack your things so you'll be ready to leave for the valley at short notice."

"I thought I'd wait in town until John gets here," Devon answered.

"If civil law breaks down here, we may have to get out in a hurry. I'd like you to be ready to go."

"Alright," Devon agreed so the colonel would go and get some much-needed rest, but she had her own agenda, and that was the one she would follow. Or so she believed.

# Saturday, March 13

In the TransCo Energy Company control room, a small red light began blinking on the animated system diagram board at the spot designated Basile Pumping Station. At the same instant, a red alarm came up on the computer display monitor reading, "02:17:16 a.m. Basile #3 compressor hi-temp," followed by a beeping audible alarm.

Six months earlier, an operator would have been on duty to acknowledge the alarm and call up the temperature readout of #3 compressor on another screen, and if the temperature were high enough he could shut the compressor down and bring on another to replace it—very simple. However, this was not possible this morning. As a means of economizing corporate operations, a recent study had indicated that only one operator was needed on duty for the midnight-to-eight shift. Unfortunately for Basile Station, that operator was firmly enthroned in the men's room, deeply regretting the extra bowl of jambalaya he had consumed before work, and the 357 Mad Dog Extra Hot Tabasco sauce he had added to it.

Three minutes and four seconds after the initial alarm, the cooling-water supply line to the #3 compressor, third-stage inter-cooler failed completely. This failure caused the spraying of water all around the room, shorting out the relay that was marked "3d stage inter-cooler hi-temp," which should have tripped #3 compressor off the line. It did not, and one minute later, the #3 compressor failed explosively, destroying itself and the two adjacent compressors and igniting a ball of blue flame that could be seen thirty miles away.

Coincidentally, natural-gas pressure in the three thirty-inch transmission mains going north along the Eastern Seaboard began to drop quickly due to the high demand on gas supplies for electric generation. All along the thousands of miles of gas mains in the system, other smaller compressors started up and pressure regulators worked in a futile attempt to stabilize the gas transmission pressure, all to no avail.

Utilities in the East and Northeast were consuming huge quantities of natural gas to run their generating plants and trying to piece their shattered systems back together. In the wave-shattered cities on the seaboard, huge gas leaks were venting to the atmosphere or burning out of control. Consumption greatly exceeded supply.

One by one, gas-supply regulators slammed shut in response to the huge deficit in supply against demand until finally, the flow of gas in the great arteries was stopped, except for the 21,000 cubic feet per second of gas the Basile turbo compressors would have supplied to the transmission mains that was creating the huge blue fireball in the dark early-morning Louisiana sky.

\* \* \*

As the blue fireball was lighting up the morning sky in Louisiana, it was already 4:17 p.m. in Nogoya, Japan, and Miiko Fujimora was kneeling in front of the small window in the tiny apartment she shared with her husband, Sonjii. Miiko was cradling her distended belly lightly in her hands, feeling the new life within her as it moved about and contemplating the fate of her unborn son. Sonjii had left for work before dawn and would not be home from work for several hours yet. Miiko had time to contemplate the future. She was deeply disturbed over the news reports of large meteorites striking the earth and causing great destruction in the coastal cities of the United States and in Europe. Malaysia had been struck, and huge oil fires were raging in the production and refining plants there. There were also rumors of a huge strike in the central region of China. Many lives had been lost, and all of these were potential customers lost to Nipponese vendors of the electronic equipment her husband designed. What would become of them if these markets were lost forever? Perhaps, she thought, new markets could be found in the rebuilding. This thought pleased her greatly.

Sonjii worked twelve to sixteen hours a day for Hitachi Electronics, and it would be unfair if his career were ruined by stupid stones falling from the skies. Miiko had paid little heed to the scenes of death and destruction that had flashed across her television screen. Hadn't she seen the same things a hundred times in the Rodann and Godzilla movies that most Japanese loved so much? Nippon itself was no stranger to natural disasters. Had they not suffered from huge earthquakes, typhoons, and tsunamis for centuries and always survived? The world would survive this also, but her concern was for her husband and her son-to-be.

Miiko also paid little heed to the four concrete domes and tall stacks of the Nagoya Electric Nuclear Generating Plant. They had been benign neighbors for so long that they were merely a part of the skyline and nothing to be concerned about. These four generating units had been operating flawlessly for almost ten years, a monument to superb Nipponese engineering as they quietly produced 4400 megawatts of energy for the power-hungry Japanese industrial giants. Therefore, she was not looking at them when a brilliant flash of light appeared above them and then flashed out, leaving behind a faint trail of smoke.

It was only when she felt the apartment floor undulate with the impact that Miiko looked up. Miiko had felt the undulation of many earthquakes in the past, but this was very different. It was a sharp, violent upheaval. Through her small window, she saw the two middle domes of the nuclear plant were gone completely and that a huge malevolent cloud of steam was rising and spreading across the city. What she did not see was that containment on the #1 and #4 units was also breached and the units were belching steam and contributing to the deadly radioactive fog.

Her building continued to shift and shake as the tectonic plates beneath her home island responded to the sudden impact. Miiko Fujimora knew the fate of her son-to-be, and of herself and several millions of other Japanese citizens who would die from this calamity.

* * *

Halfway around the world from where Miiko Fujimora was staring in horror at the rising radioactive cloud in Nagoya, it was just past eight a.m. in Broadstairs, England, where Priscilla Jameson was stretching herself out in a huge king-sized bed. The Bay Tree Bed and Breakfast guest house was snuggled down on the southwest coastline of England, and from the room, Priss had a wonderful view of the beach and the restless gray-green Atlantic beyond. She moved from the bed carefully so as not to wake Bill Appleby from his well-deserved sleep. She took the silk peignoir from the foot of the bed, draped it over one shoulder, and walked completely naked to the old leaded glass window that looked out into the English channel that connects the North Sea to the Celtic Sea. Priss was born a city girl and never tired of looking out on the vast open waters.

Old Billy Appleby, or Appleton or Applelskin, or whatever the hell Apple he was calling himself this time, was an interesting man, and a fair-to-midling lover, but he had no soul or conscience, and that made him dangerous. That was all right and good with Priss, as she had always enjoyed flirting with a little danger, and perhaps this was why she had so readily accepted his offer to spend a few days at the shore, even if it was the off-season.

Her best friend, and Billy's current secretary, Meave McCormak, had been horribly jealous of Billy's attraction to Priss and of her persistent flirting, so she had not been speaking to Priss for the past few days. As a consequence of that mood, it had been ridiculously easy for Billy to fabricate a story about work out of town and for them to slip away.

Priss had no bad feelings about stealing away her best friend's lover, because, after all, she only wanted him for a short while and then Meave could have him back. And he wasn't that great in bed, after all, but he was interesting, and currently, he was very well funded. The chill of the room was raising goose flesh on her arms, and Priscilla was contemplating a return to bed and Billy when the sky to the west lit up in a brilliant blue flash, just on and off like a photo flash.

Priscilla stared hard out over the water, blinking rapidly to try clearing the bright spot the flash had left on her retinas. She thought she could see a white column of clouds rising on the horizon in the spot where the flash had ended. "Billy...Billy. Dammit, Billy, come here and see what just happened!" Priss called, the fright obvious in her voice.

William J. Appleby roused slowly from his sleep and stared squint-eyed. All he could see was Priscilla standing nude by the window. She made a breathtaking picture with her hair all tousled from sleep and her body gleaming golden in the early morning sunlight. She was truly a ravishing and completely sexual creature, and his body immediately responded to her earthy appeal. He slowly maneuvered from the bed when Priss said firmly, "Hurry up and come look at this. I think one of your little money-makers just landed in the sea."

"What, that close?" Billy mumbled as he strode quickly over to the window. Halfway there, he could feel the timbers of the antiquated inn begin shaking under his feet from the shock of the meteorite's impact on the ancient seabed. Not even the allure of Priscilla's naked body or the morning scent of her could detract from the feeling of pure panic that rose in Billy as he looked out to sea.

For certain, there was a column of cloud rising high into the air, and a strange, almost metallic, look to the sky. He peered immediately down to the beach, and his worst fears were confirmed. In the short time since the meteorite strike at the Charing Cross book store, William J. Appleby had become quite an expert on meteorites in order to sell his shooting-star insurance policies. He had a very good and very frightening idea of what was coming for him.

The sea was rapidly receding from the beach as if a giant pump were pulling it out and away from shore. By the minute, large areas of beach and mud flat were being exposed as the sea withdrew from the land. As his eyes traveled up from the beach, Billy could see that a mountain of gray-green water was piling up far from shore where the deep water shelved onto the shore. "Tsunami," Bill muttered under his breath, lungs already frozen in fright.

"Su what?" Priscilla asked, feeling the fear in him and responding to it.

"Tidal wave, Priss, and probably the mother of all tidal waves."

Priscilla Jameson grabbed onto Billy Appleton and held him tightly for the remainder of their abbreviated lives as the 250-foot-high wall of gray-green water rolled over the Bay Tree Bed and Breakfast and over Broadstairs, then Canterbury, and then over much more of England and the coastal areas of Europe. Meave McCormak did not have to be jealous anymore. Not only were Billy and Priss out of the picture, so was she, because she and London itself were not spared the violence of the tsunami. There would also be no more of the famous Appledoorn tulips in Holland, which lies on the east side of the English Channel, for many years, as it too suffered from its own grey-green wave.

\* \* \*

"Damn, Willie, did you get the number of the truck that hit you?" asked Bud Flynn as his relief walked unsteadily up to the shift manager's console at the NYISO.

Willie Davis did not respond to the completely distasteful joke at all. He simply stated in a flat, unemotional voice, "They killed my dogs, Bud. The bastards, they killed both my dogs…Jeet and Mo are gone."

"Here, sit down," Bud said as he drew up a chair for Willie in an uncharacteristic act of kindness. "Tell me what happened."

"Some young people came by the house last night and knocked on the door asking for food. They said they'd gotten out of the city, but they never said which one, and had nothing to eat. I gave them some stuff to eat and let them wash up a little.

Then I made them some sandwiches to go, and they went off. They seemed okay enough at the time…not very polite, and a little seedy looking, but nothing to be afraid of.

"Then around midnight, they came back with a whole bunch of their friends. But they didn't knock this time; they just broke in my door and were busy raiding the house when I came down. I hollered at them to stop and told them they could have whatever they wanted, just don't wreck the place. They laughed in my face and kept trashing my house, and that's when the dogs went after them. They had a lot of guns, and they shot my dogs. They just shot them over and over, both my boys."

"What did you do?" Bud asked.

"I went a little crazy and jumped in after one of them. I never got to him, because some of the others hit me over the head, and when I fell down, they kicked me all over. Only thing I remember clearly is their eyes. Those young bastards have cold eyes, like there's no soul alive behind them, just ice-cold eyes."

"You feeling okay? We're having a hell of a day here."

"I'm alright; besides, where else am I gonna go?"

"You're sure about that, Willie? You look like hell."

"I'm sure. Just tell me what's happening."

"Willie man, I feel terrible for you, but here it is straight. Con Edison and Long Island got beat up pretty badly in that tsunami tidal wave that hit them. In fact, all the coastal utilities are badly hit. It's a lot worse than Hurricane Sandy, if that puts it in perspective for you."

"It's got to be a disaster down there then," Willie said, still sounding dazed.

"Both of their systems are down, and we've had only spotty communication with them at all, and what we do get is over the emergency radio. The damned satellite is down again. The only information we can get from that area is bad. It seems the damage is unbelievable, damn near total. The rest of our system north of Westchester County and excluding the Hudson Valley is up and running with only spotty outages around the Hudson River towns due to flooding. Restoration crews just left an hour ago to get some rest. ISO New England has lost Boston and most of the coastal cities in New England. They lost more generation than load, but like us, most of the upstate parts of New England are back on the line."

"Killed both my dogs; I just can't believe it," Willie mumbled as his mind continued to wander.

Bud grabbed Willie Davis by the shoulder and shook him a little. "Settle down, Willie, and listen up." He was getting a little annoyed with all this mumbling about two damned dogs. "Gas contracts are being cut in wholesale lots. I hear there's a problem down in Louisiana somewhere, but no more than that, so we're still short on generation, even with the lost load. You'll probably have to be in eight percent voltage reduction over the peak hours, and if you lose anything, you'll be in load shedding to cover the loss. This damned weather is causing icing problems on both the transmission and distribution systems, all over. Quebec is having severe problems with ice on their long lines down from Churchill Falls and James Bay, and they're really nervous about this K-9 SMD we've had in effect for the past thirty hours or so. Watch Quebec, because they've had to cut their deliveries without much notice. The last that I heard, there was some overheating on two harmonic filters on the HVDC at Chateauguay. That's probably from the SMD, but it might force them to reduce deliveries again. If they do, you're gonna be hurtin' for sure."

"Damn bastard kids had no souls, you know that? No souls at all."

"Hold on, Willie. I'm almost done." Bud looked Willie over once again and continued with his relief, thinking, *I don't give a shit how bad off he is, I'm gonna give him the shift and get the hell out of here.* Bud continued, unrelenting, "As I said before, we are still in an SMD of K-9. It was K-9 plus earlier. Ontario and Quebec have had the most trouble, but I've heard on the radio that some of the direct-current ties in the MISO tripped, causing them a number of local blackouts. We've still got all the gas-fired IPPs online and cranking out full load as long as the gas holds out, and I just got confirmation that all our nukes are on cold standby officially. Damned good thing we had the Indian Point units off the line before that big wave came roaring up the Hudson Valley."

"Damned kids. I gave them what they wanted. Why'd they have to kill my dogs?" Willie Davis was still less than fully coherent, and obviously not able to take over the shift. This didn't concern or bother Bud Flynn at all.

"The blackouts, the SMD, and the lousy weather are all raising hell with communications. Like I said before, the satellite backup communications are down again with no return date or time. I've been checking all phone lines hourly, so I'd suggest that you do the same each hour just to verify that the phones are still working. We are set up to start working the restoration plans with Con Ed and Long Island just as soon as we can communicate and see what's left and where they need to start from. You'll have to try to call in a crew to help with that. Everything else is in the log. You sure you're gonna be okay, Willie?"

"Sure, I'm okay. Go on home."

"You're sure now? I am worried about you."

"I'm sure. Just get the hell out of here before I change my mind."

Bud Flynn didn't need any more encouragement than that, and he quickly gathered up his things and headed for the staff door, knowing in his heart that Willie was in no condition to take the shift, but hoping Roger and the day workers would get in early and bail him out. In reality, Bud didn't much give a shit either way. He was going to high ground for a while, maybe for a long while. He knew a girl who lived out in the country up around Mt. Marcy in the Adirondacks, and he thought he'd give her a visit. *Fuck this mess,* he thought as he got ready for the two-hour drive.

Bud Flynn had not even started his car before Willie Davis began getting himself together. He was a thirty-year veteran and had weathered many storms in his life, both personal and professional, and had always managed to come through whole. He put his personal grief into its own compartment in his mind, where he could deal with it on his own time, and got down to the business at hand.

First, he reviewed Bud Flynn's shift Manager's log, then he read the log of the shift before. He scanned his computer monitors, taking note of the system voltage profile,

ACE, frequency, telemetering status or at least what was left of it, and then signed his shift on duty in the operator log.

The familiar routine was having its usual remedial effect, and Willie settled down to his shift routine. The National Grid phone rang, and Willie depressed the blinking button. "ISO, Davis," he answered.

"Hey, Willie," the National Grid system operator began without preamble. "The non-utilities can't deliver and are cutting us 300 megawatts right now due to gas fuel cuts, and Mike is taking more calls right now. It looks to me like we'll be losing a lot more."

"What are the cuts for?" Willie questioned.

"Do you mean the gas or the megawatts?"

"Either one or both. They're buying firm gas and supplying firm power. Don't contracts for firm delivery mean anything anymore?"

"Not in the new world of deregulation, they don't," Tom Agnew, the well-respected system operator, said bitterly.

"Tom, I gotta go." Willie hung up the phone and watched the system frequency meter start to drop along with his area control error. A quick mental calculation told Willie the interconnection frequency was dropping at a rate out of all proportion to the generation cuts being made. *Someone else is in trouble too—big trouble. We have to...*by then, phones were lighting up from all the upstate utilities and the generation dispatcher was waving to get his attention. Willie was reaching the end of his rope. He took a deep breath and began to deal with one problem at a time.

Finally, after fielding many calls and much excited conversation, Willie was told by the PJM shift supervisor there had been a compressor station explosion down south somewhere west of Baton Rouge in Louisiana and that gas supplies would be cut all day. Willie Davis sat for a few moments and fought to get his harried mind into the situation at hand, then he looked up at his console and depressed the hotline phone. He knew what he had to do, and he would do it.

He waited as all eight green lights illuminated on the alarm panel, then said in a completely calm voice, "Gentlemen, I'm declaring a major emergency state in effect at this time. Due to lack of generation and continued low system frequency, I am ordering all members to institute an eight percent system-wide voltage reduction. All members are to be prepared to shed customer load in the amount of any generating units lost from now until further notice. End of message."

He sat back and was just beginning to get his head together when several new alarms went off at once.

Willie Davis looked over at his frequency meter and knew there was nothing more he or anyone else could do. The system frequency of all of the continental interconnected power systems had dropped drastically and was still falling. A look at his system-voltage profile display showed Willie that voltages were also declining in response to a large loss of generation somewhere. He sat by helplessly as, one by one, generating units in New York were tripped off the line by under-voltage or under-frequency relay action, and soon, major portions of his bulk power transmission system started tripping also.

In a matter of one minute and eleven seconds, and despite all actions that were humanly possible, the interconnected power systems east of the Rocky Mountains went black.

Bud Flynn wasn't twenty miles up the highway when he noticed there were no lights on in the houses beside the road. He simply shrugged his shoulders and kept on driving north.

\* \* \*

Bruce McCartan awakened to slatted sunlight peeking through aging venetian blinds directly on him. It took him a few moments to get his mental processes working again, and a very brief peek at Gina Morrisette's smiling face and bottomless green eyes to fill in the blanks. It was obvious to him that Gina had set the blinds so the rising sun would shine into his eyes and gently wake him up. "Did you set the blinds, Gina?" he asked.

"Cheap alarm clock," she answered, still smiling.

Bruce barely remembered checking into the Super 8 Motel in Ardmore, Oklahoma, barely ten hours ago and falling directly into bed and into a deep, exhausted sleep. As he slowly rolled over and got out of bed, he mentally took an inventory of the places where his body pained him, then immediately regretted he hadn't inventoried the places that didn't hurt instead, because they would definitely make a shorter list.

"Have some coffee, and then you'll feel better," Gina said, and she was right. A big twenty-ounce container of steaming hot coffee stood on the bedside table. The first few sips were like heaven. After a few more, Bruce was feeling a lot better and began to check out his surroundings.

The motel was old, but the room was scrupulously clean. He vaguely remembered that Gina had insisted he stop right here and right now. After a long and busy day, a scuffle in an alley, and fourteen hours of driving, she had been right. His stubbornness had been endangering everyone.

Gina looked bright and chipper this morning, all freshly scrubbed and wearing one of his flannel shirts over a bright pink tee shirt. "Get into the shower quickly. It's cold water, but at least you'll be clean. Then I'll change your bandage and we can go. We're all fed, packed, and pottied, so as soon as you're ready, we're out of here."

This was a rare treat for Bruce, and his surprised expression must have shown. Gina smiled again contentedly. His ex-wife had been consistently slow to rise, and slower to get ready, and always grouchy in the morning. She had always held them up on a trip. But not Gina.

The whole family had to wait while his ex showered, applied her complete makeup, and fixed her hair. Then she would insist on a leisurely sit-down breakfast that would last another hour. By the time they got back on the highway, his children would be out of sorts and the day had started badly. It was a rare treat for Bruce to be the last up and find everyone else ready.

He showered very quickly, not enjoying the cold spray, and finished his coffee while Gina peeled off the soggy bandage covering his side and replaced it with a fresh one. "You heal up real good," she said, sticking on fresh tape.

"It's the expert nursing that does it," he said gallantly.

"Flattery will get you everywhere, but not this morning. It's time to hit the road." She was beaming up at him, liking the banter, and liking him too.

"Yes'm," Bruce said and eased on the light Henley shirt she had lain out for him to go under a flannel. Having his clothes laid out was another treat for him, and Gina's smiling good nature in the morning was unbelievable. He was beginning to think Gina was going to make an excellent addition to the trip. He was certain of it when he found the Suburban all gassed up and waiting, fully loaded, outside the motel door.

"We're all checked out," Gina said. "I kind of used your credit card. I hope you don't mind."

"I'm just surprised they honored it," Bruce answered. "It's been overdrawn and underpaid for a long time."

"They never even checked it in the office. The lights are off, so they couldn't run it through the machine. I just signed and left."

"My kinda girl." Bruce nodded approvingly. "But how did you get gas with the power off?"

"The man at the gas station had rigged up a hand pump and was doing a land office business," she answered matter-of-factly. "He seemed to be pretty proud of himself for it."

"And so should you for picking the right station."

"Thanks, but it was the only station available. The Waffle House didn't have any electricity, either, but their gas stoves still worked, so I got you a couple of bacon, egg, and cheese sandwiches for the road."

"I think I love you," Bruce said, only half in jest.

"Too soon for that, mister, but hang onto the thought anyway," Gina said, beaming at him.

Shortly, they were on the road north toward Oklahoma City, where they would catch Interstate 40 West and back into the Texas panhandle. The weather was alternating from bad to horrible, from driving rain to wet, sloppy snow that accumulated in ruts and made driving a nightmare for a Louisiana boy. "You really did well getting us up and on the road this morning," Bruce said, meaning every word.

Gina smiled, quite pleased, and said, "It's the least I could do. After all, I got quite a lot of sleep on the road yesterday evening."

The rolling Oklahoma countryside fled past their windows as Bruce pushed the aging Suburban as hard as he dared to. Ashley and Evvie were playing some sort of quiet hand-slapping game in the back seat, and Tabatha had regained her territory again, curled up asleep against Bruce's leg. Everything was peaceful.

"Maybe we could pass some time by getting to know each other better," Gina suggested.

The getting-to-know-each-other part was rich with promise, and Bruce responded instantly. "Did we, um...sleep together last night?" he asked, feeling a little foolish.

"We slept in the same bed, but we did not sleep together, if that answers your question. You were much too tired, and I don't know you that well."

"How well do you have to know me?" he asked jokingly.

"You'll know when I know," she answered seriously, but smiling.

He was smiling too, and he thought that rather strange, since he couldn't remember smiling very much at all for quite a long time.

"Suppose you start the process by telling me a little more about yourself," Gina said.

"What do you want to know?"

"Everything, so start from the beginning."

"Once, there were two people living in the Garden of Eden, and their names were Adam and Eve."

Gina smiled indulgently and said, "Not quite that far back."

"It's not all pretty, and sometimes it hurts just to think about it."

The pained expression on Bruce's face struck a chord in Gina's heart, and for an instant, it was almost as if it were her pain. "I don't want you to have to hurt any, Bruce. I know how that can feel. So maybe I should tell you some about my life.

"I was born as Regina Morrisette in Brown's Bayou. That's over in Terrebonne Parish. If you've ever been over there, you know it's pretty rural country. The nearest town of any size was Houma. My daddy was named Joelle Morrisette, and Mama was Jean. I have three sisters all younger than me, but I don't hear from them much. They are named Elizabeth, Victoria, and Mary 'cause Mama had a fascination for the English nobility and named us all for dead queens. I've always hated my name!"

"Why hate it? It's a pretty name."

"Because Mama wouldn't let my teachers pronounce it like Gina, she made them say it as Regina. She pronounced it slowly as Reg-eye-na. Pronounced that way, it sounds the same as a woman's most private part, and all through school, I was teased about it and called Regina Vagina by the older kids. When I was little, I didn't mind it because I didn't know what it meant, but when I got old enough to know, then I hated it. I made all my friends call me plain Gina."

"I'll bet that you were never plain, Gina," Bruce said, thinking she was a beautiful young woman who didn't realize how beautiful she was.

"No, I was never ugly, and that was another part of my problems. There were only two classes of people in Brown's Bayou: the two rich families whose granddaddies were smart enough or lucky enough to buy up some old useless swamp land that just happened to have oil or gas under it, and then all the rest of us. My daddy was a good man with his hands and could fix or build just about anything. He would get work on the oil rigs whenever there was any, or he would fix your car or build you a shed or a chicken coop or just about anything that come to mind. The rest of the time, he would hunt, fish and trap the bayou.

"Mama would raise a huge kitchen garden, and we'd all help in it. Daddy used to say not to stand still in the summer or Mama would can us right along with the vegetables."

"It doesn't sound too bad, Gina, just hard times, that's all."

"Not if you're Regina Vagina, growing up poor and hungry on Brown's Bayou. Not if you were skinny and gawky with a homemade haircut and clothes from Sally's Smart Shop. That was my Mama's way of saying the Salvation Army store in Houma. I was the oldest, and lucky because sometimes I would get a new dress. My sisters always got my leftovers.

"When there was no other work to be had, my Daddy could carve things out of wood that looked so real, you'd believe they were. When things were slow, he would take his boat out in the bayou and get some Tupelo wood to carve out duck decoys. He had to do more and more carving after the animal rights people from the cities up north killed the trapping trade. Before that, Daddy could always pick up some spare dollars for Christmas by running a trap line in the bayou and taking some raccoon, muskrat, nutria, or possum when they were prime. He'd sell the pelts to the fur buyer who came around late each fall. I remember he used to go on about those animal rights people something awful.

"He would say, 'Men have been trapping critters for their fur since there's ever been a man smart enough to do it and we never have run short of critters to take. Now these smartasses from the city want to give the critters more rights than most men have. So what happens? I'll just tell you what happens. The natural balance of nature is upset and we're overrun with animals. It ain't worth trapping them or even shooting them, but there's so damned many of them that they're catching the mange or rabies and dying horrible deaths to no good cause and maybe coming in to bite our children. It's a damned shame,' he'd say. He always wanted to catch a rabid coon and box it up and send it to that guy on *The Price Is Right*. Said if his kids had to get bit by one, then he should get bit too.

"After he would get the tirade off his chest, he would light up his pipe and go into his shop and carve out some ducks. Daddy never got paid for them what they were worth because the rich folks who could afford to buy them knew that we were needy, but it was something to get by on.

"Daddy married Mama when he was nearly forty years old, so I never remember him as a young man. He was mostly bald and tall as a tree, and I loved just to play around his workshop when he was carving. I can still see him in my mind, all bent over his vice, just whittling away on a duck or a snipe, his big hands making the work so fine that he hardly needed sandpaper."

Big tears were rolling down Gina's cheeks as she remembered her childhood, and it nearly broke Bruce's heart. "You don't have to do this, Gina," he said.

"Yes, I do," she said with a determined look he would get to see quite often, and she continued. "I filled out early, I guess, and that's when the real trouble started. Mama said I was just blossoming, but whatever it was, I was the only girl in my class with boobs, and all the boys liked me for it, and all the girls hated me, and I don't know which was worse. Mama and Daddy were very religious, and we went to church every Sunday. We also never had anything in the house that Daddy considered improper, and we never talked about sex at all.

"One day when I was fifteen, Daddy had to take some mallard and redhead decoys over to old Millard Jakes's place, and he let me ride along in the truck. Daddy knew he was being cheated every time he had to sell a bird to old man Jakes, but he needed the money. I think he took me just so we could talk and keep his mind off things.

"Michael Jakes was home from prep school that weekend, and he had a new red Corvette. He came over and talked to me while Daddy and Old Man Jakes were dickering over a price for the decoys. On the surface, it looked like Daddy and Mr. Jakes were friendly, but they weren't, and on the surface, it seemed like Michael Jakes was nice to me, but he wasn't nice either. He asked me to go out, and he was so damned good-looking in that car that I wanted to go, but Daddy wouldn't allow it. 'They're not our kind, Regina,' he would say, 'and don't you ever forget it, because they never will be.' But I didn't listen.

"I stayed okay until I was sixteen and all filled out and I met Michael Jakes in town one day when Mama was shopping. He asked me to go out with him again, and I said no at first, but he kept asking me, and I finally said yes, even though I knew that I would have to lie and sneak out on my daddy to do it. I got dressed up as nice as I could without making Daddy suspicious, then lied and told him I was going to a movie over in Houma with a girlfriend. Then I walked down the road to meet him.

"We did go to a movie, and he made some advances in there, but I could handle him. After the show, we went and got some burgers and stuff and then drove out on to the levee to eat. He put some liquor in the Cokes that made them taste awful sweet, but I drank it anyway and got a little woozy-headed from it. He and I were kissing and getting all worked up, but I kept saying no to him, until he finally got mad at not having his way with me. I was crying and saying no to him and begging him not to, but he just slapped me around, then did me anyway."

Bruce was amazed at the anger he felt, and he had to make a conscious effort to release the death grip he had on the steering wheel. He wanted to hold Gina and comfort her, but she was curled up against the door, in her own world, and he let her continue.

"He hurt me badly that night, but two good things came of it. One, I got sick and puked up all over his nice new red Corvette, and the second was my precious girl, Ashley."

Gina was sitting there with her jaw set and tears still streaming down from eyes that were fixed on someplace far ahead, or far behind. "He must have bragged up on what he did to me that night, because after that, every boy in town thought that he could put his hands on me, and I began to hate even going to school. Mama and Daddy kept looking at me funny too, so I guess they must have heard of it somehow, though they never said anything. Things were just awful around the house for the next two weeks, and Mama and Daddy talked quiet so we couldn't hear and fought a lot, sometimes way into the night. When I missed my period, Mama knew all about it, and I knew that I was done for. I told Mama what had happened, and she just cried and cried. It broke my heart.

"I guess Daddy did the only thing he knew to do about me. Mama packed my suitcase, and Daddy said, 'Get in the truck, Regina.' He drove me to the bus station and never said a word to me all the way. When we got there, he handed me a hundred dollars in cash, which must have been all they had, and put me on the bus for New Orleans. He was crying just like I was, and he said, 'It breaks my heart to do this, Regina, but I don't know of any other way. I've got three more daughters at home who have to grow up in this place. I'll tell folks around that you had to go up North to help out with your old grandma who is sick.' He kissed me and wiped the tears off his cheek and just walked away. He never said for me to come back, and I've never been back since." The words were running out of her like a torrent, and the tears were flowing freely down her cheeks.

"Gina, damn it, you don't have to do this," Bruce said.

"Don't stop me. I've gotta get it out and be clear." She took a deep shuddering breath and continued. "When I got to New Orleans, I was scared nearly out of my wits. I'd never been north of Houma before, and the city scared the hell out of me. There were so many nasty-looking people at the bus station. I just wanted to run back onboard and hide, but I couldn't. I had no idea of where to go or what to do. It had always seemed so glamorous on TV when girls went off to college or to get a job in the city, but it wasn't that way for me. I was just plain terrified.

"There were a lot of men just hanging around, and I could see they were looking at me and nudging each other with their elbows. I knew what those looks meant, but I didn't know what to do about it. A couple of them waved to me and started calling me sweetie, but I just kept my eyes down and walked away. That's when I heard a big old voice say right out loud, 'Well, what have we got here?'

"I looked up right into the biggest, brownest eyes I had ever seen. In the biggest, brownest face I had ever seen. 'I bet we've got a pretty little piece of white bread that's got herself knocked up and her pa's throwed her out. Am I right?'

"I nodded yes, and she surprised me by wrapping me up in her arms and hugging me tight to the biggest, brownest breasts that I have ever known. She smelled of lavender and made me feel all warm and safe. 'Not to worry, little girl, Loretta's going to take care of you.' And she did just that.

"Loretta was a hooker who worked the Quarter, and she had my apartment before I did. She took me there, sat me down, and looked straight into my eyes and gave me the first lesson in 'life according to Loretta.'

"'That bus station where you came in is just about the worst place in the world for a young girl to be at. Those men who were waving at you were all pimps and drug dealers. They would take you in, then get you hooked on junk, then put you in a hotel and use you. After a couple of weeks, they'd have you working down in the Quarter, just peddling your sweet ass off just to keep them and your habit happy. I know all about that stuff.'

"I could see Loretta must have been a beautiful young woman, because even after fifteen years on the street and gaining a few pounds, as she liked to say, she was still a pretty woman. 'What are you gonna do about that baby you got growing in your belly?' she asked plainly.

"'I'm going to have her, and keep her, and raise her myself,' I said with more determination than I really felt. I didn't have a clue as to how I was going to do all this.

"Loretta just nodded and kept looking at me. I knew there was a lot going on behind those big brown eyes. 'Reggie, this is what we can do,' she said finally. I started crying when she said 'we,' because I knew she would take care of me and help me with the baby. I just hugged her.

"'You can stay here with me until the baby comes and you can make other arrangements. You will have to work and help out while you can, and I can arrange to get you into the clinic so you can have a proper doctor. After that, then we'll see what happens.'

"She stayed with me through the whole pregnancy and held my hand in the delivery room. She held my hands and loved me, and that was all that I needed. She let me stay home with Ashley for three months because, she said, 'A baby has got to get to know her mama.' Then it was time for me to move on with my life.

"While I was pregnant, I worked at McDonald's and washed dishes and did anything I could do to earn a little money to help out. Now that I was getting ready to be on my own, Loretta took me to see her aunt Evvie, and we arranged for her to watch Ashley while I was working, though I still didn't have a job. Then Loretta took me to the Doll House and introduced me to the owners.

"I didn't want to be a dancer, and I told her so, but she just laughed at me. Loretta told me then in no uncertain terms that I was a pretty girl with no education and that in this town I had only two choices: I could show it to them at the Doll House, or I could sell it to them on the street. I've been working at the Doll House ever since."

Bruce looked over at Gina sitting there so bravely after baring her soul to him and still holding her chin high, and for the first time in his life, Bruce McCartan had the good common sense to keep his mouth shut. He simply reached across the seat and took her hand and held it tightly.

\* \* \*

"Wake up, Mark, wake up." Devon Grant was shaking Mark Person's shoulder vigorously.

"Where am I? What's going on?" Mark Persons asked sleepily, trying to get his foggy brain functioning again.

"You're in the ladies' lounge at SWPC, Colonel. You've just gotten a few hours' sleep, but there's some bad news coming in." Devon Grant's pretty face looked grim.

"What news?"

"There's been a meteorite strike in the Gulf of Mexico. It's not being reported as a big one, but it created a sizable tsunami, which has already struck the Peninsula of Yucatan." Devon was talking a mile a minute.

"What's the news from Houston?" Mark asked, his head clearing from the update.

"Nothing."

"Nothing?"

"No, nothing for the last hour. We can't raise NASA or the airport on any of the other numbers we have. We keep getting the 'can't complete your call as dialed' message no matter what number we try."

Mark Persons lowered his head into his hands and was silent for a moment. When he came up, he was full of decisive energy. "Have you tried Denver International recently?"

"Last time was a few hours ago. They had no information to release on inbound flights from Houston, or anywhere else for that matter." Devon gave a frustrated shrug.

"That does it!" Mark rose and started for the door of the ladies' lounge. "I'm going over there to find out for myself. I'll get some answers if I have to commit bodily harm on half the staff."

"Wait, Mark. I'll go with you."

"Thanks, Devon, but I think I'd better do this myself. Besides, you've been up working all night." He paused for a second, trying to think back to last night. "Weren't you going home at midnight?"

"No one to relieve me or Art, either, for that matter. We stayed the night and listened to the shuttle coming down. They got into Andrews early this morning, after some really tough problems. Not only were the communications bad, but the weather is abysmal almost everywhere in the country."

"You'd better go home and get some rest then, Devon. Is Art ready to go home? I can drop him off on my way to the airport."

"He's just shutting down now. We finally agreed there's not much sense in staying in operation here when there's no one we can talk to. We're going to get some rest and check back here later."

"That sounds good to me. Go on home and get some rest, then get the packing done for the valley that we talked about yesterday. Things are turning around quickly, and I want to be ready to go. Professor Schmidt is already there, and Tom Brooks is preparing his family for the trip."

"I know, Mark; you told me all that yesterday."

"Sorry, I guess my head is not completely clear yet. Go home anyway, Devon. I'll get Art, and I'll check with you later when I get back from the airport."

"Yes, sir, Colonel," Devon said with a mock salute. "I'll go, as ordered, sir."

"Good, I'll see you later," Mark said as he hurried down the hall toward SWPC Operations. "Get some sleep."

Devon smiled at his receding back as Mark Persons hurried away. She pulled up the collar on her storm coat and walked quickly to the employees' parking lot. The driving rain-snow mixture of earlier in the night had subsided to a steady drizzle seeming to ooze out of the heavy low clouds, almost an extension of them. Everything felt soggy as Devon climbed into her Prius and started for home. The streets were almost devoid of people and traffic this morning, and those who were out seemed to be scuttling from place to place in twos and threes or in small groups. There was an almost palpable tension in the damp air. She was delighted when she pushed her apartment door closed behind her with a satisfying click of the lock and the two deadbolts. She was so exhausted, she didn't even bother to undress but simply flopped facedown on the bed and fell immediately into a deep sleep.

Devon Grant was sound asleep under a pulled-up comforter as Colonel Mark Persons stepped out of his car and walked through the door of Denver International Airport Operations. Mark was resplendent in his full blue dress uniform with his pilot's wings and all his decorations lined up above the left breast pocket. Silver eagles gleamed on his shoulders as he approached the control tower entrance and squarely faced the security TV camera and depressed the talk switch on the intercom. "This is Colonel Mark Persons, United States Air Force. I need tower access to check an inbound flight with approach control. Time is of the essence, and I can't afford the delay in checking with individual airlines."

"Could we see your ID card, Colonel? Please hold it up to the camera."

Mark raised the photo identification card he had hanging around his neck and held it up to the remote camera. He started well away and slowly moved the plastic laminated card closer to the lens.

"That's fine, Colonel. Come upstairs and take the first right." The voice was accompanied by the buzzing of the security lock release.

Mark hurried up the stairs and knocked on the first door on his right. The sign read, "Denver Approach Control, absolutely no admittance." The door opened, and a tired-looking man in his early fifties said, "Come on in, Colonel. It's stacking up to be a quiet day here, which is a good thing, because I haven't had a relief in thirty-six hours. I'm Cliff Swanson, by the way."

"Pleased to meet you, Mr. Swanson. My children are due in commercial from Houston, and I can't get any information from the airlines. I've been calling since yesterday."

"So you decided to come right to the source."

"Yes. I'm running low on time and patience."

"I can understand this. From what I understand, if they got out of Houston yesterday, it was none too soon. We haven't had a peep out of the whole Gulf Coast for the past several hours."

"Anything inbound at all from that area?"

"The only thing we've got is a Texas Air National Guard C-130 due in just a couple of minutes. They were scheduled for Stapleton, but they're closed down."

"Did the Tex ANG say if they've got passengers aboard?"

"No word on that, sir, but if you want to talk to the crew, they'll be coming in through commuter gate C11 in the American Airlines concourse. They're going to fuel up and make a pit stop, then continue to California. If you head over there, you'll probably get there about the time they land."

"Many thanks, Mr. Swanson."

"Call me Cliff, and no thanks necessary. Hope your kids make it in alright."

As Mark sprinted down the almost empty American Airlines concourse, he could see out the windows. The squat transport airplane painted in camouflage was taxiing toward the gate. The whirling turbo-prop engines were creating shining silver vortexes in the heavy drizzle outside. Squat fuel tankers were waddling up beneath the wings of the big transport as Mark hurried through the gate and out to the front of the aircraft, waiting for the propellers to spool down before approaching. Suddenly, a movement behind a window caught his eye, and there was the face of his son Clint, who was smiling and waving to him. Not surprisingly, his son Eric was in the next window down, and in the third was a young woman whom he did not recognize at all.

* * *

Jim Gianetta sat back in his booth at the Flying J Truck and coffee shop and continued watching the two young people who were sitting a few tables over. As a long-distance truck driver for nearly forty years, Jim had spent enough time in truck stops and coffee shops to become an expert observer of people, and these two kids were in trouble.

They were very nice-looking young people and did not appear to be the type to purposely rip off a restaurant, but the boy, who appeared to be about fifteen years old, was definitely counting and recounting his money, as if he expected it to increase with the effort.

"Katie, I sure wish you had stuck with the ninety-nine–cent breakfast like I told you to. Now I don't have enough to cover the bill." He was staring down at the bill for three dollars and eighty-five cents held in one hand and the three dollars he held in the other and was wondering how he could make them balance.

"I'm sorry, Keith. I thought that it came with the meal, and I never thought they'd be that much."

"You should have read the damned menu," he said through slightly clenched teeth. "Now what are we going to do?"

"Do you think we can leave what we have and sneak out without them noticing?" Kaitlin McCartan asked her brother.

"Not very likely," Keith answered, eyeing the hostess. She had a mean look about her.

In truth, he was quite correct in his assessment of the hostess. Janet Tolliver was a woman who prided herself in her appearance, and today she was a wreck. She was also a good judge of people and had sensed there was a problem in the making, and she would just relish making a fuss today. *Who ever heard of two days of constant rain in Sparks, Nevada?* she thought. Because of this rain, her hair was a mess, and this weather was ridiculous, and her mood was as dark as the clouds. The only thing she was grateful for was that she was on the west side of the Rockies, because all reports she heard said there was no power on the east side of them.

Keith was counting his available cash for the fifth time, fighting the rising panic that was causing his breakfast to turn over in his belly, when a five-dollar bill suddenly appeared on the table. Keith looked up and smiled into the friendliest face he had ever seen. "Pay up, son, and I'll wait outside for the change. And don't forget the tip. The waitress has to make a living, too." Jim Gianetta gave him a big wink and headed out.

As the stranger walked off, Keith observed a man of medium height with gray hair, a great tan, and a big bald spot. His shoulders were broad but stooped, and his back looked powerful. His arms were long, and he rolled when he walked, like a sailor just getting his land legs back.

"Thanks a lot, mister," Keith called after him, but the stranger never broke stride or looked back.

Keith snatched up the bill and said, "Come on, Katie, and be quick about it. We've got to catch that man before he leaves."

"He said that he'd wait for the change, and I've got to go to the bathroom," Katie said emphatically.

"Go ahead, then. I'll meet you outside."

Keith darted up to the cashier and put down his breakfast check and the five-dollar bill Jim had given him. He received a sour look along with his change. Janet Tolliver was not happy about being cheated out of a perfect opportunity to create a fuss, but Keith McCartan didn't take any time to notice. Seconds after receiving his change, he was bolting out the door, looking for the kindly stranger who had bailed him out of his trouble.

From the habit of many years on the road, Jim Gianetta was doing his walk around his rig. Check the tires for cracks or uneven wear, look at all hoses and wires for fraying or breaks, check underneath the rig for fresh oil spots in case there's an oil or hydraulic leak, check all lights for broken glass or other damage. Jim had not survived for nearly forty years on the road without being a careful driver in all ways. He'd had only one accident in his career, but it had been a dandy and had very nearly cost him his life.

Jim was just bending over to check the rear brake lines when the young man came cannonballing around the back and nearly toppled him over. "Jeez, I'm sorry, mister. I didn't want to miss giving back your change," Keith said breathlessly, handing Jim three dollars and fifteen cents. "I left a dollar for a tip like you said."

Jim looked at the money and said, "Looks like you gave me three dollars too much."

"No, sir, I didn't," Keith said firmly, stretching himself to his full height. "I had three dollars; I just needed the eighty-five cents and the tip. I also didn't get the chance to thank you properly."

"You're quite welcome," Jim said, pocketing the money. "Where's your sister?"

Keith looked up and saw Kaitlin coming out the doors, lugging two backpacks and looking around for him. He waved. "Hey, Katie, over here."

She spotted him immediately and came right over. "Did you ask him?" Katie asked her brother.

"Ask me what?" Jim wanted to know.

"Well, mister, I really don't know where to start."

"Jim, son. My name is Jim Gianetta. What's yours? That's usually a good place to start."

"I'm Keith McCartan, and this is my sister, Kaitlin. We're from California, but we're on our way to Boulder, Colorado, to visit our dad."

"And just how did you expect to get there with no money?" Jim asked.

"We left in quite a hurry because my dad called and asked us to, and we only had our savings to go on. The bus fare from Palm Beach to Reno took most of what we had. The bus driver was a lady, and she and my sister talked a lot. She said it would be better for us to get off here, rather than the bus depot, and to try to hook up with a trucker that was heading east. I was hoping that you were going that way. Are you?" It was obvious that both of them were holding their breaths waiting for an answer.

"I don't know for sure where I'm headed. I was just headed over to the K-Mart warehouse to try and pick up a load. Give me a minute, and I'll call the dispatcher over there to see what he's got for me. Things are kind of crazy with the power outages in the East and the weather all over the country."

Jim disappeared back inside the Flying J, and Keith and Kaitlin waited nervously outside for him. "He seems like a nice man," Kaitlin said hopefully. "I think he'll give us a ride."

"I sure hope so."

At that moment, Jim came out of the shop with his blue eyes twinkling and a big white grin on his suntanned face. Kaitlin turned to her brother and said with a smug little grin, "Told you so."

As Jim walked back to the truck, Kaitlin unconsciously slipped her hand into Jim's and held it. Neither of the McCartan kids noticed the glint of a tear in the corner of his eye as he looked down at the small blonde head.

Jim Gianetta settled back in his seat and let the big rig plow its way at a steady seventy miles per hour going northeast on Interstate 80, headed for Winnemucca. Keith McCartan was sitting next to him and stretching upward to try to look taller and older, while his sister, Kaitlin, was curled up in the back, sound asleep already. Jim always had to move about a few times to find the spot in the seat where his back didn't hurt, and when there, he could comfortably drive for hours. The steady light rain didn't bother either him or the truck, but he was a little concerned at what he would find crossing the mountains. *Oh well, deal with that when we get to it.*

The pain in Jim's back was the result of a terrible accident almost fifteen years before. Jim had been hauling logs that summer in northern California and had been rolling downhill past Trinity Lake when a small herd of mule deer had crossed right in front of him. He had locked up the brakes and promptly skidded off the road, rolling down a steep bank. Strangely, Jim's last conscious thought had been that he wouldn't run into Sasquatch down there.

When he had awoke, Jim had been in a hospital in Redding, in a world of pain and surrounded by long-faced doctors. The prognosis had been grim. Although the team of orthopedic surgeons had pieced his bones back together, there had been no assurance he would ever walk or drive again.

The next few months had passed in a blur of anesthetics and pain, with any number of wires, screws, and pins being placed in his body only to be removed after his bones had knitted sufficiently. Still, the orthopedists could give no assurance to Jim of his mobility. The only bright side had been that there was no major nerve damage. That was when Alexandra Banks had come into his life like a miniature tornado.

Allie Banks was five feet tall in bare feet and weighed in at ninety-eight pounds, but what she lacked in stature, she more than compensated for in pure animal energy. Allie had been Jim's physical therapist, and she had changed his life.

"Hey there, big guy," she had said upon entering his room for the first time. "I understand those slice-and-dice boys are done putting your bones back together and now it's time for Allie to put your life back together. If you've got what it takes, that is." That was all the challenge Jim had needed.

"I've got all the balls you'll ever need," Jim had come back.

"That's good, Jimmy, 'cause I like nothing better than a challenge. And I don't waste my time on a quitter."

That had been the beginning of Jim Gianetta's nine months in hell. He often told people it had taken his mother nine months to make him and it had taken little Allie Banks nine month to remake him. Nine months of pain and challenge and failure and success and failure, of tears and smiles and all the things that make for success. All of this orchestrated by ninety-eight pounds of sheer determination named Allie Banks. Allie had strong hands and a stronger will as she had massaged, exercised, worked, and pushed Jim until he was exhausted. She had pushed him to the limit, then shown him that the limit was much further along than he had thought. She had been therapist, teacher, coach, and, twice when he was in the pit of despair, a best friend. Jim was special, and she had helped him succeed against all the odds.

Fifteen months after entering the hospital, Jim Gianetta had gotten a ride in a wheelchair to the door, where he had promptly stood up, turned, and gave Allie Banks the biggest hug of her life, then smiled and walked away. He had been minus a family, lost through an acrimonious divorce in the middle of his paralysis, but with the rest of his life back.

"Hey, Jim. Hey, Jim, where have you been?" Keith asked, bringing Jim out of his trance. "I've been talking to you, but you're off in dreamland somewhere."

"Sorry, boy. I was just daydreaming a little; that's an occupational hazard on this job. You can pass a lot of boring hours by dreaming inside your head."

"I just asked if you were married or had any kids?"

"A long time ago, in another life, I did. Now it's just me and this old truck. Just us. But I am thinking that there is one little gal in northern California I have to get up to see and take out to lunch real soon."

\* \* \*

Becky Crawford was trying to boil some water in a badly dented pot from the Boy Scouts of America camping kit Kenny had behind the seat of his truck. The Sterno heat was slow to bring the ice-cold water from the nearby stream to a boil for their morning coffee. They both had passed an uncomfortable night in the cab of the Happy Tyme frozen food truck, and sleep had been elusive even after the tremendous events of the day before and 500 miles of increasingly difficult travel behind them. A cold blast of wind nearly extinguished the feeble alcohol flame.

"Close that door, Kenny; you'll blow the fire out," Becky said a little tartly. "I want my coffee sometime today."

"Sorry, Becky. I think the darned weather is worse today than yesterday."

"Don't I just know it?" Becky had been out for her morning stop earlier and thought that her fanny might freeze to the metal seat in the Porta-Potty at the roadside picnic area near Wathena, Kansas, where they were parked. It was really nasty.

"Here," Kenny said as he placed a piece of folded cardboard wrapper from last night's frozen dinner around the Sterno can, cutting off any breeze and letting the heat rise up to the saucepan. In short order, the water began to boil. "Let it boil good for a few minutes," Becky said. "I don't trust using water from that stream."

"Fine, if you say so."

When leaving the Speedway the morning before, Becky had had the presence of mind to grab three pounds of coffee and some filters, and Kenny had thought to tie the coffee up in a filter like a little bag and boil it in the saucepan. The system worked well, and shortly, they were snug in the cab of the truck with the heater running and fresh coffee in their bellies. "I guess it's time to roll," Kenny said.

"I'm ready when you are. I hope Nita's not having nightmares. She looks so peaceful."

"I'm ready; let's go," Kenny said, dropping the truck into first and pulling slowly up the exit and out onto Route 36 West. Soon, they were cruising along at a steady fifty. The alternating driving rain pounded on the truck roof and kept them awake, and the heavy wet snow silently created a layer of dirty wet slush all over the landscape. Kenny briefly wondered why the slushy snow should be dirty all over. He could understand it along the roads, but even in the open fields, it had a dingy-gray look. The big old Power Wagon had no trouble with the slush-covered roads, even if they weren't plowed. Kenny took childlike glee in looking in the rearview mirrors and seeing the slush whirl back from his rear tires like the wake from the stern of a speeding boat. He grinned.

"Tell me what's so funny, Kenny. Don't keep secrets," Becky chided him.

"Just watching the slush spin off in back," he answered. "Feels like I'm driving a big speedboat in the movies."

Becky smiled. "I did a lot of thinking last night, Kenny, and realized that we really don't know much about each other."

"Yes, I know," he answered, his features beginning to change to concern with the reality of their situation. "I know."

"Maybe we could start out by telling each other about ourselves."

"Not much to tell for me."

"Yes, Kenny, I'm sure there is. I have a feeling that there's a lot more to Kenny Smith than you ever let people know." Becky reached over and took his hand in hers. "Kenny, I really want to get to know you."

"What about you?"

"There will be time later for that, Kenny, and I promise it will be worth waiting for," she answered cryptically. "I want to hear about you."

"I don't know where to start."

"Start as far back as you can remember."

As Kenny let his mind wander back to his childhood, a pained expression began to spread slowly across his face but was shortly replaced by an expression of resigned determination. "Becky, I have never told all this to anyone else. A lot of it is hard for me to remember back on. I can remember it, but it's hard times, and my mind doesn't like to look at it."

Becky said nothing and continued to listen.

"I never knew my father. He was just never around. My mother worked, and I stayed with a neighbor lady who had a lot of kids of her own. I was just another one of the pack. My mother had a lot of men friends who would visit, or stay around a while. Most of them treated me right, but the last one, he was different. He was a long-range trucker and sort of lived out of his truck. He had nothing to do with me at all.

"One day I got up and my mother had my clothes all packed. She gave me a bath and told me we were going on a nice long trip. I remember I was all excited about traveling in that big old truck with the bed in the back. I sat on my mother's lap into the city. I think it was Wichita. The man pulled up and stopped in front of this big old church. My mother was crying a little, but she took me by the hand and walked me around back and stood me by a big heavy door. She gave me an envelope and told me to give it to the man who would come. She kissed me, knocked hard on the door, and just walked away. If I live to be a hundred, I'll never forget her back as she just walked away. She never even looked back one time." Ancient bitterness was strong in his voice. Becky moved a little closer on the seat and took his hand and held it. He never noticed.

"It was a Catholic church, and the fathers were really nice to me, but I only stayed there a short time. After that, it was just one foster home after another. Some were good ones and I liked them and I wanted to stay but I couldn't. Some of them were awful and I hated them and wanted to get away but I couldn't. The last one was the worst of all, and I had to stay there the longest."

Kenny stopped talking and just stared ahead at the gently rolling countryside and the seemingly endless snow. When he began again, there was a look of barely contained anger on his face. "The last family I was with was the Sharples, John and Cora Sharples. They were cheap with us kids but not with themselves, and meaner than snakes, the both of them. We all lived on a big farm outside town, and there were rabbits and chickens and little piglets and cows and none of them were pets. In time, we ate them all.

"We all had our work to do, and the older you got, the more work you got to do. We would work in the garden all day, then work in the kitchen canning or freezing all night, it seemed. The only thing that made it bearable was a tall and thin girl named Adelade Hicks. Addie was awesome. She would go to the Sharples with our complaints or problems, but most often, nothing changed."

"Kenny, that must have been hard on you as young as you were, growing up like that."

"That wasn't the worst of it. With us young kids, old John Sharples would give us this bitter stuff to drink when a social worker was coming and then claim we was retarded. The social workers would ask us questions and make us do puzzles, but the medicine we had taken made our minds fuzzy and it was hard to think. I'm pretty sure he got extra money from the government for us, but we never saw a penny of it."

"Why did you take the medicine, Kenny? You're not disabled."

"Because John Sharples was a mean man. If you didn't do what he said, he would beat you, or lock you outside the house all night in cold weather, or make you do extra work at something nasty. If you got sick, then Addie would have to go and argue with Sharples to get medicine. She hated to have to do this.

"When I was fourteen, Addie was eighteen and left us to go away with a boy she met in town. Things got really bad after she left. The Sharples would argue all day, and then John would get drunk and beat Cora up at night. The next day, she would beat all of us kids up just to get even. I ran away three months after Addie left. I was scared for a while that the police would catch me, but I wonder if he ever told anyone I was gone. He probably just collected his money and never told anyone.

"I've been on my own ever since. I worked for three years for a Mexican man who ran a landscaping business. I stayed in a room behind his garage and did whatever he needed. That was the only time I got any real schooling. Then I bummed around for a while and wound up in Danville working for Happy Tyme Frozen Foods Company, and the rest you know."

"God, I thought I had it bad. Thank you for telling me about Kenny Smith. I'm sure that was not easy for you."

"Now it's your turn." Kenny said with a smile, grateful he was done.

"Not just yet, Kenny. You'll know when."

"Then we had better think about finding some gas cuz' we are running low" Kenny said.

\* \* \*

The first thing Janice Wharton noticed this morning was that her alarm clock sounded funny. She squinted over at it and noticed the battery backup light was on. *Hmm,* she thought, *the power must have gone off through the night.* The next thing she noticed was the sound of heavy rain drumming on the roof of her home—just a steady, hard, straight-down rain. *Rainy days and Mondays,* Janice thought as she swung her feet out of bed and felt around the floor for her slippers. Finding them, she put on her bathrobe and noticed how chilly it was in the house. The power must have been out a long time to be this cold.

Janice went quickly to the living room and turned on the gas log in the fireplace. The log ignited but was not burning with its usual steady brightness. Janice shook her head, thinking, *What else could happen this morning.?*

In the kitchen, she lit the propane stove to boil some water for coffee because the coffee maker wouldn't work without power. Neither would the TV where she usually watched Robin Meade and the CNN Headline News first thing to get a feel for the day, nor the hot water heater, so she had to forego her hot shower and wash in cold water. Neither would her curling iron work, so she had to content herself with a bad hair day. The instant coffee, when she finally got some, was grainy tasting and foamy on top. The light didn't go on in the fridge. *Damn!* she thought. *This is starting out to be a really bad day.*

By the time Janice considered herself ready to go to work, she was thoroughly angry with the power company and the gas company, too, because her gas log had sputtered down to a flicker and she'd had to shut it off. One last check in the mirror before she left told her that makeup by candlelight was not to be desired, either. In mild anger, she snatched her car keys from the vestibule table and her umbrella from the stand by the door and went out. There was a strange white van in front of the Jones' house and some men hanging around. Thinking they may have been hired by the gas or electric company to get things back to normal, she went right over to them.

"Say there, are you men going to get the power back on sometime this morning?" Janice asked curtly.

"Not today, and not tomorrow either, lady. Where have you been? Don't you know that the meteors hit?" replied a rather fresh-faced blonde man.

"No," Janice was about to say when she glanced at the Jones house and saw Burt Jones draped over the porch rail with his head bleeding badly. Her eyes flew to the open front door, and through it, she could see a man in the living room doing something to Florence Jones that was properly to be reserved for the bedroom. Come to think of it, Flo didn't seem too happy or cooperative with it. "My God, she's being raped!" It was in that moment that Janice realized how bad things were.

Janice spun around to face the nice-looking blonde man, and he punched her neatly on the point of her chin, knocking her senseless and chipping a front tooth in the process. Suddenly, she was being gagged and bound with some foul-smelling silver tape that was amazingly strong, and thrown into the back of the van like a sack of potatoes. Janice sat up to try to get away or argue with the men, but the "nice" blonde man slapped her face and used the tape to bind her hands to the car seat.

"Where's the new broad from?" asked a swarthy man who had just come from inside the Jones' house with a bundle.

"Next door. Let's go over there and have a look before we go."

"Sounds good, but make it quick. We don't want to linger in any neighborhood too long."

"I'll be right back."

The nice-looking blonde man left, and the swarthy man got in and looked Janice over. Her dress and raincoat were hiked up on her thighs, exposing more of her shapely legs than she would have liked, and he took his time enjoying the view before allowing his eyes to travel the rest of the way up to her face. He smiled, exposing dirty gapped teeth, and said, "Well, lady, how does it feel to know you're going to be tonight's entertainment?"

Janice began to struggle even harder, but the man just laughed out loud, then yelled in to the house, "Come on! We ain't got all day!"

\* \* \*

The weather in Youngstown, Ohio, was just as bad as anywhere else and John Halloran cruised around looking for a gas station. He was happy to find one only three blocks from the interstate. There was a big cover over the gas pumps, and the wind wasn't blowing the rain too far under it. *Good as any*, he thought as he pulled in.

"See if there's a key for the ladies' room when you go in the office," Sally said as John prepared to get out. "Butch and I have to use the facilities."

"It's probably going to be cold in there and no hot water. It looks as if the lights have been off for a while."

"No matter. If you gotta go, then you gotta go."

"Understood," John said as he slipped out in the rain and walked over to the station office. It was locked up tight, so John used the pry bar he carried in his hand to break the window and unlock the door. Inside was dark and oily-smelling like all service stations seem to be, and the keys were hanging over the desk with a big man and woman cut out of plywood securely fastened to them. John grabbed the female silhouette, then moved to the back wall and found the breaker panel and, with the heel of his hand, opened the main breaker with a loud click.

He then went out to the Jeep and handed Sally the key. "Keep your eyes open. I don't like the feel of this," he told her

"I don't like the feeling of having to pee, either, so move over and let me by. Come on, Butch. You can share the facilities with me."

After they left, John used the pry bar to force the front cover of the gas pump off. With quick economical motions, he took the clamp-ended lead lines from the Honda generator mounted on the front of the Jeep and hooked them to the lines for the gas pump motor. John started the generator with just a short twist of the key, then took a wire from his pocket that had two insulated alligator clips on it and manipulated the computer controls to make the pump start up. In a minute, John had precious gasoline flowing into his main and saddle tanks.

John had filled all tanks and was about to get the key for the men's room when Sally came back dragging Butch, who was beginning to act surly again with her. She helped him into the truck, somewhat more vigorously than necessary, and was about to climb in herself when a white van pulled in. The driver was a small man with a ratty-looking face, and he immediately began to run his eyes over Sally's body. "Get in. I'll handle this," John told her.

John walked over to the van and asked, "Something I can help you with, gentlemen?"

A nice-looking young blonde man got out of the back and said quickly, "We saw you gassing up, and we sure could use some fuel ourselves." He was smiling innocently.

John didn't like the looks of the whole operation but saw no way to politely refuse, so he said, "You can pump what you need. I'll keep the generator running. Then you can put what you owe on the cash register just like I did."

The man gave him a strange look for a few seconds, then said, "Sounds great to me. Pull her in there, Dick, and fill her up."

John waited at the back of the van while Dick filled the tank, and the young blonde man looked frequently over at Sally. Suddenly, there was a bumping sound from the back of the van, and John jumped a little. "What do you have back there?" John asked.

The blonde said quickly, "Oh, it's just the damned dog." He pounded on the side of the van and yelled in the window, "Shut that bitch up or I'll come in there and beat the hell out of her." The bumping stopped.

John was more than glad to see them leave, because there was something about their behavior that made him nervous. He was about to pull out himself, when an Ohio State Police car pulled up to the pumps. "What the hell's going on here?" asked the tired-looking young officer in the blue-gray uniform and campaign hat. His hand rested lightly on the handle of a wicked-looking 9 mm pistol.

"Just getting some gasoline," John said, trying hard to sound casual.

"I can see that, but how the hell did you rig that pump?"

John said, "Come over here, and I'll show you how to do it."

The young trooper was named Kyle Lenny, and he was nearly exhausted from too much overtime duty and more than a little concerned about how he was going to get some gasoline. After John filled his tank and explained how to rig the generator on the pump, the trooper was beyond happy.

"Do you know where you can get a small generator like this one?" John asked as he began unhooking the wires and preparing to stow them in the back of the Jeep.

"Yes, they've got them over at TC Crist's Supply Store."

"Show your sergeant how to do it, and then he can rig them up all over town and keep his people mobile, at least."

"Great idea," Trooper Lenny said and went immediately to his car and picked up the radio.

As John returned to the Jeep, he heard Trooper Kyle Lenny saying rather proudly, "That's right, Sarge. If you'll send all units over to Sloane's BP station on Fourth and Elm, I'll gas them up, rescue units too. If you come by here, I'll show you how it's done and you can set up fill-up points all over town. Yes, sir," Trooper Lenny said into the mike, beaming with pride. "I'll be waiting right here."

The Jeep was idling smoothly as Trooper Lenny returned and peeked in the window, giving Sally an appreciative once-over. "Well, sir, you sure made me some major points with the sergeant. You'd better be on your way out of here now. Have a safe trip." He patted John on the shoulder and backed off so John could drive away. He even waved good-bye as they drove off.

"Step on it, John," Sally said with an uncharacteristic tremble in her voice. "This place gives me the creeps."

"As you wish," John answered with an accompanying steady pressure on the accelerator. The Jeep jumped in response and seemed as if it wanted to be out of Ohio too.

\* \* \*

"It's time, Mr. President," Amos Bellinger said quietly, respecting the president's reluctance to abandon his office.

"This is unbelievable, Amos. I've just been here a few months, and now I have to abandon ship. It's simply unbelievable."

"Nobody said that life had to be fair, sir. I believe a very wise man once told me that."

"At least he thought he was wise, Amos, and that was a long time ago."

"I still haven't forgotten it, sir."

"Do I have a few more minutes, Amos?" Jameson Coleridge asked.

"Just a very few, sir. FAA command center has been alerted that we will be the last flight to take off. They are anxious for us to leave. The first lady and the others are already onboard, and the weather is worsening quickly. Very quickly."

"Alright." Coleridge rose and began to take neatly piled stacks of papers from the desk and put them into his briefcase. "All bad news, Amos; all bad and getting worse. Did you get Liz Coulter to come out with us?"

"Yes, sir. It took some persuasion to do it, and I had to promise to have her husband's unit shifted out to Colorado Springs as additional presidential security. I issued the orders and forged your signature on the order. I hope you don't mind."

"No, I don't mind at all. We owe that gutsy little woman a huge vote of thanks. She had the courage to shut down our nuclear generators well before any others did. Our Japanese allies did not heed her warnings, and now they're dying by the millions in Nagoya and the surrounding area because of it. Did you hear the latest from over there?"

"I don't think so, sir."

"Riots around several operating nuclear plants. On one just outside Tokyo, the crowd broke in and killed the entire working crew. Now they have to recruit operators from other plants to shut it down, and pray the automatic controls work until they do. They're shutting down the rest of their operating plants and hoping that it's not too late."

"We can go over the rest of the items in the air, sir. We really have to be going."

"Okay, Amos, I'm coming." Jameson Coleridge looked about twenty years older than he had just a few short months ago. Amos had known the job did that to presidents, but he had never imagined how quickly it could happen.

\* \* \*

Colonel Daniel J. Coulter had his command post set up in an abandoned day-care center just outside Newburgh, New York. Evacuees from the New York metropolitan area and other coastal cities were raising hell in the countryside, raiding and looting to survive. Dan Coulter's unit was protecting the southern approaches to Stewart Airport from the New York Thruway, east to the Hudson River. His regiment was under strength and stretched pretty thin, but because Stewart was the only operating airport in the area, it was imperative that he hold his ground. He was studying his area map for the hundredth time when a white-faced major from the New York National Guard came in and saluted smartly. "Orders for you, Colonel."

Dan Coulter's color deepened as he read the orders, then he looked up at the pale-faced officer who had brought them. "Do you know what is in these orders, Major?"

"Yes, sir. Colonel Bleeker is bringing his regiment down to relieve you in place. You are to be airlifted out with your staff and headquarters company, the remainder of your regiment to follow as soon as they are relieved. That's all I know, sir. Colonel Bleeker asks that you make all arrangements to turn over command immediately, as he will be here shortly and your reassignment orders were quite specific and urgent."

"Thank you, Major. Give my compliments to Colonel Bleeker and tell him that I'll be ready to move out as soon as his troops can take over my positions."

"Yes, sir." The major saluted and exited the command post with obvious relief.

Dan Coulter then took a moment to read over the orders he had just received. They were very clear and specific, and from General Gates himself. Undisputable. "Brownlee, get HQ Company packed up and ready to move out ASAP. National Guard is taking over our positions. Notify the regiment to be ready to turn over our positions to the guards as soon as they arrive. Make sure everyone takes their time and explains our setup before bugging out."

Major Herbert Brownlee's eyes widened, and he snapped to obey his commander's orders without question, even though he had many of them. This was considered to be a critical position to hold. That's why the 82nd Airborne had gotten the job in the first place. Now they were being relieved by National Guard and reassigned to who knew where. None of this made sense, but then again, very few things made sense any more. "Sir?" Major Brownlee asked, unable to withstand the curiosity. "May I ask what our new assignment might be?"

"Herb, we're going west to Colorado to act as presidential security."

"Sir, does that mean Washington's had it?"

"Yes, Herb, I would assume that is very much the case." Dan Coulter watched the muscles play across his adjutant's face and shared his grief and fear. Herb Brownlee's family lived just outside Washington in Fort Lee, Virginia, and if Washington was gone, so were they. Major Brownlee knew that Dan Coulter's wife was in Washington, DC.

* * *

Lieutenant Peter Krauss led his platoon off the truck even before it had come to a stop. The blue-lighted sign read, "East-Side Hospital Emergency Services." Using only hand signals, Krauss quickly dispersed his troops to cover and waited for the second part of his command to arrive. A few seconds later, two black Chicago Police Department vans pulled up and men in black battle dress spread out silently and waited. Almost instantly, a short, blocky police officer wearing three stripes squatted down next to Peter and said briefly, "What's your read on the situation, Lieutenant?"

The ramp down to the emergency entrance was lined with sick and injured people cowering against the brick walls. There were several obviously dead or badly wounded people lying in the middle of the ramp. Inside the emergency room, shadowy movement could be seen and the sounds of looting and some screaming could be heard, but all gunfire had ceased. Apparently, a lookout had reported their arrival.

"Do we have all the interior exits from emergency blocked? Sorry, I didn't catch your name," Peter said rapidly.

"Sergeant Roman Kazanske, Chicago SWAT team," came the terse answer. "And yes, I left Jeff Pilatich and his team out front, they have that side secured."

"You and your men are trained in urban warfare, Sergeant, so I'd suggest we combine our forces with you and your men in command and mine as reinforcements to each unit. You say what to do and we'll do it."

"What rules of engagement?" Kazanske asked.

"They've made the rules, Sergeant. Use whatever level of force is necessary to secure the area and prevent further loss of civilian life. Do not expose your people unnecessarily. Blow them away if you have to."

Roman Kazanske's bushy black eyebrows arched at the sheer common sense of the disposition of the situation by the young lieutenant, and he heartily approved. The soldiers were going to participate, not wait outside where it was safe, but the best-trained men would lead the assault. Good sense. "I like you're thinking, Lieutenant. Here's what we'll do."

Peter Krauss's impression was one of sheer carnage as he burst through the emergency room door in a running crouch right behind Sergeant Kazanske. He hit the floor and rolled behind a reception desk as a burst of gunfire broke out from the end of the long hall. As he was trained to do, Peter immediately rolled back out from behind the desk on his belly and let loose a short, waist-high burst from his M16 in the direction of the shots and was rewarded by a body hitting the floor.

Roman Kazanske merely grunted approval and started forward again. Peter followed, his eyes darting from left to right, taking in one scene of horror after another. Furniture, linens, and medical supplies were strewn all over the floors. A big black orderly was draped backward over some chairs with several bloody holes in the front of his green scrubs. A nurse lay curled up in the corner of the room, and dead patients were scattered about the floor. A burst of automatic weapon fire brought Peter's attention back, and he saw several youths fall from the full automatic burst of Sergeant Kazanske's MAC-10. One stopped and started to aim, and on reflex, Peter dropped him with another economical burst from his M16. A few seconds' hesitation, then up and run again.

It took only a few minutes more to secure the emergency room area and herd the few gang members who were captured outside. Pretending to check the whole area clear, Peter Krauss moved slowly from room to room. All his training had never prepared him for the scene that presented itself. Hospital staff and patients alike were strewn in disarray all over the area. Several women were in various states of undress, still lying where they had been attacked; cabinets were rifled and their contents strewn all over the floor. A drug cabinet had its door blown off and its contents gone. That was probably why so many of the gangbangers were acting wild and drugged.

In the last room, Peter found a young blonde-haired girl who very much resembled his sister strapped stark-naked to a table and stabbed repeatedly after being brutally taken. He fell to his knees on the spot and lost his supper, violently retching many times until he was completely dry. Finally, he rose, wiping his mouth on his sleeve, and made for the door.

As Lieutenant Peter Krauss went out the emergency room door into the night air, Sergeant Kazanske came up and said, "What is the disposition of the prisoners, sir?" with a respect that had been earned.

"Give them what they gave the staff inside, Sergeant."

"But, sir, they're prisoners."

"They're cold-blooded murderers and rapists, Lieutenant, and we have neither the time nor the room to deal with them. No prisoners. These shit bags are getting exactly what they deserve."

As he walked away to where the trucks were parked, Peter Krauss heard the rattle of gunfire burst out momentarily and then stop, followed by cheering from crowd gathered outside the hospital.

\* \* \*

Patsy Cox stood in the sullen rain outside the Marathon gas station in Georgetown, Indiana, just west of Louisville, Kentucky, and stamped her foot in frustration. "Why can't you sell me any gas?" she demanded of the station attendant.

"Like I told you, lady, the power's off, so we can't pump gas for anyone, even a sweet little thing like you."

"I've got to get to Colorado as soon as possible! How can I do that if I can't get any gas?" Patsy hated the whining quality in her voice.

"Not my problem." The attendant simply shrugged and walked away.

Patsy noticed a gangly-looking young man staring at her from in front of the now-dead Coke machine. She lost her temper a little and stamped her foot in frustration again. "Damn!" she yelled and stomped quickly back to the car. She got in and slammed the door a little harder than necessary. She was just about to start feeling sorry for herself when a tapping came on her window. Patsy looked up and was startled to see the young man from the Coke machine signaling her to roll the window down. She did, but just enough to talk through.

The young man smiled knowingly. "Is that a nurse's pin I see on your collar?" he asked without preamble.

"Yes, it is."

"Then I may be able to help you get some gas."

"Just how do you plan to do that?" Patsy asked, feeling her hopes start to rise.

"My mother has not been feeling well of late, and I'm not sure just what to do for her. Our place is just outside town. You've got enough gas for that?"

"Yes."

"Then if you look in on Mama, I'll give you a fill up from our farm gas tank," he said hopefully.

Patsy considered her situation for a few seconds and then decided. She rolled the window down the rest of the way and extended her hand. "I'm Patsy Cox, and I'll be glad to look in on your mama."

"Oh, gee, Miss Cox, that's just great! I'm Boyd Moon." His face was beaming with such relief and happiness that to Patsy it resembled the celestial body for which he was named. "Just follow me."

"Alright. You have the pickup truck over there?" Patsy said a bit awkwardly.

"Yup. That's it, so just follow me; it's not far," he said as he walked away from Patsy and toward his truck.

The truck's reverse lights lit up, and Boyd backed out and turned past Patsy as he gave her a smile and a "come along" wave. She knew this was a less than ideal situation, but she thought she would keep her guard up and be ready for anything. At the first hint of no gas at the farm, she had it in her mind that she would bolt out of there. Just to be extra safe, she reached in the back seat and into her pharmacopia. She expertly placed her right hand on the eight-inch medical scissors where she knew they were and pulled them out. She would hide them in her back pocket as soon as she got to the farmhouse. Just in case Boyd had other ideas, she would be prepared.

\* \* \*

Amos Bellinger rubbed his eyes in near exhaustion from the killing schedule of the past few days and the relentless flow of bad news. The president was little better as he sat and scanned more reports of trouble. They were both caught off guard when the huge aircraft suddenly bucked up momentarily, then trembled and fell, slipping sickeningly sideways. At that same instant, the red light lit on the flight deck intercom.

Colonel Richard Selner had been flying the Boeing 747-200B jet with his counterpart and equal, Colonel Douglas Lampman, for a few years. They had been the admiration of the 89th Airlift Wing at Andrews Air Force Base since the previous administration. Their pilot briefing before this flight had included a convective SIGMET, which is significant meteorological information, but this information, they had already been fully aware of. Air Force One, most people don't know, isn't technically a plane but a radio call name for any military plane carrying the president, but in this case, it was the mammoth plane that the general public was familiar with and often saw on the television news or in movies. The enormous plane that Colonel Selner and Colonel Lampman were flying in this obscene weather weighed more than 833,000 pounds and took all of their experience, flight simulation training, and concentration to keep in the air.

"Bellinger here. What the hell is happening, Colonel?"

"Sir, were hitting some really severe turbulence here, and it will only get worse for a while." Colonel Lampman said professionally.

"Where's it all coming from?"

"Sir, we are at the boundary of the two low-pressure fronts caused by the meteorite strikes in the Bering Sea and the Atlantic. The actual contact area is still one hundred miles ahead, but the turbulence is already apparent. I have ordered all passengers to buckle in and remain seated. I would appreciate it if you and the president would remain in the office and use your shoulder restraints, which are stored inside the headrest on your seats, and buckle into the top loops on your lap restraints and—"

"Colonel," Amos broke in, "can't you fly over or around this weather?"

"No, sir. The front extends from Canada to Mexico and seems to go clear up into the ionosphere. There is no option but to look for the softest spot and go through it or turn back east."

Amos looked over at the president, who had been listening on the intercom. Jameson Coleridge simply nodded. "Continue west, Colonel, and I hope that you find a really soft spot."

"Yes, sir."

Amos took a deep breath and gripped the armrests on his seat as the 747 took a sickening plunge, then experienced a brick-wall stop, followed immediately by several sickening lurches and an updraft. "Jesus, this is worse than anything I've ever been in!"

"Makes you wonder what's next, doesn't it?" Coleridge said, his knuckles white on the arms of his seat as he watched Amos hit the intercom button again.

"Colonel, God dammit, please get this bird under control," Amos demanded.

Colonel Lampman gritted his teeth and with a calm anger said, "Yes, sir," and disconnected.

As if choppering from the White House to Andrews AFB in bad weather wasn't bad enough, now the president and his trusty advisor had to endure a bumpy flight and piles of reports varying indistinctly from bad to worse.

"Amos, talk to me; it will help to pass the time," Jameson said.

"Foreign or domestic?"

"Domestic. There is scarce little we can do for our neighbors or allies these days except to save our nation and get it back on its feet so we will be in a position to help them later. I know Israel is under attack from several Arab states and they are on the brink of using nuclear weapons. I can't help them, and I can't stop them. Western Europe is devastated, and the Balkans are erupting in new ethnic warfare. I can't stop them, and I can't help them. Russia has problems with her republics, and China has taken a huge hit in Sinkiang Province. I can't help them, and I don't know if I would help them even if I could, so let's do domestic."

"General Gates's report?" Amos posed.

"As good a place as any to start, but give me an outline. I'll ask for details where I think I need them."

"All civil-defense zones reporting in, as follows.

"Civil Defense Zone East. Battered along the coastlines by tsunamis caused by the strikes in the Atlantic, and the latest hit near the Grand Banks of Newfoundland. Florida is gone for all intents and purposes, hit by the Atlantic tsunami and from the strike off Yucatan. West of the coastal mountains, there are widespread power outages, but the general reports utilities are making superhuman efforts to restore as much as possible. Weather is another big negative factor; a snow-and-rain mixture is causing highway problems and has the potential of creating considerable flooding later. Cities are the worst areas, so if it is agreeable with you, I'll deal with them in some detail later.

"Civil Defense Zone Central. The Gulf Coast from Brownsville, Texas, to Panama City and Pensacola, Florida, is devastated as far as 250 miles inland; in many cases, much further where the terrain is flat. Power outages and bad weather are again complicating factors.

"Civil Defense Zone Mountain. Texas is devastated along the Gulf Coast, but inland, they are not too bad off. The power is mostly on, with spotty outages. I never realized Texas utilities are not interconnected with the rest of the country. The weather is horrible, and so are the problems in the larger cities. The rest of the zone has power and communications, but these are deteriorating.

"Civil Defense Zone Pacific. Probably in the best shape of any part of the country. They are not interconnected electrically to the East and therefore have few power problems. Unfortunately, their weather is deteriorating and their cities are expecting related difficulties.

"Now I would like to outline the urban problems we are experiencing in a general way, since most of the problems are common to all cities and urban areas."

Just as Amos finished this statement, Air Force One lurched up and to the left and then fell straight down as if the sky was falling with her. Both men grabbed the armrests on their seats and stared intently at each other while the aircraft's engines screamed and buffeting increased as the pilots forced the nose down in hopes of gaining some airspeed and regaining the lift lost to the huge gust of wind from the rear. Just as suddenly as the fall had started, it ended with a slam that pushed all aboard down into their seat cushions. Amos struggled upright in his seat and grabbed the interphone. "What the hell happened, Colonel?"

"Wind shear, Mr. Bellinger. We dropped nearly 19,000 feet before we caught enough air to regain control." His voice sounded calm and in control, while Amos's voice was so trembly and frightened that he got even angrier.

"Just get this damned airplane under control. Remember who you have flying back here. How are the other passengers?"

"Mrs. Coleridge and all the rest are OK, sir. The crew just checked the main cabin."

Even in the difficult conditions, Colonel Richard Selner could not help himself as he chuckled at how his friend was dealing with the chief of staff in the back of the plane. "Hey, Lampman, how 'bout flying this freaking thing with me rather than kissing ass on the phone," he said sarcastically, prompting a reaction.

"Fuck you. The guy is a first-class moron. This is my last flight with him, one way or the other."

The president could see that Amos was scared, and he wanted to keep his chief of staff's mind on something else. "You might as well do the urban problems, Amos, before we run into another hole in the sky," Jameson Coleridge said in a somewhat weak voice.

"Yes, sir. As I said, the urban problems are pretty well uniform across the country. Many people tried to flee the cities for as many different reasons, but the result was uniformly the same: traffic accidents, mechanical problems, National Guard checkpoints backed up, and massive gridlock everywhere. Bridges and tunnels became the biggest bottlenecks, so people just got frustrated and abandoned their cars, taking only what they could carry.

"These evacuees are causing problems for some suburban localities, as they are unprepared for survival and the weather is uniformly bad. General Gates' people are helping localities put these refugees up in schools and public buildings and are providing supplies and medical assistance. There have, however, been many cases of looting and robbery. Loss of power seems to be a trigger for a let's-get-even-with-the-world syndrome, and ethnic and social violence is rampant in many areas. It gets worse when someone owns a grocery store, liquor store, restaurant, or pawn shop. Any place where one group feels cheated or disenfranchised by another, there is violence and the police are spread too thin to adequately deal with it.

"The urban areas that are without power are the most critical. Phone service is out. There's no television, and minimal radio communication, which can only be used if you have battery power. Most stores are closed, and the ones that are open are overcharging for the few supplies they have left, and perishables are worth their weight in gold. What I found amazing when I read these initial reports is how few people keep a pantry anymore. When I was a kid, my mother could probably feed the entire family for a month on what she had stocked in the pantry. It seems everyone runs out daily or buys food already prepared and therefore have nothing stored at home. Even people with babies only have a few days of formula on hand and nothing but disposable diapers.

"Medical facilities are overloaded with victims of violent crimes of all categories and the usual assorted ailments. What has them surprised, and me too, is the number of heart-attack victims from people climbing stairs because the elevators no longer work. There have already been a number of assorted burns and asphyxiations from people trying to heat apartments with everything from kerosene or gas space heaters to fireplaces and gas barbecue grills and just plain open fires in whatever container is available.

"There have been any number of break ins at hospitals, ERs, and pharmacies. Police and National Guard are reporting two distinct types of crimes. One, street gangs and groups of drug addicts are breaking in, stealing whatever drugs they can locate, and destroying the rest wantonly. And two, another type of theft altogether is being perpetuated by organized groups who are taking all types of prescription pharmaccuticals and medical supplies intact. General Gates believes these people are planning to use the pharmaceuticals as trade goods later on when they'll be worth much more.

"Fires have become a major problem because of broken-down or abandoned vehicles clogging the city streets. People are using many creative means of heating their apartments, and some of them get out of control and start the buildings on fire. In many cases, fire departments cannot get to the scene to fight the fire and it simply burns to the ground, putting many hundreds of people out on the street with nothing but the clothes on their backs and what they could carry in their hands. Unless and until the power is restored, the situation in our urban areas will continue to disintegrate."

"That's not a very pretty picture, Amos," Jameson Coleridge said dejectedly.

"No, sir, and it won't improve for some time to come, I'm afraid."

"Amos, do you think that things would have been better in the cities if I had announced the danger as soon as I learned about it?"

"If I thought that was the case, I would have advised you to do so. I believe we would have had all the same problems we have presently, only sooner, and we would have been less prepared for them."

"That may be true, but the power would probably be on, and that alone would have removed the fear of the dark, loss of communication, and many of the medical problems people are having. In retrospect, Amos, I think I should have called the shot when I first learned of it."

With those spoken words, the plane took another sickening dive that caused the president and Amos to both turn white, and the president threw up on the floor. The plane settled, and Amos grabbed the interphone. "Colonel, do I need to come up there and fly this fucking thing myself so we can get on the ground safely? You are aware of who is on this plane, aren't you?"

Colonel Douglas Lampman reached his breaking point and would not take any more shit from this ignorant jackass. "Listen closely, *Anus*. I am fully aware who is on the plane with my wife and two kids. I assure you they are as important to me as the president is to the world. Now leave me and Colonel Selner to do our job. I repeat, quit distracting us from doing our job. We're doing the friggin' best job we can." He hung up the phone, not waiting for a reaction.

Colonol Selner let out brief laugh and said, "You weren't shitting; you're done one way or the other after that."

Amos was not bothered by the hostile words, or by being called anus; he was bothered by the fact that he now knew for sure, they might not make it.

"JC," Amos started.

"JC? You haven't called me that in a lifetime, it seems," the president said, somewhat surprised.

"I know, but I think it is a very real possibility this is it. We may not make it through this flight, and as far as announcing the meteorites, you're being too harsh on yourself. If Ben Cohen hadn't altered his calculations, we could have made a better judgment. We thought we would not be exposed for another two weeks, and that would have given us ample time to do all the things that were planned for the people. As it is, we just have to pick up the pieces and put things back together as best we can, if we make it."

"Amos, I knew on the helicopter flight from the White House to Air Force One that we might not make it. You have been a good friend, and I hope we will be able to rebuild the country together."

The plane began to violently fall again, and this time, it was Amos who threw up while descending. Then he said, "I hope so too."

The president knew Amos had said something, but he could not hear his friend over the rattling of the shaking aircraft.

# The Epilogue

## The Next Several Days

"I'm starving," young Kaitlin McCartan grumbled as she looked in the very empty lunch bag.

"Me, too," answered her brother, Keith.

Jim Gianetta just smiled to himself, never taking his eyes off the slush-covered road. They were in Nevada on Route 95, going southwest, avoiding the high country, where Jim feared the roads would be bad. "We'll be in Hawthorne soon, and I know a gal who can maybe take care of us with some food. We'll be able to gas up there, since it looks like the power is still on in this area," Jim said.

"Seems as if you know a lady in about every town out here," Keith remarked, half smiling.

"That's a trucker's life, boy," Jim replied with a sly grin. "Got to take comfort wherever you can."

Jim Gianetta may have been sixty-three years on the calendar, but he could pass for his mid-forties. After the accident, he had taken his physical therapy and physical therapist very seriously. He remained faithful to his exercises even after his physical therapy was officially complete. This allowed his body to be in the good condition it was today.

As they reached Hawthorne, Jim could immediately see things were bad. The main street, Route 95, was a shamble of wrecked and burned cars. Several buildings were burned out, and the entire town had an odor of soggy wood ash and death. It appeared as if there had been a massive explosion in the small town. "Good God," Jim said in a low voice to no one in particular, "I never thought things would get so bad so soon."

"Jim, this place smells bad and makes me scared," Kaitlin said in a soft, wavering voice.

"I know, honey; I don't like it either," Jim replied as he put his work-hardened hand on her shoulder and patted her for comfort.

"Look out, Jim!" Keith yelled as a bunch of filthy, wild-looking men jumped out toward the truck.

The big 500-horsepower Cummins engine roared as Jim accelerated through the grizzly scene in Hawthorne, and there was no mention of hunger again until they got near the small town of Tonopah.

Tonopah, Nevada, looked to be unchanged: an old hotel, a run-down campsite, a few unpainted and aging houses and stores, and numerous piles of dirt and rock scattered across the hillsides on both sides of town showing where men were digging for silver.

Jim slowed to a stop in front of the hotel and let his eyes wander up and down the street, slowly taking in every detail. Somewhat satisfied, he reached across in front of the children and popped open the big glove box. He removed a big heavy Colt .45 automatic pistol and chambered a shell. The children's eyes widened at the look of it and what it meant—danger. "Come with me," Jim said in a new commanding voice.

They dismounted the truck and went directly up the hotel steps. The peeling paint and old wood spoke volumes of the age and rough history of the building. Jim moved quickly and went inside, paused a second to survey the big room, then turned to the right, into the restaurant. Tables were overturned and chairs were scattered and broken.

"Hey, look at this," Kaitlin said, the sound of fear gone from her voice. "The menus look like newspapers and have articles about Area 51 and flying saucers and aliens!"

"Neat," Keith replied, taking a copy for himself.

"Save them to read in the truck!" Jim said briskly. "Go over there and check if there's anything to eat in the kitchen. I have to check upstairs; things are way too quiet here."

Keith and Kaitlin responded to Jim's stern voice and moved quickly. The kitchen had been ransacked already. Pots and pans and broken dishes lay all over the floor. The cabinets and fridge were nearly bare. They grabbed what was left.

When Jim came downstairs, his face wore a pained expression and was white under his usual ruddy tan. "Let's go."

"Aren't we getting gas?" Keith asked.

"No. Now get a move on."

Kaitlin picked up a small lumpy store bag with some bagels in it, and Keith picked up a box with some peanut butter and three cans of vegetables. They all hustled out and climbed back into the truck. Jim kicked the engine over and quickly pulled out onto Route 95 and continued down the road. "There are some very bad people around here who did some terrible things back at the hotel," he explained.

Keith nodded solemnly, understanding what lay behind Jim's words. Kate said nothing, just accepting the words of the man she had begun to call Grandpa Jim.

"With our fuel situation, we will be able to make it to the town of Ely with no problem. There will be plenty of places to gas up there, so don't worry about that," Jim said, thinking more out loud to himself than to the kids. He was one hundred percent committed to getting those kids to Boulder; how they would find their father from there was another story. *One step at a time*, he thought, *one step at a time, but I will do it.*

\* \* \*

Patsy Cox was still cursing at herself hours after ripping the leather seat to her Mustang with the scissors she had forgotten about in her back pocket. After Boyd had filled up her tank at the farm, he had thanked her and simply wished her well in her travels. She had told Boyd there was no need to worry about his mom, as she was going to be just fine. Patsy had then gotten in the car and sat down, creating a seven-inch tear in the back of her leather seat. She had just been so preoccupied with her original, and now embarrassing, thoughts that Boyd Moon might have evil intentions for her that she had forgotten about the scissors.

Patsy continued driving on Interstate 64 West while reminiscing about checking Miriam Moon's vital signs and briefly getting to know her a little bit. Her temperature had been normal at 98.6, pulse fine at sixty-eight beats per minute, blood pressure normal 120 systolic over 80 diastolic, and respiratory rate at fourteen breaths per minute. All were very normal for any adult, but for Miriam, who was in her late sixties, they were excellent. She said she was tired from a long few days of spring cleaning and her son just worried too much. She was hopeful that someday her son would find someone like…

Then it happened.

One minute, Patsy was thinking about the past couple of hours at the dark, quiet, and lonely home of the Boyds, and the next instant, a huge red and yellow flower bloomed up to her right. The light was not bright and sharp like a spotlight, but rather dull and smoky like an oil lamp, but it grew fast—one second dark and now bright. Her dulled senses did not make a connection before the huge hand of the pressure wave pushed her car to the left, forcing her across the highway toward the guardrail, looming ever closer.

Suddenly, the sleep-deprived synapses in her brain all clicked closed and she realized almost too late the gravity of her situation. *Explosion!* her mind screamed. *Must be an oil tank or something.* At the same time, her body reacted without conscious thought. Her foot pressed the accelerator pedal to the floor while her hands fought the wheel to the right to counter the ever-increasing pressure of the blast wave. There was never a thought in her mind of stopping or turning back.

The five-liter V-8 engine in her Mustang responded to her need by opening the fuel injectors and drinking in a large quantity of the precious fuel from the Boyd farm. The front end of the car rose slightly in response to the sudden acceleration, and the car skidded as the rear wheels drove forward against the pressure wave. For a few slow-moving seconds, all forces seemed to be at an equilibrium and time seemed to stand still as the first red tongues of flame engulfed the car. Then suddenly, she broke through the flames. The Mustang leapt forward as it overcame the pressure of the blast, and the rear end slid wildly to the left, hydroplaning in response to her oversteering and acceleration, the tires spinning as they searched for pavement to bite.

Patsy reacted to the skid instinctively, turning left into the skid and feathering her brakes. The Mustang responded and began to straighten out as Patsy's wits returned. Another slight correction to the right to compensate for oversteering, and she was straight on the highway, headed for a bridge crossing the Wabash River. She could smell the burned paint and rubber, and her watering eyes told her that the huge conflagration behind her had spread completely across the highway; rolling red and angry flames filled the rearview mirror. She realized she had better continue to distance herself from the inferno, thinking how lucky she was that the car hadn't exploded with its nearly full tank of gas. She continued across the bridge entering Illinois, and once there, she eased off the gas pedal and brought her pride and joy to a stop along the side of the interstate. She then lowered her head to her hands and began to cry quietly.

After a few minutes, Patsy forced herself to get out and assess the damage to her car. The formerly immaculate bright red paint on the passenger side was black and blistered in spots, and the rims of her tires were badly soot-stained and slightly burned. Her side windows were coated with a thin film of burned-on black soot, but aside from that, the car seemed to be in decent condition. "I've got to keep moving," she said aloud to no one but herself. "I can't let this stop me." She began crying again but was determined to keep heading west. She got back in the battered car and continued on her way. The trip would hold many more detours and tribulations, but she would eventually fight through all of them to find a new life, a happier and less lonely life, when she reunited with the only love of her life, the new Sergeant Tommy Brooks.

* * *

The passing landscape was as monotonous as it was sodden and soggy, with water-soaked desert lands dotted with saguaro, eerie man-shaped cacti standing in puddles of water. Every so often, a depression in the low-lying land contained a small pond of water. They were driving through a sullen drizzle broken occasionally by small showers. The air itself was so humid that Bruce had to run the defoggers occasionally to keep the windshield clear.

"I thought this was supposed to be dry desert land. Why is everything so soggy?" Gina asked, feeling slightly depressed by the oppressive weather.

"It is," Bruce answered absently, "but be glad it's just rain and not snow or ice like we hit in Oklahoma."

"Why are there little ponds of water? I thought with all this sand, it would just drain away."

"Hardpan," Bruce said quickly.

"What is hardpan?" Gina asked.

"Under the sandy soil, there's a layer of heavy clay soil called hardpan. It is nearly impervious to water and holds all the rain at the surface. That's why we are seeing so many puddles."

Gina was barely listening to his answer, and added, "Can we stop soon?"

"No. We'd better keep going as long as we can."

"Bruce, we are all tired, and it would feel good to stretch our legs."

"I know, Gina, but I am afraid that all this rain might be snow in the mountains when we get further north. I don't want to get caught in the passes up there. I have to get to Boulder. You know that."

"I know. I'm sorry for complaining. Kind of selfish of me."

"That's okay. We are going to need some gas, anyway. I am hoping we get lucky and find a station with the power on. I don't want to feel like a criminal again, like we did in Oklahoma, but I will if we have to," Bruce said, still feeling a little bit guilty.

"Me neither," Gina confirmed.

Back in the small town of Purcell, Oklahoma, Bruce had been low on gas. With no power, he'd had to resort to something to get gas. He'd seen a sign for Purcell Lake and thought maybe there was a marina and he could figure something out from there. He had known it would be easy to siphon gas from a boat that was up on a trailer in the parking lot of the marina, but Purcell Lake had turned out to be more of a pond and hence had no marina. But, as luck would have it, just south of the lake was the Brent Bruehl Memorial Golf Course and the grounds maintenance crew's barns. Bruce had found several maintenance trucks and mowing tractors in the parking lot and wondered where they gassed those things up. He had looked on the side of the barn and found three twenty-eight–gallon portable gas caddies. One of them had been empty, but the other two had had more than enough to fill the Suburban up. With the foul weather, nobody had been around. Bruce had driven the Suburban next to the portable pumps and filled it up in a matter of five minutes. He had felt his Irish luck kick in.

Bruce and his new crew of girls eventually made it to Boulder in another forty-two hours and began the search for his kids. He finally found Kaitlin and Keith through a conversation that traced back to a National Guardsman he met in town. The guardsman remembered some oddities that prompted him to have a conversation with a truck driver. A semitruck in the middle of town was odd enough, but the driver had been a bit on the older side and caring for two young kids who did not appear to be his. Once the driver, Jim Gianetta, had explained who the kids were and how they had ended up with him, the Guardsman had felt a lot better. When Bruce questioned the guardsman as to where a good spot would be to look for a couple of kids, he explained that no place was yet set up, but he told Bruce about the truck driver who was helping a couple of kids find their dad. Bruce was overcome with relief and immediately knew what to look for—a big friggin' truck. It didn't take long before Bruce had found the truck and the driver he would forever be indebted to. They would all remain together for the next several weeks and survive in the hills of Colorado.

\* \* \*

To the east, Kenny Smith and Becky Crawford had left the Sunflower Motel for their one-night stay just outside Hiawatha, Kansas, on good old Route 36. Becky complained and cajoled him, throughout the trip, but Kenny did not leave his good-luck road. She couldn't complain too much, since Kenny had shown so much resourcefulness in obtaining fuel for the gas-guzzling pink truck by trading frozen food. Becky joked with him about the old truck getting thirty miles per sirloin.

They had decided earlier in the morning they would head to Colorado. They really had no good reason except that Becky had watched a television show about the

Boulder Bach Festival on TV and it looked interesting. Kenny had heard there was power in that part of the country, and he did not want to go back to Danville to try and explain his violent but necessary actions at the Speedway.

Kenny pulled into a gas station along with several other cars. There was no power, and people were getting desperate to get fuel and be on their way. A big man with a heavy beard was standing dejectedly next to a station wagon loaded with kids and supplies. He looked at the big pink truck and said dismally, "You're out of luck just like the rest of us, buddy. No friggin' power to pump with."

"Got to be something around here to help us," Kenny insisted.

"Like what?" the man asked. "There's no portable generator. We looked all around but didn't see nothing. I'm Jake Turley," he said as he and Kenny shook hands.

"I'm Kenny. No harm in looking again, is there?" Kenny said, already walking away.

Jake Turley followed as Kenny began nosing around the station. Jake lost interest after they found nothing inside the station, and he wandered dolefully back to the station wagon and began talking to his wife. Kenny went around to the back of the station to look through the scattered, run-down scrap metal and debris. Becky sat in the truck, ignoring the openly admiring glances Jake Turley was throwing her way, and silently prayed Kenny would not be too long. The mood at the station was starting to get tense, and some of the people were beginning to argue about pooling what fuel they had left to move on. Nita wriggled in Becky's lap and said, "I don't like that man, Becky; he's got bad eyes."

Becky was surprised to hear Nita finally speak and couldn't agree more with her words. She said, "Don't worry. Kenny will be back soon." Her mood brightened appreciably when she saw Kenny coming around the corner of the building, lugging some strange-looking apparatus and a length of garden hose.

"Watcha got there, boy?" Jake called.

Kenny had found an old hand pump that had been designed to pump oil out of a fifty-gallon drum, which the others had overlooked completely. "Found us a pump," was all he said. He went straight to work, and with the wicked-looking switchblade knife he had taken from the dark man back in Danville, he promptly cut off the brass fitting at the end of the hose. "Jake, see if you can get the cover off that fill line over there," he said, giving the order as if it were the most natural thing to do. The big man responded quickly, as if Kenny had been his boss for years. Several men from the other stranded cars gathered around Kenny, while the others went to watch Jake.

"If this works, we'll be back on the road in a few minutes," Kenny said as he started up the truck. He climbed down, then went around back and shoved the cut end of the garden hose up the exhaust pipe. In a matter of a minute or two, the heat from the exhaust had softened the hose just enough so Kenny could work it up on the long stand pipe from the bottom of the old pump. A hose clamp from the garage parts shelf made the hose secure. He then cut about four feet of hose off the other end and repeated the heating process, then slipped this onto the pump's outlet pipe. Carrying the whole rig over to where Jake was crouched down, Kenny saw that Jake had removed the cover off the fuel fill manifold and taken a cap off one fill line. Kenny handed the pump to two men who were following him and said, "Hold this please," and without hesitation began feeding the garden hose down the fill line. When all the hose was in the tank, Kenny began to turn the pump handle around. After a few turns, some ugly black substance started to come from the outlet hose onto the pavement.

"What's that shit?" one of the men asked with an edge of panic in his voice. The men all looked dismayed.

"They were using this to pump recycled oil out of the collection drum out back," Kenny said casually. "We've got to clean that out first, then we'll get some gas."

In a few moments, the air was filled with the sweet smell of unleaded gasoline and all the men were bolting for their cars. Kenny had to grab the old pump to prevent it from falling over. Jake grabbed onto it also and said admiringly, "That is one slick idea, boy. Where on earth did you ever see that before?"

"Never did," Kenny said. "Just making do, is all."

"Goddammed good rig for just making do."

With two men holding and one man pumping, everyone was able to fill up in short order and be on their way. Kenny relaxed considerably as their mood changed, and there was almost a carnival atmosphere as they all filled up every available container with the precious fuel. Becky felt a huge thrill of pride as she watched all the men congratulating Kenny and thumping him on the back and calling him a genius. Quiet old Kenny Smith had become the man of the hour, but he just grinned shyly and smiled a lot.

Jake and his family were the last to leave. Jake pumped Kenny's hand and exclaimed, "Boy, that was the God-dam best show I've ever seen. You made a lot of people happy today, but if you'll take a bit of advice from an old man, I'd be careful from now on."

"What do you mean?" Kenny asked.

"Power's been off for a while, and things are getting scarce. You saw how jumpy those guys were at not being able to just pull in and fill up. You've got a big truck which looks like it has food in it, a real pretty girl with you, and a pump to get gas. Soon, there'll be men that would do you harm to get what you have. Just remember that, and be safe."

"I'll remember, thanks. It was great meeting you." The men shook hands, and Jake left with his family.

"Kenny, that was wonderful," Becky said, leaning over Nita to give him a big hug and a kiss on his stubbly cheek. She was very proud of him and felt so safe with him that her heart was letting her know she was falling for him more and more.

Kenny smiled, enjoying the attention, and said, "Well, with this pump, we won't have to give away any more food for fuel. I can't believe it, but we're off to Boulder." His mind drifted a bit as he turned west onto Route 36, and he thought, *This is crazy. I am with the girl of my dreams, I'm taking care of PJ's daughter, and I am on my way to Colorado to a music festival celebrating a guy named Bach. Yup, this is crazy.*

*  *  *

"Concerning this condition which we are now living through, I have often prayed to the Lord for guidance. It is with all my heart I believe He will answer." Reverend Randy was standing and was deep in thought as he spoke to his wife. "I can't help but think of the Corinthians verses "And he said unto me, my grace is sufficient for you, for my strength is made perfect in weakness. Therefore most gladly will I rather boast in my infirmities, that the power of Christ may rest on me." He turned and faced Ruth. "May we gather strength from Paul's words in his letter to the people at Corinth and find the means to carry out his word. Ruth, I am so sorry for the dismal state I have caused us."

Reverend Randall Davis solemnly surveyed their situation. They were camped in a makeshift shelter in an I-70 roadside rest area just west of McFarland, Kansas. They had been lucky on two occasions to find gas stations with portable generators to power the pumps. The price had been steep at both locations, one in Indianapolis, and the other just east of Columbia, Missouri, but last night, with less than a quarter of a tank, and seeing abandoned cars becoming more common each hour, Randy had decided to camp for the night and wait for guidance in the new day.

Now, the day was here, and he still lacked direction. Ruth Davis straightened up to her full five-foot, four-inch height and looked up into her tall husband's eyes, so full of sadness and remorse. "You did not cause these things to happen, Randall, nor did you shirk in your duty to the Lord to warn His people. You have done as much as is humanly possible, and Jesus will not forsake you or us." Ruth drew her eyes downward and read in the faces of her sons the same confidence and pride she felt in her husband. She slipped her arms around Randall's lanky, hard frame and hugged him lovingly. Randall P. Davis was without blame.

"Thank you all for your strength, and let us pray together for guidance." The Davis family joined hands under their meager shelter and spoke to their god. When prayers were ended, Ruth Randall gently pulled her husband aside. "Randall, we need to" Suddenly, she was interrupted by the appearance of a beige van entering the rest area at high speed. The family watched in shock as the van braked hard, the side door slid open quickly, and, in the same motion, a rumpled gray bundle rolled out into the rain and up against the parking curb of the rest area. The van spun its tires on the slushy pavement and picked up speed as it fled back out onto Interstate 70. Ruth and Randy both realized immediately what the bundle was, and without any communication, Ruth hurried out to check on it as Randy increased his grip on his sons' shoulders and turned them around to face their shelter. "Boys, I need you to go out into that patch of woods and bring whatever wood you can find that you think will burn. Also check around the toilets over there to see if there are any useful items. Go and take your time to do a thorough job."

"But, Dad, what about the van?" Eli asked.

"Never mind about the van, son. Your mother and I will deal with it."

"He doesn't mean the van, Dad. He means the dead lady in the raincoat," Noah said, and Randy realized that his sons had also seen the nakedness inside the tumbling raincoat.

"Never mind about that. Just go and do as you are told." Randy spoke with unusual firmness and finality. With his large hands planted firmly on their backs, Randy propelled his sons in the opposite direction and then turned to go help his wife.

The woman in the battered raincoat was in terrible condition, but she was alive. She appeared to be in her late twenties or early thirties, and even in her present condition, she was quite attractive. Her hands were bound behind her back with duct tape, accentuating the firm fullness of her breasts, but her torso was a mass of purpling red bruises. She also had two large bruises on her face—one high on her cheekbone, and the other on her chin where a blow had split her lower lip and caused some swelling. Her eyes were open and of a gray-blue color but were glazed over and unseeing. Her ankles were bloody and still retained traces of the tape that had held them and of the struggles that had caused the lacerations there. "Don't just stand there staring, Randy; help me get her under the tarp. We must make her comfortable and decent before the boys get back."

Reverend Davis then moved quickly and scooped the woman up as if she weighed nothing. He carried her to the crude shelter they had rigged with blue tarpaulins hanging on top of the picnic area shelter. Randy opened his pocketknife and cut free the duct tape that bound her hands so she could lie flatly on the picnic table, and then he laid the knife down on the seat of the table. Ruth shouldered him aside with their first-aid kit in her hands and said a little more vigorously than was necessary, "Start that heater back up and get me some of your clothes for her to wear."

Randy Davis could accept the sharing of his clothes because it was very obvious nothing of Ruth's would come close to fitting the woman, but fuel for the radiant heater was in short supply, and he objected. "Ruth, we don't have a spare tank of fuel for it."

"Fuel be damned. This woman is freezing, and hers is the greater need right now. We're healthy and can see to our own needs. Do as I say and pile some more wood into the fire, as well, then go help the boys. Keep them busy for a while."

Randy turned the heater back on and slid it under the picnic table so the red glow could bring warmth to the naked woman, trying all the time to avert his eyes. He then put more small branches into the blackened steel standing charcoal barbecue that they were using as a fireplace inside the shelter, then moved off quickly, relieved to be away from the unpleasant nursing work his wife Ruth was already busily performing.

As Randy walked out of the shelter, he was startled by another vehicle approaching from the highway. He felt a brief surge of fear, thinking it might be the men from the beige van returning for more mischief. His senses cleared when he realized this van was a different color. It was white, and four elderly women were busily piling out of it, led by a large woman who appeared to be their leader.

Stepping over to Randy and extending her hand, she said, "Greetings. I'm Paula Patowski from Boston, and these are my friends…" Her rapid speech ended, and her eyes popped wide open as she stammered, "You're Reverend Randy? Reverend Randy!… Oh, my goodness!"

"Yes, Paula, I'm Randall Davis. Welcome to our humble camp."

While this conversation had evolved, the other women had come up and were standing close and staring. Randy nodded his head toward the ladies and extended his hand. "Welcome, ladies." His warm eyes and smile broke the ice, and all three newcomers spoke at once.

"I'm Burtha Kurtz, Reverend. I am honored to meet you."

"I'm Wilma Krauss. Likewise for me, Reverend," she managed with the biggest smile of her life.

"I'm Annie Phillips, Reverend, and I'm sorry, but we stopped here so I could pee, and I gotta go."

Randy laughed out loud, smiling from ear to ear. "The facilities are behind our picnic shelter over there, but I would recommend not using them. They are badly befouled, so outdoor relief is much preferable. The power has been off here for quite a while, and people had not stopped using the facilities. Every bowl is filled to overflowing, and the smell of human waste is overpowering. My wife, Ruth, will tell you the same thing, but she is occupied with a badly injured young woman who was dropped off just before you arrived."

"Well, doesn't sound pleasant, but when you got to go, you got to go," Annie said as she went on her way.

Noah and Eli came over to meet the ladies standing with their father, and their dad said, "These are my boys, Noah and Eli, and they can assist you with whatever you ladies might need. Is that okay with you, boys?"

"Sure, Dad. Mom told us to tell you she is done."

"Thanks, boys." Randy left to see his wife while the ladies talked with the young boys.

"Where did she go?" Randy inquired of his wife.

"She is doing a bit better and can walk. She said she had to use the restroom. I told her it would be more pleasant to go behind the building, but she insisted she would be fine. She seemed distant when I told her about the smell and the floor. Randy, she was sexually abused terribly. I feel so bad for her; she is in a zombie-like state of mind. Oh dear, let me change the subject. Who are our new friends?"

"Some ladies from Boston heading west. They recognized me and are a bit enamored with my recent celebrity status. They say they left Boston because of my words. I have a strong feeling they will be a part of our life for the near future."

Ruth chuckled a bit. "My husband the celebrity."

Ruth then spent some time introducing herself to the ladies and getting to know them. They shared some road stories with each other about the condition of the roads and sleeping in their vehicles, the lack of places to find gas, the abandoned cars on the road, the terrible weather, and whatever else they could think of.

Randy then asked Ruth where the young woman was, as it had been several minutes since she had left.

Ruth said she better go check on her and excused herself. She walked quickly to the restroom, took a deep breath, and held it to avoid the horrible smell. What she found was much worse than the smell. There on the floor was the young woman lying in a massive puddle of her own blood, with both her wrists sliced open. Next to her, lying in the blood, was Randy's pocketknife, which he had used to cut the duct tape that had bound the woman's hands together. Ruth bowed her head and said a short prayer before going outside to tell Randy.

In his sadness, Randy decided that the young woman would not be abandoned and they would stay here until proper authorities could deal with the body in a respectful manner. Reverend Randy decided this could be their new home for the next day or two, maybe even three. He mentally surveyed their belongings; they had enough clothes, they had food and water, and they would break the glass on the vending machines and take everything from those. In all of his wisdom, he was not sure if the young woman was a sign from the Lord to stay here. He and Ruth both felt that staying was the right thing to do, so it must be a sign.

Randy had been correct in his assumption about the ladies of the Boston Tea Party. They asked the Davises if they could all stay together until conditions changed, but nobody had any idea when that would happen.

* * *

The dawn broke weak and watery in Jackass Valley as well as in most of North America. The persistent low-pressure system generated by the Arctic strike continued to pour icy-cold moist air out over the continent. This terrible spring weather only added to the misery of a life without electricity, but while most Americans huddled close to whatever heat source they could devise and hoarded meager provisions, things were better than that at the lodge in the valley.

Devon was sharing a room with an unexpected guest, Elisa, who was the Persons boys' nanny. Devon and Elisa were awakened early by footsteps on the creaky stairs just outside their room. They both hunkered down under the heavy covers and hoped for a little more sleep, but to no avail. Soon, noises from the kitchen below and the smell of fresh coffee brewing drove them from bed.

In the big kitchen, Mark Persons had the wood stove crackling and a big blue enamelware coffeepot percolating away merrily. "Well, good morning, ladies," he called cheerily as they entered. "Coffee will be ready in just a few."

"G'mornin," they said sleepily and almost in unison.

Mark laughed at their morning drowse and ignored it completely at the same time. "If you'll take over the kitchen chores, I will see to getting the stoves stoked and the heat up in the lodge."

Devon was mildly surprised at the ease with which she and Elisa fell into their "traditional" female roles and moved about the kitchen getting down large bowls, mixing up pancake batter, and heating up a big soapstone griddle they had found a couple of days before. She enjoyed Elisa's company and was quick to consider the girl a friend.

Clint Persons tried to sneak past them to go out back and use the outhouse, but Elisa spotted him. "Stop right there, mister. You can set the table before you go out back."

"But, Elisa, I've really got to go bad."

"Fine, but come right back. Everyone has chores to do," she said with a little less stridence in her voice.

Clint passed Eric on the way out while Eric was carrying an armful of firewood and grumbling about his chores.

Mark had both wood stoves burning merrily, with the doors open to let the fires blaze a few minutes and get good and hot. As soon as he came back to the kitchen table, Elisa poured him his first cup from the coffeepot. "Breakfast will be ready soon, Colonel Persons."

"Elisa, stop calling me Colonel. Call me Mark. There is no need to stand on formalities here."

Elisa said, "I'm sorry, sir; it is just habit. I will work on it, Mark." Then she added a smile and returned to the first batch of pancakes on the stove.

Devon had set the plates in the warming ovens above the stove, and she took one out when she saw the pancakes were done. Elisa took the plate and put three pancakes on it for Mark. Clint returned and started setting out coffee mugs and silverware. Devon fixed two more plates and set them down for the boys. "Will Professor Schmidt be down soon?" she asked.

"No idea, Dev. He said he was going to see if he could get the radio working with a temporary antenna he rigged across the attic last night. He didn't hold out much hope, though."

"Maybe I should go up and tell him breakfast is ready."

Mark shook his head and said, "Clint, go tell the professor breakfast is on the table."

"But, Dad, I just started"

"Go," Mark said authoritatively.

"Jeez," Clint complained on his way, but the professor stopped him in his tracks as he came in through the door.

"Good morning, all," the professor said,

Elisa came in with pancakes for the professor and Devon. "Would anyone like seconds?" she asked.

Both boys were raising their heads to say yes, but Professor Schmidt broke in, "No seconds for anyone, and in the future, we'll have to be less lavish with our portions." There was finality in his voice.

"But, Professor," Devon tried, "we're well supplied and probably better off than most people this morning."

"True, Devon, but we are still expecting Sergeant Brooks and his family and your Mr. Halloran, and we don't know what others may find the valley and want to join us. Furthermore, we don't know enough about the situation outside the valley to know how long we must make our provisions last."

The mention of John's name caused a tremor in Devon's heart and a chill to travel up her spine at the thought that while they were eating breakfast comfortably, John was making his way west through ugly weather and a land with little to no electricity. She fell silent and allowed the table conversation to flow around her as her mind tried to follow John's route from New York. Vaguely, she heard talk about getting in more firewood and reorganizing supplies stockpiled haphazardly in the cellar and the barn, and she also heard some talk about whether or not the steep roof was too slippery to climb to install a more permanent radio antenna. None of it could penetrate her sudden melancholy over John Hallaron's safety.

"Devon, Devon. Earth to Devon. Come in, please."

The words being spoken by Mark Persons finally permeated her wandering mind. "What? I'm sorry, just daydreaming."

"Welcome back, Devon." Professor Schmidt smiled indulgently. "I was asking if you and Elisa would do an inventory of the food supplies we have in the house and the barn and then if you would try and work out a menu to give us all adequate nutrition while stretching our supplies as far as we can."

"Oh, yes, Professor. We can get started right after the dishes are done."

"The boys can do the dishes. I would like you both to get started as soon as possible, if you both don't mind."

The Persons boys frowned at the prospect of cleaning up the kitchen. "Have no fear, boys. I have plenty of other chores for you after the dishes are done," Mark chimed in, but his mind was also wandering a bit, wondering what was taking Tom Brooks so long to get his family here, hoping and praying that Tom's wife was strong enough to make the trip. Maybe Tom was waiting for the old girlfriend who was a nurse back east, he thought. He remembered Tommy telling him that his wife wanted him to call her. Very unlikely she would make it across the country, even if she had been lucky enough to leave before the tsunami had hit the East Coast. With that thought, Mark's mind drifted to Devon's friend and the probability that he would make it to the valley from New York. He knew it was a long shot at best. What he didn't know was the strength of John Halloran's will and determination to fight through anything.

\* \* \*

The wind made an eerie moaning sound through the branches of the row of cottonwood trees that lined the driveway, and the sleety rain mixture rattled off the Jeep's roof as John Halloran pulled up to the darkened farmhouse. He was very near exhaustion, and this seemed like a reasonable place to pull in for a rest. He and Sally had been making aggravatingly slow progress westward over the past few days. Ever since they had left Youngstown, Ohio, their progress had been marred by never-ending detours and evil weather. They had avoided large cities on the interstate since encountering a bad incident on Interstate 71 in Columbus, Ohio. It was there that they found several trailer trucks pulled across the highway in a roadblock with a number of armed men milling around. John had slowed to survey the situation when a bullet had come from behind one truck, struck and starred his windshield. John had quickly shifted the Jeep into reverse and spun it around on the wet pavement, then headed north on the southbound lanes. Thankfully, the men at the roadblock had apparently not wanted to waste any more ammunition on them, and John had escaped with nothing more than a leaking windshield on which Butch had proved himself capable by patching the hole with a sticky wad of bubble gum. They had unanimously decided to avoid the larger cities in the future and had spent many hours slogging along on state and local highways.

John's generator had proven itself to be worth its weight in gold, as it had frequently allowed them to fill up their tank at abandoned filling stations and to trade gasoline that wasn't theirs for food that they badly needed after Sally's supply of sandwiches had run out.

Now they were parked outside an apparently abandoned farmhouse twelve miles outside of the small town of Wentzville, Missouri. The lettering on the mailbox at the end of the drive said "Jonas P Wilson." Slipping out of the Jeep, John said as calmly as he could, "Let me take a look around for a bit. Maybe I can find the Wilsons. Lock the doors and stay alert; I'll be right back."

Sally slid over into the driver's seat and pushed the door lock button, happy to hear all four doors click. Visibility was hampered by fog and darkness as she passed the time by staring out into the inky blackness and continually checking the rearview mirror until she was startled by a tapping on the window. She looked quickly and saw John signaling her to unlock the doors. She slid down the window. "Well?"

"The house is abandoned and looks as if it has been cleaned out of anything useful. There is a propane stove top in the kitchen, and there is also dry wood inside on the screened porch. Let's stay," he reported.

"Sounds great. I am exhausted."

John took a flashlight, and Sally reached back to wake up Butch, who was sleeping peacefully in the back seat. "Come on, Butch. We're going to stay here for the night. Bring your sleeping bag with you."

"Where are we?" he asked.

"Somewhere in Missouri, at a farmhouse. Nobody is home."

"Oh." Grabbing his stuff, he got out of the Jeep and headed inside.

John had already started getting the fireplace going, and Sally was holding her hands out reflexively as she had done as a child in her grandmother's house. "Oh, John, this feels wonderful."

"I'm going to park the Jeep in the barn. I don't want anyone to see it outside," John said quietly.

"I'll be right here," Sally said, cuddling her backside as close to the rapidly warming fire as she dared.

John smiled at the sight and headed outside for the Jeep. The Wilsons' barn was big and old but in good repair. John pulled the Jeep up to the big sliding doors of the hay mow and stopped, leaving it running with the lights on. He got out and pushed one big door open. That was when he met the Wilson family and very nearly screamed. Hanging by the neck from the low rafters were four members of the Wilson family, all very grotesque and all very dead.

John knew he had to move quickly so as not to arouse Sally's suspicion, so he promptly climbed the ladder up to the crossbeam at the top of the hay mow and climbed out on the rafters to cut down the Wilson family. The dull thud that each body made as it hit the old wooden floor sickened him to death. He then dragged the bodies off to the side and laid them out atop some hay bales. Sweating profusely despite the cold, he looked around and found a gray plastic tarp still in the plastic wrapper and draped it over the Wilsons' bodies before pulling the Jeep inside. He already knew that, even though he was tired, he would not sleep too soundly tonight. If he allowed himself to sleep, he would dream of the family now lying under the tarp and of the evil men who had put them there. He would also dream of Devon being attacked in Boulder while he struggled across the country. He badly wanted to be in Colorado before all these rains caused flooding. *Well*, he thought, *with any luck, we'll be in Colorado tomorrow night.*

The kitchen was pleasantly beginning to warm up, and he was unpleasantly wet. Sally had dressed for bed and laid out the sleeping bags already. She had a can of Campbell's beans heating on the stove and had found some stale bread to pour them over to soak up the juice. "What took you so long out there?" she asked over her shoulder as she stirred the beans., he looked pale and out character.

"I took a look around the barn to see if there was anything useful in there for us to use the rest of the way."

"Anything worthwhile?"

John's heart sank, even as his lips formed the lie, "Nothing at all."

"Get out of those wet clothes and hang them by the stove. You look terrible, maybe these beans will be the right thing to get you looking better and warm you up. They'll be done in a minute or two."

John was tired and depressed beyond caring about niceties, he told Sally he was going to check the bedrooms for some dry clothes.

She shot back at him, "I hope they don't mind you wearing their clothes."

"I don't think they'll mind at all," John muttered, "I think they're far away from here by now."

"Why would you think that?"

"No particular reason, I just do." He said softly with a horrible sense of remorse and sadness.

Sally shook her dark red curls at his obtuse answer but didn't think much more about it. She was simply too tired. She served out the bread and beans and they all ate it under the light of two candles she had found in a kitchen drawer. When they finished, she put the dishes in the sink, and Butch headed into the main living room and immediately dropped back down onto the couch and fell into a deep sleep.

John was still trying to shake the awful sight in the barn out of his head when he went to find and roll out his sleeping bag in the study off of the kitchen because it had a carpet and it was near the warmth of the stove and fireplace. It was then he realized that Sally had zipped the two bags together.

He looked up in surprise, and his eyes met hers. "Don't get any ideas, Halloran," she said with her accustomed firmness. "I'm tired and I'm scared and I'm in need of a little cuddling, and that is all. Understand? That's all."

John cleared his throat and said with some difficulty, "Understood."

Sally blew out the candles and slid into her sleeping bag. John put some more logs on the fire and returned to the study and slid in beside her. He took Sally in his arms, and she slid back up against him firmly. She was soft in all the right places and firm in all the others. She smelled sweet and womanly, despite all the days on the road. He kept his hands securely in the non-erogenous zones and was just beginning to drift off when Sally began to cry softly.

"It's gonna be OK, Sal." John didn't sound convincing, even to himself.

"Bullshit. Nothing will ever be the same again."

"Maybe so, but"

He never got a chance to finish his statement, as Sally said through clenched teeth, her voice trembling with mixed anger and sadness, "Shut up, John. Just shut up and hold me." And in a short time, they fell fast asleep, just that way.

It was only about three a.m. on the same dreary morning when John Halloran awoke with Sally's soft, full lips pressed against his. Instinctively, he returned her needy kiss, her lips moving on his and her cheeks still wet with tears. Slowly, he realized that other parts of him were also waking up. Sally whispered to him, "I need you now, with no commitments. I just need you tonight, here and now. You've got your girl in Boulder to think of, and I've got Duke and Paul to think of; I just need you, just this once." She moved his hand to her breasts, and John found they were warm and firm as he had always imagined them. In a matter of moments, they were both naked. John was torn by his thoughts of Devon and his current strong male urge, which won over in a matter of microseconds. When they had finished, no further words were exchanged, and they relaxed in each other's arms while Sally fell back asleep and John lay staring at the dark ceiling with feelings of guilt toward Devon, guilt toward leaving his job in a time of need, and overwhelming sadness for the Wilson family out in the barn and the countless lives lost, and the many more he feared would be lost. He knew they would make it to Colorado, and they would, but he wanted to be there now—right now, dammit, as he continued to lay wide awake, staring at the darkness.

\* \* \*

Stay tuned for part II, the tale of rebuilding and surviving after the *Fury of the Fifth Angel*.